ANOTHER CHANCE

"I care about you. I've always cared about you."

"Enough to be my woman?" Charles stared down at her, his heart racing as he waited for her response.

Diane answered with her heart in her soft brown eyes. "Yes." She lifted a trembling hand to caress his high, sculpted cheek. "Please, give me a chance to show you I've changed."

Never before had Charles allowed the tenderness, the warmth of his feelings for her, to surface. He'd kept them hidden, locked inside. This once, he turned his face until he could press his mouth into the warm center of her soft palm. He tasted her with full masculine lips, then with the hot flick of his tongue. Charles groaned deep in his throat as his defenses crumbled.

SENSUAL AND HEARTWARMING ARABESQUE ROMANCES FEATURE AFRICAN-AMERICAN CHARACTERS!

BEGUILED (0046, $4.99)
by Eboni Snoe
After Raquel agrees to impersonate a missing heiress for just one night, a daring abduction makes her the captive of seductive Nate Bowman. Across the exotic Caribbean seas to the perilous wilds of Central America . . . and into the savage heart of desire, Nate and Raquel play a dangerous game. But soon the masquerade will be over. And will they then lose the one thing that matters most . . . their love?

WHISPERS OF LOVE (0055, $4.99)
by Shirley Hailstock
Robyn Richards had to fake her own death, change her identity, and forever forsake her husband, Grant, after testifying against a crime syndicate. But, five years later, the daughter born after her disappearance is in need of help only Grant can give. Can Robyn maintain her disguise from the ever present threat of the syndicate—and can she keep herself from falling in love all over again?

HAPPILY EVER AFTER (0064, $4.99)
by Rochelle Alers
In a week's time, Lauren Taylor fell madly in love with famed author Cal Samuels and impulsively agreed to be his wife. But when she abruptly left him, it was for reasons she dared not express. Five years later, Cal is back, and the flames of desire are as hot as ever, but, can they start over again and make it work this time?

Available wherever paperbacks are sold, or order direct from the Publisher. Send cover price plus 50¢ per copy for mailing and handling to Penguin USA, P.O. Box 999, c/o Dept. 17109, Bergenfield, NJ 07621. Residents of New York and Tennessee must include sales tax. DO NOT SEND CASH.

Forever After

Bette Ford

PINNACLE BOOKS
KENSINGTON PUBLISHING CORP.

ZEBRA BOOKS are published by

Kensington Publishing Corp.
850 Third Avenue
New York, NY 10022

First Printing: December, 1995

Printed in the United States of America

To Mary Pittman. Your friendship and kindness over the years means the world to me. Thanks for all the encouragement and endless hours of proofreading duty.

To Connie, Sally, Dennis, Randy, and Tom. Your support and relentless critiquing skills are legendary.

To Bill . . . with love.

One

(Day 1, Saturday: Departure)

The cruise ship had been a beehive of activity when Diane Rivers had boarded earlier that afternoon. Exuberance and excitement were in the fragrant sea air as they left Miami on a fifteen-night Caribbean cruise. Yet Diane's heart wasn't racing with exhilaration despite the fact that this was her first real vacation. It was pounding with fear.

As Diane dressed in her cabin for the evening ahead, she acknowledged that she had good reason to be scared. She was more frightened now than she had been the day she'd left home at sixteen, fed up with fighting off her mother's men. She'd struck out on her own and never looked back.

Diane had done well for herself professionally. She'd managed to work her way through college with the help of modeling and waitressing jobs and hard-earned scholarship money. She'd even gone on to obtain a master's degree in business. She taught business and computer classes at Lawrence, a private high school in Detroit, as well as an evening class at the local community college.

She wasn't part of a large, nurturing family, like Heather Gregory-Montgomery. Nor did she belong to a small, close-knit extended family, as did Charles Randol. The three had been close friends and had worked together at Lawrence.

No, Diane belonged only to herself, for she refused to

lay claim to the poverty and grief that had marked her girlhood.

Charles . . . the name slipped past her lips as she smoothed the back of her close-cropped black hair. The front was fluffy and curly, while the sides and back were straight and followed the graceful lines of her head.

Diane at thirty-two knew she was striking. Her flawless, creamy toffee toned skin, her lovely topaz eyes, and her full, lush lips caused far too many male eyes to linger over her African-American beauty.

She sighed heavily, placing the styling brush on the vanity. She'd been stalling, hoping for a dose of courage. There was no way she was about to spend the next two weeks aboard this ship locked in her cabin, terrified of Charles's reaction when he discovered she'd followed him. Grabbing her red beaded evening bag, she refused to take another glance in the mirror. She wore a red tuxedo suit. The lapels and the short straight skirt were satin. This was as good as it got.

"Wish me luck, Heather," Diane said to her absent friend. Heather had encouraged her every step of the way, certain in her belief that Diane and Charles belonged together. Trouble was, Heather was so happily married that she'd lost touch with reality. Charles would not be pleased.

Pausing only long enough to check her purse for the key, Diane closed the cabin door firmly behind her. She didn't need to remind herself that she was the last person Charles wished to see . . . ever. He'd made that abundantly clear. But there was nothing he could do to get rid of her, short of tossing her overboard. Given time, maybe—just maybe—she could convince him he'd been wrong about her.

The elegance and beauty of the luxury liner with its finely woven carpets, fresh-cut flowers, and elaborate works of art prominently displayed were wasted on Diane. Lost in thought, she was oblivious not only to her surroundings, but to the frequent masculine glances she received as she made her way to the lobby, where the welcome aboard *bon voyage* cocktail party was in full swing.

What if she'd made an error in judgment? What if Charles wasn't traveling alone? It was possible he had a female companion with him. Diane swallowed with difficulty. The thought was too disturbing to consider for long. She'd known she was taking a huge risk from the very first, but she'd come anyway.

Charles was a reasonable man. If nothing else, he had to give her a fair hearing—didn't he?

With her heart fluttering in her chest, she looked around for a familiar face. At six feet four, Charles would be easy to spot. After nearly an hour of straining her neck, she still hadn't spotted him. She was almost relieved when the crowd began moving toward the dining room.

Diane's breath quickened with expectation. The dining room like the rest of the ship, was lavishly appointed. The very real possibility of seeing Charles left her trembling in anticipation. For no matter how she assured herself that she was strong enough to face him, she didn't completely believe it. His disapproval could easily destroy what she was just beginning to acknowledge to herself.

"Good evening," she said, reaching her assigned table.

"Good evening. I'm John Pondexter, and this is my wife, Beverly. We're from Orlando." The elderly couple beamed at her. "These are our twin daughters, Gwendolyn and Margaret."

"How do you do?" she said, taking one of the two empty chairs. "I'm Diane Rivers."

"Where are you from, my dear?"

"Detroit." Diane's gaze methodically traveled over the room. Where was he? She forced herself to smile in hopes of hiding her growing anxiety and disappointment.

"This is our fourth cruise. We love it so much we just keep coming back." The couple laughed brightly. "Although this is the first time for our girls." The "girls" were clearly over fifty and wore identical blue velveteen ruffled dresses.

"Is this your first cruise, my dear?" Beverly asked her.

"Yes," Diane managed, determined to concentrate on more than the empty chair next to her. Surely there hadn't been a mistake with the tables? She'd specifically requested to be seated at Charles's table. Where was he?

Besieged with doubt, she wondered if she was about to make a fool of herself. At the moment, this brilliant idea appeared to be a complete waste of not only time, but money. She shouldn't have come . . . she shouldn't have come . . .

When she'd managed to speak to him on the telephone, while he was still in the hospital, he'd been bitterly cold. Evidently, he preferred to think the worst of her, so why didn't she just let him? Why in the world did she even want the man? Why hadn't she just left well enough alone? Once he made up his mind, it was nearly impossible to change his viewpoint. Talk about mule-headed.

But Charles wasn't like any of the men Diane had dated. Although he was sophisticated and charming, like the upwardly mobile types she preferred, he was much much more: He was genuine. There was nothing phony about him. He didn't put on an act, nor did he pretend to be something he was not. He was a strong man a woman couldn't help but admire.

He'd been wrong about her . . . dead wrong. All she had to do now was convince him. So where on this blasted ship was he?

"No!" Charles Alexander Randol III screamed in protest as he tossed on the bed, fighting to slow the fast-moving car. He repeatedly pumped the useless brakes, as he had done on that fateful night. His body strained with tension as he crashed through the guardrail, plunging down the slope into a tree.

Charles woke with a jerk, his breath fast and heavy. His torso, wracked with pain, was drenched in sweat. "It's over," he reminded himself. His thoughts were filled with the harsh memory that had put him into the hospital. The car accident had left him laid up with cracked ribs and a punctured lung.

He groaned as he slowly dragged himself up and into a sitting position. He was sore all over. "Damn!" he swore, as he eyed the travel clock on the nightstand. He'd intended only to take a nap, but apparently he'd been asleep for hours. His stomach chose that moment to remind him that he'd slept right through the dinner hour.

Well, he'd come on this floating hotel for rest, and it looked as if he'd get more than his share. It must have been that pain pill that had put him out so soundly. Why hadn't he flushed them down the toilet the day he'd left the hospital?

He'd let his sister and Heather talk him into taking this stupid cruise. Both of them claimed to know what was best for him. What did a man alone need with moonlight and stars?

What he needed was a tall beer, a thick steak, and time alone to forget. Hell, who was he kidding? He wanted some time away from Detroit and temptation. A bit of a diversion. Two weeks away from the big "D" was what he needed. Or more important, he needed to get away from haunting thoughts of a beautiful dark-haired witch who liked to play with men, using them for her own amusement and then tossing them out with the trash when she was tired of them. There was always some new sucker drawn in by her flawless beauty. But he knew she wasn't capable of love. She didn't understand the meaning of the word. And the word commitment wasn't part of her vocabulary.

Charles hadn't allowed himself to see Diane in over a

year, but he'd forgotten nothing about her. She had called a few times and had even sent flowers while he was in the hospital. But he knew from painful experience not to let her get too close. She had managed to sink her hooks into him once. He vowed it'd never happen again.

Yet no matter how many women he dated these days, Diane was never far from his thoughts. She inhabited his house, his office, his empty bed. For the first time in his adult life, Charles found all his emotions and sexual desires centered on a single woman: Diane Rivers. Frankly, he deeply resented it. Damn it! Oh, how he resented her. He knew her game. Hell, he'd even called her on it. Yet regardless of his resolve, he ended up still longing for her. He couldn't seem to get over her.

By the time Charles had showered and dressed, his stomach was making demands he could no longer ignore. As he approached the elevators, he realized he was moving more easily; the ache in his chest was barely noticeable. He smiled. He was definitely on the mend. He found a buffet set up near the pool on the top deck. He filled his plate, enjoying the wide variety of food available even at this hour.

Later, he wandered into a lounge on a lower deck. He made himself comfortable at the bar. As he leisurely sipped on a beer, he was able to relax for the first time in a long time. Perhaps this wasn't so bad. He could get in some swimming and snorkeling, as well as a little blackjack.

Out of the corner of his eye he took note of several attractive unescorted women sharing a nearby table. Two were eyeing him with frank interest. Charles's teak-brown skin, thick, close-cut black hair, and long, lean body held a certain appeal to women. Judging by the attention he was getting, he knew he didn't have to worry about being alone unless he desired it.

But at thirty-four, he'd been around that particular block a few too many times. He was dog tired of playing the dating go-round. He wanted more, much more. He was ready to fall in love and commit to one special woman. He wanted a loving home that included a family of his own. The single life no longer held the appeal it once had.

A long, leggy beauty with soft dark-brown skin, big, beautiful dark eyes, and long black curls managed to catch his gaze. Her smile was an open invitation. Charles automatically returned the smile before refocusing on the nearly empty glass in his hand. She was gorgeous. But he wasn't the least bit tempted. His taste ran toward soft, full curves and creamy toffee-toned skin . . . Damn! When would he learn?

His plans for the community center should be occupying his thoughts. He'd helped organize and develop a mentoring program targeted at young black males between twelve and seventeen in the city of Detroit. With the help of his fraternity brothers, it looked as if they were beginning to make some headway. There was still so much that needed to be done. The situation with the black male in America was something he took seriously. Issues that affected black men weren't just a black problem. To Charles's way of thinking, they affected the entire nation. Now, he had the means and the know-how at least to try and make a difference. As much as he cherished and respected the black female, he believed that only a man could teach a boy to become a man.

Of course, it had been expected that he would follow in his late father's and his uncle's footsteps by taking over the managing of Randol Pharmaceutical. Sports were his passion, and coaching seemed a natural outlet for that interest. His family had indulged him by allowing him to play for a time after college. They didn't take his coaching at Lawrence seriously.

Last fall, when his uncle had taken ill, Charles had had no choice but to take over the family pharmaceutical business. Family came first. Besides, he'd always known he would eventually head the firm his grandfather founded some forty years ago. It had been time for him to face up to his responsibilities.

There was only one person at Lawrence he didn't say goodbye to when he left . . . Diane. He needed to get his life back on track . . . needed to heal emotionally. Diane wasn't interested in "happily-ever-after," or at least, not with him.

For years he'd dared to dream that she might be his woman. But it had turned out to be just that . . . a fantasy. Diane wanted only one thing—to add his name to her long list of conquests.

He'd hungered for her from the moment they'd met at a staff meeting nearly eight years ago. And she'd been friendly . . . too friendly. Most of the men on staff couldn't seem to say enough good things about her, while the females couldn't stand her.

He had to admit that she was an excellent teacher. He admired her professionalism and her camaraderie with the students. At first, like the other men, he couldn't see past her beauty. It wasn't long before they started dating. They quickly discovered they made better friends than possible lovers. Charles had had no alternative but to accept that while his kisses left her unaffected, hers aroused and thrilled him to the core. They remained friends until his final year at Lawrence.

Everything finally came to a head on a perfectly normal spring day during lunch in the teachers' lounge. He'd been sick to death of her throwing her male friends in his face. On this particular day, he'd reached his limit.

So instead of joining Heather at the table they normally shared, Charles had gone to another table and eaten with other colleagues. Diane had been sitting with Heather. It was far easier to avoid Diane altogether than to listen to her boast of meeting yet another new man. Charles wanted more than a platonic relationship . . . he wanted Diane.

Diane didn't understand the change in him and talked

Heather into finding out what was wrong. Against his better judgment, he let Heather talk him into having a frank conversation with Diane.

To his surprise, he found himself giving her an ultimatum. Continuing as they were was not an option. When she refused to date him exclusively, preferring their friendship, he opted to bow out of her life. He was not about to beg for her love. He'd learned the hard way that although Diane was a beautiful and extremely desirable woman, no sane man would put his heart into her hands for safekeeping.

"Sir, the lady sent this over," the waiter said, as he set a freshly drawn beer on the bar in front of Charles.

Charles lifted a brow. His gaze strayed to the women at the nearby table. "Which lady?" he asked, certain he knew. Hell, yeah. It was way past time he got Diane out of his system.

"The one in the red suit. Over there, against the wall."

Charles followed the man's gesture to the opposite corner of the room. The soft lamp glowed above her smartly cut dark hair, displaying her soft, flawless skin and large topaz eyes.

Diane lifted her chin, and her mouth formed a welcoming smile. Although she was trembling, she knew she looked cool and in control. She had perfected the facade over the years.

Two

It took Charles a few painful seconds to realize that his eyes weren't playing tricks on him. His disbelieving gaze wandered over Diane from the top of her short, curly hair to her long shapely legs, crossed at the knee. The red dinner suit did marvelous things to her lovely brown skin. She was stunning.

His nostrils flared as if he were attempting to inhale her scent. His physical response to her was immediate. He was hard and uncomfortable. One look at her and he was so damn hungry all he could think about was burying himself in her moist warmth. He trembled with hot expectation. Hell!

Even in the relatively dim interior she created a stir. He didn't have to look around. He knew she was the recipient of many appreciative male gazes. That was a given with her. Diane drew men like bees to a honeycomb.

In spite of her smile, Charles could see the tremor of her full red-tinted mouth. Lips so sweet that no man could forget the taste. She was dangerous.

He swore beneath his breath as he slowly rose to his feet, buttoning his sports jacket in hopes of hiding his erection.

He'd been too long without a woman. Why else would his pulse beat so wildly in his throat? He attributed the weakness in his limbs to the pain medication he'd taken early that morning.

* * *

Diane had come into the lounge after the floor show feeling very lonely and uncertain. She'd been so caught up in her thoughts of him that she couldn't recall what she'd eaten for dinner or what the show she'd seen had been about. As she looked up to order a glass of wine that she didn't really want, she saw Charles enter the lounge. It seemed like an eternity since she'd last seen him, even longer since they'd really talked.

The trouble was there was so much about herself he didn't understand, so much she could not share with him. At fifteen, Diane had lost her baby fat. Her body had ripened into a tiny waist, full curves, and long, shapely legs. Suddenly, she was no longer safe. She was forced to fight to maintain her virtue. She'd learned early that men weren't to be trusted. It was an unforgettable lesson. Time and experience had served to further narrow her meager supply of trust. It wasn't until her senior year in college that she felt save enough to date. During her years away from home, she gained confidence in her ability to take care of herself. She didn't waste her time with men who could not accept "no."

Once she'd started teaching, she began dating in earnest. She found safety in numbers. After a few dates she moved on. No serious involvements for Diane. And truth be told, she relished the masculine attention she received. For the first time, she'd felt truly feminine, at ease with her own womanliness. Over the years she'd perfected the art of juggling men. She'd gotten too good at it, according to Charles. Now, she didn't even have his friendship. He'd turned his back on what they had.

Diane was deeply in love for the first time in her life. Unfortunately, she discovered her feelings long after Charles had issued his ultimatum. He had since quit his teaching job at Lawrence. In fact, she hadn't seen him since Heather and Quinn's wedding, a year and a half ago.

It was only recently, since his accident, that she'd come

to recognize the full extent of her feelings for him. Oh, she'd been in love with him for a long time. She just hadn't been strong enough to trust her feelings.

Perhaps she'd let too much time pass? Although he was acting like the most opinionated, arrogant, smart-alec black man she had ever had the misfortune of meeting, she knew how tender and compassionate and caring he could be. She would make him change his opinion of her, make him give her a second chance. She would!

It had taken all her resolve to send that drink over to him. As he approached her drink in hand, her stomach muscles tightened even more. She felt as if she'd swallowed a mass of silken butterflies. Her heart sank when she saw that his beautiful black eyes were flashing sparks of absolute rage. He might not be what some would call a conventionally handsome man, but she found his strong brown face, high cheekbones, well-drawn African features, and full sensuous masculine lips extremely appealing. He moved with a smooth, athletic grace she'd come to associate with him alone. He was a charismatic man.

His navy blazer, teamed with ivory trousers and open polo shirt, only hinted at the sleek, well-muscled strength of his wide shoulders, long torso, and muscular thighs. But his eyes were his most arresting feature. They were very, very black. When he was pleased, they seem to twinkle with merriment. When he was aroused, they smoldered with dark flames of desire, and when he was angry they flared with fury, as they were doing right now. He slowly moved toward her table.

"If I didn't know better, I'd think you were following me," he said in his naturally deep, gravelly baritone. His eyes mocked the playfulness in his tone.

"Hello, Charles. It's been a while. Please . . . join me." She smiled, lifting her chin while nervously swallowing the lump in her throat. She'd waited and planned too long for this moment. She didn't intend to let his anger stop her.

"What are you doing here?" he asked, taking the empty chair across from her. His brow was creased in a heavy scowl.

"Cruising the Caribbean. What else?"

"Yeah, what else," he repeated. "Well?"

"Well, what?" She tried to laugh, but it came out sounding weak, even to her own ears.

It was clear that this line of questioning was getting him nowhere fast. He wasn't sure if she'd followed him or not. Yet how could she have known his plans? Heather, he deduced. Who else?

Heather knew how badly Diane had hurt him. Charles didn't think for a moment that she had betrayed his confidence. They'd been friends too long. He also knew she wouldn't be above a bit of matchmaking.

Damn! He had told her his plans were confidential, hadn't he? Maybe not. Why should he? He'd never considered the possibility of Diane being on the same cruise. It could be a coincidence. Yet he had serious doubts about that. There was another very real possibility . . .

"Where is your man? A woman like you is never without one."

Diane should have been prepared for this, especially considering the way they had parted with so much bitterness and anger between them.

Charles waited, his eyes never leaving her lovely face. Knowing Diane, a man was always involved. She collected them like trophies. Was there ever a time when she didn't have a lover?

"It is good to see you again also, Charles." She smiled while clenching her small evening bag tightly in her lap. This was worse, far worse than she'd imagined.

"Cute, but not very informative."

"I didn't see you on the plane. But then, I left on Friday. When did you leave?"

"Let's stop playing games, doll face."

"Don't call me that!" she snapped. "That's your name

for Heather, not me." She was unable to admit even to herself the jealousy she sometimes felt over the closeness Heather shared with the man of her own daydreams.

"Sorry," he said. "I forgot for a second that I'm not talking to a friend."

"That was your choice, not mine. You didn't want my friendship, remember?" She swallowed the tears burning her eyes. She'd promised herself she wasn't going to cry.

"Why are you here?"

Diane fingered the rim of her wineglass. She might be foolish for coming, but she was no fool. It wasn't in her best interest to answer. She didn't recognize this angry, bitter man. Where was the playful, tender, kind man she had known for so many years?

Forcing herself to smile, she said, "It's spring break. Even hardworking teachers get time off. My plans are to relax and enjoy myself. I'm sure you're here to do the same. If you will excuse me, I'll say goodnight."

Charles wasn't ready for the conversation to end. He was no closer to getting a straight answer out of her than he'd been when he'd walked over to her table. "I'll escort you to your cabin."

Close to dissolving into tears, she said, "That's not necessary."

"I'll walk you, anyway."

Diane gave in with a shrug. It was pointless to argue. He was determined to have the last word.

Despite the tears that threatened to flood Diane's eyes, she noticed it was a lovely night. A soft, warm breeze caressed their faces. The stars seemed much bigger and brighter, in spite of the almost full moon. The sounds of the sea were soothingly close. Despite the lateness of the hour, the deck was crowded.

Diane wondered how many times in the past few weeks as she'd prepared for this trip she'd imagined herself alone with him on a night such as this. In her fantasies, he was always smiling down at her with love in his eyes, the dimples in his cheeks engagingly evident. Tonight, Charles's features were arranged in distinct displeasure. Evidently, he found nothing positive in her being on board. Even though she had tried to prepare herself for his anger, it hurt deeply.

Charles was oblivious to the pleasant sounds of the ocean as it lapped against the ship. His breathing was quick and uneven, his body was taut with tension and desire. In spite of his anger, he wanted her so badly he hurt.

"Start talkin'," he said, once they were finally out of earshot of the crowd. His hands were shoved safely into his pockets, where he couldn't do anything stupid like touch her.

"Will you look at those stars!"

"Diane! I'm having a difficult time believing our being on the same ship is an accident. I think I deserve an explanation."

"I disagree. But I will repeat the only one I am prepared to give tonight. I'm here on vacation, and I plan to enjoy every second of it."

A muscle jumped in the side of his neck. He looked as if he might be grinding his teeth.

Diane sighed. "Charles, we haven't seen each other in so long. Can't we at least be cordial to one another?"

"Not a damn thing has changed between us."

Diane's throat ached from suppressed tears. She was weak with relief by the time they reached her door. "I'm sorry you feel that way. Goodnight."

"Aren't you going to invite me in?" Charles studied the soft lush curves of her mouth.

Diane didn't see the hunger in his gaze, for she concentrated on maintaining her composure. It took her longer than necessary to retrieve the key to her cabin from the bottom of her small evening bag.

Made impatient by her delay, he demanded, "Well?"

"I'm tired. It's been a long day." How much more of his anger could she take?

"I have a few things to say that I'm sure you don't want the good people on this ship to hear. Or is your lover in the cabin? Are you afraid he won't appreciate you returning with another man?"

Diane gave him the key. "Here, go on in." She waited until he'd unlocked the door and they were inside before saying, "As you can see, I'm traveling alone." She stood with her arms folded beneath her breasts.

Charles swallowed with difficulty. He was determined to stare her down. Unfortunately, he couldn't get past the ripe fullness of her breasts. She was a statuesque woman, tall enough to fill a tall man's arms to perfection. Her body was wonderfully soft and lush.

But she had never given him the opportunity to prove he could make her forget every man she'd ever known. She'd allowed him a few sweet kisses, nothing more. There wasn't a doubt in his mind that he was man enough to pleasure her in ways none of her lovers had bothered to learn. The difference was the depth of his feelings for her. Naturally, that was all in the past. Unfortunately, his body hadn't gotten the message. His manhood pulsated with a timeless need. All she had to do was lower her soft brown gaze in order to see what he couldn't hide.

His voice grated with a disappointment he couldn't begin to explain. "Heather told you my plans. What I don't understand is why it would have been of interest to you. Why did you follow me?"

His coldness finally got to her. Diane's voice was brimming with unshed tears. "Why are you treating me this way? Sure, I've made mistakes in the past. But I never deliberately took advantage of our friendship. I have always valued you, Charles. I know there were things you didn't like about me. But I've had time to think. Lots of time. Charles, I've changed."

"Was that little speech suppose to make up for the past?" He leaned against the door, his arms folded against his chest when he really felt like ramming his fist through the damn wall. This woman had managed to turn his emotions inside out with the mere blink of her long, silky lashes. He wasn't about to open himself up again to her particular brand of torment.

"Neither one of us can change what happened between us. Please, Charles. We were friends once. Maybe someday we can be again."

Charles reacted as if she'd slapped him. His mouth twisted into a harsh sneer. "When in the hell are you going to get around to acting like a grown-up? Do me a favor, okay? Stay the hell away from me." He jerked the door open and walked out, slamming it behind him.

She sobbed, tears running down her cheeks as she sank down onto the narrow single bed. She'd gambled and lost. She'd risked all for nothing. Diane cried out her disappointment, burying her face in the pillow. The warm, sweet man she'd grown to love had become an embittered stranger, someone she no longer even recognized.

She'd been so hopeful when she'd boarded the plane, sure she could change his mind. It wasn't that she thought he would drop at her feet. In truth, she'd been ready for his anger. She'd just expected it to give way once he'd gotten over the shock of seeing her again. Maybe then he'd realize she'd changed.

But his anger had been as hot and cutting as it had been almost two years ago, when he'd told her he never wanted to see her again. For him, nothing had changed. He resented her today as much as he had back then.

(*Day 4, Tuesday*)

The sun glinted off the water. The air was heavy and fragrant. Birds flapped and called overhead. Diane, like her fellow passengers, was caught up in the excitement of arriving at their first port.

"Can I interest you in sharing a cab?"

Diane glanced back over her shoulder to the woman she had met on the second day out while lounging around the pool. Diane was one of the few women not intimidated by the other's dark sultry beauty. Jeanette Parks was tall and shapely, with long black hair and exotic African features. They had taken an immediate liking to each other. They'd shared two fun-filled evenings enjoying the ship's nightlife. Like Diane, Jeanette was traveling alone. Jeanette's idea of a good time was attracting as many men as she could. There was no shortage of available men. Diane was not the least bit jealous of Jeanette's popularity. She saw qualities in her new friend that were very familiar.

Since Diane had realized she'd fallen in love with Charles, her whole demeanor had changed. Unfortunately, her appeal to the opposite sex hadn't diminished. She found herself devoting too much time to avoiding unattached men and their unwanted attention, while being ignored by the one man who mattered.

After two full days at sea, Diane hadn't caught more than a glimpse of Charles's strong features across the dining room. He'd gone so far as to change his table assignment. They hadn't spoken since that first night. Diane's disappointment and fear had grown with each passing day. How could one perfectly wonderful man turn into the most muleheaded fool on earth?

Seeing Diane's frown, Jeanette quickly added, "If you have a better offer, girl, you know I'll understand."

"Hi, Jeanette. On your own this morning?"

She laughed, linking arms with Diane. "It happens. No luck with tall, dark, and gorgeous?"

Diane shook her head with a dejected little sigh.

"Cheer up, sugar. It ain't over yet." Jeanette laughed.

Talk about a small world. Jeanette had told Diane about

the fine *thang* she had tried to pick up in the lounge their first night at sea. He'd turned out to be Charles.

"Ready to go ashore?" Diane asked.

"Girl, yes! Aruba, here we come. Shall we shop until our feet are bloody, or go sightseeing, perhaps check out the local men?"

"Both!"

Armed with sun hats, suntan lotion, cameras, and comfortable shoes, the two had no trouble finding a cab ready to take them all over the island. Oranjestad in Aruba was everything the brochure had promised and more. The trouble was, despite her best efforts, Diane couldn't forget that her daydreams had always included sharing the excitement and adventure with Charles.

On Wednesday, after a marathon round of shopping, Jeanette and Diane had lunch at a quaint outdoor café before touring the historic forts in Willemstad, Curaçao.

It was later that evening, at the "Singles Get-Together," that Jeanette had leaned over and whispered in Diane's ear, "Hey, isn't that your man at the bar? Girl, he is lookin' awfully lonely to me. You oughta do something about that."

Diane looked up from her fruit drink. She'd been absorbed in twirling the orange and pineapple slices on the swizzle stick. They shared a small table with three of Jeanette's men friends. The band played golden hits from the sixties and seventies.

Charles was seated alone at the bar, his back to the band and the dance floor.

"Stay out of it," Diane whispered back.

Jeanette laughed. "Will you wake up? There are women all over this room eyeing that tall, sweet thang. But the man spends his time watching you when he thinks you aren't lookin'. When you goin' to do somethin' about it?" When Diane didn't answer, Jeanette asked, "He's no stranger, is he?"

"An old friend."

Jeanette giggled. "He's certainly not old and definitely not friendly. Give it another shot. What can it hurt?"

Diane knew what would hurt . . . her heart. Nevertheless, she said, "Yeah, I think I will."

"Good luck," Jeanette said, giving her hand a squeeze.

Diane moved with graceful strides to the end of the bar, where Charles seemed lost in thought. He wore an almond-colored silk shirt and matching trousers. A black sports jacket covered his broad shoulders.

Charles sensed rather than heard Diane's approach. He didn't move a single muscle when she took the stool next to his. If there had been any doubt in his mind as to her identity, the sweet fragrance of crushed lilacs mixed with her own unique body chemistry told its own tale. She was breathtaking in a simple white silk sheath. The deep V neck shimmered with sequins. Her feet were encased in white strapless high-heeled sandals.

He signaled the bartender. "The lady needs a drink."

"I'll have whatever you're drinking," Diane said softly.

"What's wrong, sweet cheeks? Getting bored with the selection of men?"

"As a matter of fact, I am bored. Haven't had a good fight in three days. Thought it was about that time, if you know what I mean."

Three

(Day 7, Friday: At sea)

Diane held her breath, not certain what to expect. She knew Charles was blessed with a keen sense of the ridiculous. But where she was concerned, the man tended to have a one-track mind.

Charles found himself rumbling with laughter. After days of being exposed to Diane's natural grace and beauty, he knew he was weakening. Despite his better judgment, he yearned to talk to her, spend time with her.

"Let's dance," he said gruffly, as if he had to get the words past a constriction in his throat. Taking her hand, he led her onto the dance floor.

Every night of this blasted trip he had lain awake wanting what his mind told him he couldn't have, what his heart and body told him was necessary for his continued survival. Hell! He was the only one suffering. He was tired . . . tired of trying to convince himself that she didn't matter to him. For well over a year he'd denied the truth. Charles still cared about Diane. In fact, he'd never stopped wanting her. Despite heartache, hurt feelings, and injury to his pride, his feelings for her hadn't diminished.

For once, he'd allowed himself to focus on nothing more than how badly he needed to hold her. Lucky for him, the band was playing a slow, dreamy tune, for he couldn't seem to breathe until her soft, sweet curves were pressed close against his long, hungry length.

Charles suppressed a groan. He was aroused. It had begun the instant her soft hand had brushed his. The strength of his desire pounded with the thunderous force of an African drum in the quiet of a star-filled night . . . relentless. He ached to make her his.

This once, he didn't bother with examining his motives. There would be plenty of time for that later, when he was alone. Now, he would savor the sweetness of holding her close to his heart.

They danced several slow songs without speaking. Eventually, as the tempo in the music picked up speed, Charles asked, "Would you like to catch your breath?" even though the last thing he wanted to do was release her.

"I'm fine." Her warm breath bathed the base of his throat. "How are you? The pain all gone?" She was afraid of disturbing the frail truce they'd managed, but she had to know.

"It was Heather," Charles chuckled. "You two have been discussing me, haven't you?" He didn't wait for an answer before he asked, "Tell me, did you two plan this little rendezvous?"

"You don't understand . . ."

"By all means, explain," he said, as he guided her with rhythmic ease.

Diane looked up at him. But she was unable to tell if his eyes were gleaming from anger or humor. Sighing, she rested her cheek against his wide chest. "I'm sorry you were injured, Charles, but . . ."

"But what, Diane?"

"Why did you refuse to see me? Everyone at Lawrence was welcome to visit you while you were in the hospital. Everyone except me!"

"You know why," he said harshly, refusing to be swayed by the hurt evident in her voice. Hell! He was already weakening. He unconsciously tightened his arms around her small waist. Her soft breasts were pillowed on his chest.

Unable to conceal her emotions, she whispered, "I care about you."

They stopped moving. At first, Diane thought it was because of what she'd said, but then she realized the music had stopped.

Charles didn't let go. His hands remained at the base of her spine, just above the flare of her shapely behind, as he stared down at her without saying anything. When the band started again, with an old Four Tops tune, he moved with her in time to the music.

"Charles?"

"I heard you."

Trying to deal with her disappointment and apprehension, she reminded herself of the need for caution. "So, old friend, how are you?"

"Much better."

"I was so worried when I heard about the accident. You could have been killed."

Charles was warmed by her concern. "It's taken me a while, but I'm back on my feet. This little vacation should do the trick. Are you enjoying the trip?"

"Oh, yes. This is my first cruise."

"Any seasickness?"

"None, thank heavens. Chucky," she paused, ". . . won't you tell me how it happened? The crash, I mean."

He shivered, realizing how much he enjoyed her calling him by his childhood name and savored the soft, silky intonation of her voice. He imagined her moaning his name as he licked her full breasts then slowly laved each hard nipple in turn. The thought sent a shot of white-hot heat straight into his groin. He was forced to swallow a groan.

As close as they were, there was no way Diane could fail to note the prominent ridge of hard male flesh pressed against her. She was flattered. He felt something for her. It certainly wasn't love, but at least she knew that he still found her attractive, even desirable. His arousal served to heighten her own awareness of him.

"The incident is over, and as far as I'm concerned, best forgotten."

"But Chuck . . ."

"I prefer Charles," he lied.

Although disheartened, she forced a smile and tried for a light tone. "So, do you miss the classroom, Mr. Vice President of Randol Pharmaceutical?"

Charles chuckled. "I miss Lawrence. I don't miss teaching. I've been coaching during the week at one of the community centers."

"Can't give it up, huh? Must be in the blood."

"Must be," he smiled. He couldn't hold back the enthusiasm he felt for the project. "My frat brothers have decided to take an active role in our black community, not merely by financing projects, but by developing and participating in a mentoring program with African-American teenage boys."

"That's fabulous. And knowing you, I'm sure you've had a hand in every aspect of the program."

Charles grinned. "We've been able to reach some boys with heavy-duty problems. Our efforts are working, and that's all the thanks I need."

"Congratulations," Diane smiled. "That many nights doesn't give you a lot of time for a social life." When he didn't respond, she said, "In a minute, you're going to tell me you decided to embrace celibacy for nearly two years." She tried to sound as if she were teasing, but she was serious. She wasn't stupid. She needed to know if he was involved with another woman. After all, Heather could be wrong.

"Why the sudden interest in my love life?" He held his breath, waiting expectantly.

"Why not? We're not exactly strangers, are we?"

Charles wasn't about to let her know that for almost three years he'd been without a woman. He'd done without because he couldn't have the woman he wanted . . . he couldn't have Diane. Even he hadn't realized just how possessive or particular he'd become until he'd acknowledged his feelings for her.

He had fallen head over heels in love with the woman. It had happened so quickly, so unexpectedly, that he'd hadn't been prepared for it. For too damn many years he'd accepted her sweet smiles and friendly companionship as a pitiful substitute for the fierce love and passion he craved. He was no wimp, but in order to be close to her, he'd been willing to swallow his pride and pretend. He'd pretended until he'd felt as if he were being eaten alive with jealousy and sexual desire for her.

While she enjoyed his friendship, she went to bed with other men. It wasn't until he'd bowed out of their so-called friendship that he was able to regain his self-respect. She had put him through hell. He vowed that never again would he permit a woman to emasculate him the way he'd allowed Diane to.

Yet here he was again, hanging on her every word, while painfully aroused from the simplicity of holding her. No, damn it! Not this time.

He hissed, close to her ear so they wouldn't be overheard, "I don't believe I asked you who you are sleeping with, lady?"

She whispered back, "It's an easy enough question to answer. I'm not dating anyone, and I'm not sleeping with anyone, either."

Charles couldn't believe his reaction to that simple statement. Despite the pain she had caused him, despite the resentment and anger that wouldn't let go of his vitals, he couldn't escape the fact that he ached for her.

Devastated by his silence, she swallowed down the tears rising in her throat. "Okay, Charles. You win."

"What is that supposed to mean?"

"It means I won't bother you again."

"Did I say you were bothering me? Let's just dance, okay?"

As one slow song moved into the next and the next, Diane relaxed and concentrated on nothing more than enjoying the moment. As his hard-muscled thigh slid between hers, Diane bit back a moan. She couldn't hide the tremor in her limbs or the sensitive tips of her breasts.

Diane caught herself just in time, an instant before she rubbed her hard nipples against his chest and pressed her feminine mound against his blatant masculinity. What was wrong with her? She was a heartbeat away from throwing herself at the man's feet. She must be losing her mind!

Diane felt like shouting her relief when the bandleader announced they were taking a break and Charles stepped away. She could breathe again.

"Let's get some air. It's too warm in here."

Charles nodded, following her without comment.

The trade winds were wonderfully refreshing. The sky was deep and rich as sapphire. There was not a cloud in sight. Charles and Diane walked around the deck until they found a relatively isolated spot. Pausing at the rail, they stood staring out into the distant horizon.

Diane inhaled deeply, savoring the sound and smell of the sea.

"Feeling better?" he asked, his voice deep and husky. The breeze wasn't doing a thing to cool his overheated system.

"Mmmm." She tried to smile, but couldn't quite manage it. "The sunsets have been breathtaking. I've never seen anything so beautiful."

"Yeah." He didn't tell her how often he thought of her then, and yearned to share the experience with her.

Her heart fluttered, but she had to know. She just had to. "Why tonight, Charles? Why did you ask me to dance?"

"I thought it was obvious," he snapped, impatient with his raging hormones and his vulnerability to this exceptionally beautiful woman. He shoved his hands into his pockets. "Let's walk."

They'd nearly circled the deck in silence when she said, "I'd really like to know why."

"There are some things a man can't hide. You felt my erection on the dance floor. I want you. But that's nothing new. I've always wanted you," he said harshly, his voice edged with bitterness.

Diane was grateful for the darkness. He couldn't see her blush. She hadn't expected him to be quite so blunt. "Oh, really? You've been avoiding me for days . . . no, since you left Lawrence."

"I'm flattered you even noticed my absence. For a sexy woman like you, there's no shortage of available men, not even on this floating hotel."

She stopped suddenly. "Don't! Don't do this to me!"

"Do what?"

"Bring other men into this conversation. This is about you and me."

"There never was a 'you and me,' Diane. That's the problem. You wanted my friendship. I wanted a lover . . . a relationship"

"I want that, too," she said, with a tremor in her voice.

"Like hell! All you want is a boy-toy, someone who will play the game your way. Well, I'm no boy, and I'm certainly nobody's toy. You know nothing about love or commitment, lady."

"That's not true!"

"Oh?"

"Yes! I'm not like that. I've changed."

"Oh, yeah? You expect me to believe that? I've got eyes. Men follow your sweet behind like bears searching for honey." Charles's nostrils flared with temper. He wasn't about to let her twist him into knots again.

Diane hid her trembling hands behind her back as she faced him with her shoulders square and her chin lifted. She forced herself to meet his challenging black eyes. "I'm not responsible for other people's behavior. But I'm taking responsibility for my own." She swallowed quickly. "I've made mistakes. Yes, I've avoided emotional involvement in the past. We both know that. I'm not trying to pretend it didn't happen. But I care about you. I've always cared about you."

"Enough to be my woman?" Charles stared down at her with his heart racing like a galloping bronco as he waited for her response. He didn't even try to feign indifference.

Diane answered with her heart in her soft brown eyes. "Yes."

"I'm not interested in sharing," he shot back.

"Neither am I."

Charles wasn't quite ready to believe what he was hearing. He'd waited too long for those gut-wrenching words. It would hurt too much if she changed her mind later. No! He wasn't going to try to predict the future. He had to deal with the here-and-now. She'd make her choice. The ball was in his court.

Diane lifted a trembling hand to caress his high sculpted cheek. A tender gesture. "Please . . . give me a chance to show you that I've changed."

He flinched at the action and she moved to withdraw her hand. "No . . ." he said in a hoarse whisper. His hand captured her slender fingers and held them against his face. "Don't pull away."

Never before had he allowed the tenderness, the warmth of his feelings for her to surface. He'd kept them hidden, locked inside. This once, he turned his face until he could press his mouth into the warm center of her soft palm. He tasted her with full masculine lips, then with the hot flick of his tongue. Charles groaned deep in his throat as his defenses crumbled.

His voice was vibrant with emotion when he said, "Let's get out of here before I do something really asinine."

Diane nodded, her senses alive with a sizzling desire unlike anything she'd ever experienced. "Where . . . ?"

"You'll see," he said thickly, threading his fingers through hers.

Charles didn't let go of her hand until they'd reached his stateroom. Nor did he speak. By this time, Diane was trembling with fear of the unknown. It was just as well he didn't give her an opportunity to absorb the beauty and opulence of his suite. She didn't even hear the door swing shut behind them before she was pulled against him. He'd flung his jacket into an armchair and crushed her against his silk-covered chest. There was no time to prepare herself for the firm warmth of his mouth as his full masculine lips covered hers.

He explored the succulent sweetness of her lush mouth, relearning the texture, the shape, and the utter softness of her lips. Her soft moans of pleasure heightened his enjoyment. Charles found he had to taste Diane . . . taste her as he had been yearning to do for so damn long.

His tongue was like damp, soft velvet as he followed the generous curves of her mouth. He reacquainted himself with her soft upper lip before licking her fleshy bottom lip. His stroking tongue thoroughly investigated the enticing seam between her lips. Her soft, husky moans sent him over the edge. He slipped inside, finding the sweetness he craved. Oh, she was as ripe and sugary sweet as dew-kissed strawberries.

Diane gasped, melting against Charles, unable to contain the pleasure he gave her. She'd never felt like this before. Their kisses in the past had always been brief exchanges . . . never with such white-hot need.

Charles suckled her bottom lip, gently worrying it with his teeth before soothing it with his tongue, then repeating the process on her top lip. Oh, yes! She was sweet . . . so sweet. Unable to contain himself, he plunged his tongue deep inside her mouth, over and over again, while imagining what he wanted so desperately to do with his shaft in her tight, wet sheath. Diane almost fainted when he gave her the fullness of his tongue, rubbing it against hers. She clung to him, overwhelmed by the primitive fire he kindled within her. Charles was the first to pull back, allowing them both the liberty of breath.

He said her name, sexual tension evident in the dark tone of his voice. His nostrils flared as they filled with her scent. He was swollen, aching for still more of her sweetness . . . more of her incredible heat. She felt so soft and pliable in his arms . . . so right. He'd nearly lost control when she'd rubbed her breasts against his chest.

Dizzy with longing, Diane was forced to lean against him for support. Her long, dark lashes slowly lifted, offering him the beautiful depths of her large topaz eyes. Her eyes were as faceted and mysterious as the brown stone they resembled. But there was no hardness, only her magical warmth. She was the most desirable, responsive woman he'd ever known. He wanted her so badly his jaw ached from clenching his teeth.

"Should I apologize?"

She shook her head, momentarily lost for words.

He caressed her beautiful creamy tan face, trailing a lean dark finger down her cheek to her small chin. "I love the taste of your mouth, Diane. I'd be lying if I said I didn't want to taste every last inch of your beautiful body . . . tonight. I want you, baby. But what we both need is time."

She surprised them both when she said, "I want you, too."

"Don't tempt me," he whispered. "We need to really talk."

"No . . ." Diane brushed her lips against his, which would have been impossible if he had not dropped his head, thus allowing her access to his mouth. "When we talk, we fight. I don't want to argue. Honey . . ." she said nervously. ". . . If we just made love."

Charles shivered with anticipation. But he refused to let his engorged flesh do his thinking for him. There was just too much he didn't understand. With his hands balled at his sides so he couldn't touch her, he stepped back, purposefully putting more space between them.

"Why the change in attitude? There was a time when you wanted no part of me except as your buddy. In fact, you said . . ."

"I know what I said," she whispered defensively. She closed her eyes briefly, calming herself. It seemed that if she wanted her dreams to come true, she had to take yet another risk. In a soft whisper, she said, "I was afraid. You wanted so much from me. Don't you see . . . ?" she stopped suddenly.

Charles frowned, waiting for clarification.

Diane moved closer to him and thus robbed him of coherent thought. Her breasts nearly touched him. He could see the outline of her nipples against the soft fabric of her bodice. Unable to look away, he couldn't help wondering about the hue of her nipples. Were they a deep, rich ebony, or lush chocolate brown, or the dark hue of ripe raspberries? He ached to see every inch of her. He knew he wouldn't be satisfied until he knew all her sweet secrets.

"I . . ."

Charles placed a wide palm against the small of her back sending her off-balance and into his body. With her softness crushed against him, he groaned an instant before he took her mouth. He ravished its sweetness the way he wanted to bury his erection deep inside her heat.

"Yes . . . oh, yes," he whispered, as he felt her trembling response. He intended to make her wet, dewy with hunger for him . . . only him. He forgot about questioning her motives . . . he forgot everything but the sizzling intensity of his own desire for Diane.

"I've missed you so much," she managed between his hard, sweet kisses.

"Diane . . ." he said huskily, his mouth devouring hers. It wasn't enough. He needed more . . . more of her. His lips slid down her throat. Her skin was as soft and smooth as satin, he thought, as he tongued the hollow at the base of her neck. He cupped her wondrously lush breasts, stroking the nipples with his thumbs.

"Charles!"

He stopped as he realized she was trembling like a leaf in a whirlwind. It took only an instant to recognize the rapid change within her.

"What's wrong?"

"Nothing," she whispered, unable to explain.

Sexual frustration and doubts from the past caused him to gruffly demand, "You're pushing me away again. Am I wrong? Didn't you agree to become my woman—my lover?"

"Yes. But . . ." she bit her lip thoughtfully. "It's happening so fast. Give me a moment to get used to the change."

He scowled but said nothing as he walked past the small sitting area, which consisted of a sofa and armchair, to the floor-to-ceiling patio door that led out onto a tiny private veranda. But his mind was not on the beauty of the sea. He stared down into the churning water, hoping time and space would calm his raging desire for Diane.

She stood watching him, terrified by the possibility that she'd really angered him this time. She waited with a heavy heart. It was all her fault. She was a coward. Once again she had let her fear control her.

After several long agonizing moments, he said, "You're right. It's happening too fast." Slowly he turned to look back at her.

"I should say goodnight," she whispered unhappily. Better to leave before he threw her out for leading him on. She didn't dare meet the smoldering passion in his eyes.

Charles sighed heavily. "I'll walk you to your cabin."

"I'll be fine on my own."

"My aunt would be horrified if I didn't," he said, with a sudden cocky smile. "Won't take a moment."

The smile reminded her of the dear friend that she'd cherished and trusted. He didn't breathe easy until he'd escorted her through the door and into the hallway. They were silent until they reached Diane's cabin on a lower level. At her door, Charles leaned forward to briefly brush her mouth with his.

"Breakfast at eight, followed by a fun-filled day in Port of Spain?"

She smiled radiantly. "I look forward to it. Charles, I'm sorry about . . ."

"No need to apologize. We'll take this one day at a time, okay? See you at eight. Sleep well."

Diane was still smiling when she let herself inside. She couldn't seem to stop. Happiness bubbled with a wonderful effervescence inside of her. He wasn't angry! He was even willing to give her time to adjust to their new relationship.

She was still humming to herself when she came out of the shower and prepared for bed. It was only as she lay in the darkness that the old, painfully familiar doubts emerged.

She'd been so proud of herself when she'd gone to his stateroom. She'd wanted to be alone with him as much as he'd wanted it. She'd even allowed him to touch her and caress her. It wasn't until he'd seemed close to losing control that her anxiety had surfaced.

But miraculously, he hadn't held it against her. Perhaps he'd found nothing unusual in her behavior? Oh, she hoped so! Things hadn't ended badly. She'd been silly to panic, she'd forgotten she was with Charles.

She'd spent her entire life building up walls around herself. She hadn't allowed anyone to get so close . . . not Heather, who she loved and trusted like a sister . . . and never a man.

Charles was different from other men. He was her friend. He really cared about her. It didn't matter to him how she looked on the outside. Charles was the only man she'd ever been close to, the only man she truly felt safe with.

Yet Charles was one-hundred-percent male. And that male part of him wanted to know the female part of her. When the time came for total intimacy, would she be able to let him make love to her? She wasn't sure! What if she couldn't? What then? Would she lose him forever?

Diane's eyes filled. No . . . no . . . she mustn't lose him. She told herself she would do whatever it took to keep him. Anything!

When he'd first given her the ultimatum, she'd lost it. She'd been so terrified. He'd always been so generous to her, sharing so much of himself. He wasn't afraid to show his gentle side, his tenderness. Not for a minute did she suspect he'd be cruel enough to walk out of her life. She hadn't meant to hurt him. He didn't understand that she hadn't rejected him. How could she when he meant so much to her?

Yet it wasn't until after their separation that Diane had recognized the sheer depth of her feelings for him. She loved him with all her heart. With him she didn't have to worry about her physical beauty. He cared about the woman she was on the inside. With him she could be herself. He was a man who could be trusted. A man she could depend on.

Their estrangement had been the loneliest time of her life. She'd missed him desperately. His disappearance from her world had been devastating.

There were things about her that Heather and Charles could never know . . . horrible things. They were both from middle-class homes and had grown up comfortably, securely surrounded by loving families. They had no comprehension of the hell she had survived. And as much as she loved them both, she knew she could never share the ugly, hateful parts of her past with either of them.

If only she weren't so deeply in love with Charles. She shivered with terror at the thought of his disappointment and disillusionment if he ever knew her secrets. Her whole life was a lie. But that was her choice. It had nothing to do with Charles or what she felt for him. Nothing!

She had to be strong. She could give him what he wanted. Those first few moments in his arms weren't frightening at all. They'd been wonderful. His kisses were electric. They exceeded her wildest imagination.

For the first time in her life, she felt beautiful . . . adored by one special man . . . her man. Diane placed a hand over her heart, acknowledging the pleasure she'd found in his embrace. Her body had felt so soft and pliable in his arms. Her breasts had felt so heavy, her nipples had ached for his touch. She had wanted to feel his hands on her body . . . his mouth . . .

Yes, she had wanted that. She'd been so moist in her womanly center that she'd found herself craving the hard pressure of his thigh between her legs. She had just managed to stop herself from rubbing herself against his thigh. Although she yearned to love and be loved completely as a woman, she was still unsure of herself.

It had been her experience that only women like Heather found that special kind of deep happiness with a man. Not women like her or her mother.

No! She wasn't like her mother. She might look like her, might even even attract men like her. That was where the similarity ended. She couldn't be like Lillie! Never . . . like her!

Four

(*Day 8, Saturday: Port of Spain, Trinidad*)

Charles wondered if an hour and a half of sleep qualified as more than a catnap? He'd tossed and turned restlessly before finally dropping off around four.

He was up and circling the jogging track by five-thirty. As he worked his body, his head raced with thoughts of Diane. She'd turned him down once and he'd sworn he'd never be fool enough to give her another opportunity. Wounded pride had been the enabler that had allowed him to keep his distance. He'd told himself she was all wrong for him.

Was he yet again about to shoot himself in the foot? Or was he just addicted to Diane's unique brand of heartache? Damn it! He was tired of fighting his feelings for her. He couldn't sleep, he couldn't enjoy the food or any of the other diversions available on board this luxury liner. Yeah, he wanted her, badly. Could he ever really trust her to keep her word? Would she disappoint him again?

He was no closer to an answer by the time he started swimming laps in the pool. He had known from the first how deeply she affected him. Yet it wasn't until their estrangement that he'd accepted how much she really meant to him. He would never forget the day he'd erupted with fury because she stubbornly clung to their friendship, refusing to even consider more. Even though he'd turned his back and walked away, the pain of losing her hadn't ever disappeared.

By the time he'd showered and changed into jeans and a blue-and-white sport shirt, he was thoroughly annoyed with himself. Once again he was focusing on the past. Hell! He'd made mistakes, too. He had been the one to strike out with angry, cruel words.

The Diane he had spent time with last evening was different. She was more open, more giving than ever before. She had even gone so far as to agree to his terms. She deserved a chance to prove that she had changed. She sure in hell had responded to his caresses and kisses. He just had to take care not to move too fast. They both needed time to adjust to this new situation. His heart accelerated at the thought of seeing her again.

"You're early." Diane joined him at one of the small tables on the sun deck.

His smile was warm and welcoming. "Yeah. I've been up for hours. Trying to keep the old bod in shape." His voice dropped when he asked, "How are you?"

Diane laughed, her lovely peach-tinted lips drawing his appreciative gaze. "Great! But you look a little tired. Are you sure you didn't overdo your workout this morning?" She looked fresh and lovely in bright orange shorts and a camp shirt.

"A few turns around the track? You're starting to sound like my baby sister. That girl acts like she's four years older than I am, rather than the other way around," he chuckled.

Diane smiled, wishing she'd had an opportunity to meet his family. They hadn't had an intimate relationship. She suppressed a sigh, realizing she wanted to know everything there was to know about him. "How is Eliz? How are her boys?"

"Nosy," Charles said with a hearty laugh, his eyes dancing. "Both of my nephews have really grown. You'd think Eliz has enough to do with keeping track of her family and working for the company. But no, she still manages to find time to try and run my life." He paused before asking, "How's your mom?"

Diane frowned, suddenly fascinated with her hands held tightly in her lap. "Busy. She's in New York, shopping and taking in the shows. About what I said earlier, I didn't mean . . ."

"I'm not offended, Diane." He lifted her chin so he could see her eyes. "In fact, I'm pleased by your concern. Hungry?"

"Uh-huh." She smiled, about to rise.

"Relax," he said, sliding his chair back. "I'll get it. What would you like?" he gestured toward the elaborate breakfast buffet.

"Grits with cheese and sausage."

They both laughed.

"I don't think they have that."

"Pancakes and strawberries."

"No eggs and bacon?"

"Boring."

"Be right back."

Charles filled both their plates and returned. They were halfway through their meal when he asked, "When are you going to admit it?"

"Admit what?"

"How we managed to be on the same cruise ship at the same time."

"You still think I followed you?"

"Yeah," his eyes glinted with laughter. "Admit it."

"Never."

His laugh was deep and throaty, and Diane was thrilled that his keen sense of humor was evident. This was the Charles Randol she had fallen in love with. This was the man who had always been there for her. He was strong and dependable.

Perhaps they could have a new beginning. She was almost

giddy from the possibility. Dear God, don't let me mess this up, she thought.

"What's wrong?"

Diane blinked, realizing how closely he'd been watching her. "Tell me about the accident . . . please."

He sighed heavily before he began. "I left the community center late that night. I was tired. I suddenly realized I was speeding. When I tried to slow the car, the brakes failed. I ended up going through the guardrail and into a tree."

She touched his hand. "You're lucky to be alive!"

"It was an accident. I'm almost back to normal. Let's talk about you."

Diane nodded. She pushed her plate away, her appetite gone. "I've been fine . . . working hard. Tell me about the kids at the center?"

"The kids I work with there don't come from two parent middle-class homes like we do, sweet cheeks. Most of them come from families with no male in the household. Don't get me wrong, I'm not saying every single-parent household fails."

Diane knew all about a single-parent household. She also knew about poverty and neglect. But unlike Charles, she hadn't read about it; she'd lived it. She shuddered, pushing back the memories that were no longer a part of her life to a place she never intended to revisit. She'd made a new life for herself.

". . . Some of the boys at the center are gang members."

"Charles! You can't be serious . . ." She didn't share Charles's and Heather's eagerness to get involved with the downtrodden. It was what she had done her best to forget. Why couldn't they see that putting themselves at risk didn't change a blasted thing?

"I'm damn serious about helping these kids. And I'm not about to let a few thugs get in my way. We're losing another generation of African-American males. Somebody has got to do something about it. Can you imagine how I felt after reading Kunjufu? In my view the brother is the leading educational consultant and author on the subject. Di, I had to become involved." When he saw the worry etched across her soft brown features, he said, "Let's talk about something a bit more pleasant . . . a bit more personal." He took her hand. "Have you given what we talked about last night more thought?"

"Don't change the subject. This kind of stuff can be dangerous. I couldn't bear it if anything bad happened to you."

"I won't take unnecessary risks . . . I promise."

Diane sighed. It looked as if she would have to be satisfied with that. But she still didn't like it . . . not one bit.

"Now, about last night. Have you thought about us?"

She nodded; her pulse accelerated. "That's all I've been able to think about. I . . ."

"Hello, you two," Jeanette Parks said, with a wide smile. "Up early, I see, Diane."

" 'Morning, Jeanette." Diane offered a welcoming smile before she introduced the two of them.

"My pleasure," Charles said, having risen to his feet. "Enjoying the cruise, Ms. Parks?"

"Without a doubt. Please, call me Jeanette. We're practically old friends. I saw you sitting at the bar our first night out."

Charles blinked in surprise, suddenly realizing that Jeanette was the gorgeous leggy woman who'd eyed him with frank feminine interest. The instant he'd noticed Diane, all else had gone right out of his head. Naturally, he'd seen the two of them together on several occasions, but he hadn't made the connection until now.

"Care to join us?" Diane asked.

"No, thanks. I need to get changed. A very nice man has persuaded me to go sightseeing with him today. Trinidad awaits! Have fun, you two." She squeezed Diane's shoulder before she hurried on.

"I don't doubt that for a minute," Charles murmured beneath his breath as he sat down.

"Doubt what?" Diane sipped papaya juice.

"Your friend's power to persuade. Every time I see the woman, she's with a different guy. She's got to have a revolving door on her cabin."

Diane swallowed with difficulty. That was exactly what he had always thought of *her.* How had Diane forgotten so quickly? She felt as if her heart had crumbled into a thousand tiny pieces as she very carefully folded her napkin and placed it beside her plate. She said, "If you will excuse me, I . . ."

"Where are you going?"

"I don't want an argument." Her eyes filled with tears. Quickly, she turned her face away. His hand on her arm prevented her from rising. She hissed, "In another minute you'll be comparing me to Jeanette."

"No, baby. I didn't mean anything. It was a stupid, thoughtless comment. I wasn't even thinking about you."

"Just last night you said . . ." She could not go on. She bit her bottom lip in hopes of controlling the tremor.

"Yeah. I've said some cruel and mean things out of jealousy." He sighed, before he went on to say, "We both know how to hurt each other. In fact, we're damn good at it. But, baby, that was before . . . before we talked." He tilted her chin so she was forced to meet his eyes. "I want another chance with you, Diane. I want to start again. And I want it to be right this time. I think we can make it work, baby."

Diane was trembling. She said, in a whisper, "Oh, Chuck. I don't know if it's possible."

"If we both want it and we're honest with each other, I don't see why not. Everything is possible, sweet cheeks. Let's pretend, we met last night. Let's use this cruise to really get to know each other. What do you say?"

She'd waited an eternity to hear him say those magical words. Nonetheless, fear swelled inside of her . . . momentarily overshadowing even her love for him. Their estrangement had been a living hell. At long last, he was reaching out to her. Was she strong enough to try?

Diane visually caressed the lines of his face, lingering on his beautiful eyes as if she could find the courage she needed from within their ebony depths. Sincerity and determination were evident in the angles of his strong jaw.

"Diane?"

His entire body was taut with tension as he waited for her response. It seemed like a lifetime before she slid her hand into his.

"Yes. Let's try."

His smile was warm. "Great. Ready to tour Trinidad? I know of a tiny, out-of-the-way restaurant that serves the best chowder in the Caribbean. Interested?"

(*Day 10, Monday: Cabrits, Dominica*)

"I'm warning you! If you know what's good for you, you'll stop!" Diane tried to sound stern but was giggling so hard, she could hardly make it out of the surf. "Charles!" she screeched from over her shoulder, as she raced ahead of him along the nearly deserted beach. "I'm not playing!"

With a broad grin, he easily eliminated the distance between them while admiring the way her suit clung to her sweetly shaped behind. Her bright pink two-piece suit was splashed with orange and red flowers. Although it was cut high at the thigh, a wide band modestly encircled her small waist. His large hands clasped her thighs. Thrown off balance, Diane would have fallen head first into the warm sand if Charles hadn't twisted his body so she landed on top of him. Her soft upper torso sprawled across his chest, her head cushioned on his wide shoulder.

"Say it!"

Laughing, Diane could barely talk, but she did manage

to get out, "Never!" She gasped, trying to catch her breath, shouting "Okay! Okay!" as one of his hands trailed upward. "Charles! No . . . please don't tickle me. I'll embarrass myself."

Charles watched her through sparkling dark eyes. The joy and laughter he saw on her face left him breathless with happiness. Being with this new, wondrously unguarded, warm, vibrant Diane the last few days had given him more pleasure than he thought possible. He found himself eager for her companionship and fascinated by her thoughts. She filled the empty spaces inside him.

Who did he think he was kidding? He'd given her his heart years ago. It was a wasted effort to try and reclaim it. Hell, how dense could he be? He was no monk. Yet he'd lost his appetite for other women. Oh, he noticed their beauty, but he didn't burn to make love to any of them. Only one woman consumed his thoughts, occupied his fantasies, invaded his dreams, and inflamed his senses into sizzling-hot need . . . and that woman was Diane. The most casual caress of her hand against his skin was enough to quadruple his heart rate. He was thrilled by their reconciliation.

Their being together had intensified his yearning to claim her for his alone. Yet they both needed time. Time to get to know and understand each other. He wasn't about to let his raging hormones jeopardize their newfound closeness.

Nevertheless, Diane had to know how desirable he found her. He'd been semi-aroused from the instant she'd removed the bright pink walking shorts she'd worn over her swimsuit. The Caribbean sun had deepened the toffee tones of her skin to a toasty brown. As he gazed down at her, he imagined cupping her soft breasts, which were covered by an annoying bra-like top. He could almost feel their hard, full tips. Her soft limbs rested between his muscular thighs. She was wondrously soft. Charles was fascinated with the way a bead of water rolled down her smooth throat before eventually disappearing between the lush swells of her breasts. As he pressed his face to her neck, his nostrils filled with her unique and feminine scent . . . pure seduction. He said her name seconds before his lips sampled hers in an intoxicatingly slow assault on her senses.

Diane sighed, opening her mouth for him, then gasped in delight as he licked her lips with the velvet tip of his tongue before dipping inside to stroke her tongue, then suckle. Diane moaned her pleasure. Her hands slid along his strong neck, over his shoulders, and down his back. She trembled from the shock of her own burgeoning desire. She could feel the firm pressure of his need for her against her thinly covered mound. Oh, she ached. Unwittingly, Diane lifted herself against his arousal. Goodness! The way he made her feel . . . forgetting all but her longing to be loved by him.

"Awww . . ." He tore his mouth from hers and eased from beneath her. He quickly rolled up to his feet. He raced into the surf and plunged beneath its surging force.

Trembling, Diane slowly sat up, locking her arms around upraised knees. With her chin propped on her knees, she concentrated on taking slow, deep, calming breaths, determined not to fret about her unusual behavior. They were on a public beach, and she hadn't wanted him to stop. She'd grown so needy of his hot, sweet kisses that she'd begun to expect them as her due. For the first time in her life, she wanted to share her body with a man. She loved him with all her heart. She wanted what every woman wants, to make love with her man. The trouble was, Charles was not yet hers. Just how did a woman let a man know she was ready to become his lover?

"It's getting late. We should be getting back to the ship," he said softly, reaching for a towel.

She jumped at the sound of his voice. Her nerves were raw.

Misunderstanding her frown, he teasingly asked, "You don't want to be stranded here, do you?"

As long as she was with him, it wouldn't matter. But she didn't dare voice her thoughts. Things were going so well between them, she was afraid to press her luck.

She watched as he pulled on a pair of cutoffs over his trunks and a short-sleeved pale blue knit shirt over his head. Diane began collecting towels, suntan lotion, a cassette player, and tapes and tossed them into a large straw totebag. Her walking shorts were the last thing she pulled on before running a comb through her short, damp curls.

Thank heaven for perms, she silently prayed. A quick glance into her compact confirmed that her lips were so swollen and pink from his kisses that she didn't need to apply color.

Lately, he'd made a practice of kissing her. He always seemed to stop abruptly, leaving her hungry for more. Charles never bothered to explain, nor had he asked more of her than those sweet, hot exchanges. It was her own responses which caused alarm. The second he took her into his arms, she forgot everything—her inhibitions, her fears, her doubts. It was as if her brain switched off and her body went into fast-forward. Charles was always the one in control, while she was like moist clay in his hands.

A populated beach wasn't the place for a romantic interlude. What about last night or the night before that, or even the one before that? He had made a habit of leaving her at her door, with her mouth tender from his kisses and her breasts aching for his touch.

"What have you decided?" he asked, once they were settled in the back of a taxicab, speeding toward the wharf. "Trinidad or Barbados or Dominica—which has the best beach?"

They both enjoyed swimming and water sports. Between local art exhibits and restaurants and shops they'd managed to sandwich in time for a visit to the glorious beaches in each port.

Diane giggled. "What a question! The entire trip has been a dream come true. I'm so glad I decided to come."

"Me, too." He gave her hand a squeeze. All too soon the taxi eased to a stop at the crowded wharf. Fishing in his pocket for his wallet, he boasted, "We made it with fifteen minutes to spare."

Diane was dismayed by the intimacy of her thoughts about Charles. After years of evading intimacy, she was the one left disappointed and craving more.

There was no misunderstanding; his conditions for reconciliation included commitment and intimacy. Had something happened in the last few days to cause him to change his mind? Had he decided against deepening their relationship?

"Face it, girl," Diane chided herself. She loved him so much she was willing to accept whatever terms he was offering. Her pride was no substitute for the pleasure she found in his arms. Had she forgotten how fortunate she was that he'd given her another chance? She had gambled when she'd decided to take this trip. So far, she had been lucky.

As he escorted her aboard the ship, he asked, "Shall we meet in the Rendezvous Lounge for a drink before dinner? Six-thirty?"

"That doesn't give me much time."

"You don't need much time, you are already gorgeous."

Diane smiled, warmed by the compliment. "I really enjoyed myself today. Thanks for showing me around the island. I know you've seen all this before . . ."

"My pleasure, sweet cheeks," he teased. It had been sheer joy. Although Charles had traveled extensively, this was his first cruise. Thanks to Diane, he was rediscovering the magic and beauty of the Caribbean. "Now, get moving. No more excuses."

She waved before hurrying on to her cabin. She took

special care with her appearance as she prepared for the evening ahead. She selected a yellow silk sheath of a dress that stopped a good two inches above her knees. Thin straps held the low bodice in place, while the soft fabric draped low in back, almost to her waist. It was impossible to wear a bra with the dress, and Diane was very conscious of her bare breasts. Her undergarments were limited to yellow lace bikini panties and sheer-to-the-waist hose. Cascading gold-beaded drop earrings glimmered whenever she turned her head. Her hair was soft and fluffy, curled just enough to frame her oval face. Charcoal-gray eyeshadow deepened the beauty of her eyes while touches of deep rose at her cheeks and on her lips seemed to heighten the richness of her skin. She was dabbing a bit of Joy behind her ears and her knees when the knock sounded.

"Hi," Diane said, her heart racing.

"Hi, yourself." Charles smiled, his dimples prominent. He leaned down to place a soft kiss on the supersensitive side of her throat. His hungry gaze leisurely traveled down her shapely frame, lingering on the top swell of her full breasts, then moving down past her hips to her beautifully shaped long, sexy legs to her small feet encased in strappy yellow high-heeled sandals. The color of her dress seemed to enhance the brown warmth of her skin. He swore beneath his breath, wondering if he would be able to keep his hands to himself.

Diane nervously smoothed her dress. "Will I do?"

"You're beautiful."

Heat flooded her face. "Thank you. You look very handsome yourself." She appreciated the way his cream suit and bronze silk shirt open at the throat complimented his long, muscular frame.

"Thank you. Hungry?"

"Mmm. Excuse me, Mr. Randol, but it was my understanding that we were meeting in the lounge?"

Charles smiled. "Couldn't wait."

When he didn't cross the threshold, Diane lifted an elegantly curved brow. He didn't make an effort to come inside.

"I'll be ready in a second."

"No rush." His smoldering gaze followed the.delectable sway of her behind as she walked to the dresser.

She quickly stuffed compact, lipstick, handkerchief, and key into a small gold-and-pearl-beaded evening bag. Turning, she smiled. "All set."

Charles breathed a sigh of relief when they were finally out in the corridor and on their way. A few more minutes in the privacy of her cabin and he wouldn't have been able to maintain his resolve. Damn it, he was teetering; a tiny nudge would no doubt send him over the edge. He wasn't sure how much longer he could go on ignoring his desire for her. Hell, he had no one to blame but himself. It had been his idea for them to focus on getting to know each other all over again. Now, he was the one back to feeling incredibly frustrated.

He was so blasted needy . . . desperate to make her his woman. He had to be absolutely sure this time. He couldn't afford another mistake with Diane. It was up to her to let him know that she wanted him as much as he wanted her. So far, she'd been as shy as an inexperienced girl, totally confusing him. He told himself over and over again that when the time was right, she would let him know. He just hoped he could wait without making an issue of it. The decision had to be hers.

Charles tucked her hand into the crook of his arm. "Did I tell you about the time I nearly burned down the chemistry lab?"

"What!" Diane giggled. "It's a wonder they let you out of college."

"No mystery there. My dad was a very major contributor to the university."

"Are you serious?"

"The chemistry building was named after my grandfather, Charles Alexander Randol. So you see, I didn't have an option as to what school I attended."

Diane knew he came from a well-to-do family. "I don't think you ever told me that before. It was your grandfather who started the family business, wasn't it?"

"Yeah."

They shared a booth in one of the lounges with floor-to-ceiling windows. The night view was enchanting.

"All the Randols attended Howard," he said thoughtfully.

"Big mistake. Central State is the best," she said, toying with her wineglass.

"Spoken like a proud graduate," he teased.

Diane giggled. "Eliz majored in accounting and business administration, if I recall. Didn't she meet her husband at Howard?"

"Yeah. I owe her. If she hadn't taken up the cause, I wouldn't have been able to play so long at Lawrence. She now heads the accounting department at Randol."

"Really? She's certainly moved up quickly. I know you must be very proud of her," Diane said wistfully, aware of the love the siblings shared. They'd always been so close.

"I must admit, the brat has done well for herself. It was rough after our folks died. But we were lucky."

Diane silently agreed, aware that his father's younger brother, Alex, and his wife, Helen, hadn't hesitated to make a home for them. They raised both Charles and Elizabeth like their own. Diane asked, "Did you aunt and uncle have kids of their own?"

"No, unfortunately not." The brothers, his dad and uncle, had been close, business partners as well as friends. "My sister and I often wished growing up that we had cousins. It certainly would have taken some of the pressure off."

"Pressure?"

"Uncle Alex and Aunt Helen had very high expectations for both of us. Eliz was to marry well, and I was to someday head the family business." He laughed. "Eliz, at least, did her part."

Diane was shocked. He'd never told her that he felt like this. She'd always assumed that he'd been content. She said, "I'm sure your aunt and uncle are very proud of you. You're an excellent educator. You care about kids. And the community work you've done can only be applauded." She blinked in surprise, realizing she meant every word.

Charles was touched by the sincerity in her voice. "Giving back to the community has always been important in my family, mainly due to Aunt Helen's charities. The Black United Fund has been her favorite. I think I've told you that business is Uncle Alex's passion, just as it was my father's and grandfather's." She nodded. Then he said tightly; "I know I would have been a disappointment to my old man. It's only since I was forced to take over because of my uncle's illness that I've redeemed myself."

She heard a measure of hurt in his voice. She whispered, "Why are you telling me this?"

He laced her fingers through his. "I want an open, honest relationship. Okay?"

Diane wasn't sure if she could handle the emotional intimacy he craved. It was totally beyond her experiences. Nodding her agreement, she sent up a silent prayer for courage.

Five

(*Day 10, Monday: Late evening*)

It was late when they strolled the decks enjoying the balmy breeze and the moonlight.

Charles said, close to her ear, "Tell me something new about yourself."

Diane's entire body went rigid for a moment. "Like what?"

He shrugged. "You never talk about your childhood. I know you grew up in Chicago. Why didn't you go back home after college?"

Diane forced back a shudder. She swallowed with difficulty. Her heart felt as if it had turned over in her chest. It took her a few precious minutes to calm herself enough to think. She couldn't afford to make any stupid mistakes. Fortifying herself and silencing her conscience, she knew it was too late to consider honesty. She had chosen her path long ago when she'd vowed to never look back . . . the past was gone. It belonged to another life . . . another Diane.

Diane lifted her chin and told him the story she'd claimed as her own when she'd left home. "I wanted a change. I was eager to prove myself. Detroit seemed like the place. As you know, my parents were divorced and my mother and I have never gotten along. Childhood wasn't fun, not with my parents always fighting. After my dad was killed in that car accident, I had no reason to go back to Chicago."

"I'm sorry." How had he forgotten? He hadn't meant to bring up painful memories. Stupid! He remembered her telling him that she never really knew her father, that he had never taken time with her when he was alive. "My mother's working on her fifth or sixth husband at the moment. I've lost count," Diane said casually.

The entire time she was talking, her eyes were locked on the distant horizon. She found it impossible to look directly into his dark handsome face and lie.

Charles's large hands settled on her soft shoulders. He caressed her arms. "Your mother must be beautiful, like you."

Diane was momentarily stunned by the comparison. She closed her eyes, biting her lips in order to contain the depth of bitterness and resentment she felt because her mother was the kind of woman who sold her body. Lillie was the last person Diane wanted to resemble.

"Tell me . . ." he said, in a soft, deep voice, " . . . what you want more than anything else in the world."

Diane stared down into the midnight-blue depths of the rushing water far below, exposing the vulnerable lines of her graceful neck. She'd been happier with him these past few days than ever before. Just being with Charles filled the dark emptiness inside her.

"Di?"

"I might have everything I want right now."

His warm breath caressed her skin before his generous mouth brushed her nape, his tongue sending chills up her spine. "I hope I'm included in that everything?"

Suddenly feeling very open and exposed, Diane knew she was moving into dangerous uncharted waters with this special man she loved more than she'd ever dreamed possible. She loved him with all her heart, her soul.

"Have you enjoyed these past few days as much as I have?"

"Oh, yes," she whispered, barely able to vocalize her joy. If only she could contain the fear of losing him.

"But is it enough? Do you want more, Diane? Do you want me?"

Charles held his breath, his heart slamming against his chest with the force of a sledgehammer. His hands were at her waist. He eased her back until she rested against him, her back to his front, her soft hips against his engorged sex. He could no more deny his need than he could harness the flow of the sea. His head was lowered, his mouth a breath away from the side of her neck.

"Chuck . . ."

He released a rush of air from his lungs. "Tell me."

Diane was trembling so badly she wasn't sure if she could speak, let alone formulate a coherent thought. His arms surrounded her, his large hands spanned her midsection just below the swell of her breasts and above her flat stomach.

"Tell me you want me as much as I want you. I'm trying, baby, to take this slow. Give us time to really put the past behind us. But I'm reaching my limit. All I can think about is how much I want to make love to you." His voice sounded gruff, even to his own ears.

If not for his support, she would have fallen. Yet she had to see his face, his eyes. She turned until her eyes could search his. What she saw there made her tremble. He cared about her . . . really cared about her. Her lips parted and she stood on tiptoe to move her mouth against his warm masculine mouth.

When she spoke, her voice was husky with feminine desire. "I want you, too. Make me yours."

Charles covered her mouth with his, his masculine possession unmistakable. He coaxed her until her lips opened for him. Diane pressed even closer to him, loving the spicy aftershave he favored that blended so wonderfully with his own special scent. His body was so firm, so welcoming, so exciting, and yet comforting. Charles groaned his pleasure . . . lost to everything but the woman in his arms.

Murmuring voices of an approaching couple penetrated the sensuous haze encompassing them. They parted out of necessity. She gripped the guardrail for support.

Charles was no less shaken. He balled his hands into potent fists of frustration and unfulfilled longing, ramming them into his slack pockets. The scowl on his face was proof positive that he didn't appreciate the intrusion.

"Come on, baby. We need some privacy."

He led the way to his stateroom rather than her cabin.

Diane didn't question their location. Her stomach was a mass of nerves. It seemed as if she had waited forever to hear him say those wonderful things. Oh, yes, she craved his caresses, his lovemaking. So why couldn't she stop trembling?

He'd been up front about the type of relationship he wanted. There was never any doubt on that score.

Unfortunately, she couldn't harness the fear. She'd lived with her appeal to the opposite sex since puberty, when she'd begun attracting not only the boys at school, but her mother's men. Over the years, she had learned to protect herself and stay out of intimate situations with men.

All that was about to change, and Charles was the one responsible. What had begun as a friendship had evolved so slowly that Diane hadn't been aware of falling in love with him. It had taken years, but now she understood what all those love songs were about. She understood what it meant to want to place someone else's happiness above your own.

As she stood just inside the door, watching Charles, she knew he wasn't the source of her discomfort, nor was she uncomfortable with the way he made her feel. She'd had plenty of time during their separation to come to terms with the depths of her feeling for him. What she hadn't come to terms with was her fear of sex. Not that she was naive, for she'd known about sex from the time she was a little girl, when she'd seen her mother with a man. The problem was that she'd never experienced it. Charles's intimate caresses and seductive kisses were the only ones she'd known. She was too ashamed to tell him that she was a thirty-two-year-old virgin.

After years of perfecting the art of keeping men at arm's length, Diane wasn't sure she could go through with her heart's deepest wish. Could she take Charles inside her body and let him do to her what she'd seen done to her mother? No, she mustn't think about Lillie. Not now, she begged of herself. Please, not now . . .

It seemed like such an ugly, dirty thing. What if it destroyed the beauty of what she felt for him? What then? Common sense told her that what they shared could never be ugly or dirty, but the harshness of what she'd seen and heard as a child seemed to haunt her as an adult.

She didn't have a choice. Charles would leave her if she didn't give him what he wanted. He'd never accept a refusal a second time. He wanted a relationship with her, a relationship that included sex.

Instead of sliding her arms around his trim waist and seeking the remembered heat of his mouth, she wandered around the sitting area, touching the freshly cut flowers in a crystal vase on the end table near the sofa. She lingered, studying the oil painting of the sea mounted on the wall.

Charles frowned, disturbed by her apparent nervousness. She practically jumped out of her skin when he cupped her shoulders. "What is it? You're as tight as a coil."

"I'm just a little tense," she whispered. Hearing the concern in his voice, she impulsively rested her cheek against his chest. "I love you."

His heart raced with joy. "That was worth a lifetime of waiting." His eyes caressed her. "I love you, too." He placed a strong hand beneath her chin, lifting her face so he could look at her. "What we've shared these past few days has been very special."

"Yes," she whispered, unable to believe her good fortune. He loved her! "You've made me very happy."

"Do you mean that?" His voice was thick with emotion.

"Yes. It's been wonderful. I've missed you so much."

His black eyes seemed to scorch her with the heat of his need. "I've waited an eternity to have you, but I want the words, Diane. Please, tell me it's me you want . . . only me. I'm not willing to share you ever again."

"Only you, Chuck . . . only you." Diane had gone up on tiptoe, her arms encircling his neck. Her sweet lips tasted his, their softness an irresistible enticement. She sipped at the corners of his generous lips before growing bold enough to slip her tongue into the hot recesses of his mouth.

Charles's response was immediate and utterly male. He opened his mouth to permit her to enjoy him fully while trying to ignore the dictates of his own hardening flesh. He groaned, pulling her close until her breasts were pillowed on his chest. He was more than ready to finish what had been started in the moonlight.

He held nothing back as she suckled his lower lip. He shivered, gently caressing her from her nape to her full, womanly hips. Her sweet moans of pleasure were almost his undoing. He deepened the kiss while moving her in his arms so that he could cradle one of her breasts. He gently rubbed the hardening peak against the silk of her dress. Diane experienced heat deep within her feminine core that seem to flare outward along her nerve endings.

"Diane . . ." He broke the seal of their lips only to return again and again for yet another intoxicating kiss. "I don't want there to be doubts about what we both want. If you want me to stop, tell me now."

She instantly stiffened. His mouth tightened and his eyes cooled. He dropped his arms to his side. When he attempted to step away from her, Diane tightened her hold around his waist, refusing to let go. Her lips were soft against the base of his throat in spite of the tremors that shook her limbs.

"Please . . ." Her hands were clumsy, her fingers unsteady, as she slid them down his chest. She began unbottoning his shirt. It took a few minutes to complete the task before she could place her cheek against his bare, warm flesh. "Please, don't go all cold on me. I hate it when you do that."

"I want to make love to you, but as usual, you're giving me so many mixed signals, I don't know what you want." He sighed. The fight slowly went out of him as her soft hands caressed the broad plane of his chest.

"I want you to make love to me."

Charles released a gruff moan of relief an instant before he hugged her tight. He bent, lifted her off her feet, and carried her to the sofa. He sank down onto the soft cushion with her draped across his lap.

"Show me, Di . . ." he murmured. He pressed his lips against her throat. "Show me that you want me."

There was no hesitation as she sought his enticing mouth, eager for more of his kisses. Her lips seemed to flower beneath his; her sweet tongue played with his. She didn't give herself time to think past the excitement of the moment. He filled her heart and her daydreams until there was no room for anything else . . . even fear. Her hands were soft and delicate as she explored his wide shoulders, his throat, and his hard-muscled chest. Remembering how she relished his caressing her nipples, she worried his tiny ebony nipple with the tips of her fingers, then her nail. He shivered with pleasure; his body throbbed with the power of his desire. Diane smiled at his obvious enjoyment. Her confidence and her own excitement grew as she repeated the caress, tonguing his nipple.

"Baby . . ." His hands were at her nape and he forced her mouth back to his. They exchanged a hot, deep kiss.

They were both breathless when they stopped. Charles slid the straps off her shoulders and watched in fascination as the cloth slipped down to pool at her waist. He could only stare at her beauty. Her breasts were full and perfectly formed. Her dark brown nipples were large, like thick drops of delectable chocolate. He couldn't wait to taste them . . . taste her. He didn't have to touch her to know her skin was softer and silkier than the cloth that had tantalized him, yet kept her hidden from him all evening. He ached to fill his hands with her softness, to palm and squeeze her breasts. But a tiny whimper from her brought his eyes back to hers. They were so large, and they were filled with anxiety.

He smiled at her, his voice a husky caress. "You are so beautiful, so exciting. I want you so badly." He held her close. He wanted it to be good for her . . . so good that she'd never regret her decision.

Charles's mouth returned to hers and he gave her a long, leisurely kiss. They had wasted so much time. They needed to be together. Eager to see all of her, he eased the dress away from her hips until it dropped to the floor. Then he rolled the pantyhose down her long slim legs. When he saw that tiny bit of yellow lace shielding her soft, fleshy mound from his gaze, he had to fight the urge to rip the damn things from her body. Carefully, he eased them down her legs. She was trembling . . . badly. He assumed it was from sweet expectation.

"Chuck . . . please," she begged. " . . . Kiss me." She was scared, so scared. She needed the assurance of his mouth on hers. Then she couldn't think, couldn't do anything but feel the searing heat of desire.

Charles didn't require a second invitation. His mouth went to hers and he sipped at her lips . . . nipping and licking her tantalizing full mouth. He didn't stop until she melted against him, her hips unwittingly moving against his thick shaft. He ached to give her the steel-hard friction she craved. She wasn't the only one on fire . . . hell, no. He was burning to be inside her moist sheath. But first he had to taste her, every sweet inch of her.

Diane blushed when he explained exactly what he longed to do. She surprised herself when she made no effort to shield herself from his hot male gaze.

His brown body was like a magnet drawing her to him. "You're wearing too many clothes," she complained, her mouth hot on his throat as she licked his skin. She heard his deep, throaty chuckle and she smiled, for she knew she had said the right thing. She slid off his lap to the carpet, her body between his strong, muscular thighs and her hands at his waist. But her hands were trembling so badly that she couldn't seem to undo the black eelskin belt at his waist.

Charles rose to his feet and quickly removed slacks and shoes and socks. He wore only black silk bikini briefs that barely contained his blatant masculinity.

Taking her hand, he pulled her to her feet. He held her against his side, loving the feel of her in his arms. With his mouth mesmerizing hers, Diane didn't even realize they'd reached the bed until she felt herself falling onto its firm support. Charles followed her down, returning again and again to the sweetness of her mouth as he filled his hands with her breasts. He savored the silky texture of her skin as he kissed his way down her body. Her breasts were wondrously soft. He bathed them with his tongue, irresistibly drawn to the dark, hardening centers. Her moaning response heightened his own enjoyment. He laved a nipple until she gasped out his name. Only then did he suck the chocolate peak into his mouth to apply an exquisite suction that left her whimpering with pleasure.

Lost in a world of sensuality where each new sensation was more exciting than the last, she didn't think she could bear any more pleasure. Charles relinquished her nipple. Before she could catch her breath, he moved to the other breast, repeating the delicious torment. As primitive desire burned uncontrollably within her womb, she parted her legs and rubbed her damp curls against his thigh.

"Did you like that? Did you like the feel of my mouth on your breasts, sweet cheeks?" he murmured, as he squeezed and caressed her shapely bottom. He shocked her when he turned her over and kissed the round firmness. "You have the sexiest behind. Watching you walk across the room makes me burn."

Diane was beyond words. Suddenly he wasn't there any longer. She opened her eyes in time to see him thrust his briefs down his long legs. Her eyes went wide with shock and uncertainty. Charles was a powerfully built man, an athlete. His upper body was strong, lean, and muscular. His sex was thick, heavy with desire.

Charles was so overwhelmed by her beauty that he didn't notice her fear. He covered her body with his as he sought and reclaimed her mouth. He kissed her until she was warm and pliable in his arms. Eventually, he dropped his head, returning again and again to her aching, firm nipples until she was moaning deep in her throat, calling his name. His large-fingered hands caressed her waist, her stomach, before moving lower. Diane cried out when he cupped her sex, gently stroking the dark, thick curls covering her mound, then squeezing her softness while with tender fingertips he applied a subtle pressure to the ultrasensitive nub. Thoroughly enchanted by her damp heat, Charles didn't hesitate to familiarize himself with the enticing feminine folds. She was so creamy and so wet that his shaft pulsed impatiently. She cried his name, shivering from his intimate caresses.

"Does it feel good, baby?" She was so unbelievably tight . . . so arousingly wet.

She whimpered her enjoyment as she moved against his ever-stroking finger as his thumb applied the exact pressure she craved.

"Tell me, baby . . . tell me how it feels," he whispered

close to her ear. His deep caress never eased, but moved faster and deeper as he tongued her nipple.

Diane was on fire. She sobbed out her sweet agony as the pressure built inside her. Suddenly, her entire body erupted and she convulsed wildly in his arms. Slowly a delicious warmth blanketed her. Diane pressed her face against his throat as she gradually recovered her breath.

"I've never known such pleasure," she whispered, as she caressed his chest.

"Touch me," he whispered against her lips. "I want so badly to feel your soft hands on my body."

She longed to return the pleasure he had given her. Her soft hand stroked his flat nipple. When he trembled, she stopped.

"No . . . don't stop . . . lower, please," he said, his voice thick with desire. Her hands moved lower, exploring the hard planes of his flat stomach. Charles held himself rigid while his body screamed for more. But he didn't make a sound until she neared the dense ebony hair surrounding his sex. Impatient for her touch, he took her hands in his and demonstrated how he needed her to hold him, stroke him. "Yes . . . oh, yes." His entire body quivered in reaction as she gloved his shaft. The pleasure intensified . . . his heart rate surged so dramatically that he knew he was dangerously close to losing control. Suddenly, he held her hands in his, giving her a hard, tongue-thrusting kiss.

"Didn't I do it right?"

Charles would have chuckled, but he couldn't find his voice. Finally he managed to say, "Yes, too well."

He reached into the nightstand, searching until he found what he was looking for and ripped open the foil package and prepared to join his body with hers. When he turned to her he licked the sensitive spot behind her ear while caressing her soft brown thighs. He covered her mouth with his, plunging his tongue into her mouth as his muscled thigh parted hers even more, spreading her wide. Charles settled between her thighs, stroking her moist feminine heat with the broad tip of his sex. He groaned her name as he caressed her.

Diane's breath came quick and uneven as she clenched his forearms, her eyes closed. She ached for and was terrified of his masculine power. "Please . . ." she begged, certain she would faint if he didn't do the worst and get it over with.

"After tonight there won't be any doubt about who you belong to. I'm going to make you mine, baby," he whispered, his mouth against hers.

"Hurry . . ."

Charles had no intention of rushing their joining. He had waited too long to have her. Gritting his teeth in determination not to rush, he slowly entered her body. He suddenly stopped in shocked dismay when he encountered a natural resistance. "What the . . ." he gasped aloud.

Needing the unyielding pressure of his manhood, she was so aroused that she arched her back, lifting the lushness of her breasts against his chest while instinctively tightening her inner muscles around him. Charles groaned his pleasure as she milked him, his resistance crumbled, and he plunged, tearing through the delicate membrane until he was fully lodged deep inside of her. Diane had cried out against the searing pain his hardness caused her.

"Forgive me . . ." he whispered, holding himself as still as he could in hopes of giving her body time to adjust to his size, as well as him gaining some measure of control over his relentless hunger to take her hard and quick. Her tight, wet heat was his undoing. He began to thrust slowly and as deep as he could without causing her pain.

Diane trembled as the scorching flames of desire eased the burning pain as his stroking invasion demanded more and more from her. He groaned her name repeatedly. She had no idea what he sought as he began worrying the ultrasensitive nub, the heart of her desires, with his thumb while continuously thrusting in and out of her body. That spiraling sweet tension she had felt before in his arms began to build once again, only this time it was stronger, and it came from deep inside her feminine core. Suddenly, Diane screamed his name as she reached a shattering climax a few strokes before his own exultant climax. Shuddering from the intensity of their release, Diane and Charles clung to each other.

Charles's pulse had barely slowed when he demanded, "Why, Diane? Why didn't you tell me?"

Six

"Why didn't you tell me you were a virgin?"

There was a heavy silence that Diane didn't even try to fill. She was overwhelmed by what had just happened between them. She had thought she knew what to expect. But she hadn't been prepared for the blazing hot pleasure or the lingering contentment which followed, a contentment that Charles evidentally didn't share. She yearned to hide from the condemnation she thought she heard in his voice as she struggled to find an answer.

Eventually she said, "I didn't think it mattered."

Charles couldn't believe her reasoning. Knowing would have saved him countless hours of anguish. For years, he'd been tormented, envisioning her making love with every man she'd dated. He had blamed her, left her for nothing. Well, not quite nothing, since she hadn't been willing to see only him. The things he had thought, the cruel accusations he had made, had caused them both needless pain.

"It mattered, Diane, because I care about you. Everything about you matters to me. It would have saved us so much grief."

Diane was at a loss for words. It was happening too fast. Her whole world felt as if it had been turned upside down. She didn't understand her own emotions, let alone his. She'd been alone for so long. She was not prepared for this kind of caring. It was all so new to her. She had no frame of reference . . . no comparison. He was handing her what she had longed for for too long. She was what was important to Charles. She hadn't made a mistake in trusting him with her heart, with her body. Why was he angry?

"Perhaps I should have told you," she said, so softly that he barely heard her. "But that shouldn't make you angry. You're supposed to be relieved that I didn't sleep with half a dozen men."

"I'm not angry with you because you were a virgin. I guess I'm upset that you didn't trust me with the truth. You lied to me by keeping this from me."

Tears flooded her gaze and she turned away. Suddenly Diane was ashamed, embarrassed by her nudity. She grabbed the sheet and quickly tugged it over herself as she eased toward the edge of the bed.

Caught up in his own sense of betrayal and feelings of downright stupidity, he didn't take note of the hurt in her brown eyes. "Where do you think you're going?" He knew he sounded angry. But damn it, he had a right to his feelings. How could they ever have a future if she didn't trust him?

But she was already on the floor, yanking at the sheet in an effort to free it.

"Diane!"

"No!" she hissed at him, as she rounded the foot of the bed. "You've said enough for both of us. Too much, in fact." Her face burned as she searched the floor for her panties.

Oblivious to his own nudity, he reached down for her. Catching her by the shoulders, he pulled her up and held on. "Why? Why did you let me think you were sleeping around?"

"I'm not responsible for your beliefs! What did I do that was so terrible? Make love with the one man I care about? I did nothing that deserves this kind of anger." Suddenly she was livid. "Let me go!" Planting both hands against his chest, she pushed hard. He didn't budge. Blinded by tears, she was forced to stop and brush them away. "What in the hell did you do with my panties?"

"Baby . . ." he said, his heart melting. Finally, Diane had admitted that he was the only man she cared about. Furthermore she'd proved it. She had chosen him to be her lover . . . him.

"Don't you baby me, you big jerk! This is a big ship. If we work at it, I'm sure we don't have to see each other—ever!" She spotted her dress, but he held on to her. "Will you let go of me?"

"Never," he said, as he swung her up into his arms. She kicked and hit at him, throwing him off balance. They came down on the bed together. The heavy weight of his muscled thigh across hers held her in place. "Stop it. You're gonna hurt yourself." His voice dropped and he chuckled throatily. "Never mind. Don't stop. I like the way you feel." His eyes were twinkling with amusement.

Diane was furious. But she stopped instantly when she realized she was rubbing her nipples against his chest and the soft curls covering her sex against his inner thigh. He was aroused.

"I hate you!"

"Well, I'm crazy about you, sweet cheeks," he said, rubbing her hips. Charles chuckled watching her blush. He grinned realizing how lucky he was. Instead of yelling at her, he should be kissing her pretty feet. He was the only man she cared enough to give herself to.

"I don't see anything funny."

"No? How about me? I've been a jealous fool."

Diane turned her head away. He sighed. When he lifted his thigh, he was relieved when she didn't attempt to leave his side. She wouldn't look at him, either.

"Why? Central State had no shortage of men; for that matter, neither does Detroit. Why did you wait so long?"

"What difference does it make?" she said cautiously.

"I'd like to understand."

"I've never been in love before. It just seemed pointless without the love."

"You made me very happy tonight," he said, his voice heavy with emotion. "I'm so glad you waited, and I'm thrilled that you chose *me* to be your lover. I should have told you that earlier. Can you forgive me?"

"No!" But it didn't come out with the vehemence she'd intended. She was surrounded by his blatant masculinity. All she had to do was relax and she'd be back where she wanted to be, in his arms.

Charles kissed her along the side of her neck down to the base of her throat. Diane trembled, responding in spite of herself to his warmth and tenderness.

"Diane . . . let me hold you . . . please," he said, against her throat.

Diane moaned softly, her arms going around his trim waist as she clung to him. He showered her with gentle kisses, craving her warmth and sweetness.

"Chucky . . ." she whispered, returning his kisses. Her soft hands explored the hard planes of his chest and stomach, needing to love and be loved by him. Oh yes, this was what she wanted . . . what she'd always wanted . . . Charles. Unfortunately, it had taken her years to discover it. She had once foolishly turned her back on his love because she'd been afraid to show him how she felt about him.

When his lips opened over hers, sliding his tongue into her sweet mouth, he gave her the rough heat of his stroking tongue. Diane was lost in a sensual maze. His hot, wet tongue moved down her body across her shoulders to the fragrant valley between her breasts. Eventually he licked the ripe outer curve of a breast.

"You're so lovely," he murmured. He caressed the soft skin along her rib cage, down her flat stomach, and over her beautifully round behind. He palmed her, squeezing.

When he smoothed up the sensitive baby softness of her inner thighs, Diane closed herself off to his caress.

"I only want to touch you, baby. I know it's too soon for more. I'm sorry I had to hurt you. Are you very sore?"

Diane blushed, shocked by his candor. She finally mumbled, "I'm fine, but I need to freshen up."

Charles knew better than to suggest the obvious—that they both take advantage of that huge tub in the next room. His breath quickened and his sex lengthened at the thought. He ignored his desire in deference to her modesty.

"I'll wait for you here."

Diane's face became even hotter when she asked, "Do you mind if I take the sheet?"

Charles hid his smile. "Use my robe. It's on the hook inside the door."

"But . . ."

"Why don't I order a snack? It should be here by the time you finish." He turned his back to her, reaching for the telephone on the nightstand.

Diane didn't waste any time. She hurried into the bathroom. Leaning against the sink for support, she stared at herself in the wide mirror. She didn't look any different. Her dark eyes were large with disbelief and confusion. She'd gotten what she'd wanted . . . well, almost. Her knees were shaking so badly she had to hold on to keep from falling. Her life had changed drastically, and she was still scared . . . scared of her vulnerability . . . scared because a part of herself must always stay hidden.

Suddenly, she smiled, thoroughly pleased with herself. There was an unfamiliar ache deep inside her womanly center. She'd done it! She had done the wild thing! What's more, she had loved every minute of it. Well, maybe not every second. It had hurt badly at first . . . but then . . . oh my, the fireworks had begun.

It wasn't at all what she'd expected. She was so glad that it wasn't the dirty, disgusting act she'd witnessed as a child.

As she watched the tub fill, she remembered waking from a bad dream. She could not have been more than six at the time. She had tiptoed into her mother's room seeking comfort, something she'd never found there. Lillie hadn't been alone . . . which wasn't unusual. What was different was that the door had been left open. Diane had been terrified, certain the man was hurting her mother. Lillie had been furious when Diane had hurled her small body at the man's bare back, kicking and biting him in her determination to make him leave her mother alone. Lillie had flung her away, screaming at Diane to get the hell out and mind her own damn business. Diane shuddered, sliding into the soothing warmth of the water, surpressing the hated memory. It was best forgotten. Now was all that mattered.

Tonight had been so special. Not even the past could shatter her happiness. Charles had made it special for her. More important, she knew that she had pleased him . . . pleased him in ways she hadn't dreamed herself capable of. She had taken him inside her body and loved him. She pressed her cheeks, certain she was blushing. Despite the inital pain, it had been almost magical. And she couldn't wait to see him again.

She emerged from the bathroom, swamped by his beige silk robe. The silver tray on the nightstand boasted a crystal bowl filled with fresh strawberries, a bottle of champagne, and two crystal fluted glasses. Charles was right where she'd left him, stretched across the king-sized bed, only now he wore navy silk pajama bottoms. The only light came from a lamp in the sitting-room area. Diane spotted her dress, panties, and pantyhose neatly folded in a nearby chair. She blushed.

He held out a hand to her. She came down beside him, lacing her fingers with his. They smiled at each other.

"What took you so long?" he complained, smoothing dark curls away from her forehead.

"Miss me?" she teased, pressing her lips against the side

of his neck as she snuggled against his side, not wanting to think past the sweetness of the moment.

Her soft breath on his chest sent shivers of desire flaring through his system. His hands were gentle on her back as he caressed her. "Yeah. Can I interest you in a glass of champagne?" he asked, although he didn't particularly want to move. He liked having her here, curled against him. He wasn't thrilled about the material separating them, but he was determined to give her the time she needed to get used to him. He smiled to himself as he recalled the wonderful gift she had given him. His heart swelled with love.

"Why not?"

As Charles poured, he watched her. She was propped against the pillows, her soft breasts doing exciting things to his robe, her large nipples clearly outlined against the silk.

"You look better in that robe than I do," he chuckled at her look of surprise. He handed her a glass and sat facing her. The dish of strawberries rested between them on the bed.

"Shall I offer a toast?" She smiled playfully, realizing how happy she was.

"Please," he grinned.

"To us . . ."

"Yes . . . to us."

They clinked glasses. By the time she'd drained her glass and they'd emptied the bowl, Diane was so sleepy she could hardly keep her eyes open. Charles's eyes were dark and loving as he relieved her of the glass before moving to turn off the lamp. She curled up against him as if they'd been sleeping together since the beginning of time. It felt right to lie with her cheek over his heart.

"You're awfully quiet," she whispered. "Are you sleepy?"

He kissed her palm before placing it over his heart. "Feel that. Feel how my heart is racing. I'm not the least bit sleepy. I've waited for what seems like forever to have you in bed with me. Do you have any idea how I've fantasized about this?"

She snuggled closer to him her arms clasped around his waist. "I didn't know, but I'm glad." She'd never felt so safe, so protected, as she did right now with him. He cared about her . . . even loved her a little.

"Di, help me understand. Why me? Why now?"

"I told you . . . I love you."

"We've been friends for years. We've loved each other for years."

"No, not just loved each other. This is different. I don't just love you, Charles. I'm in love with you."

For an instant, Charles forgot to breathe. He recovered enough so when he crushed her to him he was careful not to hurt her. Not being able to see her had been a living hell for him. He'd given up hope of ever having the kind of devotion and love he craved from her. Here she was, handing him both on a silver platter.

"Oh, Diane . . . baby." He kissed her over and over again.

Diane responded wantonly to his male sweetness. His tongue swept inside her mouth . . . he took . . . he caressed . . . he savored. Charles nearly forgot his decision not to make love to her again tonight. He ended the kiss, then hugged her to him.

"Chuck . . ."

"Mmmm?"

"Did I please you? In bed, I mean. Did I satisfy you?"

"You're kidding, aren't you?" He'd never wanted a woman more, nor had he known such pleasure with another. Diane was special.

"I thought . . ."

He nestled against her throat. "Yes, absolutely. You're so special . . . so hot and wet and tight. Oh, baby . . . I want you now," he said close to her ear. "I want to make you scream my name again as you climax. I'm already hard just thinking about being inside you."

Thrilled, Diane began to explore his chest and taut stomach. The instant her soft hand reached his waistband he released the snap, allowing her access to his body. Diane hesitated an instant before exploring the dense thicket of black hair surrounding his sex. He recovered his sanity and caught her hand before she could stroke the length of his pulsating organ.

"No, baby. I can't stand that."

"But you said . . ."

"Yeah, I know."

"You didn't mean it."

"I meant it . . . every word. It was wonderful . . . you were wonderful."

"You just don't want me to touch you," she whispered.

"It feels good . . . too good. I can't take the softness of your hands without exploding . . . climaxing. I prefer to be inside you, baby. But it's too soon for you. I've already hurt you once tonight. Let's just take this one step at a time, okay?"

Diane blushed profusely. She didn't know what to say. She flushed with excitement at being with him. She pressed her lips against his ever so briefly.

Charles held her close but did nothing to complete their intimacy, pretending her cushiony soft breasts with their chocolate-brown tips weren't driving him nuts.

"Diane, I want you to promise me something, okay?"

"Yes."

"This is important to me."

"What?"

"I don't want there to be any more secrets between us. I want us to be up front with each other. I care about you, woman. I don't want anything or anyone to come between us. And secrets do that."

Diane's heart suddenly started pounding with dread. How

could she keep such a promise? There was so much about herself she could never tell him, so much she hadn't ever told anyone. Charles wouldn't understand. He'd grown up in a loving family with comfort, while she'd grown up with uncertainty and fear. What did he know about poverty? Or being totally alone in the world with no one to care whether you lived or died?

She wanted his respect. She'd worked hard to turn herself into the well-educated woman she faced in the mirror every day. She couldn't go back. And if she told him about the past, she would destroy any chance they might have for a future together.

"Diane . . . I want that promise."

What choice did she have? She loved him; she had to say the words and pray that he never discovered the truth. "I promise."

"Honey, you're shivering. Are you cold?"

"Hold me . . . please."

He held her close. His head was full of plans for their future. He drifted off to sleep with a smile on his full lips.

When he woke the next morning, he was alone. The pillow next to his held the imprint of her head, and her sweet scent lingered. He scowled with disappointment when he discovered she'd left without waking him.

Diane was so tense that by the time she'd joined Charles for breakfast, she wasn't sure she'd be able to eat. Her stomach was a tangle of butterflies. Uneasiness had sent her hurrying from his bed at the break of dawn.

"Good morning," she mumbled, unwilling to meet his dark, intense gaze as she took the chair across from him.

It had taken all her strength to face him again. She would be crushed if he was disappointed, or worse, regretted their lovemaking. It was all so new to her! How would a sophisticated woman handle a situation like this? She certainly wouldn't be terrified to see her lover. Diane was being silly and she knew it. There just didn't seem to be a whole lot she could do about it.

A frown drew his heavy brows into a straight line. "How are you?"

Diane, busy smoothing the napkin in her lap, said, "I'm fine. How are you?" She looked everywhere but at him.

"Did you get any sleep?"

"A little." She couldn't control the flush that rushed over her features. She wore a pretty blue sundress which did delightful things to her soft brown skin and left the creamy expanse of her arms and her shoulders bare. But it was her trembling pink-tinted lips that captured his attention. Suddenly, her soft, generous mouth formed an enchanting smile as the memory of their sweet kisses filled her thoughts and her large topaz eyes finally met his.

Charles's frown vanished.

"How about you? I mean, you were sleeping soundly when I left."

"Why did you leave?"

"Good morning. Coffee?" A waiter picked that moment to appear.

"Diane?"

"Tea for me, please."

"Sir?"

"Yes, thanks," Charles said. Then he realized that his hungry stare was contributing to her embarrassment. He pushed back his chair. Nothing this morning was going the way he'd like it to. She was uncomfortable in his presence. He wasn't sure how to handle the situation. Just the thought of losing her now disturbed him . . . perhaps terrified was the more appropriate word. Was he expecting too much too soon? "I'll get our food. Preferences?"

She shook her head. "No, thank you. I'm not hungry."

"Fruit?"

She shrugged. She didn't breathe easy until he walked

away. He was surely angry now. She was making such a mess of things. Diane felt like dropping her head in her hands and having a good cry.

He glanced at her from the breakfast buffet. He had rushed away before he'd done something that would really embarrass her, such as sampling her beautiful mouth the way he'd been yearning to do from the moment she'd joined him at the table. His preference had nothing to do with food.

He ached to hold her. He didn't relish the idea of sharing her with anyone. Charles would much rather have awakened with her still in his bed. He would have made slow, leisurely love to her this morning. Then, later, he'd have gladly ordered anything she wanted from room service. Their meal should have been in the privacy of his stateroom, where he could have indulged them both. He would have dearly loved to feed her all the pancakes and strawberries she could hold, but from a tray in his bed.

If he had his druthers, they'd spend the entire day in bed with him introducing her to the art of lovemaking. He had only one goal, to cement their relationship.

Whether she knew it or not, she was his woman now. She had made the decision last night when she'd given herself to him. Hadn't she told him she was in love with him? He wasn't about to let her walk away from that commitment. Yet she was tense this morning . . . too tense. Did she regret what had happened? It was too late to turn back the clock. They were lovers, and he intended to keep it that way.

He approached her chair from behind. His mouth settled briefly on the soft skin on the side of her neck before he put a plate down in front of her. It was brimming with her favorites.

"Charles!"

"Eat."

"I can't possibly eat all this."

"Eat what you can," he said, taking his seat. He began telling her about his most recent visit to St. Maarten.

The impersonal topic seemed to ease her nervousness. Diane was smiling when they finished their meal. A smug smile warmed his African features as he escorted her out of the dining room.

"Do you need to go back to your cabin?"

"Mmmm, I have to get my purse and hat. It won't take a minute.

"No rush. Philipsburg is not going anywhere."

"Shall I meet you on the dock in, say, ten minutes?"

"I'll go with you," he offered.

"That's not necessary."

"Oh, but it is."

Diane nodded and began telling him about the changes at Lawrence since he'd left. "I won't be long," she said, unlocking the cabin.

Charles held her hand before she could rush away. "How much longer do I have to wait?"

"I'll hurry . . ."

He tilted her chin up. "I'm referring to a proper good morning."

Diane blinked in dismay.

"Let me show you what I mean."

He opened his arms to her and she came into them. Their lips met tenderly. "Hi," he whispered in a deep masculine tone that sent tingles along her spine. "Oh, baby," he sighed, holding her close. "That's what I've been wanting since I woke and found you gone." He gave her a hard, tongue-thrusting kiss before he dropped his arms. "Ten minutes," he said, closing the door behind him.

Seven

(*Day 11, Tuesday: Philipsburg, St. Maarten*)

"Chuck! Will you quit?"

He grinned roguishly, recalling the way she'd said his name last night as he'd filled her body with his.

"Charles!"

"What, sweet cheeks?"

"Quit staring at me as if I were a slice of homemade poundcake," she whispered.

From Wathey Square they strolled onto Front Street, where the lanes were lined with boutiques. The sun was high overhead, not a cloud on the horizon. It was a picture-postcard day.

"I happened to love the sweet, buttery taste of poundcake," he teased, watching with pleasure as she blushed prettily. He didn't dare tell her how he longed to take his time and taste every inch of her soft, delectable body.

Her pulse quickened at the heat in his gaze. Her eyes locked with his. She remembered how he had sampled her . . . he had licked the soft, full curves of her breasts before he'd laved the hard tips.

Diane felt her nipples pucker against the soft cotton of her sundress. The aching peaks hardened as if eager for Charles once again to take them into the warmth of his mouth and suckle them as he'd done last night. Diane suppressed a husky moan.

He tenderly caressed her cheek. "Why wouldn't you let me buy that necklace for you? I know you liked it."

Diane was clearly shocked. He was referring to a very costly double strand of long, perfectly matched pearls with a heart-shaped diamond-and-ruby clasp they'd seen in a jewelry shop earlier. "It was far too expensive."

"You loved it. Besides, I want you to have it. A reminder of our time in St. Maarten." He recognized the change in himself. He was a wealthy man and could easily afford to indulge himself. He had chosen not to live that way. Yet because of his feelings for her, he wanted to give her things, lovely, expensive things. He wanted to please her.

"I couldn't." She shook her head firmly. Becoming a kept woman was not high on her priority list. She longed for his love, nothing more.

"They would have looked lovely next to your skin." His voice deepened as he visualized Diane wearing the pearls and nothing more.

"Look!" Diane stopped suddenly. "Isn't that beautiful?" she said, admiring a robe displayed in the boutique window. She didn't wait for an answer, but grabbed his hand. "Let's go in. I want to see what they have. I want to get a gift for Heather."

"You go ahead, sweet cheeks. I'm thirsty. I think I'll backtrack to that sidewalk café we passed earlier. Why don't I wait for you there?"

Diane smiled, deciding he'd probably be uncomfortable waiting while she shopped for intimate apparel. "Half hour?"

"Take as much time as you need. We're not due back at the ship until five."

"But I thought you wanted to visit Fort Amsterdam?"

"There's no need to rush. Remember, we're on vacation." He brushed her lips with his before he turned and headed back the way they'd come.

Determined not to waste a second of their time together,

Diane hurried inside. A ceiling fan cooled the interior and whirled the subtle scent of expensive French perfume in the air.

"Good day, madame," a very lovely older black woman greeted her with a wide smile and a distinctly Dutch accent. Her long braid was twisted into a chignon and she wore a colorful silk caftan.

Diane spent an enjoyable hour examining and trying on an array of fine garments. Even as she attempted to hurry, she found herself speculating on whether an item would appeal to Charles. They were lovers now. Their entire relationship had altered in the space of less than twenty-four hours.

Diane finally selected a red silk lace-edged teddy and matching floor-length robe. They looked as if they had been made especially for her. The workmanship was exquisite. Diane couldn't resist adding a very short black lace nightie to her purchases. She turned a blind eye to the total as she included a pale blue silk nightgown for Heather. She was so happy, she refused to think about anything other than the wonderful man waiting for her. As she hurried along the walkway, she realized she didn't want to waste even a minute away from him.

Charles was lounging at the outdoor café, joking with several of the local men, when she arrived breathless. There was a shopping bag at his feet.

"Sorry I took so long."

"Don't apologize," he said, getting to his feet. His smile was warm and welcoming as he held a chair for her. "What would you like?"

"Anything cold," she laughed.

That evening they spent a few fun-filled hours in the shipboard casino. Charles was thoroughly enchanted with her. She was breathtakingly beautiful in a cream silk jacket and wide-leg pleated evening pants. She surprised him when she refused to allow him to stake her. Although she insisted that gambling was a complete waste of hard-earned money, she laughed with excitement when he insisted that she play his cards at the blackjack table and they won.

It wasn't long before the casino paled in comparison to the dance floor . . . any excuse was a good one when it came to holding each other close.

The music was slow, romantic, and seductive. Charles held her close to his heart. Diane tried to express what being here with him meant to her, but Charles pressed his fingertips against her lips to halt the words.

"Sweetheart, it doesn't have to end."

Diane smiled indulgently. "I'm afraid it does. Next Sunday this wonderful ship will be docking in Miami. I hate to be the one to tell you this, honey, but we have to get off and fly home . . . to the real world of responsibilities and work."

Charles's eyes were far too intense for the light-hearted exchange. "No, you're wrong. What we have doesn't have to ever end, not unless we want it to. I'm in love with you, Diane Rivers, and I want you to marry me."

As the band played "My Girl," Diane didn't move so much as a muscle. Her legs were suddenly trembling so badly she was certain she'd have collapsed if he hadn't been holding her.

"Say something."

"You can't . . ." she stammered.

"I want you to be my wife. Tomorrow isn't soon enough for me."

Diane bit her lip, suddenly realizing her mouth had to have been hanging wide open. Had he really said he was in love with her?

"Do you love me, Diane? Or was that something you said in the heat of the moment?"

"Yes . . . I love you."

"And I love you. All you have to do is say the word and we can get married as soon as I can make the arrangements." He smiled down into her soft dark eyes. "The Virgin Islands are the perfect place for a wedding. We can get married in St. Thomas and stay on for a short honeymoon, then fly back to Miami on Sunday." Charles whispered close to her ear, "It's up to you, my love."

Diane shivered.

"Marry me, baby. I want to spend the rest of my life with you."

"Yes . . ." she said breathlessly, throwing her arms around his neck. She kissed him right there on the dance floor oblivious to everything around them. She didn't give herself a chance to think . . . to worry . . . to doubt. Charles loved her and was offering her everything she had ever wanted . . . a home . . . maybe even a family, someday.

Neither one of them heard the music stop or the band announce they were taking a break. Diane and Charles stood locked in each other's arms, unable to look further than each other's eyes.

"As soon as I can arrange it?" he insisted.

"Oh, my love, yes." Her eyes were brimming with tears.

His own eyes were sparkling with emotion as he took her hand and led her off the dance floor and out into the corridor. They'd barely cleared the door before he pulled her into his arms. He couldn't wait a second longer to savor her soft, enticing mouth.

"Oh, sweetheart . . ."

Diane clung to him. Eventually he lifted his head and rested his forehead against hers. They were both laughing when they noticed there were people all around. Lucky for them, no one was paying much attention.

Charles took her hand, tugging her along with him.

"Where are we going?"

"Anywhere we can be alone."

She had to hurry to keep up with him, but she was too happy to complain. When they reached the elevator, Diane whispered, "When did you know?"

He smiled down at her, asking softly, "How I felt about you?"

She nodded.

"I've known for a long time, almost from the first."

Shocked, Diane whispered, "So long?"

"Yeah."

"That would make it years ago."

"Yeah . . . I know."

"Was that why you were so angry with me? Why we had that terrible argument before you left Lawrence?" she asked, once they were alone in the elevator.

The confrontation had come on a perfectly normal spring day in her classroom at Lawrence. He had given her one choice: either she started dating him exclusively, or he would opt out of her life completely. Friendship was no longer a consideration.

"I couldn't stomach the idea of you being with other men." His intentions had not been to hurt her. He couldn't take it any longer.

"It was very disturbing at the time. It forced me to see your viewpoint. I'd become too comfortable with our friendship," she said, as the elevator doors opened. When they reached the outside deck, it was crowded with people. It seemed like everyone had had a similar idea. Seclusion was hard to come by, especially on such a glorious night as this.

"Thank God it's all behind us. Perhaps I should warn you, I'm a bit mule-headed. A Randol family trait."

Diane giggled, holding onto his arm.

"You like babies, don't you?"

Diane stopped suddenly. They had been circling the deck.

"What's wrong? Am I taking you too fast?"

"Yes! My head is spinning. I still haven't gotten used to the idea that you've been in love with me all this time.

Honey . . ." her voice trailed away. She stood on tiptoe, her arms around his neck. "Pinch me so I'll know I'm not dreaming."

Grinning, he shook his head. "I'd rather kiss you. That is, if I can find a place to do it privately."

"Let's go to my cabin."

"Don't tempt me."

"I just thought . . . you might want to . . ." She stopped, her face flushed with embarrassment.

"Make love?" he said, his voice thick with desire.

"I didn't say that!"

"You don't want to?"

"Of course, I do."

"Sweetheart, I'm trying to use my head and not the other part of me that is hard and hungry."

"Oh!"

"Did you think one time would satisfy me?" His laughter was deep and sensual. "Baby, you have a lot to learn about your man. I have a hearty appetite where you're concerned." He pressed her mouth briefly to hers. "Come on."

They finally found a secluded corner. They claimed side-by-side lounge chairs before sharing a long kiss.

"Well?"

"Huh?"

"You interested in babies?"

"As long as they're yours . . . yes." Her heart fluttered with excitement. More than anything, she wanted to have a family with him. "I hope I get pregnant right away."

Charles smiled, warmed by the possibility. "I'd like that, too. We've wasted enough time already."

Diane sighed happily.

He squeezed her. His voice a seductive whisper, he said, "I'd like to make love to you every night . . . make you climax like you did last night."

Diane found herself blushing like a young girl. She buried her face between his shoulder and his neck.

Charles, his gaze filled with longing, asked, "Are you interested?"

"Very much so."

His kiss was deep and enticing; his body throbbed with unfulfilled need when it finally ended.

Diane was clinging to him when she whispered, "Let's go to my cabin."

He shook his head. "I don't trust myself."

"What do you mean?"

"I want the next time we make love to mean forever. I want us to be married."

"But why?"

"I don't want you to have any doubts about me or how I feel about you. It's too important. So tonight you'll sleep in your bed alone and I'll do the same in mine. Then, in the morning, we'll talk."

"So you think I'm going to change my mind?" She didn't wait for his response, but rushed on, saying, "Well, I'm not. I love you. I want forever, too."

"I'm so glad to hear that."

"Stay with me tonight," she urged. "We don't have to . . ."

"Uh-uh. I can't sleep with you without wanting to make love to you. Besides, aren't you tender from last night?"

Charles was charmed by her innocence as she hid her face against his chest. "Baby, I'm already your lover, and soon I'm going to be your husband. There's nothing we can't talk about."

Diane loved the feel and the strength of him. He was her world. She would do anything to make him happy. There was no doubt in her mind that she would be the kind of wife he deserved. She had made a new life for herself. The street life of her past couldn't touch her now. It was finally over, and her future was rich with promise.

"I have something for you."

Her lashes went wide with surprise. "You don't have to give me anything. I've never been happier."

"Diane, now is not the time to refuse." He reached into his dinner jacket and pulled out a small white velvet box. "I hope you like it."

"Oh, Chucky!" She threw her arms around his neck, placing a series of kisses against his throat. "I love it."

He chuckled. "You haven't opened it yet."

"I love it because you gave it to me."

Charles was thrilled. He had met enough materialistic women to last him a lifetime, women whose number-one interest was his family background and his net worth. Diane was the only woman he'd given his heart to years ago. She was worth the wait . . . more than worth it. He was looking forward to spending his life attempting to make her happy. Impatient with the way she was staring at the box resting in her palm, he used his thumbnail to lift the lid.

"Oh!" Her eyes filled with tears.

"Do you like it?"

She nodded, brushing at her damp cheeks. "You're so good to me." She loved him so, yet she still couldn't quite believe that he wanted her to be his wife.

Charles's heart was brimming with emotion as he removed the ring, a heart-shaped ruby surrounded by marquise-cut diamonds. He placed it on her finger. "I love you," he said huskily as his mouth settled over hers.

He shivered from the sweetness of her lips. She pressed her breasts against him, running her hands over his arms and back.

"Oh, Diane . . ." he groaned, deepening the kiss.

Diane opened her mouth for him, sliding her tongue over his fleshy bottom lip. Charles shuddered as she invaded his mouth, her soft tongue doing marvelous things to his senses and destroying his equilibrium. He craved more . . . much more. He suckled her tongue, intensifying the exchange.

He was soon shaking with the force of his need for her.

He wanted her . . . every delectable inch of her. He consoled himself with the thought that once they belonged to each other he would take her over and over again.

Diane whimpered in protest when he broke the seal of their mouths. Charles would have laughed if he hadn't been so painfully aroused . . . thrilled that she wanted him as much as he wanted her.

"Why did you stop?"

Charles did laugh then, a deep, throaty sound. "I only have so much control, baby. Soon . . . very soon," he promised. "Love me?"

She smiled against his lips. "Very, very much."

"Good," he whispered. "If I can arrange it, we can be married tomorrow night."

"So soon . . . ?"

"Too soon?"

She shook her head. "I'd marry you tonight if I could."

Satisfied, he said, "And once we're married, nothing can keep me out of your bed . . . flood . . . famine . . . nothin'."

They shared several hot, sweet kisses.

"If we keep this up, I won't get any sleep tonight."

"I can't wait to sleep in your arms. 'Mrs. Charles Alexander Randol.' I love the sound of it," she sighed dreamily.

For a time they sat quietly relishing the night and each other. Diane shivered with sweet expectation.

"Come on. It's time we got you inside."

Arm in arm they left the smell of the deep, fragrant sea and the beauty of the night.

"Have you ever been to St. Thomas?"

"Nope."

"Good!" She smiled up at him. "We can discover the island together."

Charles seriously doubted there was a thing on the island he wanted to explore more than his future bride. He wanted to learn all of her sweet secrets. He longed to become a master at pleasuring her.

They'd barely closed the door to her cabin when she asked, "Last night," then hesitated.

"Aw, last night," he echoed, his breath warming her neck.

"It was . . ."

"What?"

"Pure magic," she said, flushed with embarrassment, but needing to know more. "Was it enough to keep you satisfied?"

Charles gazed into her eyes, which brimmed with uncertainty. "You are more than enough to keep me sated. Where are these doubts coming from?" His large hands cupped her shoulders.

"I know you've been with other women. And marriage is for a lifetime. I don't want you to be disappointed."

"On that score you have nothing to worry about. Yes, there have been others. But I'm in love with you. That's what makes it special between us—our love."

She smiled. "I'm so glad you feel that way."

"I've never felt this way about anyone before."

She held him, her arms around his waist, her cheek pressed against his chest.

"I know it hurt last night," he surprised her by saying. "I promise I'll make it better for you the next time."

She quivered in his arms, her body tingling with excitement. "Chucky."

"Oh, baby. That's how you said my name when you climaxed. It sends shivers all through me," he whispered, his large hands caressing her back. He gave her a soft, tender kiss. It ended much too quickly, to Diane's way of thinking. Charles's hands dropped to his sides. "Start packing, darlin'. We want an early start."

"I'll be ready."

"No doubts?"

"None."

He said, close to her ear, "Very soon, my love, we will belong only to each other. On our wedding night, I'll show you how much you mean to me. Sleep well." He closed the door silently behind him. Diane stood with her hands pressed to her lips, wondering what she'd done to deserve such joy.

(*Day 12, Wednesday: Saint Thomas*)

"Oh!" Diane exclaimed, throwing her arms wide at the spectacular view. "St. Thomas is a perfect place for a wedding. It's too beautiful."

They stood on the patio of one of the secluded villas that overlooked Magens Bay. Each villa afforded privacy and a breathtaking view mere steps from the powder-soft sandy beach and deep blue of the sea. The complex featured world-class restaurants, tennis courts, an exercise gym, a pool, and all the amenities of a luxurious hotel.

Charles pressed his lips against the side of Diane's neck. "Too beautiful? I suppose that means you like it?"

"Mmm." Diane leaned back against him. They had both slept very little the night before. When dawn lit the sky, they were both up, eager for the new day . . . their wedding day.

They'd been busy since the ship had docked in Charlotte Amalie. They didn't have to have a blood test, but they did have to apply for an application that normally took eight days. Luckily, Charles found a way to get around the waiting period.

"One of us needs a wedding dress."

"You?" she teased.

"Very funny. Love me?"

"Yes . . . yes . . . yes . . ." Diane turned, brushing her mouth with his. "I can't believe it. It's happening so fast. Are you happy?"

"I will be in a few hours, when you're wearing my wedding band. "Let's get busy. While you shop for your dress, I'll find us a nice chapel. You won't be disappointed, I promise."

Before she could collect her thoughts, he kissed her, a gentle caress of their mouths and soft brush of their tongues. Smiling, they laced fingers, her small hand almost completely covered by his. They walked past their luggage in the marble foyer and hurried out into the sunlight.

Eight

(Day 12, Wednesday night: Saint Thomas)

Their wedding was very simple and very beautiful. It was a candlelit service at a small, flower-filled chapel on the hill overlooking the bay.

When Charles kissed his new wife at the end of the ceremony, he discovered tears trickling down her cheeks.

"I hope those are tears of happiness," he whispered close to her ear.

"Oh, yes . . . my love," she said, with a tremendous smile.

He didn't have a chance to say more until they were alone on their way back to the villa. "Are you all right, baby?"

She squeezed his hand, but she didn't say a word. She couldn't. She was choked up with emotion. She was astonished when her new husband lifted her out of the car and carried her inside the villa.

She hugged him tight as her slim legs slid down between his muscled thighs. Her mouth tantalized his too briefly before she followed the foyer into the spacious living area still carrying her bridal bouquet of pale pink orchids.

Charles's heart ached with love and pride as he studied her. She had never looked more beautiful. She took his breath away. Her dress was knee-length, with layer upon layer of soft white chiffon that floated with her every movement. Her hair was brushed to one side, a spray of pink baby orchids pinned above her ear. Pearls surrounded by gold studs adorned her earlobes.

He watched as she kicked off her white high heels and walked barefoot to the French doors that opened out onto the veranda. The soft hum of the ceiling fans overhead were the only sound in the villa. He longed to go to her, but he sensed she needed a moment to collect her thoughts.

He followed the foyer toward the back of the central hall. A round dining table in front of another set of floor-to-ceiling glass doors was set with fine china and crystal. A bottle of champagne rested in a gold ice bucket, with two fluted crystal glasses nearby. On the side table a covered serving tray held cold lobster salad, crisp salad greens, and, a bowl of fresh fruit. Satisfied that all was to his specification, he walked back to the living room and found Diane in the exact same place, staring out at the sea. He dropped his white dinner jacket over the back of one of the overstuffed cream sofas before approaching his bride.

"You're awfully quiet." His large dark hands settled at her waist.

"I know," she said softly.

"Having second thoughts?" His heart pounded uneasily.

She shook her head. "I think I'm in shock," she whispered, leaning back against his strong chest. "I can't believe we're actually married."

"Believe it." His voice was husky as he slid his hands around her and held her close, his mouth leaving warm kisses against the side of her throat. "Diane Randol."

Diane shivered in reaction, closing her eyes against the sweet pleasure of all her dreams coming true. She'd given up hope of ever being able to trust a man. Love was an elusive treasure she'd never counted on.

"Do you like your wedding ring?"

"Oh, honey, it's the most beautiful thing I've ever seen." She held up her hand to admire the wide gold band completely encircled with square-cut diamond baguettes, teamed with the ruby engagement ring. She was overwhelmed by his generosity. "The rings are much too costly. What if I lose them?"

"Don't worry. I'll buy you new ones," he chuckled.

She turned in his arms. "Thank you. I love them and I love you."

"You're trembling," he said, running his hands up and down her chiffon-covered arms. "Scared?"

"Of you?" She shook her head. "Never." She moved away, looking around the beautifully appointed room. It was sheer opulence; Charles had spared no expense. Her normal confidence had suddenly vanished. She felt totally out of her element. She must fit in his world. This was bigger than fitting into the educational world she'd been trained to understand. It was much bigger, and so much more was at risk. He headed a large corporation. He was part of a loving community-minded social family. What did she know about society functions?

"What's wrong, baby? You've been upset since we returned to the hotel complex. What is it?"

She nervously clasped her trembling fingers together, letting out a slow breath. She was unexpectedly terrified of the future . . . terrified of the unknown. She felt as she had when she had left home for good. What if she embarrassed him? She was petrified of losing him. After all, what she knew about marriage could fit into a thimble.

"Tell me what's bothering you," he urged.

Diane took a step away from him, but she didn't answer his question.

Diane watched as he slowly removed his tie and released the top three buttons of his shirt. The silk shirt was white, a stark contrast against his deep complexion and black hair. It seemed to enhance the richness of his smooth skin, his strong corded neck, and his broad shoulders. Her eyes lingered in the opening of his shirt, imagining the heat of his wide chest with its ebony nipples. She remembered how he'd trembled in reaction when she'd caressed him there.

"Di?"

Diane took a deep breath before she whispered, "I can't seem to stop worrying."

"About what? I know I rushed you into marriage. But I promise you, I'll never do anything to hurt you."

"Charles, it's not you. It's me." Because her eyes were glued to the floor, she missed the look of love and concern reflected in his dark gaze. "I don't want you ever to regret marrying me." There was just so much he didn't know about her . . . so much she could never tell him.

With his mouth warming the base of her throat, he whispered with absolute certainty, "Let's take this one day at a time. Okay?"

"Uh-huh," she nodded, comforted by his confidence, his warmth, and his love.

Charles assured himself that all she needed was time . . . time to get used to being his wife. He had swept her off her feet with his enthusiasm. Yet to him it seemed as if he'd waited a lifetime to make this woman his wife. He'd given up hope, telling himself that he would find someone else, someone who knew the meaning of the words love and commitment. These past few days had given him back his dreams, given him back his love.

"The hotel has provided a wedding supper. Shall we celebrate?"

"Let's." She gave him a beautiful smile.

With Diane seated on his lap, they shared a plate and a single glass of chilled champagne.

"Had enough?"

"Mmmm," she mumbled, her head against his shoulder, her thick black lashes lowered. Daintily, she covered a yawn. She was curled like a sexy kitten in his lap.

"Champagne and not enough sleep seem to be taking their toll on you, Mrs. Randol."

She smiled, loving the sound of her new name. "You consider one shared glass too much?"

"Evidently," he chuckled, relishing her feminine scent. He carried her into the bedroom. "Shower or bed?"

"Short nap," she murmured. She was too sleepy to be embarrassed as her husband removed her wedding finery, pulled back the bedclothes, and tucked her in.

When she woke at dawn, she realized she'd slept through their wedding night. She lay with her head pillowed on Charles's shoulder, one arm thrown across his trim waist and her leg nested between his thighs. Diane blushed when she noted he was nude, while she wore nothing more than the sheer white lace teddy she'd worn beneath her wedding gown.

Cautiously, she eased away from him, careful not to disturb him as she slipped out of bed and tiptoed into the bathroom. One look in the full-length bathroom mirror told its own story. She'd not only ruined their wedding night, but she hadn't creamed the make-up from her skin. She was a mess. A quick shower was refreshing, but it didn't remove the concern over disappointing her new husband.

"Good morning, Mrs. Randol," he said in a deep, husky voice when she returned wrapped in a pink towel.

"Good morning . . ."

"Come here." He watched as she approached the bed. One hand stroked the soft skin of her inner thigh while the other tugged the towel free. He pulled her down onto the bed. His dark eyes smoldered as he studied her lovely features. The feel of her caused his shaft to pulse with urgency.

"Did I wake you?"

"No problem." His eyes lingered on her soft, full lips.

"I fell asleep on you last night, didn't I?" She frowned. "Oh, honey, I'm so sorry. I spoiled our wedding night."

Charles cradled her chin as he looked into her eyes. His kiss was thorough. "I'm not complaining." Then his open mouth trailed down her throat, his tongue hot and tantalizing.

Diane trembled with spiraling excitement. He lifted her

until she lay on top of him, their bodies touching from chest to hip, her legs resting between his wide-spread thighs, the prominent ridge of his sex against her stomach.

"I love you so much."

"Show me," he said huskily, sampling the sweet-smelling soft skin behind her ear.

Lovingly, she traced his firm, full lips with her tongue. He moaned deep in his throat, but made no move to deepen the exchange. She suckled his tongue while caressing his smooth chest. When she teased his nipple with her nail, then soothed it with the warm wet wash of her tongue, Charles knew he was close to losing control of himself. He was hard and throbbing, ready to bury himself deep inside her.

"No more," he groaned, an instant before plunging his tongue into the honeyed depth of her mouth. She was soft and pliable in his arms. Charles rolled over, positioning Diane on her side.

"You're so beautiful . . ." he murmured, gazing down at her.

"No," she shook her head. "You're the beautiful one." She ran her fingertips over his hard, flat stomach.

Charles grinned, closing his eyes at the wondrous softness of her hands against his skin . . . close, but not close enough. Suddenly, he caught his breath as she shyly caressed his sex from the sensitive tip over the broad crown down the pulsating shaft and beyond to the fullness below. He groaned thickly, taking her soft hands and moving them to his chest until he could regain control of himself.

He began stroking her from her smooth throat to her soft, curvy bottom, squeezing her softness, relishing the feel of her. Diane gasped out her pleasure when he cupped a breast, smoothing over it before tugging on the sensitive nipple, then rolling it between his fingertips until it stood out, hard and throbbing. He caressed her until Diane called out his name, begging for his warm, wet mouth.

"Feel good, baby?" Charles sucked the hard peak into his mouth, applying a wonderful pressure that sent hot pleasure flowing throughout her body, pooling in her womb. He didn't stop until she was arching her back and rubbing the thick, damp curls covering her mound against his hard muscled thigh. Diane was out of her mind with yearning by the time he spread her thighs and caressed her intimately. She cried out as he rhythmically squeezed her softness. She was panting when he parted the dewy, fleshy folds.

She was so wet that his body's response was immediate. He quivered with a driving need to bury himself deep inside of her sweet fire, but he told himself, not yet. He longed to taste her fully, to learn all her intimate secrets. He slid down her body until her legs rested on either side of his shoulders.

"What are you doing?"

"Loving you . . ." he said, using his thumb to apply pressure to the sensitive bud, then stroking her. Diane soon lost her ability to think, to speak, only retaining an overwhelming sense of feeling. She did manage to whimper when he replaced his hand with his open, wet mouth. He was ruthless in his efforts to thoroughly lose himself in her sweetness. He laved her over and over again until she screamed out his name in a heart-wrenching moment of utter bliss.

Charles didn't give her time to recover. Unable to wait an instant longer, he sheathed himself in her sizzling heat. His passion was raw and unrelenting and it rode him mercilessly, but he refused to give in to it. He intended to make it special for her, so very special that she would know only absolute pleasure. He gave her all his love, all his hopes and dreams for the future, holding nothing back. Soon they were hurling together toward that ultimate pinnacle. They reached it as one sharing a fierce, shatteringly sweet climax that left them shuddering in each other's arms.

A soft breeze fluttered in through the open window. Charles moved his hand soothingly along Diane's spine. Neither spoke or moved away from the other for some time. When Charles disengaged himself and rolled to his side, he didn't release Diane.

"How are you? I didn't hurt you, did I? I mean, I wasn't too rough?"

Diane smiled, her eyes soft and brimming with love. "I'm fine . . . better than fine. Honey, it was . . ." Words failed her.

Charles chuckled. "So good it left you at a loss for words?"

"Something like that." Diane pressed her mouth into his collarbone. She moved her fingers into the thick hair at his nape. "Will it always be like that?"

"Better." Charles stretched. "Come on."

"Where are we going?"

"To shower . . ."

"I just did that," she teased, allowing him to tug her along.

"Not with me, you didn't."

The shower was warm and wet and wonderful as they soaped and kissed each other.

"I think I like this marriage stuff," she whispered, as her husband toweled her dry.

Charles lifted a brow. "Gonna keep me?" he asked, hugging her close.

His smell of toothpaste and soap and aftershave lotion were wonderful, Diane decided. "Yeah. I think so." Her stomach growled just then.

"Hungry?"

"For you . . ."

When she slid her tongue into his mouth and rubbed her breasts against his chest, he felt himself thicken and lift.

He brushed his lips over hers. "We need food to keep up our strength," he groaned, but he carried her back to their bed instead of to the kitchen.

It was much later, after a breakfast of fresh fruit, warm rolls, and hot coffee on the patio, that Charles placed a square velvet-covered box beside her plate.

"Your wedding present."

"I didn't have time to get you a gift."

"Oh, I already had my gift . . . and I hope to continue

enjoying it for the next forty or fifty years or so." He teased and laughed when she blushed. "Open it, sweet cheeks."

Diane slipped off the peach satin bow. Slowly she lifted the lid. A double strand of lustrous cultured pearls were nestled inside, secured by a heart-shaped diamond clasp surrounded by deep-red rubies. It was the necklace she'd admired in St. Maarten. There were also heart-shaped ruby earrings surrounded by diamonds.

"Oh!" she gasped, her eyes filling with tears.

Pleased, he secured the clasp around her neck and placed a soft kiss against her cheek. Her arms locked around his neck, and she pressed a dozen kisses against his lips.

"Thank you."

"One request?" he said, his voice heavy with emotion.

"Anything."

"Wear them for me . . . with nothing else."

"Gladly."

Friday was their final day on the island. They roused themselves enough to explore the world outside their villa. They decided to play tourist and took a leisurely drive into Charlotte Amalie, followed Veteran's Drive to tour Bluebeard's Castle, then Drake's Seat, which provided a spectacular view of Magens Bay and the nearby islands. They walked hand-in-hand through Emancipation Garden. It was a bright and cloudless day which ended far too quickly.

Soft ripples of the sea had lapped at their bare feet after they had taken a final swim and stroll along the deserted beach. Diane's mood was reflective as they enjoyed what was left of their time in St. Thomas.

"A penny?"

She smiled. "I'm not sure I want to go home. I've been so happy here."

"Me, too." He hugged her to him. "We'll come back again."

"Promise?"

"Promise."

Diane was almost asleep when Charles joined her in their moonlit bedroom. She sighed as she settled back against his chest, his arms wrapped around her. She smiled dreamily. He smelled so good, like sandalwood soap combined with his own wonderfully male scent.

"I don't think I'm ready to go back to work on Monday."

"You don't have to unless you want to."

"Oh, yes I do. Have you forgotten Mrs. Silvers?" Diane asked, referring to the principal at Lawrence, his old boss, her current boss.

He chuckled. "She's something, all right." Then he said softly, "It will be my pleasure to provide for you," before kissing her neck.

Diane couldn't imagine herself not working. She'd been working since she was a teenager. "Have you forgotten? I'm a career woman. I like what I do. Furthermore, I'm good at it."

"Yes, you're an excellent teacher. I've seen you in action. But sweetheart, you do have a choice. It's no longer necessary for you to work."

In a way, he was right. Charles could easily take care of her. She wore his ring and had vowed on their wedding day to share her life and her body with him. But one thing hadn't changed: she was still her mother's sole source of support. Even if she didn't love her work, she would never let him support her mother, even indirectly.

"If you like, I can invest your income. We could use it to set up a trust fund for our children."

"It's something to consider. About these babies, how many do you have in mind?"

He shrugged. "Five or six to start with." He laughed at her wide-eyed look of disbelief.

"I can't wait," she whispered dreamily. She could envision little girls with his eyes and rich brown skin.

"Let's get to work," he murmured, his wide-spread hand smoothing down her rib cage, over her silky-smooth stomach, and down to the triangle between her soft thighs. He smoothed over the nest of her thick curls, squeezing the soft lips together while using his thumb to worry the tiny center of her arousal.

"Chuck . . ."

"Hmm," he said, as he licked her nape while he continued his assault on her senses.

Diane's breath quickened as she moved her hips against his stroking hand. "Oh," she moaned, when he cupped a breast and tugged at the sensitive nipple. As his maddening strokes intensified she stiffened, trembling all over as she reached a climax . . . pleasure spreading to every cell in her body. She would have turned in his arms, but Charles held her in place.

"I want you," she persisted, hearing his heavy breathing and feeling his arousal against her back.

"You're going to have me," he whispered roughly, lifting her thigh. "Just hold still."

Suddenly, he was where she wanted him most as he slowly penetrated her, filling her, cherishing her, his mouth on her neck, his hands squeezing her breasts, his palms teasing her nipples. Diane closed her eyes and concentrated on following his lead. She moved with him, matching him stroke for stroke as he lost himself in her magical heat . . . Soon there was no beginning . . . no end . . . there was only their glorious union.

"Love me . . . love me . . . love me," he insisted.

"Yes . . . oh yes . . ." she breathed, as she heard his hoarse shout and felt the force of his release.

His kiss was almost as hot as the liquid fire he so easily aroused within her. Diane knew she could never stop loving this wonderful man. She promised herself that she would do everything within her power to make him a good wife.

"Go to sleep, baby. That plane leaves awfully early tomorrow."

Nine

Diane watched, melancholically, as the sparkling blue of the ocean far below disappeared from view.

"Why so sad?"

She turned, finding a smile for her new husband. "Not sad, just thoughtful. I didn't want to leave. I guess I don't want our honeymoon to end."

Charles laced his strong brown fingers with hers. "It's not ending, sweet thing. Our life together is just beginning."

"You're right," she smiled.

"Did I tell you how irresistible you look in that outfit?"

"Uh-huh . . . but you can tell me again." Diane laughed softly, looking down at her rather ordinary strawberry linen jacket, which she had teamed with cream silk slacks and shell. She suspected it was the rubies and diamonds in her ears matching the stones in her wedding rings that enhanced her appearance. She was unaware of the richness of her smooth brown complexion or her thick, curly black hair.

"Su-per-fine," he crooned, close to her ear, his ebony eyes twinkling with humor.

"I like the way you think, Mr. Randol," she giggled.

"And I'm wild about you, Mrs. Randol. Would you care for a demonstration?"

"No!" she blurted out, then blushed, afraid to look around in case they'd been overheard.

"Why not?"

"You know why!"

Undaunted, he brushed her generous rose-tinted mouth with his. What began as a simple caress quickly deepened. He claimed and suckled the sweet bounty of her tongue. When the kiss ended, Diane was weak with longing, while Charles was breathing hard, aching for more.

He almost laughed aloud. His breathing was not the only thing hard. He shifted uncomfortably in his seat. The odd thing was, he was not one for public displays, yet when it came to Diane, he quickly lost his head.

She whispered, "Have you no shame?"

He chuckled, "None. Being married to you has been worth all the hell you've put me through to get you."

Diane playfully hit his arm. "You're terrible!"

"No, just extremely grateful that I was the one who caught you. Love me?"

"Oh, yeah," she whispered, stroking his wide palm.

Diane still pinched herself when she woke each day beside Charles. She'd never known such happiness. When she'd boarded the plane for the cruise she'd had no idea she would return as Mrs. Charles Alexander Randol.

"I'm looking forward to you doing just that when we get home." His eyes were dark and seductive.

Diane blushed and Charles laughed throatily. He ordered two glasses of champagne from the cabin steward.

"What's this?" she asked, when he placed the long, slender velvet box in her lap. The jeweler's name on the box was familiar.

"A keepsake."

"I have you. I don't need anything more," she insisted, staring into his eyes.

"I'm so glad you feel that way, sweet cheeks. But I intend to keep right on spoiling you. I don't want you to regret the way you married me."

"Why would I?"

"Don't all little girls daydream of a big, lavish wedding with lots of bridesmaids and bridal showers and an elaborate wedding reception? My sister, Eliz, must have had twenty bridesmaids. It turned out to be a sorority event."

"I'm not a little girl, Mr. Randol. I haven't been for a long, long time," she said with a tilt of her head.

"I rushed you into marriage. Heather and your mother weren't there to share our happiness. You think I don't know how selfish I've been? I wanted you so badly that I didn't give you time to think. Monday I became your lover and Wednesday I became your husband."

Charles hadn't been willing to gamble on losing her. Once had been more than enough. He had pushed her out of his life because he couldn't handle her involvement with other men, only to learn later that he'd been completely wrong about her. She had proved her love for him, first by allowing him to become her only lover, but by also becoming his wife. With her beauty and sweet appeal, Diane could have had any man she'd set her sights on. He was nobody's fool. He'd move heaven and earth to make her his before they returned to Michigan—and reality.

"I have no regrets. You've made me so happy." Her eyes were bright with love. He'd come back into her life and filled it with sweet promise.

"I'm glad," he whispered gruffly, emotion clogging his throat. "Open your gift."

Diane fingered the box as she considered the sweeping changes in her life. She'd never known anyone like Charles, never been on the receiving end of so much generosity and unselfish love. There was so much he didn't know about her . . . there were so many secrets buried in her past . . . things she could never tell him. The necessity of those secrets weighed heavy on her heart. She had waited a lifetime for the joy and love they shared. She'd be crazy to let the past interfere with their future.

"Di . . ."

"I'm scared to open it. I can only guess at the cost.

Chuck, there are people living on the streets of Detroit without even a pillow to call their own."

He knew he was overwhelming her, but he couldn't help it. She meant the world to him. This was his way of making up for the heartache she had suffered as a result of his coldness and his cruelty. "If it makes you feel better, I'll donate the price of this to one of the homeless shelters when we get home. Okay?"

She nodded. Slowly she lifted the lid to discover a double-strand pearl bracelet with beautiful heart-shaped ruby clasp surrounded by diamonds, completing her wedding set. Her eyes flooded with tears as she lifted her face toward his. The hard, reassuring pressure of his mouth on hers told her all she needed to know.

He was grinning for all he was worth as he secured the bracelet on her slender wrist.

"To us," he said, huskily clicking the crystal champagne glass against hers.

After a sip, they spent a considerable amount of time smiling at each other, oblivious to their surroundings. Charles couldn't resist placing a lingering kiss on the side of her throat just below her ear. He watched her dark, silky lashes drop seductively as she shivered.

His breath quickened as he recalled with deep pleasure every one of the sensitive areas on her lush brown frame. The side of her throat was only one of those places he had tongued early that morning.

They had made hot, sweet love in the shower before they'd had to hurry in order to make it to the airport on time. Charles promised himself that tonight he would make amends for the morning's haste and make slow, leisurely love to Diane.

"Chuck . . ."

"Hmm?"

"I'm glad our wedding was private. I thought it was perfect. Didn't you?"

"Yes . . . perfect," he agreed with a smile. But she was frowning. "What?"

"Must you go back to the community center?" she asked in a tight whisper.

His bewilderment was stamped across his strong features. "You know how important, how *necessary,* the work is to me."

She nodded. "Honey, I support what you're trying to do, but aren't we talking about late nights in a high-crime area? I couldn't stand it if anything bad happened to you." His safety was more important to her than admirable goals.

"There's nothing to worry about."

"Nothing? What about the possibility of gang violence?"

"I don't take risks. I work with kids, not thugs, but if one of the gangs is willing to participate at the center without causing trouble, we'd welcome them. That's the goal, to show the kids there's another way of making it in this world."

She had fought her way out of poverty and she knew she was stronger because of it. Her past was just that—something she had willingly left behind. Her concern was for him alone. "You're my number-one priority. I want you safe. I'd like to have you around, not only to father our children, but to raise them, too. I want to grow old with you."

"Baby, don't worry. I'll be careful, but don't ask me to give up the mentoring program."

As she looked into his eyes, she knew his commitment was unshakable. She nodded.

He put an arm around her and held her close, her cheek against his muscular shoulder.

"You're going to be so busy with your workload at the company and at the community center. Are you sure you've got room in your life for a wife?"

"As long as that wife is you, I'll find time." He couldn't stop himself from fingering her fleshy bottom lip. He ached to take it into his mouth and suckle, tasting her until she quivered in his arms, opening her soft, sweet lips to the deep invasion of his tongue. Charles sighed heavily, preparing himself for a long wait.

Even at night, Metropolitan Airport was a beehive of activity. Diane was exhausted by the time they climbed into the limousine Charles had waiting at curbside.

"Your place or mine?"

"Yours. It will take me a while to pack all my things and close up my condo."

For the first time she considered the possibility of selling the condo. It was her first real home . . . completely hers. It had taken her months of searching and years of saving before she'd found the ideal home.

They were speeding along Interstate 94 when Charles said, "It shouldn't be difficult to find a buyer for your place. It's in a great location. I'll have my attorney look into it for you. Baby, you really don't have to do your own packing. That can easily be arranged."

Her arms were crossed tightly beneath her breasts and she stared straight ahead.

Charles looked at her expectantly. Finally he asked, "What's the matter?"

A tight-lipped Diane refused to so much as look at him.

"Would you rather we stayed at your place? Is that what this is about?"

"If I let you, you'd probably try to take over my whole life!" Diane snapped. She was suddenly hugging the opposite door. "I'm used to making my own decisions. I bought the condo . . . I'll decide if I want to sell it."

He studied her profile. "Baby . . . cut me some slack here. I only wanted to make things easier for you."

Diane slowly released the breath she'd been holding. Lacing her fingers through his, she said, "I'm sorry. I overreacted."

It seemed as if there were some things they hadn't gotten

around to discussing. Both of them had full lives before they married . . . full, separate lives.

Charles tipped her head toward his, but he didn't take a kiss. He was so close, his breath teased her mouth. It was Diane who bridged the space between them, savoring his full masculine mouth.

She teased, "In all the time we've known each other, I've never been to your place. Why is that?"

"I have no idea." He shrugged, lacing her fingers with his.

"What's it like?"

"It's brick and mortar, and a monster to keep up. I inherited it. Our family was one of the first African-Americans to own property in the area."

Diane discovered that Charles's description was a gross understatement. The Randol home was a stately manor house, a definite showplace. Even by Bloomfield Hills's lofty standards it was impressive. Diane was given the grand tour of its eight bedroom, indoor pool, ground-floor library, recreation room, extensive grounds, four-car garage, and separate servant's quarters. Charles had also failed to mentioned he'd inherited a live-in cook, maid, and manservant.

"You're awfully quiet," he said. They were downstairs in the huge family room on the side of the house that accessed the pool.

"Just thoughtful. You have a lovely home." Diane didn't want him to know how overwhelmed she was by the rapid change in her life. When she'd left for the cruise, she had never expected to return married.

"Excuse me, sir," asked the impeccably tailored elderly manservant. "May I get something for you or Mrs. Randol?"

"Diane?"

She shook her head, nervously rubbing the goose pimples on her bare arms. What had she gotten herself into? She felt completely out of her element.

"Nothing, thanks, Sheldon. Goodnight to you and Mrs. Sheldon."

Sheldon nodded his woolly snow-white head. His dark face beamed. "Once again, I would like to offer my wife's and my own best wishes to you both."

"Thank you," Charles grinned, momentarily removing his gaze from his wife.

Sheldon quietly closed the oak-paneled double doors behind him.

Diane stood in front of the huge stone fireplace where a fire burned cheerfully in the grate.

"My staff is impressed by your beauty," Charles said, from directly behind her. His large hands rested against her spine, just above the lush swell of her hips. He inhaled deeply, lured by the sweetness of her feminine scent.

"Your staff will no doubt need oxygen before breakfast. Not a one of them is under ninety. Who takes care of whom?"

Charles roared with laughter. "The Sheldons and their daughter, Rose, have worked for my family long before my sister and I were a twinkle in the old man's eye. Hell, they took care of my father and uncle when they were boys. They've taken good care of the Randols for more years than I can count. I wouldn't dream of asking them to retire. Every few weeks a cleaning service comes in and does the heavy-duty stuff."

"What you really mean is that you take better care of them than they take of you." Turning toward him, she slid her arms up to encircle his neck. "Oh, honey, you're such a sweet man."

He rested his chin against the top of her soft curls. "This is your home now. I want you to make as many changes to the place as you'd like."

Diane wondered how her pale modern pieces would fit in the heavy, dark, traditional decor. "Tell me about the portrait above the mantel."

"My parents, my sister, and me. That was painted only a few weeks before my mother died. She had a stroke." The Randols' closeness and love was unmistakable. It came from the heart.

Diane hadn't a clue to what that type of loving support and nurturing felt like. Yet it was something she was determined to give to her own children someday.

"How old were you?" She smiled, seeing the making of the man in the child's dark eyes and engaging dimple-cheeked smile.

"I was ten, Elizabeth was six. She barely remembers our mother," he said, with a degree of sadness. "My father died less than two years later. He drank himself to death, grieving for our mother."

Diane hugged him, kissing the base of his strong chin. "I'm sorry, honey."

For just an instant Charles welcomed her comfort before he collected himself. Pointing out one of the antique gold framed photographs on the mantel, he said, "That's Aunt Helen and Uncle Alex. And here's Eliz with her two boys and her husband."

"She's very beautiful."

Charles's eyes twinkled when he said, "Don't tell her that! I can't wait for you to meet my family. Eliz and Aunt Helen are going to be as crazy about you as I am," he went on to say. "I'm looking forward to meeting your mother. We'll have to call her and tell her our news."

Just the thought of a face-to-face meeting between Charles and Lillie was horrifying. Diane couldn't control the tremor that shook her entire frame.

"Cold?"

"Must be the change in the temperature," she hedged.

Charles added a pine-scented log to the fire. "Let's cuddle on the sofa." Once they were comfortable, with her curled against his side and his arm wrapped around her, he said, "Sweet cheeks, you might as well prepare yourself.

Aunt Helen and Eliz don't need much of an excuse to throw a party. A few close friends to those two can mean a cast of thousands."

"Do you really think they'll want to give a party in our honor?"

"You bet. Probably a huge reception, would be my guess."

"Honey, you're scaring me. We've been married less than a week." She shook her head vehemently. "Charles, I don't want a party. I don't want anything. All I want is you."

His mouth was possessive. "Make love with me, Mrs. Randol," he whispered. He had her blouse open before she could gather her thoughts. When he unhooked her bra and warmed her full breasts with his hands and then his wonderfully wet tongue, Diane forgot everything but her love for him.

It was much later, as she lay in their king-sized bed, listening to his even breathing, that she fretted over the possible ramification of their hasty marriage. It wasn't that she didn't want to meet his family; she did. She hoped they would like and accept her.

What she didn't want was to draw attention to herself with a wedding reception. How in the world could she explain her mother's absence? Hadn't she told enough lies already? How many more would she be forced to tell? She hated lying to him. Yet what choice did she have? There was no way he'd have married her if he'd known about her mother and their background She wasn't ashamed of the fact that it was humble. She'd worked hard to overcome it. That she could explain. How many times had she come home from school and found her mother passed out cold? No amount of shaking or calling could bring her around. How do you explain that your mother sold her body, not because she had to, not even because she wanted to, but because it supported her fondness for alcohol and drugs?

Tears trickled down Diane's cheeks. She turned her back

to her husband and bit her lip to hold back the sound of her sobs. She stopped breathing when Charles stirred beside her. He rolled toward her. He didn't wake, but he didn't settle, either, until his arm was around her waist. His open palm rested on her stomach. Diane lay perfectly still, her back to his front, her hand over her mouth, determined to swallow her tears. By taking slow, deep breaths, she managed to calm herself. She was just scared and tired from the long flight. It would be all right. Everything would be fine.

She would focus on cherishing every precious moment she shared with her husband. They would make beautiful babies together. Someday they would have a family of their own . . . a real family. She wouldn't let anything or anyone destroy their happiness.

Diane had never had a real home. They'd lived in cheap hotels or rundown apartments. Her first memory was of being alone at night . . . scared of the dark . . . scared of the sounds just beyond the door . . . terrified of the strange sounds coming from her mother's room. Everything had changed for her when her little brother had been born. Diane had loved him from the first instant she'd seen him. After that, she wasn't alone at night . . . Danny was there. Diane used to cuddle with him through the night . . . taking care of his every need. He'd been such a sickly baby. And as they'd grown older, they'd not only cared for themselves, but for their mother too . . . when Lillie had been beaten up by one of her men or been too drunk or strung out on drugs to take care of herself.

It was in school that Diane had learned that she was different from other children. To compensate, she'd learned to make up stories, to pretend she had a mother who took care of them and cooked for them and a father who loved them dearly. She lied to her teachers, she lied to her classmates. She made up whole stories about her wonderful mother and father, who never managed to find time to attend parent-teacher conferences or school functions because they worked so hard. She was a bright child and an excellent student. She watched and learned.

She did everything early. She learned how to make peanut-butter and jelly sandwiches, and she learned how to beg money from her mother in the morning before she went to school so she could shop after school for their evening meal at the corner store. She also learned never to get in trouble in school, never to cause undue attention to herself.

The most stable time of their life had been when her mother had been in rehab. Danny and Diane had been placed with Lillie's sister, Jean. It wasn't so much that she wanted two extra mouths to feed, but the money from the state came in handy, especially since she had five kids of her own.

Aunt Jean didn't love them like her own, but she was very good to them. She saw to it that they had three regular meals a day and that Diane could go to school without having to worry about Danny or her mother. Danny received the medical treatment he needed. Diane really excelled in school. There were trips to the library and to church on Sundays. There were family picnics and occasional shopping trips for new shoes and clothes. To this day Diane was grateful to Aunt Jean.

"Can't sleep?" Charles asked quietly.

"No. Did I wake you?"

"I'm not sure what woke me," he said stroking her soft, smooth skin from her stomach to the tight, soft curls between her thighs. He cupped and squeezed her softness before worrying the tiny heart of her desire. When he slid a finger deep inside, she was damp and welcoming. Her sensuous moans caused his heart to skip a beat.

"Yes?"

"Yes . . ."

Ten

When the doorbell chimed, Diane, stretched out on one end of the long sofa that she shared with her husband, asked, "Expecting company?"

Charles's long legs took most of the length, but he was quite comfortable with the way her soft legs rested on his thighs.

"Nope. You?" He grinned, looking up from the real estate section of the Sunday newspaper.

"Very funny. Honey, you're not going to wait for that poor little man to answer the door, are you?"

He chuckled, "You bet I am. Sheldon guards his duties and doesn't take kindly to any fool who gets in his way."

Diane was clearly horrified and was about to tell him so when Heather Gregory-Montgomery rushed into the family room as fast as her petite, very pregnant frame could make it. Her shoulder-length black braids framed a flawless golden-brown skin. She was followed by her tall, dark-brown-skinned husband, Quinn.

"What is going on?" she demanded in no uncertain terms. "I swore Charles said you two got married, but he hung up so fast I thought I heard wrong. Well?"

"Hello, doll face, Montgomery." Charles's eyes were twinkling as he came to his feet after exchanging a quick glance with his bride. He gave Heather a kiss before offering Quinn his hand. "Come in. Have a sit-down."

Heather and Diane exchanged a hug. Diane affectionately patted her stomach. "How're you feeling, girlfriend?"

"Forget about me! What's going on?"

Diane glanced at her husband. "When did you speak to Heather?"

"This morning, when you were in the shower." He placed a possessive arm around Diane's waist. "I forgot to mention it."

Diane blushed when she realized what had interrupted his telephone call. He'd been on the phone when she'd returned to the bedroom, wearing his short terrycloth robe. The robe hung off one shoulder, leaving much of her chest exposed. Charles had taken one look at her soft breasts and replaced the receiver. He'd then pulled her back down onto the bed, refusing her food unless she made love with him yet again.

Diane was beaming as she held out her left hand. Both women squealed like teenagers, laughing and hugging each other all the while.

"Congratulations, man." Quinn smiled, shaking Charles's hand.

The two women were still laughing. Finally, Heather launched herself into Charles's arms. He received a hug and kiss in return.

"Oh, I am so happy for you two!" Heather beamed.

"Time to come clean, doll face. Did you put her up to following me on the cruise?"

Diane and Heather exchanged a look before Heather shrugged, "Maybe, maybe not. Hot damn!"

"A man likes to do his own choosing, ladies," Quinn said, with an I-told-you-so smile across his dark handsome face.

"That's right!" Charles nodded.

"Huh!" both women said at the same time.

"Where's Cindy?" Diane asked, referring to Quinn's teenage daughter from a previous marriage.

"She's spending the weekend in Wilberforce, touring the black colleges," Quinn said with a proud smile. "I can hardly believe my baby will be off to college next year."

"Our baby, sugar," Heather reminded him.

"Wilberforce?" Diane yelled, "As in Central State?"

"You got it, roommate!"

Both women giggled, shouting in unison "For God! For Central! For *State!"* like two former cheerleaders. Their husbands rolled their eyes, but both grinned indulgently.

"It's not definite, but I am keeping my fingers crossed," Heather confessed. "I must say, I've never seen either of you so pleased with yourselves. Married! Now, tell me all the details!"

Quinn grinned roguishly at his wife as he helped her into the leather loveseat. "Sweetheart, there might be a few details that they won't want to share." He took the cushion next to hers, his arm resting casually around her shoulders.

"Soooo, when was the wedding?" Heather prompted.

"On Wednesday evening, in St. Thomas. We stayed until yesterday and managed to squeeze in a short honeymoon." Diane, seated beside her husband, blushed. "Charles was wonderful. He arranged everything. The chapel was really beautiful. It overlooked the bay."

"How romantic! I just knew you two were meant for each other." Heather couldn't be more pleased, her two dearest friends were happily married.

"Yeah," Charles murmured, brushing his lips against his wife's ever so briefly.

When Diane's heart stopped racing and she was able to string a full sentence together, she said, "I hope you're not upset because we decided on a private ceremony."

"Of course not, especially if you two let us, your family and friends, give Diane a bridal shower and the two of you a fabulous reception." Heather's eyes gleamed with excitement while Diane's heart filled with dread.

"Heather, you know what the doctor said," Quinn interrupted.

"Is something wrong?" both Diane and Charles asked simultaneously.

"No! I'm fine," Heather said, while absently stroking her very swollen stomach. "We found out we're having twins, so I do have to take extra care, eat right, and get enough rest."

"That's wonderful!" both Charles and Diane said at once.

"We're thrilled," Heather admitted.

"I'm the one who has to make sure she doesn't overdo," Quinn reminded his wife.

"Sweetheart, planning a wedding reception and a bridal shower does not require physical labor, for heaven's sake!" Heather said.

It was all Diane could do not to show her agitation. She tried to sound carefree when she said, "We appreciate the offer, don't we, honey, but it's not necessary. We had a beautiful wedding."

"My wife has been gracious enough not to mention that I was the one who rushed the wedding. When Diane said yes, I couldn't wait to make her mine," Charles confessed, with eyes only for Diane. She had supported him then; he would support her now. If she didn't want the reception, it was fine with him.

Quinn asked, "What did your families say?"

"You two are the first to know," Charles grinned.

"What a compliment! Thank you," Heather said, her eyes suddenly filled with tears.

"Are you all right?"

"Quinn, I'm fine. Just happy."

"Heather, we've put you in the middle through our entire roller coaster relationship. It's a wonder you're still speaking to either one of us," Charles teased.

"That's for sure! Both Charles and I have appreciated your support and love."

"How could I not want my two friends to have the kind of happiness Quinn and I have?" Heather laced her fingers with her husband's. "Enough of the mushy stuff. How many guests are you two planning on inviting to the reception?"

Charles and Diane were so engrossed in each other that they missed the last.

"Chuck!" Elizabeth Alexsandrea Randol-Bennett exclaimed, as she hurried into the room. "You look fantastic!"

Everyone but Heather came to their feet to greet the tall, slender brown-skinned woman whose long black hair was beautifully arranged in a coil at her nape. She was elegantly dressed in an ivory silk blouse, ivory leather slacks, and several long strands of gold chains, mixed with a single rope of cultured pearls arranged gracefully around her neck and diamonds glimmering in her ears and on her fingers. Eliz dashed over to give her brother a hug and a kiss.

"Hi, kiddo," Charles said, easily lifting her off the floor. He dwarfed his five-ten sister by several inches. "Where's Bernard and the kids?"

"Having Sunday brunch with the dragon queen, where else? Heather and Quinn, it's good to see you both! How're you feelin'?"

"Great!" Heather laughed and exchanged an affectionate kiss on the cheek.

Elizabeth didn't hesitate to greet Quinn with a hug. Turning back to her brother, she beamed. "Hope I'm not interrupting. I couldn't wait to hear all about the cruise." Her eyes were on the beautiful woman at her brother's side.

Diane's heart had stopped the second the lovely woman had flung herself into Charles's arms. The family resemblance was remarkable, from the regal bone structure to the unblemished richness of their skin tones, from the dimpled cheeks down to the mischievous glint in their dark eyes.

Charles reached out to take Diane's hand and tugged her close. "Eliz, this is Diane Rivers-Randol, my wife. We were married in St. Thomas on Wednesday evening."

Elizabeth stared open-mouthed for a few seconds before she cocked her head to one side and stated with indignation, "Diane Rivers! I don't think that's very funny, big brother. Will you ever stop teasing?"

"It's no joke, funny face." Charles grinned, not the least bit disturbed by her frankness. "It didn't take long for us to realize that we loved each other . . . moonlight, the trade winds, and being water-locked on the Caribbean did the trick."

"I don't believe this! You married the woman you told me not less than two weeks ago you couldn't stand the sight of?" Eliz said, both hands firmly planted on her hips.

"He did!" Heather declared emphatically. "Isn't it wonderful?"

Diane was thoroughly humiliated, but having long practice in pretending, she managed to prevent herself from complete embarrassment by bursting into tears.

Charles felt his wife tremble. He noted the defensive way she lifted her chin. Tightening his hold, he encircled her waist. His voice was taut and deadly serious. "I would appreciate it, Elizabeth, if you'd let my wife know how welcome she is in our family."

Elizabeth blinked, suddenly aware of what she had done with her infamous runaway tongue. She'd insulted her new sister-in-law and infuriated her beloved brother.

"Since we all missed the nuptials, Quinn and I have decided to give Diane a bridal shower and a wedding reception with both families. Haven't we, honey?"

Quinn nodded. "The happy couple just have to give us the guest list."

It was clear from her brother's expression that if Elizabeth didn't say something pretty quick, she would be the one not receiving an invitation to either event.

"That's so exciting. Heather, I'd love to help." Elizabeth turned to Diane. "I apologize. I didn't mean to put my foot in my mouth. It happens . . . often. Welcome to the family.

I do wish you and Chuck all happiness." She held her hands out to Diane.

Diane smiled stiffly, clasping the other's hands. "Thank you."

"And you, big brother . . . much happiness." She kissed him and hugged him tight, wiping at her tears. "Married! I can't believe it!"

Close to Diane's ear, Charles asked, "You okay, baby?"

She nodded, smiling for him, not wanting him to know how terribly upset she really was. His sister clearly didn't approve of her. Apparently she knew how deeply Charles had been hurt by Diane in the past. Diane hadn't realized until now how much Charles's family's acceptance meant to her. She lifted her chin, telling herself to get over it. She had Charles. He was her family.

"Diane, I bet your family was as surprised as I am," Elizabeth said.

"I haven't had an opportunity to tell my mother." Diane swallowed, quickly adding, "She's traveling. I hope to hear from her soon."

"Chuck, what about Aunt Helen and Uncle Alex? Have you told them?"

"Not yet," Charles responded absently to his sister's inquiry. His gaze was focused on his wife. He didn't like what he saw. She was unhappy. Even though she hid it behind a generous smile, he saw it in her eyes.

"Why don't we call the folks and invite them over? I'm sure Aunt Helen has some wonderful ideas about the wedding reception." His sister moved toward the telephone on the mahogany table behind one of the twin sofas. Pausing for a moment, she went on to say, "I wonder what Mrs. Sheldon has planned for lunch? She's the perfect housekeeper. 'The more, the better' is her motto." Elizabeth was in her usual take-charge mode.

Diane felt like wringing her hands and screaming at the top of her lungs for the others to stop. She didn't want this fuss. All she wanted was to love Charles and for the rest of the world to leave them in peace. Elizabeth was his sister, and this was her childhood home, and Charles was her only sibling. Being a part of his life was so vastly different from what she'd been expecting . . . the wealth . . . his standing in the community . . . his close ties to his family.

Suddenly, she was panicky that she would never fit in. How long would it be before her husband realized it as well? How long before he recognized his mistake in marrying her?

Charles nonchalantly took the phone from his sister and replaced the instrument. "Diane and I will tell the folks in good time, Sis. As far as lunch, not today. We have planned to spend what is left of the last day of our vacation alone. I'm sure you understand. Technically, we're still on our honeymoon."

"Enough said." Quinn got to his feet. He helped his wife rise, even though she clearly wasn't ready to leave. "Congratulations again, you two." He slapped Charles on the back while Heather and Diane hugged.

"I brought you a surprise from the islands. I'll bring it by later in the week, if that's okay?" Diane said to Heather.

"Thanks. I'm so happy for you two." Heather whispered back in Diane's ear, "Don't worry about Eliz. She'll come around."

"Thanks for everything. I love you."

Heather grinned. "Don't get mushy on me, girl. You'll make me cry." She kissed her friend's cheek. "Eliz, it's been a pleasure." Heather offered her hand.

"Mine as well. Take care of that little one."

"That's my specialty," Quinn said with a grin, "taking care of them."

"Give Cynthia our love," Charles and Diane said at once, then laughed.

While Charles escorted them out, Diane was left alone

with her brand new sister-in-law. The two women eyed each other warily.

Elizabeth broke the silence. "It was such a surprise to discover that my brother's married." She paused, then went on to say, "I just never expected the two of you . . . Oh, dear! I guess what I'm trying to say is that I love my brother, very much. All I want is for him to be happy."

Diane could see that Charles's sister was disturbed by their marriage and apparently didn't think he could find happiness with her. Elizabeth made no bones about the fact that she didn't like Diane.

Although Diane knew she would never do anything to deliberately hurt Charles, it was obviously what Elizabeth feared most. Diane also realized how foolish she'd been to hope that she and Charles's sister could someday be friends and perhaps become close like real sisters. Talk about wishing for the moon.

"You made quite a few assumptions on a fifteen-minute acquaintance," Diane said, head held high, her cool demeanor very much in place.

"I suppose I deserve that. I just wished you two had . . ."

"What?" Charles asked. He came over to sit down beside his wife.

"Waited to marry, at least until you returned home." Elizabeth laughed. "I can't get over the fact that my big brother has finally decided to settle down. After all these years of hearing you swear no one woman could satisfy you."

"I was a fool." Charles took his wife's hand into his own. He played with her fingers as he would have preferred to toy with her soft mouth. He ached for the tantalizing taste of her, longed for her to plunge her tongue into his mouth, overwhelming his senses. Desire flared as he sat studying Diane's lips.

"How did you both manage to be on the same cruise

ship? Did either of you know the other was planning to take the cruise?"

"Luck. Pure luck," Charles said, fascinated by the way Diane moistened her lips. She was wearing an orange shade of lipstick. He knew for a fact that her tangerine jumpsuit concealed a peach lace bra and panties. The large, dark tips of her breasts were veiled by two thin layers of fabric.

Charles surprised both women when he brushed his wife's lips against his own before he said, "Go home, Eliz."

Diane couldn't believe what she was hearing. She couldn't so much as form a protest because he'd dropped his head and trailed kisses down the side of her throat, concentrating on the most sensive spots.

"Oh, and Sis, next time, call before you come over."

Diane gasped, shocked by his callousness. He was infuriated with his sister. Judging by the hurt look on Elizabeth's face, Diane decided it was a very short leap until Elizabeth blamed her for the discord between brother and sister. The siblings had always been very close. Elizabeth was gone before Diane could free herself from her husband's mouth.

"Charles, that was mean."

"No, it wasn't. It was necessary. We're husband and wife, and I will *not* allow anyone to come between us, not even my well-meaning, yet meddling sister."

"I don't want to cause a rift between the two of you."

"You haven't. I'm sorry, sweet cheeks. Eliz hurt you. I didn't like that."

Diane slid her arms around his neck and hugged him close. "Our marriage was a shock. She spoke without thinking. Now she probably thinks she's no longer welcome here in her family home."

"You are my wife, Di. I won't let anyone hurt you . . . not even my own sister," he said, rising to his feet and bringing her up with him.

"Charles . . ."

"Leave it. I'll handle Eliz. Now you, Mrs. Randol, can

handle me," he said throatily, as he ushered her out of the family room and up the staircase toward their bedroom.

Oh, yeah! He might handle Elizabeth, but Diane knew who Elizabeth would blame . . . and it wouldn't be her precious brother!

Eleven

Charles slowed the car to enter the underground garage beneath Diane's high-rise condominium complex. He parked in the space beside her red Buick Skylark.

"Are you sure you want to be bothered? Packing is no fun," Diane said, as she searched for her keys in the bottom of her shoulder bag.

"Why would I mind?" Charles opened her door before he went to retrieve the empty suitcases from the trunk.

"I guess I was a little surprised that you volunteered to help and wanted to stay the night at the condo. I really only needed enough to wear to work tomorrow. I can always come back."

He pressed the button for the elevator. "Baby, you're forgetting something, aren't you? You no longer have just yourself to depend on. We're a team." His hand rested on her nape. He worried the soft skin as the elevator climbed toward the tenth floor.

Diane was tense as she let them inside her one-bedroom condo. She busied herself switching on lamps and opening the glass doors to let in some fresh air.

It was as she'd left it, spotlessly neat except for the fine layer of dust that had accumulated since she'd been away. Butter-soft beige leather armchairs faced a matching sofa, positioned on a large beige, rust, and blue Oriental rug. Crystal lamps with pinch-pleated oat-colored shades stood on glass end tables. The walls were lined with pale pine bookshelves. One wall was dominated by a huge oil of the Sahara with Black African nomads seated on camels.

"I always liked that painting," Charles murmured thoughtfully.

Diane said absently, "Honey, would you check the refrigerator? I'm sure I cleared it out. But I was in such a rush to get out of here. Who remembers?"

While he headed for her sunny gold-and-beige kitchen, Diane hurried into the bedroom. She raced for the answering machine on the nightstand. She popped out the tape of incoming messages and had barely tucked it into the zipper compartment of her purse when she heard her husband's voice behind her.

"Refrigerator is fine, nothin' but beverages in the bottom, but the freezer is packed."

"Good," she said, dropping her purse on the floor and moving toward the dresser.

"Where should I put this?" he asked, referring to the empty cases. The things she had taken with her on the trip had been stored in the huge walk-in closet of the bedroom she now shared with her husband.

"The armchair is fine." Diane sorted through a rainbow of lace bikini panties and bras.

"Why not donate the frozen food to one of the homeless shelters?"

"What a great idea!" she exclaimed, recalling the kindness she had been shown when she was a teenager living in the YWCA, after she had left home for good. Her boss at the diner had made sure she had plenty of food between her shifts. "I think I have another suitcase in the bottom of the closet."

"I'll get it."

She studied the pale pine queen-sized bed, which was covered with a gold floral comforter and dust ruffle. Lace-edged pillow shams were propped against the headboard. She decided they were much too feminine to use in their bedroom. Maybe in one of the guestrooms? Surely all of them didn't have king-sized beds?

"Now, what do you want me to do?"

"Would you pull out my navy suit, the red suit with black trim, the cream wool suit, and the melon suit from the closet?" Diane laughed at his befuddled look. "In the left side of the closet are suits and dresses. Honey, pick any you like."

"Melon? What kinda color is that?"

"Orange," she called after him, laughing. Working together, they soon filled all the suitcases.

"Charles, about your sister . . ." she began, only to be interrupted by him.

"Leave Eliz to me."

Diane couldn't help feeling responsible. She couldn't just sit back and let their closeness vanish. "Your sister didn't mean any harm. Honey, please, you have to give her time to adjust to our marriage."

She knew that once Charles had an idea in his head, it was damn near impossible to change his mind. Not so long ago, his mule-headedness had been directed *her* way. It had taken hard work and persistence to convince him he'd been wrong about her. Diane was frightened that his stubbornness could cause a lasting rift in his relationship with Elizabeth.

"My sister was quick to judge, and damn rude."

"She was being protective of you. She adores you, honey."

"Di, love isn't the issue. I didn't pick her husband for her. I had faith in her judgment. Nevertheless, I kept my thoughts to myself. I expect the same respect from her."

Diane paused in her folding and found that he'd made himself comfortable on the bed. She laughed. "What happened to teamwork?"

He shrugged. "You know, I've often fantasized about being here in your bed with you." His lids were half closed, heavy with desire.

"Fantasized, about me?"

"Often."

"I never suspected it."

"I didn't want you to know. I had it bad for you, baby. I ached to be inside you," he confessed, his voice gruff with desire.

Diane blushed. "When did you have these fantasies?"

"All the time . . ." He chuckled. "During teacher's meetings. At lunch, sitting across from you." He confessed softly, "I couldn't seem to think of anything but how much I wanted you."

"So while Mrs. Slivers was going on and on about raising test scores you were thinking about . . . making love?"

"Absolutely."

She giggled. "Have you no shame?"

"Not when it comes to you." He surprised her even more when he confessed, "I wanted you so badly that I gave up sex entirely when I couldn't have you."

"You've been celibate?"

"For almost three years. Even before I left Lawrence."

"You are so wonderful," she whispered. She would have never suspected it.

He was the only man who'd ever made her feel safe. He didn't view her as some kind of a beautiful plastic doll without a brain in her head because of the way she looked. She had always been free to be herself around him.

"I love you," she said, looking down into his eyes.

"I love you . . . so *give.*"

"Huh?"

"When are you gonna tell me what's bothering you?"

"What are you talking about?" Her legs were so wobbly that she sank down onto the foot of the bed.

"You've been jittery ever since we left the house. Yet you won't talk about it." When she started to protest, he held up his hand. "I know we've been married less than a week, but give me some credit. We've been together twenty-four hours a day. I know something is wrong."

Diane nervously twisted her wedding rings. Finally, she blurted out the first plausible explanation that popped into her head. "I hate the way you let your sister leave today. It was wrong to expect her to be pleased that we're married. All she knows about me is what you told her . . . and it wasn't complimentary."

"Did you think I would sit back and let her hurt your feelings?"

"Charles, I'll get over it. I'm not made of glass."

"You shouldn't have to take that kind of stuff from her. You're my wife. That's all she needs to know."

"Why are you so stubborn? Were you born with this horrible trait?"

"Yeah. Just lucky, I guess," he grinned.

"Lucky! You're like a dog with a bone when you get some stupid idea in your head. You were wrong about *me,* remember?"

"I don't like to think about how cruel I was. I hurt you."

"You were hurting, too. I can understand that now. Honey, Eliz is your baby sister. I know how much you love her. That's all that should matter. You two are family."

"No one is more important to me than you are, Mrs. Randol!"

Elizabeth certainly was not high on Diane's list of wonderful people, but she was Charles's sister, which meant she mattered to him. Diane felt compelled to say, "Honey, Eliz wasn't on our honeymoon. The last she heard, I hurt her big brother. It took us time to work things out. Give her some time to adjust to our marriage."

"Okay." Tired of the subject, he said, "Remember that first night when you sent that drink over? Were you scared?"

"Terrified."

"I wanted you so badly my teeth ached."

"What I remember was that you were so ticked you couldn't see straight." Diane found she could laugh about it now.

"Nevertheless, I was thrilled to see you."

"Oh, yeah?" she teased. "I expected you to throw that drink in my face."

"I was rude, but not quite that crude."

"All I could think about was you telling me you didn't want anything to do with me . . . ever."

"Giving you up was the most difficult thing I've ever done. Did Heather tell you I was in love with you? Is that why you came?"

Diane gasped. "Heather *knew* how you felt?"

"Of course. She's my best friend. My sister knew, as well."

Diane groaned, certain Elizabeth was bound to hate her for life.

"I'm shocked you hadn't guessed."

"I had no idea. Honey, I'm so glad."

"I wanted you then almost as much as I want you now." His body throbbed with the potency of his need for her. Charles's breath quickened at the rawness of his desire. He had it bad. He was worse than a starving man at a banquet. He couldn't seem to stay away from her. "Are you, too sore, baby? Because I want to love you right here in your bed . . . love you the way I've fantasized."

Diane was trembling with the sweet expectation of his lovemaking. His name was a husky whisper issued from her throat.

His smoldering gaze stroked her soft brown length. His woman was all satin-smooth skin and soft, sexy curves, but she was more than that: she was warmth and love. She was excitement and joy. She was his friend and his companion. She was comfort and titilation.

Diane couldn't believe her own boldness as she stood up,

unashamed to untie the sash at her waist and let the cream wrap dress drop to the floor. She wanted to feel his hot, dark eyes all over her body. She was as hungry for him as he was for her.

She watched as he stripped, then reclined on the bed, his skin dark and enticing against her pale gold sheets.

"One of us is wearing too many clothes."

"Think so?" she whispered, as she went to him. She encircled his waist, pressing her face between the place where his shoulder and neck joined.

He kissed the base of her neck while unhooking the front clasp of her bra. "I hate this thing." He flung it away. His hand claimed the bounty he'd bared. He caressed her softness before eventually sliding his thumbs beneath the waistband of her lace panties. They went the way of the bra, onto the carpet.

He rained kisses over her perfect features, from her eyelids down her nose to her mouth. He traced the shape of her generous bottom lip with the tip of his tongue. "Can we?"

Her dreamy eyes looked into his with confusion. Her soft hands were stroking his wide, hairless chest. His skin was smooth and muscular and so incredibly warm. He quivered when she worried a flat nipple with her nail.

"Baby, you didn't answer me." His wide palm cradled her nape. They exchanged a deep but all-too-brief kiss. Diane wanted nothing more than to slide her tongue over his lips, then quickly inside. Charles groaned, longing to intensify the kiss, but not daring to. He held her close but just beyond the heat of his mouth while one long-fingered hand followed the natural dip of her spine to cup and squeeze her lush curves. "Is it too soon?" he queried, barely able to hold himself in check. He had no choice. She came first with him.

Diane blushed, hiding her face against his throat. "I'm a little tender, but I don't care . . . I want you."

One kiss led to another and yet another, each deeper and longer than the one before it. With his eyes closed, Charles savored her sweetness as she lay on top of him, her breasts on his chest, her thighs nestled between his, his shaft throbbing against her stomach.

He fingered her soft heat.

"Chuck . . .

"Open for me . . ."

She shuddered in response, spreading her thighs, opening herself to him, needing to have him fill the void.

The bedside telephone rang. Diane was oblivious to all but the intoxicating heat of his arousal stroking her intimately.

By the fifth ring, Charles sighed wearily, "Answer the damn thing."

"The answering machine will pick it up," she whispered breathlessly, arching her back and rubbing her aching breasts against his chest. The blasted thing kept right on ringing. Diane suddenly remembered she hadn't inserted a new tape.

He swore, yanking the telephone off the hook and placing it against her ear.

"Hello?" Diane managed, her voice filled with dread.

"Sweetheart, you're back. When did you get in?"

"Greg?" she blinked incredulously, then glanced at Charles. His face was against her neck, but she could tell by the tight way he held his mouth that he was not pleased.

"Who else? I tried last night, but I got the machine. Too tired to pick up? How was the cruise?"

"Let me call you tomorrow."

Diane's total concentration was on her husband. She watched a muscle tighten in his jaw as if he were grinding his teeth.

"I missed you. When can I see you? Can I come by tonight?"

"No . . . this isn't a good time. I . . ."

He took the telephone from her. "This is Charles Randol, Diane's husband. I suggest you forget this number." He slammed down the receiver.

"Why did you do that? What did you think? That I was about to invite him over?" Diane asked, pulling the sheet over herself.

Charles's emotion inflamed from agitation because of the call to cold fury at the way she hid her body from him. She stared accusingly at him with lips swollen from his kisses, her cheeks flushed from his lovemaking. She was gorgeous, too damn beautiful. She attracted men without even lifting a finger.

He wasn't the kind of man who sought a trophy on his arm. All he wanted was for Diane to love him as much as he loved her. The way he saw it, the competition should have ended the day he'd placed his ring on her finger. She had made a promise to him, and he'd be damned if he'd let her break it.

"You don't have to do a thing, do you? Men flock to you like little lost sheep. Just who in the hell is Greg?"

"Gregory Johnson . . . a friend. Why are you so angry?"

"You took your own sweet time getting the man off the phone, yet you couldn't take another second to tell him you're married. Why?"

"That's not something you just blurt out. Greg has been a good friend."

"Are you telling me that you intend to keep your men-friends?"

"Why not? What difference does it make?"

"What difference does it make?" he roared, flinging the sheet away and towering above her. Jealous rage battled with sexual frustration.

"You have friends. I haven't asked you to give them up because of me."

"You're a married woman! And you'd better start acting like it."

Diane glared at him, "That was exactly what I was doing when you picked up the blasted telephone. It could have rung all night, for all I cared!" She turned her back to him.

But he was too damned angry to give half an inch. Diane had his nose so wide open . . . He knew he was jealous. And he couldn't seem to help it. He'd had too much practice at it since Diane had come into his life. She had put him through enough hell before they were married for him suddenly to pretend it didn't matter.

"It looks to me as if you have some telephone calls to make, Mrs. Randol. The sooner you get started, the better. We're married. I won't share!" Charles shoved his legs into the jeans he'd left on the floor before heading for the living room.

"You have no right . . ."

"No right!" He stormed back to the bed, one hand on a lean hip. "Lady, you are my wife . . . my woman. I'm the one with exclusive rights!"

Charles let out a guttural sound as he stalked away without looking back at the woman who had exclusive rights to his heart. Marching to the refrigerator, he grabbed a beer and then flopped down on the sofa. Switching on the television set, Charles was determined to ignore the dictates of his body, which demanded he complete what he'd started. He was alarmed by the extent of his vulnerability to her.

He'd never been jealous with any of the women he'd been involved with in the past. He was naturally easygoing where women were concerned. But not with Diane . . . never with Diane.

As he sat brooding, he was haunted by the way he'd rushed her into marriage. It ate at him. Damn that phone call! It had served to remind Charles of how skillfully Diane had used other men to protect herself from him.

Diane hugged the pillow to her breasts for a long time. Eventually, she got up, found a nightgown, and slipped it on. Climbing back into bed, she switched off the lamp, making a point to keep her back to the door.

They'd been back one day and already their marriage was unraveling, she decided in misery. Eliz hated her, and now he was furious with Diane because of a stupid telephone call from a man she didn't even care about. Why was he acting this way?

She'd made some mistakes in the past. Would those errors in judgment eventually cost her her husband's love and his sister's respect? Tears burned her eyes, but she refused to let them fall. She had done nothing wrong. Nothing!

When the telephone rang again, Diane expected Charles to charge into the bedroom and take it out of her hand. But the only sound coming from the living room was the eleven o'clock news.

"Hello?"

"Where the hell have you been?"

Not now, she almost groaned aloud. Not with Charles in the next room. Goosebumps pimpled her bare arms. She whispered, "What do you want?" Her eyes were glued to the partly opened door.

"What do you think? Mama needs some money." It was Lillie.

"I gave you enough to last until the end of the month."

"Well, it didn't. Where you been? I've been trying to reach you for over a week."

"Never mind that. I can't keep giving you money." But Diane knew she was in no position to argue. "I won't be able to see you until Wednesday. You'll just have to wait."

The profanity that poured from the phone didn't affect Diane. She was used to verbal abuse. What she wasn't used to was having an angry husband a few feet away, possibly listening to every word.

"I'm not a kid anymore. We both know you depend on

me. I don't have to give you a cent," Diane hissed in a whisper.

"Yeah? Are you threatening me? You think I won't show up at that school of yours. Let them fancy friends of yours see where you really come from." Lillie laughed, nearly choking on her own wit.

"The choice is yours," Diane whispered, her anxiety increasing with each heartbeat. "But you'll lose. Without a job, I can't help you or myself. I'll meet you on Wednesday at the usual place at four." Diane didn't wait for her mother's reply; she hung up.

Curled into a ball, this time she didn't even try to stop the tears as they ran down her cheeks, soaking her pillow. Lillie was why she hadn't wanted Charles to come with her to the condo. If they were to have a future, she had to make sure he never found out about Lillie.

She was asleep when her husband slid into bed beside her. Even though he ached to hold her, he held on to his jealousy and resentment instead.

Twelve

Diane woke with a splitting headache and a deep attitude. She groaned softly, taking particular care not to wake the hard-headed man beside her. Padding soundlessly into the bathroom, she stared wearily into the mirror. She was a mess! Her hair was standing all over her head like she'd stuck her finger into a light socket, and her eyelids were puffy and swollen from crying.

Damn him! The honeymoon wasn't just over . . . it was dead! She stepped into the shower, letting the hot water soothe the stiff muscles in her neck and back, easing the tension from her body. Unfortunately it couldn't wash away the heaviness in her heart.

The things he'd accused her of were all true. She had used men to buffer the unnerving feelings he alone aroused in her. Perhaps it had been foolish to think he'd forgiven her. Evidently, she'd been mistaken in the belief that they'd started anew. As much as she wished it to, their marriage could not change the past. He intended to go right on tossing the past into her face whenever something went wrong.

It wasn't right! She'd given him no reason to doubt her loyalty to him. He *knew* she wasn't promiscuous. And he knew she loved him . . . loved him with all her heart.

Diane was shaking with anger as she switched off the shower. There was no excuse for him using what had happened before they were married to hurt her! Didn't he realize how unfair that was?

By the time she'd finished blow-drying her hair and curling it with an electric curling iron, she was oozing with righteous indignation, but beneath the anger was a full measure of hurt feelings.

Her whole life had changed drastically in just a few short days. For the first time since their wedding, she wondered if her husband really loved her. How could he and believe the worst?

Refusing to give in to the nasty urge to slam the bedroom door as hard as she could behind her, Diane carried her clothes into the living room and finished dressing there.

She was sipping hot, fragrant coffee when she glanced up and met her husband's dark, brooding gaze. One bare, powerful brown shoulder was anchored against the doorjamb. She turned her gaze away from the muscular lines of his bare torso, long legs, trim hips, and prominent sex, all tucked into tight-fitting jeans.

" 'Morning." His voice was deep and throaty, his mouth grim as his eyes journeyed leisurely over her soft curves. The classic black suit she had teamed with a softly draped cream blouse did marvelous things to her beautiful skin. Not that she needed help to be beautiful . . . what she needed help with was keeping men at a distance. If she felt she wasn't up to the challenge, Charles intended to take care of that little matter himself. "Any more of that?"

Diane retrieved a cup from the cupboard. She placed it on the counter beside the coffeemaker. "Help yourself." She dumped the rest of her drink into the sink and rinsed out the cup.

She was relieved when he moved toward the counter so she could leave the kitchen without having to touch him. She reached the doorway, then suddenly changed her mind. Facing him, she said, "About last night . . ."

"Leave it," he bit out harshly, swallowing the too-hot beverage and nearly burning the roof of his mouth. He'd be damned if he'd allow her to weaken his resolve and twist his emotions into knots. He'd made himself clear when they'd started again. He wasn't about to share her with another man. She was wearing his ring, damn it!

"Fine!" Diane snapped. "I'll see you tonight."

"Where?"

"Where do you think?" She didn't wait for his response. She retrieved her purse and briefcase from the bedroom. She was lugging a suitcase and garment bag, along with her purse and briefcase.

"Leave them. I'll take them with me. I have to go back to the house anyway to change for the office."

Diane dropped the luggage right where she stood, barely missing her feet. What did he think, that she was planning on staying here? The arrogant jerk! She was the fool to marry him in the first place. Talk about mule-headed!

Diane searched her handbag until she found an extra set of keys. She dropped them onto the coffee table before leaving the apartment without another word to her husband.

Charles's disposition hadn't improved one little bit by the time he reached his corner office on the top floor of Randol and Randol Pharmaceutical in Southfield. He was engrossed in his correspondence when his sister walked into his office. As was her custom, she didn't bother knocking on the open door.

"Hi! I'm surprised to see you here. I thought you would still be honeymooning." Her smile was wide, but her eyes were worried and questioning.

Charles frowned. He didn't particularly care to be reminded that his bride had slept on the far side of the bed or that they'd barely exchanged a half dozen words that morning. It was the first time he'd started the day without a morning kiss and without the delightful temptation of their remaining in bed together. He'd exercised his male rights. He'd been the man, made his point in no uncertain terms. Instead of feeling strong, he felt more like a casualty of war.

"Hey." He waved toward the coffeemaker and mugs on the side table.

"No thanks." Eliz's normally happy-go-lucky brother looked none-too-happy this morning. Her spirits sunk. "Sooooo, you still mad?"

When his frown deepened, she wished she'd taken a less direct approach. Well, her foot was halfway in; she might as well finish the job. "Chuck, I'm sorry. I didn't mean to upset her."

"Her name is Diane."

Elizabeth winced at the pointed rejoinder.

"It was just such a shock. You *know* I don't mean half the things I say."

Charles raised a brow. "Since when?"

"I'm trying to apologize."

"I know that. But this is one time when your runaway tongue has hurt. I'm not happy that my wife was the target."

"Charles, please—I didn't mean to make an enemy of my brand new sister-in-law. I've waited years to see you happily married."

"I picked the bride, not you."

Charles wasn't thrilled to see tears gathering in his baby sister's eyes. "Look, I know we've always been close. And I've encouraged you to speak your mind. We've always been able to be straight with each other. Sis, I married Diane because I love her. I've been in love with her for a long time, even if I wasn't about to admit it," he paused, making sure there was no room for misunderstanding. "You were shocked yesterday . . . but no one, not even you, will get away with being rude to my wife. If you can't be pleasant to her, then stay the hell out of our lives."

Elizabeth couldn't believe her ears! He had married the two-timing hussy; now, suddenly, *she* was suppose to develop selective amnesia? Who was he kidding? But the set of his jaw convinced Elizabeth that he was serious. She'd always loved and admired her wonderful big brother. Yet she knew she couldn't stand back and watch him get hurt without trying to protect him. What choice did she have if she wanted a relationship with him? She swallowed with difficulty, determined not to verbalize that in her opinion, he'd made a horrible error by marrying Diane. She knew she just had to keep her thoughts to herself. There was no way she was going to let her brother walk out of her life.

She said, "I'll make it up to Diane. I can't promise to like her like a sister, but I love and respect you enough to try to be considerate of her." Despite her doubts, Elizabeth believed a family always stood together. She just prayed that she would not end up picking up the pieces when that fast-tailed witch broke her brother's heart.

"I appreciate that." Charles's face eased into a warm, engaging smile. "I'm hoping you two can come to love each other. We're family."

"Yes, family." She was so relieved that he wasn't still angry with her that she rushed over and gave him a grateful hug. She didn't dare think about where she was suppose to find all this sisterly love for someone she didn't trust as far as she could throw her.

"Charles!" Alexander Randol boomed. "What's this I hear about a wedding?" He was a tall, heavy-set man. He shared the same warm-brown coloring, wide smile, strong features, and striking good looks as his niece and nephew. His once-thick black hair was now heavily peppered with gray.

Charles's eyes swung to his sister. She had guilt written all over her pretty face. Charles couldn't help laughing. He rose. At six-four, he was only an inch taller than his distinguished, elegantly groomed uncle. Charles beamed as he accepted the bear hug and hearty handshake from his mentor and surrogate father.

"Well, boy, what do you have to say for yourself?"

"It's true. Diane and I were married this past week in Saint Thomas."

"Congratulations, son!" he said, pumping his hand. "When will Helen and I get a chance to meet the bride? She must be a beauty, to have you acting so impulsively."

Charles grinned. "Soon," he promised. "I know you and Aunt Helen will love her."

"Of that I have no doubt. Elizabeth said something about you working together at Lawrence?"

"Yes . . . we've known each other for years."

"Good. I like the sound of that. I can tell you that your aunt has a few choice words for you, my boy. If I were you, I'd call her before the day is out." Alex chuckled, softening the fine lines of his face. "Yes, sir. I suppose you two are probably still honeymooning. But I wouldn't wait much longer, if I were you, to contact your aunt."

His uncle might have run the company for years, but it was his soft-spoken wife who ran him. The two were still very much in love. Unfortunately, while they'd had no children of their own, they had Elizabeth and Charles. Everyone seemed satisfied with the arrangement.

"I'll call right away."

"Good. How are you feeling? Completely recovered?"

Elizabeth was ashamed to realize that in the excitement of his marriage, she had forgotten about his reason for taking the cruise in the first place. "Yes. How are you?"

"Great! Marriage must agree with me," he laughed, determined not to recall the way his wife had looked at him this morning. They would patch up their differences, and soon. Maybe he had overreacted? Had he been a bit possessive?

"Glad to hear it. Well, I'll let you get back to work," he said, waving toward the stack of correspondence on Charles's desk. "Come along, little girl. I want you to have a look-see at these new production figures."

Charles was reaching for the telephone when his private

line lit. "Hello?" His heart pounded expectantly. He quickly dismissed a twinge of disappointment at the sound of his aunt's genteel, deeply southern voice.

"Aunt Helen, I was just about to call. How are you, sugar?" he teased.

It was silly to have expected Diane to call. She would be busy all day with her classes . . . too busy to take five minutes to let him know she was thinking of him. But then again, he was the one who had gotten wildly jealous and laid down the rules and then refused to discuss what happened. While she was the one who'd kept all her sweet kisses and her feminine warmth to herself.

Maybe she had a right to be ticked. Well, he was not about to let her wrap him around her pretty little fingers. They were married! He'd be damned if he'd share his wife with another man. The sooner she understood that, the better. He'd just give her a little time to see reason.

"Charles . . ."

"I heard you, dear. Yes, I can't wait until you meet Diane. Sunday dinner? Sounds good to me." Charles sincerely hoped he and Diane would be on speaking terms by then.

Diane couldn't remember a more hectic day. It seemed as if every single person at Lawrence felt the need to offer lengthy congratulations on her marriage. Not that she wasn't appreciative of their best wishes, but the very last person she wanted to think about was her new husband, the jerk.

Charles hadn't so much as called her all day. Not that she could take phone calls during class, but she had study hall duty and a preparation period and a lunch hour. The man had worked at the school almost as long as she had. Surely he hadn't forgotten the blasted telephone number?

The harder she tried not to think of him, the more he seemed to pop into her head. By the time her last class ended, she was ready to scream from the strain of pretending to be happy. Why had she taken that call? Should she have hung up? Even better, why hadn't she been fast enough to put a new tape in the answering machine before he'd come into the bedroom? Shoot, she'd been shaking so badly from worry that it was her mother on the phone that she hadn't given a thought to the possibility of one of her male friends calling. And that was all any of the men she dated were to her . . . friends.

Charles knew that! She hadn't given him reason to fly off the handle. Where did all this possessiveness and jealousy come from? She hated being angry with him . . . hated knowing he was equally angry with her.

After school, Diane went back to her place. She changed into her sweats before starting to pack. She was beat by the time she reached her new home. The backseat and trunk of her car were loaded with boxes. With her heart pounding with the possibility of seeing her husband and facing his anger, she went into the house.

But Charles wasn't home. Sheldon informed the disappointed Diane that he'd already left for the community center. Diane couldn't bring herself to ask Sheldon to help unload the car, but help he did, without her asking. She had a solitary meal in front of the television in the family room before exhaustion sent her to bed earlier than usual.

She tried to stay awake in hopes of spending time with Charles. In spite of everything, she missed him terribly. She fell asleep and was very disappointed when she realized, early the next morning, that he had already left for the office. Evidently, he was still angry. What other reason could he have for not waking her? She was left with nothing more than a vague awareness of him beside her during the night.

Diane was caught off guard when Heather called on Wednesday and asked her to stop by on her way home from work. She was so insistent that Diane decided to stop, even though it would make her late for her meeting with her mother.

"Hello, Mrs. Thornton. How are you?"

"Just dandy. Please, come on in, Mrs. Randol. Mrs. Montgomery is expecting you."

"Thank you."

The housekeeper gestured toward the living room to the left of the foyer.

Diane was shocked when she was greeted with a chorus of "Surprise!" from all the female staff members at Lawrence.

"Oh! My goodness!"

Heather beamed as she made her way slowly over to Diane.

Diane hung onto her dear friend tightly, tears in her soft brown eyes. "I don't believe this!"

"Every bride must have a shower. With a new husband around, there's no such thing as too much lingerie!"

Diane laughed. "You are supposed to be resting!"

"I am. I didn't do any thing harder than picking up the telephone."

"Thank you." Diane kissed her cheek before guiding Heather to a comfortable lounge chair and ottoman. She wiggled her finger at her. "Don't you dare move."

Suddenly, everyone was talking at once. Diane enthusiastically greeted her co-workers. She couldn't quite hide her shock when her new sister-in-law appeared carrying in a tray of hot hors d'oeuvres.

"Congratulations!" Elizabeth said.

"Thank you. It was nice of you to come."

"I wouldn't have missed it for the world."

Diane smiled and tried not to remember how upset and disappointed Elizabeth had been when she'd learned of the marriage. Diane didn't let her uneasiness with Elizabeth show. It wasn't easy, considering the stupid quarrel that had effectively driven a wedge between Charles and herself.

Diane oohed and awhed and giggled along with the other ladies at the the array of feminine lace and silk teddies, nighties, slips, and panties. She had to dab at tears time and time again. She was overwhelmed by the friendship directed her way. She reminded herself that much of the display was for her husband's benefit. Charles had been a well-liked and respected member of the faculty.

By the time the party broke up, Diane had had enough pretending to be carefree to last into the next century. Charles was so pleased by their marriage that he spent his every waking hour at the office or at the community center.

At the door, Diane hugged Heather. "I can't thank you enough. The party was a wonderful surprise."

"I'm glad you enjoyed yourself. I can't tell you how happy I am about your marriage. It took a few years, but finally you two came to your senses and realized how much you love each other. I have to confess that I've known all along that you two were right for each other."

Diane had gone to Heather for help when she'd first noticed how cold and out of character Charles had been acting toward her. Knowing how he felt about Diane and suspecting that Diane returned those feelings, Heather had encouraged him to speak openly to Diane about his needs.

Diane's eyes burned with unshed tears. "You have been such a good friend to both of us."

Heather saw her troubled gaze linger on Elizabeth. "Don't worry about that one. She's coming around. She's just a little protective of her big brother."

"She doesn't approve of me."

"Give her time. When I called to invite her to the shower, she insisted on pitching right in and helping out. I think she's sorry about the other day. It was an awkward beginning, nothing more."

"Perhaps. Charles was furious. I know it isn't my business, but I just don't want there to be an estrangement between them, especially because of me. From what I understand, they've always been close."

"Yes, they have. Don't worry. One day soon, Elizabeth will love you just as I do. Now remember, if you and Charles change your minds and decide you want a wedding reception, Quinn and I will be thrilled to host it."

Diane hugged her again. "Thanks for everything. I love you."

"Ditto!" Heather waved as Diane left loaded down with packages.

It was after nine, much too late for Diane to meet Lillie. Even though Diane didn't expect Charles home until late, she was upset when she arrived and he wasn't there to greet her.

Thirteen

Diane slammed the car door as she hurried toward the section of Chene Park where she normally met her mother. She didn't have to wait. Lillie was already there. One look at her tight mouth revealed her mood.

"Where the hell have you been? I waited over two hours for you yesterday and you didn't show."

Lillie Rivers was an older version of Diane. The two looked so much alike they could have been mistaken for sisters. Lillie's thick, shoulder-length black hair was streaked with gray at the temples and her body was still as slim as her daughter's. The major difference was that Lillie had survived a hard life, and the signs of it were etched into the harsh lines of her once beautiful face. Today she was dressed in a skin-tight short black lace dress that bordered on garish.

"Calm down. I couldn't come yesterday. Something came up at the last minute and I had no way of getting in touch with you. I'm here now. What's so urgent?"

"Don't you take that high tone with me! I'm still your mother."

"Please, don't make me laugh. You haven't ever been a mother to me, so shall we get down to business here? How much do you want?"

Lillie didn't bother to look for the pain in her daughter's eyes. "I called you last night, but your damn number has been disconnected. What's going on? How the hell am I supposed to reach you?"

"Let's stop wasting time." Diane reached into her purse and handed her a sealed envelope. Lillie grabbed it and ripped it open without delay.

"Why the extra?"

"I won't be able to come as often as before. And you won't be able to contact me," Diane said, with absolutely no emotion in her voice. "From now on, you will have to wait until I contact you."

"Now, look here, I'm not about to put up with this kind of mess!"

"Now, *you* look! I don't owe you anything. You're lucky I even speak to you. We both know if it wasn't for me, you'd be living in the streets!"

"What's going on?"

"My life is none of your concern."

"You uppity bitch!"

"You don't know the first thing about me. You've never taken time to care what I do." Diane suddenly realized her heart was racing and her breathing was uneven. She forced herself to calm down before saying evenly, "All I ask is that you respect my privacy. I will continue to support you as long as you remember that. You take one little step over the line, and you can forget this meal ticket."

The two glared at each other. It was Lillie who broke the silence.

"You may be ashamed to admit it, but you are my child and you came from my body. That counts for somethin'."

"Please! I have more respect for any stranger on the street," Diane snapped, hating that she allowed herself to so much as care what happened to Lillie.

"Why did you have your phone disconnected?"

"My life has changed. I'm married now, never mind to whom. I'm not about to let you ruin that for me."

"Married some rich son of a bitch, hmm?" Lillie grinned, staring at the sparkling stones on Diane's left hand.

"Don't get any nasty ideas, Lillie. Yes, you brought me into this world. I can't change that. Unfortunately, you've never done a damn thing for me since. I'm the one who built a better life for myself. You had nothing to do with who and what I am today. And I sure as hell didn't ask you to follow me to Detroit."

"So your new husband won't be too pleased by his mother-in-law?" Lillie roared with laughter.

Diane shuddered, terrified by the mere thought. "Don't play with me, Lillie. My marriage is not your concern. We stick to the same rules as before. I'll continue to pay your rent and your expenses. But don't come to my job or call me there. Remember, if you expose me, it'll be the last time you ever get a nickel out of me!"

"And what if I have an emergency?"

"If I were you, I'd take real good care of myself."

"You're full of bull! Do you hear me?" Lillie screamed at Diane. "I need a phone number, or your precious new husband may not be the only one to find out about you. How would you like for those professional friends of yours to find out where you come from, girl?"

"Don't you dare threaten me! You're the one who'll wind up with nothing!" Diane spun on her heel and walked away as fast as she could. She didn't look back. Her spine was stiff, her body tight with anger and grief. Because of Lillie she was forced to tell lies to the very people she loved and respected most. It wasn't fair!

Tears were streaming down her face by the time she let herself into her car. She was shaking so badly it took a moment before she had herself under control enough to start the car. The tears flowed freely, yet Diane couldn't explain why she was crying. Hadn't she come to terms with her mother years ago?

She'd worked hard for everything she'd accomplished; no

one had given her an easy ride. Working full-time while taking a full load of college classes hadn't left her any free time. During all these years of struggle, she'd had no one to depend on but herself. Finally, she had someone in her life whom she truly loved and valued. Her mother wanted to destroy her happiness, wanted to drag her back down to the same gutter they'd crawled out of. No way! Diane wasn't about to sit idle and let her, and she wouldn't even consider losing Charles. She meant every word she'd said; she would gladly cut Lillie off before she'd allow her to come between her and Charles.

Charles . . . she sighed his name with longing. How she missed their closeness . . . their talks . . . their loving. It was through Sheldon that she'd learned Charles was involved in a late-night basketball tournament at the community center. The week was slipping away and still they hadn't resolved their disagreement.

Lost in thought, Diane didn't pay attention to the taxi that was following her progress through the early evening traffic.

On Thursday, Charles was no closer to forgetting his jealousy than he'd been on Sunday night. He just couldn't seem to let go of his anger.

Even though they'd slept in the same king-sized bed, that one telephone call had been as effective as placing a brick wall down the middle of it.

Was his pride the only thing keeping his arms empty?

It was after one in the morning when Charles climbed the stairs and quietly approached their bedroom. Since he was coaching, there was no way he could have gotten out of the late-night games. Charles told himself he preferred to return home after Diane had gone to bed. It made things a whole lot simpler.

But despite his declaration, he missed her terribly. He

hadn't realized how much he'd hoped that just this once Diane would wait up for him until he entered their room and found her asleep. He was tired of doing without her sweet, sweet loving. If anyone was acting like a fool, it was him. He was the one lying awake beside his woman night after night with a hard-on.

The bedside lamps were switched on as well as the television set mounted on the built-in wall unit. Diane lay curled on her side, sound asleep. An open book lay beside her. Charles sighed, turning off the set. The navy comforter was at her waist, revealing the pale blue lace nightgown which barely contained her luscious breasts. She didn't stir. He placed her novel on the nightstand and turned off her lamp before moving into the connecting dressing room. The plush cream carpet underfoot absorbed the sound of his footsteps.

Closing the dressing room door carefully behind him, Charles flicked on the light. He was pleased that her dresses, suits, blouses, and slacks filled one side of the long room. Her white wicker bureau and dresser stood beside his own heavy dark oak bureau. He opened a drawer, then smiled as he gazed at the array of her silky underthings arranged neatly inside. If asked, Charles wouldn't have been able to put into words why the physical evidence of Diane's presence in his home filled him with such deep satisfaction. Nonetheless, it was a fact.

He showered and reentered the bedroom with nothing more than a towel around his waist. Carefully he got into bed and turned out the light, plunging the room into darkness. He didn't try to sleep. Instead, he lay on his back, his hands behind his head, concentrating on the sound of his wife's soft, even breathing. Eventually, he turned on his side toward her, but he made no move to touch her.

Perhaps she sensed his presence, because she moved toward him. In fact, she didn't settle until her sweet, sexy behind was cradled between his thighs. They lay spoon-fashion. His aroused shaft hardened even more. Charles swallowed a throaty groan, placing his arms around her, a soft full breast warmed by his cupped palm. It was a long time before he was able to drop off to sleep.

"Diane."

"Hmm," she mumbled, pressing her face into the pillow.

Tempted to caress her soft shoulders, instead Charles said, "It's almost seven. If you don't get a move on, you're going to be late for your first class." He busied his hands with knotting his necktie. He was no fool. If he so much as touched her, he would wind up in bed with her, deep within her hot, womanly center . . . that was, if she would let him near her.

"I'm awake," she mumbled, sitting up. She saw that he was already dressed. Normally he was up and gone before she got out of bed. She supposed with his heavy workload, starting before office hours enabled him to finish early enough to spend time at the community center.

The trouble was, they hadn't spent any time *together.* It was the first time she'd seen him the entire miserable week.

"You look familiar. What is your name again?" she said sarcastically, furious with him and self-conscious about the way she looked. Her hair was no doubt standing up all over her head and her gown suddenly seemed too short and much too sheer. How in the world were they ever going to solve their problem if they never saw each other? How were they going to make this marriage work? Surely they couldn't go on like this for much longer.

"Very funny." He didn't look amused. Nevertheless, he took note of how lovely she was drowsy from sleep . . . and how sexy. He hadn't seen her like this since their first morning back from their honeymoon. His body reminded him of just how many seconds, minutes, and hours it had been since they'd made love. He'd missed her. He was forced to clear his throat before he could speak. "We don't have time to get into another argument," he said tightly. "You'd better hurry. The clock went off fifteen minutes ago. I thought you heard it." He shrugged into the jacket of his navy pinstriped suit, which he had teamed with a cream silk shirt and a red-and-navy striped tie.

He looked good . . . so good. She sighed as he seemed to make a point of keeping his back to her as he pocketed his wallet and change. They were like perfectly correct strangers. They hadn't talked . . . they hadn't made love in days . . . she missed her husband . . . her lover . . . her friend.

Unable to gaze at her lush, sweet mouth without reaching for her, he said gruffly, "Oh, I forgot to tell you about the dinner dance tonight, a fundraiser for the community center."

"How could you forget something like that?"

"I had other things on my mind." A muscle jumped in his jaw.

"Do you want to go?"

"I have to. I'm on the executive board. Besides, my fraternity is sponsoring it. I've invited Jeff Jenkins and his mother to come as my guests."

"That's the young man you told me about, isn't it?" Diane asked, as she reached for her robe on the padded bench at the end of the bed.

Charles swallowed, unable to look away from the outline of his wife's large nipples. His body swelled with erotic anticipation.

"Charles?"

"Yeah. I'm late—I've got to get out of here." He was already reaching for the doorknob. "I know this is short notice, but can you make it? It would mean a lot to me."

Diane couldn't meet his gaze. She didn't want him to see her disappointment . . . her hurt. Somehow, she managed to make her tone as polite as his. "Of course. Is it formal?"

"Semi. I'll pick you up at seven."

"Pick me up?"

"Yeah. I've got racketball with Quinn after work. I'll shower and change at the club. 'Bye." If he had bothered to look, he'd have seen tears sparkling in her eyes.

She had been furious with Charles for waiting until the last minute to tell her about the dinner dance. Fortunately, she didn't have to run around after work looking for a dress. She'd bought a new dress for their final night on the cruise and hadn't gotten a chance to wear it. A dress, with any luck, that might cause her husband to wake up and take notice.

Instead of admiring the graceful lines of the form-fitting black velvet sheath with its heart-shaped neckline, Diane frowned at the fatigue she saw in her toffee-toned skin. Smoke-colored eyeshadow, rose blush and lipstick, and the feathery ebony curls could hide only so much. She looked how she truly felt—exhausted. Friday night. She'd much rather curl up in an armchair in front of the fireplace with a book than face a room full of strangers.

Diane had chosen to wear the earrings and bracelet that Charles had given her on their wedding trip in hopes of lifting her spirits. She had just reached the bottom step when Charles let himself in with his key.

"Hi." His dark gaze traveled over her soft curves. "Pretty dress."

"Thank you. Do we have time for a drink?"

Charles met her gaze with surprise, since Diane very rarely drank. "Sorry, we're already late. Are you ready?" He placed his sports bag on one of the armchairs which flanked an ebony lacquered table in the hallway.

It was bad enough that he hadn't reached for her to share even a brief kiss. Did he have to look away, too?

"Yes." Handing him her black velvet evening cape, she

PHOEBE
CONN
BELOVED
BESTSELLING AUTHOR
SHANNON
DRAKE
PRINCESS
OF FIRE
GENTRY
Jo
Goodman
FOREVER
IN MY
HEART
Now, for
the first time...
You can find
Janelle Taylor, Shannon
Drake, Rosanne Bittner,
Sylvie Sommerfield,
Penelope Neri, Phoebe
Conn, Bobbi Smith,
and the rest of
today's most popular,
bestselling authors
...All in one
brand-new club!
Introducing
KENSINGTON CHOICE,
the new Zebra/Pinnacle service
that delivers the best
new historical romances
direct to your home,
at a significant discount
off the publisher's prices.
As your
introduction,
we invite you
to accept
4 FREE BOOKS
worth up to $23.96
details inside...

told herself that now wasn't the time to get into an argument. But she was sick and tired of being treated so coldly. She had done nothing wrong. If she'd wanted to be with Greg, she could have married the man months ago when he'd asked her. Greg knew the score . . . he knew that they were only friends.

Charles saw the flicker of emotion which sped across her beautiful features. He was trying his best to maintain some semblance of control over his emotions. He'd done enough ranting and raving on Sunday night. It had only served to make her furious with him. He knew he owed her an apology. And he intended to give it to her, later, once they were alone.

She looked so good and smelled so wonderful. He yearned to pull her into his arms. It had been a long, empty week. All he wanted was to be alone with his wife. They needed to spend time with each other. Hell, he ached to have his woman back.

His hands rested momentarily on her shoulders in the thick pile of the soft wrap. The fabric could not compare to the softness of her bare skin. Briefly, he allowed himself the pleasure of inhaling her scent. His betraying body tightened, his shaft thickening with desire.

Charles lowered his head until his open mouth touched her neck just below her right earlobe. He heard her soft gasp. He comforted himself when she didn't pull away from him. In fact, she leaned back against his chest for an all-too-brief instant. He fought the urge to devour her soft, rose-tinted lips. One kiss wouldn't be enough . . . could never be enough. He'd been without for too damn long. If he touched her, they could forget about the dinner dance, because he wouldn't be able to stop until he was deep within her moist, tight heat.

Stepping back, he realized his hands were shaking. He quickly shoved them into his trouser pockets. After nearly a week of doing everything he could to hold on to his anger, despite his relentless hunger for her sweet mouth and her soft body, he knew he was damn lucky she'd allowed him to touch her at all. It was a wonder that she'd agreed to go with him tonight.

Charles didn't understand the strong sense of possessiveness or jealousy he felt toward her. This wasn't the first time it had happened. But it had taken him by surprise. He expected their marriage to change all that nonsense. But it hadn't. Even though she wore his ring, he was terrified of losing her.

"You're going to like the Jenkinses. Jeff is sixteen. He's a junior at Cass. His mother, Anthia, has been raising him alone."

A picture of her own brother formed in her mind. Diane smiled, wondering how different her life would have been if her brother had lived. Maybe she and her mother could have had a relationship? Maybe she could have felt something for her mother other than shame and resentment?

Fourteen

Anthia Jenkins nervously smoothed the deep ruffled flounce of her white dress. The soft polyester felt and looked, she hoped, like silk. At least, that was what the saleswoman had assured her at the resale shop. Was it appropriate for a dinner dance?

She'd done her own nails and hair, using the last of her paycheck for a new shirt and tie for her son, Jeffery. Anthia knew she was attractive. Her small, curvy body seemed to attract the male eye, especially when she wasn't interested. And lately she had not been interested in any of the men she'd met.

Was she setting herself up for disappointment by putting so much emphasis on this one evening? She couldn't help it. She wanted everything to be perfect . . . as perfect as her limited funds would allow. Her job barely covered the cost of their one-bedroom apartment, food, and clothes. It certainly didn't provide for the high-priced clothes and videogames her teenage son longed to have. Nor would it stretch to accommodate the price of community college for her.

Jeff had his heart set on going away to a black college, and Anthia wanted it for him just as badly. She wanted him to have not only the skills, but the confidence and assurance that such a background installed in the school's graduates.

"Jeff? Are you ready? Charles will be here any minute."

"Almost," he called, from behind the closed bathroom door.

Anthia sprayed herself lavishly with cologne before grabbing her everyday black leather purse and coat. She didn't own a dainty evening bag or evening wrap.

At thirty-two, she was weighed down by the strain of trying to raise a male child alone. It had been so much easier when her mother had been alive. Anthia had someone to guide her, someone to share the worries. If it hadn't been for her mother's help, she would not have managed to finish high school and then start college. But Anthia had been forced to give up her college courses after her mother's death—and her dream of becoming a lawyer. She'd settled for being a secretary in a law firm. And it looked as if she wouldn't be able to resume her own education. Taking care of her boy, keeping him away from the gangs, and keeping him in school had left her physically and emotionally drained. She didn't even have a personal life, but she knew she was lucky. She had a job and she had a good kid.

"Jeff!" she yelled, her patience nonexistent as she entered the living room and saw the mess he'd made of it. True, it also served as his bedroom at night. "You want Charles to think we live like pigs?" she fussed, as she rushed around, picking up clothes and athletic shoes and shoving them into the hall closet.

She'd spent the last hour getting ready, hoping to make a favorable impression. Now she'd end up messed and sweaty. Her soft, amber-toned skin was flushed when her young son finally made his appearance. Her thick shoulder-length black hair had probably lost all its curl.

"You called?" Jeff Jenkins was a handsome boy. Too handsome, Anthia thought with impatience. Girls were constantly calling the apartment asking to speak to him . . . regardless of his ten o'clock curfew.

"What have you been doing? Didn't I tell you to pick up this room?"

The tall, slender youth shared the same skin tone and thick black hair as his mother. While her features were small and feminine, his were distinctly masculine but equally appealing.

"Sorry. I'll take care of it. You're looking good, Ma."

Anthia was too tired to worry about the hard edge to her voice. "It's after six-thirty. Charles will be here any minute. Do you ever listen to me, boy?"

Why didn't he understand she only wanted the best for him? She had been hoping to take a second job to build a nest egg for his future. But how could she, when she worked such long hours as it was? What she needed was a man . . . a good man to share the load—a man like Charles Randol, she thought. Love was not necessary. She'd learned the difference between love and sex at the tender age of sixteen. She'd fancied herself in love with Jeff's father. Today, she could barely remember the features of the teenager who'd fathered her child.

Jeff didn't have a father or grandfather, not even a wayward uncle. That was why she'd enrolled him in the mentoring program at the community center. Her sole aim was to keep him off the streets and out of trouble . . . away from people like his friend Eddie Walker. The boy was nothing but trouble.

"Mr. Randol has taken a lot of time with you. He's showing you how to make something of yourself. Why do you still hang around with Eddie? He ain't nothin' but trouble."

"Don't start on Eddie, Ma. He's my friend," Jeff said bitterly. "I'm supposed to put him down 'cause you say so? That ain't fair! I'm not a baby anymore. Besides, you used to like Eddie. You and his grandmother used to be friends."

Anthia had no idea why she had even brought up the boy's name. Kids like Eddie were the reason they left the old neighborhood. "Hurry and straighten this room," she snapped, then rushed into the bathroom and slammed the door behind her.

He swore beneath his breath while finishing the room. It wasn't his fault he didn't have a bedroom of his own, a place to keep his stuff. He was almost grown, a foot taller than his mother. But he had no privacy, no place to entertain his friends.

Why was she on Eddie's case? He hardly saw Eddie anymore, not since Eddie had started usin' and hangin' with a rough crowd. But Jeff and Eddie were still friends. They'd grown up together. Shouldn't matter who he hung with. His mom knew he was clean, never messed with the stuff. Jeff had his head on straight and he knew how to use it. Why didn't she give him any credit?

Jeff had never told her how he'd tried to get Eddie to join the community center. All the fellows liked Charles. Charles was all right. He paid attention to the guys, really listened. That made all the difference. Jeff often found himself telling Charles about problems in school, problems with his mother, even about the girls. It was easier to talk to him because he was a man. As his granny would say, Charles was "good people."

When Anthia returned, she didn't say a word about the now tidy room. "Remember, there are going to be some very important people there tonight. Mr. Randol has gone to a lot of trouble for us. We don't want to do anything to embarrass him or ourselves," she said nervously smoothing her dress. Charles Randol was the kind of man a woman could lean on; you didn't worry about him disappearing into thin air. She lifted her chin, telling herself she was just as good as any of those uppity black women men like Charles Randol hung out with. Just as good.

"You haven't said a word since we left home," Charles said softly, having parked the car in the narrow drive of the two-family flat. The houses were close together, with very little yard between them. The Jenkins house was situated on the northeast side of Detroit in a low-income neighborhood.

"Diane?"

"I'm fine," she said softly. "Just a little tired. It's been a long week." She didn't add how lonely it had been without his smile and tender love.

"I'm sorry I didn't tell you about this charity thing until the last minute."

"It's done. Let's forget it."

"Baby, we need to talk. I've been thinking about . . ."

"Hi." The tall, lanky youth stood beside the car.

Diane's heart sank. She was frustrated by this intrusion. She was beginning to wonder if Charles regretted their marriage. The mere thought of that was terrifying.

"Hi," Charles asked. "Where's your mom?"

"She was right behind me a second ago." After a curious glance at Diane, he said, "I'll go see what's keeping her." He disappeared in a flash.

"You're going to like Jeff. He's a great kid. He deserves a fair shake."

"Everyone does. You're a very special man, to care so much," Diane said, her eyes warm with love and respect.

Charles's heart skipped a beat as he responded to the softness in her voice, something he hadn't heard all week. "It's payback time, Di. I never knew what it was to do without. I've always had enough food, money, a roof over my head, someone to care whether I failed or succeeded. The Detroit gas and electric company was never a threat in our household. We had it all."

"You were lucky, yes, but what's more important, you care about other people. That's what makes you so special to me."

Charles smiled, a slow, easy smile, something he hadn't done much of lately. Diane's heart began to pound so loudly in her chest she wouldn't have been surprised if he'd heard it. They were both so busy staring into each other's eyes that neither heard Jeff or his mother's approach.

"Good evening," Anthia said softly, in a deep, feminine tone.

"Hello." Charles turned in his seat and smiled at the lovely woman who slid in before her son. "It's good to see you." Charles noted her studied glance at Diane. "Anthia, I'd like you to meet my bride, Diane. Sweetheart, this is Jeffery Jenkins and his mother, Anthia Jenkins."

Diane turned with a smile. "Good evening. It's a pleasure to meet you both. Charles has told me so much about you."

Well! He hadn't said one word about even being engaged, Anthia fumed. Bride! When had he gotten married? He'd only been away a few weeks.

"Congratulations!" Jeff said with a wide grin.

"Yes, congratulations," Anthia said, with a forced smile. "Charles, I'd no idea you were planning to marry."

Charles chuckled. "We surprised everyone, didn't we, sweetheart?"

"To say the least," Diane said, remembering his sister's reaction to their marriage.

"All set?" Charles asked, before setting the car into motion.

The dinner dance was being held at the Western Hotel in downtown Detroit.

Diane was just as surprised as the others by the crowd. Charles was telling Jeff about his fraternity, which had sponsored the event, as he helped Diane with her wrap. Jeff quickly followed his lead, assisting his mother with her coat.

"You look lovely tonight, Anthia," Charles said, with a wide smile, his hand resting comfortably in the small of Diane's slim back.

Diane could have cheerfully stomped on his foot. He hadn't commented on how she looked tonight. Oh, no! He'd been too busy avoiding her all week. They hadn't made love; they'd hardly even seen each other. He was right, Anthia Jenkins had a spectacular figure and was gorgeous in her low-cut dress.

Diane lifted her chin a notch, taking note of the flirtatious glance the other woman gave her husband. That little hussy was not trying to hide her interest in Charles. Her soft black eyes hadn't left Charles's long, lean, muscular length for an instant. Diane couldn't help but agree that he was wonderfully attractive in his custom-tailored black tuxedo. The stark white pleated shirt was stunning against his deep-brown skin.

Charles ushered them inside the ballroom, stopping often to make introductions. He seemed very pleased when he was congratulated on his beautiful wife and his pride seemed to ease Diane's nerves somewhat.

They shared the table with Dexter Washington, the director of the center. The tall, attractive, light-brown-skinned man was a close friend of Charles's as well as an associate. They were also introduced to the two teenage boys and their parents. Charles had just seated the ladies when another man approached.

"Charles, my man," Doug Henderson offered his hand. He was an influential and successful real estate agent. Although Doug was also a frat brother, he wasn't a friend. Doug was well known for his prowess with the ladies.The bronze-skinned man with thick black hair and steel-gray streaks at his temples was aware of his appeal to the opposite sex. Doug and Charles had often dated the same women, although Charles frequently succeeded where the other man failed, a fact that seemed to bug the hell out of Doug. "Two beautiful women! Not fair."

"It has been a while," Charles said, not pleased by the gleam he saw in the other man's eyes as his gaze lingered a bit too long on Diane. "How's business?"

"Introduce me," he said, oozing a boyish charm. After the introductions were made, Doug gasped, "Wife? How lucky can you get? You're actually married to this exquisite woman?"

"That's right," Charles said, with a touch of impatience.

Doug offered his best wishes. Much to Charles's annoyance, he didn't seem to be in a particular hurry to return to his own table. He remained to make casual conversation about the community center while his gaze returned time and time again to Diane.

Charles's veneer of politeness was rapidly disappearing when they started serving the formal dinner and Doug reluctantly left.

As the meal progressed, Charles kept a light banter going while taking pains to include Jeff and Anthia in the conversation. Thank heaven, they were spared the usual long drawn-out speeches. It was a fundraiser for the center, and everyone seemed intent on having a good time.

Charles was keenly aware of the interested looks Doug still sent Diane's way. By the time the tables were cleared and the dancing had started, Charles's temper was near the boiling point.

"I didn't expect quite so many people." Anthia leaned toward Charles, offering a tempting view of her cleavage.

"I think we're going to be thrilled, once the tally is done. What do you think, Dex?"

"I agree with you. The turnout is more than we'd hoped."

"Jeff and I certainly appreciate the help the center has given us."

"Jeff has done the real work. He's been working extremely hard to prove himself," Dexter said softly to Anthia.

Anthia touched Charles's hand where it rested on his wineglass. "We were so worried about you after the accident. How are you?"

"Great."

"Charles, it's such a relief to know that you've fully recovered."

The attention the other woman was dishing out by the

bucketfull was beginning to get on Diane's nerves. She said firmly, "I couldn't agree with you more. I'm so glad it's behind us." Her smile was forced. Anthia was getting a little too touchy-feely.

Charles casually eased his hand away from Anthia's. "Thank you, ladies. I must say, I'm flattered."

Diane leaned forward to brush her lips with his. "You deserve it, honey."

Charles blinked in surprise, yet was extremely pleased by her attention. He looked down on her small features, his gaze resting on her mouth. He'd missed her softness and sweetness . . . missed them desperately.

Doug chose that moment to appear at Diane's elbow. "Charles," he said, staring at Diane. "You don't mind if I borrow your lady for a dance?"

Charles minded very much, but he recognized it was neither the time nor the place to acknowledge it. "Ask Diane. The choice is hers."

"Diane?"

She glanced at her husband's expressionless face before she reluctantly agreed, allowing the other man to escort her onto the dance floor.

As Doug's hands settled around her waist, she recalled the cruise, and the pleasure of being held in her husband's arms. She and Charles fit together perfectly. The last time they had danced was under the Caribbean stars. They had been so happy then, so very much in love. It had been a magical time. Was it truly over?

"Enjoying yourself?" Doug asked with a wide grin.

Although he was a handsome man, Diane found his features were too refined . . . almost pretty. Judging by his air of confidence, Diane suspected Doug was used to female admiration.

"Yes, very much."

Diane watched as Charles escorted Anthia onto the dance floor. The petite beauty smiled up at him. When she threw back her head, laughing with sheer enjoyment, Diane found herself grinding her teeth together. She was so engrossed in watching the two of them that she missed a step and came down on Doug's foot.

"Forgive me."

"No problem." He smiled gallantly. Charles Randol had all the luck. He could afford to devote so much time and money to the community center. Charles had the connections in the business community to make an event like tonight possible. He was an excellent coach before he'd gone into the family business. He had it all, Doug decided, including marriage to the finest sister in town. "I must say, your marriage was a shock. I never expected that old skirt-chaser to settle down. I can sure understand the reason when I look at you. You're a very beautiful lady."

"Thank you. My husband and I used to work together at Lawrence High School. Are you married, Mr. Henderson?"

"No, and the name is Doug."

Diane smiled, deciding Doug would be perfect for Anthia.

"I don't know how he has kept you such a secret. None of the brothers knew he was even thinking about jumpin' the broom."

"Love happens when least expected," Diane said, recalling the excitement of their cruise.

"What do you teach?" Doug wondered aloud.

"Business and computer classes. But tell me about yourself. Are you from Michigan? I think I detect a southern accent."

Chuckling, he said, "I'm originally from Atlanta. I started my own firm a couple of years after leaving the South. At that time the Midwest seemed like a perfect place to set up shop. The car industry was really booming back then."

Although the music stopped briefly before starting again, Doug didn't relinquish his hold on Diane.

"Atlanta? What a lovely place. Are you involved with someone special, Doug?" She smiled speculatively. Anthia evidently was interested in finding a well-heeled man, and Diane fully intended to assist her in her efforts.

"If you weren't a newlywed, I'd think you were up to something, pretty lady."

"My turn," Charles said, a hard edge to his voice. A muscle jumped in his cheek. Not waiting for an answer, he took Diane into his arms.

The band was playing a soft, romantic tune. Diane relaxed in the security of her lover's arms. She had been aching to be held against his body. She sighed softly.

Unfortunately, it was hardly an ideal moment. Charles hadn't spoken a word since he'd taken her away from Doug.

"Honey?" She asked.

When he didn't respond, she tilted her head back so she could see his face. His features looked as if they had been carved out of granite. "What's wrong?"

"Not here," he whispered, his hand tightening against her spine as they circled the crowded dance floor.

"Something's wrong."

"I hear my wife propositioning another man. What could possibly be wrong?" he said between clenched teeth.

"That's not true!"

"What do you call it when you're questioning the man about his sex life?"

"I call it eavesdropping and then jumping to the wrong conclusion. But then, that's something you're quite good at, isn't it?"

"Don't get huffy with me. I've had enough of your flirting to last me two lifetimes."

"You're being unfair! First you get angry over a telephone call from a friend . . . a friend who, by the way, had no *idea* I was married. Now this! Why are you treating me this way? If I wanted Greg, I could have married him the last time he asked me!"

Diane was livid. She'd have left him on the dance floor if he hadn't held on to her.

"Stop it!" he said, around a forced smile. "The song will be over in a minute."

"It can't be soon enough for me." She kept her face averted so he couldn't see her blink back tears.

Fifteen

Neither one of them spoke, yet their bodies moved against each other in a sensuous caress, reminding them both of what had been painfully absent.

"Why were you questioning Doug about his sex life?"

"I didn't use that word. I asked if he was seeing someone."

"Why, damn it?"

"I've fallen in love with him, of course," she insisted with a saccharine smile, her lovely eyes flashing daggers at him. "Oh, what does it matter?" She refused to voice her own insecurity when he'd been dancing with Anthia.

"It matters," Charles said dryly. He closed his eyes, allowing himself to do nothing more than touch her while inhaling her special scent. Finally he said, "I'm jealous. I can't seem to help it. I don't know why you're so upset. You've given me plenty of practice. For years you've thrown man after man into my face. What the hell do you expect from me?"

Her voice was brimming with emotion when she said, "It seems as if we've made a mistake . . . too much moonlight and too many candlelit dinners." Diane walked away from him, not bothering to see if he was following. She paused at their table long enough to ask Anthia, "Would you care to freshen up?"

Anthia blinked in surprise, but didn't hesitate. She nodded, picking up her purse.

"Please, excuse us, gentlemen." Diane swept by her husband, head held high.

They had to thread their way through the crowded ballroom and into the hallway. Neither spoke until they reached the ladies' room.

It was Anthia who asked, "Is something wrong?"

"Yes," Diane said, standing in front of the long mirror above a row of sinks. "But that's not why I asked you to join me." Diane waited until a woman finished with her hair and left and they were finally alone. "This is about my husband. He's no longer available."

Anthia's dark eyes went wide with shock. "I-I-I-I'm not . . ."

"You are, and we both know it. Look, I know what it's like to have to make it out here alone. I also know that men like Charles seem like an easy way out. I'm letting you know up front, you'll be making a serious mistake by going after my man. You see, you have to go through me to get to him, and I'm not about to move out of your way."

Anthia nodded, respect shining in her eyes. Her voice was edged with defensiveness. "What do you know about raising a child without a man? You probably come from the same cushiony place that he does. You think I don't know those are real diamonds and rubies glimmering on your ears, girlfriend? You paid more for that dress than I paid for rent this month."

"We're talking about money. Yes, it does make life easier, but never enough to make you happy. I should know. I've been on my own since I was your son's age. I know what it is to wait tables, to go to bed so tired you can't see straight. I also know what it takes to get ahead in life. Yes, I've finally made it. I didn't trade on my looks. I used my brain, girlfriend. I put myself through college. It was the hardest thing I've ever done." Diane paused to make a point. "I married Charles for one reason. I love him. I'm not interested in the money. It just happens to come with the package."

"Why should I believe you?"

"You don't have to," Diane shrugged. "If you're interested in doing more than taking phone messages, call me. There are grants out there for folks willing to work and study. Last semester I taught business courses at night at W.C.C.C. Call me any time. I'll hook you up with the right classes."

"You willin' to help me, after . . ."

". . . You made a play for my man?" Diane shrugged. "We all need help from time to time. Besides, you and I understand each other."

Anthia laughed. "You'll scratch my eyes out if I look at him too hard, right?"

"You got it," she said, taking a lipliner and lipstick out of her purse. "Tell me, what do you think of Doug Henderson? Kind of cute, don't you think?"

"Fine," Anthia giggled.

"And single," Diane supplied, with a smile.

"Are you sure?"

"Positive."

The two discussed the man's attributes as they repaired their make-up. Diane's demeanor was calm when they returned, her anger and disappointment pushed to the back of her mind.

Charles was in conversation with Dexter and Jeff. He sensed Diane's presence even before he saw her. She was breathtaking. He loved her so much that she made him ache with longing, while at the same time she infuriated the hell out of him. When she refused to meet his gaze, he simmered with frustration. Her smile was warm and generous to everyone except him. For the next hour and half, Charles circulated with Diane at his side, concentrating on securing financial backing for the community center. As the evening drew to a close, both Charles and Dexter considered it an astonishing success.

Charles's heart jerked in his chest when he felt Diane's soft breath close to his ear. "It's late. Can we leave soon?"

He nodded. Her earlier declaration weighed down his spirit. They had hardly seen each other this week. He'd been impossible to live with. He didn't even recognize himself in the angry man he'd become. She was right . . . he was so caught up in his own jealousy, his own fear, that he'd forgotten everything else. He was embarrassed by his loss of control on the dance floor.

Doug Henderson! Where was his mind? She had just met the man. Charles had no cause to accuse her of anything. She wore his ring and she spent her nights in his bed. Jealous fool! If he didn't start thinking with his head, he'd lose her. Their marriage license didn't come with a guarantee.

When they stopped to drop the Jenkinses off, Charles was surprised to hear Anthia and Diane arrange to meet for lunch the following week.

"Warm enough?" he asked, as he guided the car back into traffic. The streets were busy in spite of the lateness of the hour.

"I'm fine, thank you," she said frostily.

It was worse than he'd suspected. Not only was she hugging the door, but she seemed to be fascinated with the passing scenery. Sighing, he put on an Aretha Franklin tape. Soon music filled the void. Charles concentrated on his driving, assuring himself that they would talk once they were home.

Yet he couldn't help speculating over what she'd meant when she'd said they'd evidently made a mistake. Was she regretting their marriage? How had she put it? Oh, yeah, too much moonlight and too many candlelit dinners. What had she meant?

By the time Charles parked the car in the circular drive

and they entered the house, Diane still hadn't said a word. He watched as she walked past him toward the staircase.

"Nightcap?" He stood at the entrance to the family room.

Diane didn't so much as glance his way. She shook her head as she began mounting the stairs.

"Di! We have to talk about this."

"Not tonight. Perhaps in the morning."

"Now," he said, a bit more sharply than he'd intended.

"We said it all on the dance floor. It's late and I'm tired. I'm going to bed."

"You might have said it all, but I haven't. I'd appreciate it if you came into the family room and shared a nightcap with me."

"At the moment, I'm not interested in sharing a damn thing with you, including a bed."

Charles swore. "Oh, yeah, that's really going to settle a hell of a lot, isn't it?"

He jerked open the door to the family room and disappeared inside. His suit jacket sailed into one of the empty armchairs near the fireplace. He'd be damned if he'd follow behind her like a sheepdog in heat!

She hadn't really planned on joining him, but after she showered and moisturized her skin with scented lotion, she realized he was right. They needed to talk. She pulled on a yellow lace slip of a gown and the yellow silk robe.

Charles wasn't in front of the fireplace, where fresh logs rested in the grate ready to be lit. His outer things had gone the same way as his black silk socks and briefs—into the armchair. The only sound in the room came from behind the glass doors that led to the indoor swimming pool. Diane hesitated before stepping down the two shallow steps onto the blue-and-green tiled flooring. The vertical blinds on the surrounding glass walls were closed against the spring night. The only light came from overhead.

Her heart pounded with trepidation as well as appreciation as she watched her husband's long, powerfully muscled frame glide through the water. She stayed where she was for some time before she slowly crossed to one of the emerald-green canvas chairs and perched on the edge, where a towel was draped over the back.

She didn't have long to wait. Charles spotted her from across the length of the pool. His eyes never left her as he swam to the edge. He used his powerful arms to push himself up and out of the pool. A stream of moisture cascaded down his long, bare body. Diane caught her breath at his brown perfection.

He ran his gaze over her. The fluid fabric clung rather than concealed the softness of her body. Her nipples were pouting against the fabric. Her pink-painted toenails peeked out from beneath the hem of her robe. Her small feet were bare.

They stared at each other, neither making the effort to shatter the electric silence that hung like an invisible curtain between them. Without speaking, Charles reached for the towel and began toweling himself dry. When he was finished, he casually looped the towel low on his slim waist.

Hiding her trembling hands in the pockets of her robe, she refused to stare at the wide expanse of his chest or the width of his shoulders or the thickening of his manhood beneath the towel.

Taking a deep breath, she asked, "What did you want to talk about?"

Charles surprised them both when he pulled Diane into his arms.

"What are you doing?"

"What I should have done days ago," he said, his mouth covering hers in a hot, hungry kiss. "Feel, baby. Feel how much I've missed you, how much I need you." He explored her soft lips with his tongue until she sighed, opening for him. His tongue slid into the warmth of her mouth, filling it as he longed to fill her body with his sex.

"Chuck . . ." she whimpered, when he briefly lifted his mouth from hers. "We must talk."

"What I must have is you." He lifted her into his arms and carried her through the house. "It has gone on too long."

"This will solve nothing."

"It will solve everything," he grumbled, mounting the stairs two at a time, not stopping until he reached their bedroom. The lamps were lit.

"Charles!"

He kissed her until she swallowed her protests and moaned with the urgency of unfulfilled desire. Her small hands caressed the long line of his back. Diane pressed soft kisses across his wide chest.

Charles quivered with the force of his need and the intense pleasure of having Diane back where she belonged. He wanted her so badly he hurt from it. Unable to wait a moment longer, he undressed her. His hands weren't rough, but they weren't tender, either.

Diane was a mass of raw nerves as he licked the hard, elongated tips of her breasts, circling, tonguing each in turn, savoring her sweetness before he took a nipple deep into his mouth and sucked. She cried out from the pleasure, sending shock waves racing to every cell in her body. The pleasure only accelerated as he palmed the damp curls between her thighs, rhythmically squeezing her softness, then stroking his long fingers over the fleshy folds. Diane didn't think she could bear much more. Charles didn't hesitate to caress the hidden layers of softness or worry her ultrasensitive nub. He stroked her as he continued his hot attention to each breast.

"Please . . . I need you . . . now."

Charles had no intention of denying either of them. He repositioned himself and slowly penetrated her heat, filling her completely. Diane cried out, unable to contain the thrill of once again having his demanding strength deep inside.

He loved her with each steel-hard thrust of his body, his hands palming her breasts, gently tugging the hard tips. Charles increased the pace while Diane clung to him, responding to his power . . . his maleness. Their release was raw, quick, and simultaneous . . . sheer joy.

It was a while before Charles recovered enough to disengage himself. He lay on his side, facing her. Diane had barely caught her breath when she slowly opened her eyes to his persistent gaze.

His voice was gravelly when he said, "I have to know if you meant what you said. Have you decided our marriage was a mistake?"

"I never said that."

"Then what were you talking about on the dance floor?"

Diane sighed, not able to met the force of his dark, questioning eyes. How could she explain, when she wasn't quite sure herself what she meant? She had been so miserable this week. All the bright, glittering dreams of a new life together were disappearing like autumn leaves on a dark, windy night.

"I know I rushed you into marriage . . ."

"Chucky, I wanted it as much as you did."

"Then why?"

"I was upset and I was hurt. I have no regrets about our marriage."

Charles swallowed the fear. Tilting her head back until he could look into her eyes, he said, "You scared me." Rather than being the angry declaration he'd intended, it was released from his throat in a raw whisper.

"I'm sorry."

"You own my heart and I can't get it back. I gave it to you unconditionally a long, long time ago."

"I married you because I love you. Why can't you believe that?"

He frowned, concentrating. It took him a while before he could put his feelings into words. Finally, after what seemed like an eternity to Diane, he said, "My intellect tells me one thing while my emotions tell me something entirely different. Di, we have a history. Sometimes, it's difficult to separate what's happening now with what happened then."

"Are you saying you can't forgive me for those earlier mistakes?" Yes, she had deliberately tried to make him jealous, and she'd succeeded beyond her wildest dreams. It had proved to be worse than unleashing a hungry bear.

"I can't forget it."

"That's not fair! You know what you thought about me wasn't true. You know I never slept with any of those men." Her vision blurred as tears filled her eyes.

"Diane, for years you went from one man to the next. There was always some poor sucker waiting to get next to you," he growled impatiently, despite the pain he saw in her eyes. He had to finish. "When that phone rang Sunday night, it brought back all those bitter memories. You're a married woman. My woman."

"I know that."

"Oh, really? What about Doug?"

"How can you ask that? I've done nothing wrong. You're punishing me because of how I hurt you in the past."

Charles stared at her, wondering if that was what he had done. Finally, he said, "I never looked at it quite like that." His brow, came together in a heavy scowl. "I guess I didn't think . . . I just reacted. I'm sorry. I've let this thing go on and on." He stroked her cheek, then whispered, "Maybe if you weren't so darn beautiful, I wouldn't have to worry."

Diane reacted as if she'd been struck. "I can't help how I look!" Her thoughts instantly flew to Lillie . . . the beautiful whore.

"Baby, I was teasing. Don't pull away. This is about how I feel, knowing that so many men find you attractive. I can't seem to forget that I was the one you once pushed out in the cold. You're right. It should stay in the past." He sighed.

"This isn't your problem. It's mine. I've been so jealous that I haven't been thinking straight."

Diane lifted her hand to his cheek, roughened by the late-night stubble. She caressed it, her eyes brimming with tears. "I love you. Don't you know that yet? We belong to each other." She encircled his neck, lifting her lips to his.

"Oh, baby . . . baby," he groaned, crushing her softness to his hard length. He ravished her sweetness as one lengthy kiss flowed into the next. When the kiss ended, he buried his face against the place where her shoulder and neck joined, his tongue heating the tender skin. "I'm sorry," he whispered huskily. "Forgive me."

Her smile was radiant. "I love only you. I have no room in my heart or in my life for another man. You, my darling, are my lover . . . my friend . . . my husband," she said, snuggling even closer.

"I've been cold and distant." Charles had suffered a string of sleepless nights while he'd lain beside her, watching her through the night, aching for her comforting warmth.

"Yes, you have," she murmured, kissing the highly sensitive base of his throat. "I've missed you so," she whispered, caressing and smoothing his wide chest.

"I've missed you more," he echoed. "Do you know what you put me through each night?" he chuckled.

"What did I do?"

"Even in a king-sized bed, you always managed to find me."

"That's because you are so deliciously warm, my love."

He lifted a brow, laughing. "Really? Warmth is the reason you rubbed your sexy behind against my shaft until I was as hard as a steel rod?"

"I didn't!" she blushed.

"You did . . . you *do,*" he amended, hugging her close "Diane, no one ever made me feel the way you do. Wild and crazy in love, blind with jealousy. You drive me nuts."

"You drove your ownself nuts. If I wanted Greg why would I have married you?"

"Good point."

"Greg is a friend . . . nothing more."

"I want our marriage to work." His voice was husky with the intensity of his emotions. He was pained by the possibility of her regret, yet unwilling to hide from it. There could be no secrets between them. "I hate fighting with you, baby."

"Me, too," she insisted. "I love you so much."

Charles stared down into her eyes for a time as if he could find all the answers in their lovely depths.

"Show me." Charles's mouth settle on hers in utter persuasion, as if she needed to be encouraged to open her lips to the exquisite stroking of his tongue. "I need you . . ." he whispered. "Let me . . ." he managed, before he claimed her mouth yet again and again, ". . . show you how badly I've missed you."

He gathered Diane even closer, thrilled by the feel of her warmth pressed against his arousal, her breasts wondrously soft on his chest. She felt good . . . so good. As he kissed a path down her neck, she trembled with desire. When he retraced the same journey, only this time with the wet, rough surface of his tongue, Diane shivered in response. Her soft, fluttery moans blended with his deep, throaty groans as excitement flared, bursting into red-hot need as he urgently filled her.

As hard as he tried to control the need, the obsession, to thrust vigorously within her, his body took over his mind and he gave all he had to give. Diane accepted him gladly and matched each pulsating thrust with a purely feminine tightening. Charles lost it then . . . he poured out his love . . . he gave her his all and in doing so sent them both into a wild, incredible release, hers an instant after his.

It was later, as she nestled against him, her lids heavy with sleep, that she recalled how frightened she'd been that night in the condo. She'd been terrified that the caller might be her mother. She hadn't been able to think clearly. Perhaps if she had, she'd have been able to defuse the situation before it had exploded into such a full-scale argument.

"Di?"

"Mmm."

"We're building a new life together. And I'm not saying that we shouldn't maintain old friendships. I don't want you to think I'm trying to control you. But I want our relationship to come first. I won't accept second place with you ever again. That I couldn't tolerate."

"Honey, you're the most important part of my life."

Charles swallowed the lump in his throat, kissing her tenderly.

"I need the same commitment from you."

"You already have it," he murmured.

"No, I don't. Aren't you forgetting the community center?"

"What about the center?"

"It takes so much of your time. I want us to spend more time together. Charles, you leave in the morning before I'm awake. I know it's so you can put in the time necessary to keep the business thriving. What about *us?* We don't see each other all day long, and when you get home, I'm asleep. I never saw you this week. I didn't get to tell you about the bridal shower Heather gave me. Nothing."

"This week was an exception. We had late-night basketball playoffs. Besides, I was angry. I stayed away until I knew you were asleep. I'll do better. I can try to make it home by ten . . . ten-thirty."

"That's still not much time for us. Do you have to go to the community center right after work? Can't you come home and eat dinner here with me? I need you." Diane was trembling. She'd never felt so vulnerable.

Charles felt her tremor and heard the worry in her tone. "Okay, dinner at six."

Diane let out a happy giggle, placing a series of kisses on his jaw and down the side of his neck. Charles chuckled at the sweet brush of her soft mouth across his skin. She was like champagne—bubbly, playful, and thoroughly intoxicating.

"Oh, I forgot to tell you—my folks are eager to met you. We're expected for Sunday dinner."

"They know?" Diane asked with a sinking heart.

"Yeah. Eliz can't keep a secret. Not to worry. It will only be Aunt Helen, Uncle Alex, Eliz, and her husband. Her kids usually spend Sundays with their grandparents." He kissed the top of her head. "I can't wait to show you off. Too bad your mother isn't in town. Then both sides of the family could get to know each other."

Diane forced herself not to shudder, her face hidden against his chest as she fought the terror invading her body.

Sixteen

"What do you think?" Diane asked her husband for the fifth time. She turned slowly, modeling a cream dress.

"I love it, just like I loved the other four before this one. Baby, you look wonderful. Will you please stop worrying?"

She'd been fine all morning. They'd gone to church for early service, had a leisurely breakfast, and spent the rest of the morning relaxing. It wasn't until it was time to dress for their dinner with the family that she'd become jittery. Diane seemed terrified by the prospect of meeting his aunt and uncle. What Charles couldn't figure out was why. Diane was not an insecure person. Besides, his folks were down-to-earth, generous people. It wasn't a question of acceptance. Uncle Alex and Aunt Helen would love Diane because he loved her and had chosen her for his bride.

Diane was ready to scream that she needed to look her best, confident and self-assured, the perfect complement to her husband. Suddenly, she yanked down the zipper, shimmying out of the dress, then tossed it onto the pile on the chaise longue in the corner of their bedroom.

"Di, we don't . . ."

She hurried back into the dressing room, leaving him standing in the middle of the floor, talking to himself. For once her thoughts were not on him. They were firmly rooted in her own insecurities.

Charles swore beneath his breath, completely mystified about how best to handle a frantic woman. This marriage thing was more complicated than he'd imagined. But then, Diane had given him more pleasure, more happiness than he'd ever dreamed possible.

Crossing to their dressing room, he said, "I'll meet you downstairs." He thought she mumbled affirmatively beneath the folds of a lavender dress.

As he paced the foyer, he wondered if he should call his aunt and let her know they'd be late. The house was only twenty minutes away and they had plenty of time . . . that is, if they left within the next fifteen minutes. Yet at the rate they were going, they'd be lucky to make it for dessert and coffee. No sense in ruining a perfectly good meal because Diane couldn't make up her mind.

Charles had just picked up the telephone in the hallway when he heard Diane's heels on the stairs. He decided not to make any comment when she appeared in the same pleated peach dress trimmed in cream that she'd discarded two outfits ago.

Diane waited expectantly. But Charles merely smiled, cupping her elbow in order to guide her out the door to the car parked in the drive. It wasn't until they were under way that she said tightly, "You don't like it, do you?"

Charles knew better than to pretend ignorance. He gambled by saying, "You look very nice, sweet cheeks. That color does wonderful things to your complexion." When she remained silent, he sighed, "You look almost as good as you did last night."

"Last night?"

"Mmmm, when you emerged from the tub . . . all wet and soft and so feminine . . . with absolutely nothing between the two of us."

Diane was too tense to respond to the deep sensuality in his baritone voice. "I want your family to accept me."

"You sound as though there's something wrong with you."

Diane blinked back tears. "I meant, I want them to like me."

"They will, I promise."

Elizabeth Randol-Bennett stood on the wide patio that overlooked the rear view of her aunt and uncle's property. She didn't see the rolling lawn or the extensive garden. She was so lost in thought she jumped when her husband, Bernard, brushed his mouth over her neck.

"What's wrong?"

"Nothing."

"Your aunt had been calling you for some time now," he said, as he smoothed his large hands down her soft arms.

"Oh! I should go see what she wants."

"Not until you answer me. What's the matter?"

Elizabeth sighed, leaning back against her husband's long, lean length. "I didn't realize I was so transparent. I suppose I'm not looking forward to this dinner. In fact, I'm dreading it."

"You could be wrong about her," Bernard said, knowing how she felt about her brother's new wife.

"Perhaps . . . but I doubt it. I don't trust her."

"You don't *have* to trust her. Why don't you try trusting your brother? Charles is no fool."

"Ha! When it comes to that woman, he can't see past her beauty. She's not good for him. Look how she hurt him! You tell me what has changed. *What?*"

"I haven't got a clue. Furthermore I'm not about to hazard a guess. I'll tell you this, sweetheart. If you value your relationship with Charles, you'll accept her as his wife."

"I don't think I can," Elizabeth said, so softly that Bernard barely heard her. "I'd better go and see what Aunt Helen wants."

* * *

The Bennetts' custom van was parked in the wide circular drive when Charles eased to a stop behind it. Turning off the ignition, he glanced at his wife's lovely profile. She was staring straight ahead, her hands clasped tightly in her lap.

"Baby, we don't have to do this today. We can always call and give our excuses."

Diane looked at Charles. "I'm being silly, aren't I?"

Charles knew there was no correct answer to that one. She was trembling with fear. He suspected there was more to it than she was willing to reveal. He felt helpless when he said, "Baby, this can wait. We really can do it another time."

She shook her head firmly. Taking a deep breath, she opened her door and got out before she could change her mind.

Charles pocketed the keys before hurrying around the car to walk with her to the wide double doors. Before the bell could sound more than once, the door was opened.

"Welcome . . . welcome," Alexander Randol boomed in a deep, throaty voice, his smile warm and engaging. He was tall and distinguished, and the family resemblance was unmistakable. "You've done well for yourself, son." He winked at his nephew. "Come in, come in. We're thrilled to have you, my dear." He didn't give Charles time to make the introductions. "You must be Diane. It's a pleasure . . . a pleasure. Just call me Uncle Alex." He beamed as he held onto Diane's hand. He called from over his shoulder, "Come on out here, Helen, and see this pretty gal our boy brought home."

Diane lifted her chin, determined not to give into her nerves. She took comfort from Charles's hand on her waist.

Helen Randol was a petite woman, a very elegant and youthful-looking sixty-something in a pale yellow, short-sleeved linen sheath. A long strand of perfectly matched pearls were roped around her graceful neck. Her thick dove-gray hair was swept up in a French roll that complemented her small features and good looks. She was everything Lillie, Diane's mother, was not.

"Darling," she gushed, rushing over and lifting her cheek for her nephew's kiss. "It's so good to see you. You know, I should be angry with you for waiting so long to come and see us after your trip. This must be your bride. Hello, Diane. Welcome to our family."

Diane was touched by her graciousness and her warmth. She could see why Charles and his sister thought of them as adopted parents. Elizabeth stood nearby with her husband. Introductions were quickly made.

Dinner was an elaborate affair. The dining room table had been set with the finest crystal and bone china. Unfortunately, Diane was so tense she couldn't enjoy the sumptuous meal. It wasn't until later, when they were all seated in the spacious, beautifully furnished living room for coffee and dessert, that Diane was able to relax somewhat. She shared a velvet loveseat with Charles.

Helen Randol gave her nephew a pointed look. "I shouldn't even be speaking to you. Running off and getting married with only strangers to wish you well!" She clicked her tongue in mock reproach, but her gaze was warm.

Charles reached for his wife's hand as he felt her whole body tightened. "Aunt Helen, I'm sorry if you feel slighted. Diane and I couldn't wait . . . being together was all that mattered. We did have a very beautiful private wedding and a very romantic honeymoon in Saint Thomas. The only thing we regret was having to leave after only a few short days."

Diane's large, dark eyes locked with Charles's. His love and support were easy to discern. When she smiled, a sweet radiant smile, his heart quickened with gladness. She was unaware that the others could not fail to see the love they shared.

"I told you, honey, there's no need to worry," Alex reminded his wife softly.

"Yes, *Alex*. I can see. Diane, Charles, we missed the wedding, but we *insist* on giving you a wedding reception. Is three weeks from Saturday too soon? I thought a dinner dance would be perfect . . . naturally, it must be a formal affair. We'll have a wedding cake and a jazz band. As for the menu, I think . . ."

"Hold it!" Charles interrupted. His wife was digging her long, peach-tinted nails into the palm of his right hand. He stroked a thumb soothingly over the back of her hand in an effort to calm her. "We appreciate the thought, Aunt Helen. Diane and I don't need a reception. Our wedding affirmed our love. Privacy is important to us. We're happy, and that's all that's really important."

"Darling, we're all family here. We have something to celebrate. Diane, dear, I'm sure your family feels the way we do. I'm sure your parents, especially your mother, must be just as disappointed as we were to miss the wedding," his aunt insisted.

Diane panicked even more at the mention of her mother. Calling on the inner strength that had gotten her through the rough years, Diane said what she felt she had to. "My father has passed. My mother was pleased when I told her about our marriage. She understood completely why we didn't postpone the ceremony."

This was news to Charles. She had said nothing to him about speaking to her mother. He couldn't help wondering why. She knew how eager he was to establish a relationship with her family.

"My dears, we'd like to share in your happiness. What about all our friends?"

"Aunt Helen, we appreciate both your and Uncle Alex's love and support. I'm thrilled by the way you've welcomed Diane into our family."

"Surely you have other family members, Diane?"

"No, I'm afraid I don't," Diane said evenly, all her efforts focused on maintaining the polite facade. Her heart was heavy with thoughts of her little brother.

Charles continued to hold her trembling hand in hopes of reassuring her. He knew that Diane and her mother were not close. She spoke of her mother only when asked directly. She never volunteered any information about her childhood. Charles knew it hurt her to talk about the past, so he'd never pressed the issue.

"Helen, we must respect the children's wishes," Alex said gently, but firmly. Changing the subject, he went on to say, "But we aren't going to *completely* overlook celebrating." He went over to the bar and lifted a champagne bottle from where it had been chilled in a silver ice bucket. He popped the cork and quickly began filling fluted glasses. Elizabeth helped pass them around. Once everyone had been served, Alex, raising his glass, said, "To the newlyweds. May you enjoy all the love and happiness that Helen and I have shared these past forty-seven years."

"Here! Here!" Bernard Bennett chimed in.

"To the newlyweds!"

Charles was relieved that the subject of a wedding reception had been dropped. Now Diane could relax and enjoy herself.

Bernard asked, "How's the mentoring program going?"

"Great. Thanks for the check you sent over. It went to buy computer equipment. We're hoping to start a computer lab during the summer."

"Good idea. Perhaps I can talk some of the doctors at the hospital into sending in a few more checks. Most of them have benefited from some program or another in the past."

"Thanks. We need the money. But we need the help more. If you have a few hours you can string together each week, we could use more volunteers."

While Charles and Bernard discussed the community center, Elizabeth began clearing.

"Leave it, dear; I can take care of that later."

Elizabeth kept right on working. "You've done enough today. The meal was fabulous. Won't take me a moment to take care of these few little dishes."

"You're an excellent cook, Mrs. Randol," Diane said.

"Please, call me Aunt Helen. And thank you for the compliment, but I only planned the meal. The credit belongs to our housekeeper and cook, Mrs. Samuel. She leaves right after dinner on Sunday evening. She enjoys spending time with her son."

Diane tried to hide her embarrassment as she rose to collect the few remaining dishes. She couldn't get used to the wealth and influence that the Randols seem to take for granted. Surrounded by love, neither Elizabeth nor Charles had ever known any other way of life. Things might have been different if Danny had been a part of a family like the Randols'. He'd have received the medical attention he so desperately needed. He might even be alive today.

Elizabeth was loading the dishwasher when Diane brought in the last of the coffee cups and saucers. "Here, I'll take those."

"It's no trouble."

"No, don't be silly. I don't know why Aunt Helen doesn't hire more help. Mrs. Samuel is like family. We don't expect a guest to work off her supper." Elizabeth blushed, realizing what she'd said. "I mean . . ." Then she stopped abruptly, leaving the thought unspoken.

"I know what you meant, Eliz. Believe me, no offense was taken." Diane looked around the spotlessly clean kitchen, hoping to find something that needed attention. The kitchen was immaculate. She didn't need reminders that she was an outsider . . . not a true member of this close-knit family.

"I hope Aunt Helen didn't upset you! I tried to prepare her, but she just refused to take no for an answer." Elizabeth gave Diane a concerned look. "I hope you didn't feel pressured, especially when you two have already decided against a wedding reception?"

"Eliz, let's be frank with each other. I know you can't forgive me for hurting Charles in the past. I also know you don't think our marriage will work," Diane said quietly. "I am sorry. It's wrong for Charles to force-feed you large doses of me. You're entitled to your views."

"That's not the point. Chuck married you, and I, like everyone else, have no choice but to accept it."

"You don't have to like it or me," Diane said evenly.

It took Elizabeth a long time to answer. Finally she said firmly, "I want my brother to be happy. What I feel or don't feel about you is immaterial. I won't do anything to jeopardize my relationship with my brother. He's too important to me."

The two women stared at each other. Diane managed to keep the hurt from showing while Elizabeth concentrated on her own fears. His sister was terrified of losing her brother, while Diane yearned for acceptance. Evidently, acceptance and approval were in short supply.

Elizabeth had everything in the world going for her. She had lived a charmed life, compared to Diane. Yet they both loved Charles. Funny, how things turn out sometimes. They had both lost their mothers . . . Diane had lost hers to substance abuse, and Elizabeth had lost hers to death. But that was where the similarities ended. Elizabeth had been loved and adored by her family. She didn't know what it was like to be hungry or to do without.

Diane envied her poise and self-confidence. She didn't have to worry about fitting in. Her husband's family no doubt loved her as much as her own family.

It was Diane who said, "I like your aunt and uncle very much. They're charming. It's wonderful to see a couple still very much in love after so many years."

For the first time, Elizabeth offered a radiant smile. "Thank you."

"You have a very nice husband," Diane said, striving to hide her disappointment that they could not be friends.

"Bernard's a very special man. I know how lucky I am." She sighed, "Look, Diane. Perhaps, I shouldn't have said what I did when we met."

"No, please don't say any more. We've been honest with each other. If there's nothing else that needs to be done, I'll join my husband."

Diane put the marking pen and homework papers she'd been correcting in her briefcase. Charles was already in bed, reading.

"You've been awfully quiet since we got home." He watched as she slid into the opposite side of the bed. His eyes lingered on the swell of her breasts above the pink lace of her nightgown before lifting to her lovely face. He thoughtfully decided she was even more beautiful without make-up. He never tired of looking at her. Her soft skin and feminine scent sent the blood rushing to his groin. Would he ever get enough of her? For once, he chose to ignore the demands his body was making to bury himself deep inside her moist sheath.

He waited until she snuggled close, her head resting on his shoulder.

"Feeling better?"

"About what?"

He shrugged, "My family. You were a bit nervous."

"I'm fine."

Charles switched off the lamp, plunging the room into near darkness. The only light came from the nightlight near the door.

"I know we didn't do much talking last week, but Di, I wish you'd told me about your mother's call. I was hoping to speak to her. You know, introduce myself over the telephone."

For a moment, a brief second in time, Diane considered telling Charles everything. He loved her; he was bound to understand. But by the time she'd said his name aloud, her courage had deserted her and the fear that had become her companion had taken over. Diane took a deep breath as she prepared to do what she'd always done . . . lied.

"That's sweet of you. Unfortunately, my mother telephoned while you were at the community center. I'm sorry I forgot until your aunt asked about her. Please, don't be mad, honey. My mother and I are just not close, not like your family."

Diane detested the lies. She hated deceiving him, but she had no choice. She couldn't reveal why there was no love between her and Lillie. How could she tell someone like Charles that her mother had sold her body? When things were really bad, she had used both alcohol and drugs. How could she describe what it was like when Lillie had been using? She had ruined not only her looks, but nearly lost her life. He couldn't begin to comprehend what it had been like when Lillie couldn't even care for her own needs, let alone her children's.

Today, with his family, Diane had felt as if she were on the outside of a glass wall looking in, close enough to see, but never close enough to become a part of all that warmth and love. It hurt. She comforted herself with the thought that someday she'd be the mother of Charles's children. Together they would make a family of their very own.

Charles sighed, kissing her temple. "I wanted your mother to know she doesn't have to worry about you. I intend to do everything I can to make you happy. We should think about inviting her here for a long visit soon."

Diane shivered with dread.

"Cold?" he said, pulling the comforter over them both. "Better?"

"Yes . . ."

Seventeen

Diane stood back, surveying their handiwork. The dining and living rooms had been painted a pale ivory, and a honey-beige carpet had been laid. Her pale furniture barely filled the huge rooms. Nevertheless, Diane was pleased. There was a warmth and comfort she found appealing. She had plenty of time to find just the right pieces to complete the spacious rooms.

"Well? Do you like it?" Diane asked.

Charles smiled indulgently from where he sprawled on the sofa. "If *you* like it, I like it. Just don't ask me to move this blasted couch again!" He chuckled good-naturedly. They'd been arranging furniture and pictures all morning.

"What kind of answer is that?" She'd followed him into the hallway.

"It's the best I've got," he said from over his shoulder as he headed for the staircase.

"You don't like it, do you?" she called after him.

"What do I know about these kind of things? I've got to get showered and changed. It's after three, and I'm due at the center at four."

"Oh . . ." she said, unable to hide her disappointment.

Half way up the stairs, he turned and bounded back down. "What's wrong, sweet cheeks?"

"Nothin'."

"Can't fool me. Give."

"We've been married less than a month. I can almost count on one hand the evenings we've spent together."

Charles frowned heavily. "I made dinner every day this week. Baby, you know I try to give you all my time once I'm home."

"I know. But we haven't had a romantic evening since we returned from our honeymoon."

"Yeah, I know. There are just not enough hours in the day." His mouth was warm and seeking over hers. Diane moaned, melting against him. She wrapped her arms around his waist, her mouth open and sweet beneath his. The kiss ended all too quickly. "I haven't been paying enough attention to you."

"I didn't say that." She shivered, recalling the intensity and sweetness of their lovemaking. "You were so very *attentive* last night."

He grinned, "No complaints in that department?"

"None. Honey, I want us to spend more time together. We're both so busy during the week."

"How does a romantic dinner sound? Dancing and candlelight?"

"Dinner at home sounds more appealing. Just the two of us, in front of the fire . . . no servants . . . I'll cook."

Charles laughed. "You cook?"

"I do. Stop acting like that! I've cooked for you before."

"You mean the coffee you made the morning we stayed in your condo? You were barely speaking to me, as I recall."

"Don't remind me. All you wanted was coffee. You're acting like I can't fry an egg without a cookbook."

Charles eyes twinkled with humor. "I didn't say that. Sure you wouldn't prefer to eat out?"

"I rather be alone with my man. Besides, I can't wear the red teddy in a restaurant."

He groaned, his mouth hot and demanding over hers. "Baby, we can eat cornflakes and bananas, for all I care.

I'll be home by eight. Don't start the Luther tapes without me."

Diane's eyes were dark and dreamy as she watched her husband mount the stairs two at a time before disappearing from view. She hugged herself, still not believing her good fortune. Charles loved her as much as she loved him. It was true they had problems, but so did all couples. The doorbell chimed as Diane was walking past.

"I'll get it," she called to the elderly Sheldon when she heard his slow footfall in the hall. She mumbled beneath her breath about that poor dear man running around answering doors when there was absolutely nothing wrong with her legs, or Charles's, for that matter.

Lillie Rivers stood on the front stoop.

"What!" Diane gasped, glancing nervously over her shoulder. Thank God the hall was clear, she thought. Quickly, she stepped outside, closing the door behind her. "What are you doing here? How did you find me?"

"Don't be mad. I know you don't want me here. But I had to see you," she said, unsteady on her feet.

"How did you find me?"

"I followed you here. Nice place. You've done well for yourself, sugar. My little gal done real good." She grinned, wiping at her tears.

Her crying didn't impress Diane. Nothing Lillie said or did impressed Diane, not after all the sad years of neglect. The only person her mother cared about was herself. Diane was not about to let her mother mess her life up because of some thoughtless whim.

"You've got to get out of here before my husband sees you. I can't talk to you here," Diane whispered in near panic. Charles was showering this very minute. How much longer did she have before he was dressed and came looking for her?

"I need money. I wouldn't ask, but . . ."

Diane could smell the alcohol on her breath, but she was

too terrified of discovery to worry about the fact that her mother had evidently started drinking again. "Lillie, I gave you enough to cover the cost of food and rent for another month. What did you do with it?"

Lillie sneered, "Hell! I don't have to explain to you."

Diane knew she was in no position to argue. "Don't move." She rushed into the house. Where the world was her purse? Upstairs in the bedroom, probably. Then she remembered the money Charles kept in the drawer of the lacquered table in the hallway. It was for household emergencies. She was having an emergency right now, one in which she had only minutes to get her mother the hell away from here. As she yanked open the drawer, she almost stopped breathing. For a second she thought she heard her husband's footsteps on the stairs. She listened intently. Nothing but the sound of the old house settling. She grabbed the money, barely remembering to count it, so that she could replace it later. She was a nervous wreck by the time she returned to her mother.

She practically threw the money at her. "Here. Now go."

"Thanks, baby."

"I'll meet you on Wednesday at four in the park. And Lillie, I want to see a receipt from your apartment manager."

Lillie swore nastily. "Look, just because you're livin' high on the hog, in this fancy house . . . that don't mean you better than me, girl. We're the same, you and me. The same!"

Diane, on the verge of tears, said in a frantic whisper, "Never! I'm not like you! Get out of here before you ruin everything for me. Or is that what you want? Do you want me back in the gutter with you? Huh?"

Diane tensed. She heard Charles calling her name. *"Go!"* she pleaded. Even though her heart was pounding with fear, for she expected Charles to open the front door any second, she waited until her mother was in the back seat of the cab she'd hired and moving down the road before she stepped back inside. "I'm here."

"Going somewhere? I thought I heard the bell." Thank goodness he didn't wait for an answer. "Don't be upset, baby. I forgot that I invited the swim team over for spaghetti and fixings after the meet tonight."

Diane was so busy hanging onto the door handle to keep from falling that nothing seemed to matter. "When?" was all she managed.

"Tonight, after the swim meet. Not to worry . . . I told Mrs. Sheldon. She'll take care of the food."

Diane knew she should be annoyed with him for waiting so late to tell her, but she was too upset about her mother to tell him that he should have consulted with her first, not Mrs. Sheldon. Aparently, he had dismissed their plans for a romantic evening together. However, now she didn't have the stamina to be angry with him.

She was overwhelmed by how close she had come to disaster . . . how close she had come to losing everything she cared about . . . losing Charles. There was no doubt in her mind that he would not want to be married to her if he knew the truth about her background. It wasn't because she thought he was a snob. She knew better. Nor was it because she was not proud of her own success. Diane was so shamed by the evil and hopelessness of where she came from that she feared that if it was revealed, Charles would lose all respect for her. There was nothing to keep her mother from dropping by any time she chose. Well, Diane must make certain Lillie understood the consequences of her behavior when she saw her on Wednesday. Lillie had put them both at risk by coming to her home.

"Di?"

"I'll see you later." She accepted the kiss he placed on her lips before he hurried out.

* * *

"Hey . . . man," Eddie Walker called, leaning out his car window.

Jeff Jenkins glanced back over his shoulder. "Hey, Eddie," he paused, shifted his athletic bag from one hand to the other.

"Where you headed?" he asked, ignoring the blaring car horn behind him.

"The center, man. Got a swim meet tonight."

"Hold up, Jeff." Easing the car over to the curb, he waited until Jeff was beside his car.

"What's up?"

"I have a business proposition to put to ya, blood." Eddie said with a smile. He and Jeff had grown up together, living in the same apartment building until Jeff and his mother had moved out of the old neighborhood.

"Naw . . . I don't think so." Since Jeff had started at the community center, he had made new friends—friends who were into sports and girls and school, guys who had big plans for the future, a future that didn't include the bad stuff going on in the streets.

Eddie hopped out of the car and rounded the hood. He stopped next to Jeff, leaning against the passenger door. "Got no time for a homey? Ain't good enough for you no mo', man, since you been hangin' at the center?"

"Naw, it ain't like that." Jeff could tell from Eddie's pinched, wild-eyed look that he was still using.

"You got any money, man? A twenty'll do."

Jeff shook his head. "All I have is five, and you can have that. But this is the last time, Eddie."

"Hey, thanks. You still my partner . . . still my man. Look, I appreciate it." Eddie smiled, palming the money quickly.

"Look, man, I gotta go. I have to meet the others on the swim team. Gonna beat the hell out of those guys from Grosse Pointe."

"Swimming! Hell, what kind of sport is that? Punk

stuff!" Eddie said, unable to hide his resentment. He hated the way Jeff had changed. He was different now.

They had been close, real close, for a long time. That community center and that Randol guy had Jeff so messed up in the head that he'd turned his back on his *real* friends. Randol this, Randol that was all Jeff ever talked about nowadays.

Jeff shrugged, then started walking on, refusing to get into an argument. They'd been tight until Eddie had started hangin' with the neighborhood boys. Jeff's mother had gotten him out of that area before he'd had time even to think about joining a gang. The next thing he knew, he was going to a new school and at the center every evening.

"Look, man . . . I-I-I'm sorry," Eddie said, hurrying after him. "Hey, wait up. I have a proposition for you."

"Not interested."

"Wait, Jeff. We go back a long ways, man. I wouldn't ask this of you . . . but I need a favor."

"What's wrong with Mark and DeJuan?"

Eddie shrugged. "They ran into a little trouble with the man. No big loss. Both of them are so strung-out on crack they ain't good for nothin'. Got so bad, they spend more time usin' than conducting business, my man. I'm the only one left got his head together."

Jeff had his doubts, but refrained from commenting.

"Let me give you a lift. Save the bus ticket for another time." Eddie laughed uproariously. "Come on, blood. You still my main man."

Jeff glanced at his watch. He was already late. If he didn't hurry, the team would leave without him. "Okay."

Eddie grinned, pleased with himself. "Hop in. How's your old lady? She found herself a man yet? Probably not, too busy tryin' to run yo' life."

Jeff ignored the second question. His mother's personal business was none of Eddie's concern—friend or no friend.

"She's fine. Really busy, now that she's got this new job, working downtown."

"That's all right, man. You have to come by the crib. Big Mama is always asking about ya'."

Eddie's grandmother had always been especially kind to Jeff. He sure missed her peach cobbler. That woman knew she could make some peach cobbler. Absorbed in the passing scenery, it took Jeff a couple of minutes before he realized they were headed away from the community center, not towards it.

"Where you goin', man?"

"One stop, and then we'll head for the center. Won't take a second. I need to get some smokes. Okay?"

"Sure." Jeff said, although he was furious, but his affection for Eddie ran deep. Eddie had been there for him. It was Eddie who'd showed him the ropes in middle school. It was Eddie who'd come to his rescue when the big guys had started picking on Jeff.

While Jeff excelled in school, Eddie did as little as possible. Eddie's goofing off was really stupid, to Jeff's way of thinking, especially considering that Eddie was a real whiz in math. Eddie got decent grades without putting in any study time, just from what he picked up in the classroom—when he bothered to show up. About the time Jeff was accepted at Cass Technical High School, Eddie started getting friendly with members of the gang. Soon he quit school and started using. Eddie had gotten into a few scraps, but nothing serious, thank goodness. Eddie was okay.

It wasn't his fault he didn't have a mom like Anthia on his back twenty-four-seven. Nor did he have a coach like Charles sticking his neck out for him. Jeff wondered: if he really tried maybe he could convince Eddie to try the community center.

Jeff was so absorbed in thought that he didn't notice they had circled the same block twice before Eddie slowed the car and eased to a stop outside a convenience store.

"I'll be right back. Do me a favor, will you, bro? Get behind the wheel and keep the motor runnin'. This old thing might not start up if I cut it off." At Jeff's look of surprise, Eddie grinned. "It's an old piece of junk. But hell, it's moving."

"No problem," Jeff said, sliding over. "But you'd better not be trying to pull nothin' on me, man."

"Naw! Be right back."

"You've got five minutes. Then we ride."

"Right." Eddie grinned, jumping out and heading for the nearly deserted store. One hand deep in his pocket, he used the other to pull his knit cap down on his head.

Jeff's fingers drummed on the steering wheel. He tried to ignore the feeling . . . the bad feeling that Eddie was up to something. Because of the glare of the sun, he didn't have a clear view of the store or of the clerk behind the counter. All he saw was Eddie standing by the back cooler. Minutes ticked away. Then a woman and little girl came out of the store. Then an elderly man left while Eddie seemed to be fascinated with the soft drink section. After a few more minutes passed, Eddie was at the counter with his back to Jeff. But he didn't seem to be in a hurry to make his purchase and leave.

Growing tired of waiting, Jeff jumped out of the car, leaving it running, with the keys in the ignition, and headed for the store. "Hey, man, what's the problem?" he asked.

Eddie sent a quick glance over his shoulder. The guy behind the counter was holding his hands out in front of him, not moving a muscle.

"This fool is scared." Eddie laughed through the folds of the scarf over the lower half of his face. He tossed something at Jeff, his eyes never leaving the clerk, who seemed too scared to move. "Hold this while I get my money."

Jeff's reflexes were superb. He caught the gun without thinking. He froze, suddenly realizing what was going on. "Are you nuts, Eddie? I don't want any part of this."

"Just point it, fool. And keep your mouth shut," Eddie said, backhanding the man and shoving him aside. He began filling a bag with the contents of the cash register.

Stunned, Jeff watched as Eddie kicked the guy on the floor. "Let's get out of here."

The man on the floor reached under the counter for the silent security alarm and a gun.

Eddie was out the door first. Jeff was several steps behind when he heard a loud *pop* and felt a searing pain burning down the center of his back into his legs. He crumpled like a rag doll on the dirty linoleum floor.

"Where's Jeff?" Charles asked, as the boys started piling into the van.

The fellows looked at one another. Finally, Luis, a short, thin kid, spoke up. "He's probably just late, Mr. Randol. When Bob and I stopped at his place, he said he couldn't leave the house until his mom got home. Said he'd meet us here."

"I saw him get in a car with Eddie near the bus stop. Maybe he changed his mind about the meet?" Brent added.

Mike groaned. "Eddie's trouble."

"Who's Eddie?"

"Just some crackhead from Jeff's old neighborhood," said Dexter Washington. "Jeff mentioned trying to get him involved in the center." Dexter had been managing the community center for several years. He'd grown up in a rough eastside neighborhood.

"I hope he can. The kid needs to know there are other options."

"He'll be hard to convince."

"Why do you say that?"

Dexter shrugged. "He's dealin', man."

Charles was frowning. "Jeff doesn't usually run with that kind of crowd."

"Naw. But they been tight since the cradle, man," Luis supplied.

Glancing once more at his watch, Charles said, "We may have enough time to drop by his place before heading on out. Okay, fellows, let's put a move on it."

Jeff wasn't at home. Anthia was insistent that Jeff had left home on his way to the community center. Dexter and Charles exchanged worried looks.

"Think we should call the police?" Charles asked Dexter, as they walked back to the van.

"What good would it do? The kid's late, not missing. Hit it, we got a meet to win."

"Yeah," Charles said, putting the van into gear. But he couldn't dismiss Jeff from his mind in spite of the team's first win.

Everyone was ready for food by the time Charles pulled into his own winding drive. Charles just hoped Diane was ready.

Diane met them at the front door dressed in a red jogging suit. Charles loved the color on her but still couldn't help feeling disappointed that it couldn't be the sexy red lace teddy.

"I hope everyone is hungry?" Diane said with a smile, once the introductions were made. "Come on. Everything is set up in the dining room."

A hefty buffet had been laid out on the side table: spaghetti, meatballs, corn on the cob, seven-layer salad, loaves of garlic bread, and soft drinks. Chocolate layer cake and homemade vanilla ice cream rounded out the meal.

Before the dessert had disappeared, the boys were laughing and talking while Heavy D played in the background. After tons of food, the fellows played videogames and pool in the recreation room.

"Thanks, baby." Charles leaned over and kissed Diane's neck, taking the heavy tray of dirty dishes from her. "Everything was great. You and Mrs. Sheldon did a fantastic job."

Diane laughed, happy at his obvious approval. "It was fun. Maybe we can have a little swim team of our own someday. What do you think?"

Charles grinned, his voice suddenly huskier, deeper. "Sounds good to me. I won't be gone long. We can discuss it in detail when I get back," he whispered close to her ear. "Say, in bed?"

"Maybe . . ." She began with a smile.

"Maybe? I don't like the sound of that."

"Get out of here. The others are waiting for you."

"Leave the dishes. I'll clean up when I get back."

"Forget the dishes. I have something else for you to focus your attention on . . . me." She formed the last word silently, her soft lips as ripe and luscious as a succulent strawberry.

Charles pressed a quick, hard kiss against her mouth. "Hold that thought. I'll be back as soon as I drop the others off."

Eighteen

Diane tried to force herself to relax, to concentrate only on the moment . . . nothing more. Yet her thoughts returned time and again to her mother. She still couldn't believe that Lillie had actually followed her home from the park where they usually met. Why? Why was she spying on her? Lillie had never done anything before to jeopardize their arrangement. Yes, lately she'd been tossing about threats, but they both knew she had just as much to lose as Diane. So why now?

Since Lillie had followed her from Chicago, she had gone out of her way not to interfere in Diane's private life. Lillie had been clean and sober for several years now. What had changed? What had triggered her drinking? Had she started drinking in earnest again? With Lillie, drinking was the first step toward using drugs. Years ago, when things were really bad, heroin had been Lillie's chosen drug. Diane knew better than anyone that Lillie was a recovering addict. What she didn't know was what had caused her mother to put them both at risk.

"Enough!" Diane mumbled aloud, impatient with her thoughts. Nothing could be solved tonight. When she saw Lillie on Wednesday, she had better be ready to do some explaining. Diane wasn't about to allow her mother to endanger her relationship with Charles.

When Charles entered the bathroom, Diane was up to her creamy neck in warm, frothy water.

"Hi," he said, pausing in the open doorway to enjoy the sweet picture she made.

Diane blushed. "Hi yourself." Somewhat uncomfortable at being caught nude while he was fully dressed, she couldn't meet his warm regard.

He grinned, amused by her modesty after their weeks of shared intimacy. He was pleased when she made no effort to conceal her beauty from him. They belonged to each other, no secrets and no regrets. They were a team now.

"Care to join me?" Her voice was soft, seductive.

He chuckled. "Hmm, the offer is tempting." He walked slowly over to where she relaxed in the wide, square tub, the whirlpool jet causing a froth of bubbles to play peek-a-boo over her lush curves. His image filled the mirrored walls surrounding the tub on three sides. Slowly, he rolled up the sleeves of his chambray shirt before he dropped down until his face was within mere inches of hers.

"Very tempting," he whispered, an instant before he teased her mouth briefly with his, then reached for the bath sponge on the ledge. He soaped it with the lilac-scented soap she preferred. His dark eyes moving over her toffee-toned beauty. He watched as her large nipples pouted even more beneath his heated gaze. Ignoring his body as it prepared to become a part of hers, Charles began washing her neck, her shoulders, and her back, moving the sponge in easy circles over her silky skin.

"Mmm," she moaned. "Do you think the boys enjoyed themselves?"

"Yeah, especially if you consider inviting themselves back as any indication," he laughed. "I received some very flattering comments about you, sweet thang. 'She's all right for an old chick,' " he mimicked.

Diane giggled, then sighed with pleasure as her husband replaced the sponge and began caressing her with his large hands. She moaned, trembling with sweet expectation as he smoothed down her spine to cup and squeeze her lush behind.

"Chucky . . ."

"Huh," he mumbled throatily, as he moved up her legs to the baby-soft length of her inner thighs. His hands slowed even more as he soaped the apex of her thighs. Charles fingered the thick nest of curls, rhythmically squeezing her fleshy mound until her moans told him she wanted more. He slowly parted the puffy folds and caressed her slowly. Diane gasped as he slid a finger deep inside her feminine passage. He stroked her as thoroughly and almost as deeply as he intended to fill her with his body.

Charles gloried in the realization that her inner warmth was much hotter and wetter than the water surrounding her. He used his thumb to worry the feminine bud at the top of her mound. He applied gentle, steady pressure while he continued to stroke deep inside her body, his mouth warm on her neck. Diane lay securely against him, her back pressed against his chest, oblivious to everything outside the pleasure he gave her. Charles closed his eyes and enjoyed her sobs of wanton pleasure. He didn't stop until she cried out his name in a throbbing, intense release. He held on to her as her trembling stopped and her breathing calmed.

Diane turned in his arms until she could press her breasts into his damp cloth-covered chest. She was a quivering mass of nerves as she plunged her tongue into his mouth, stroking his tongue with hers over and over again. She caressed his lengthening arousal. The hot feel of him increased her desires. Diane whimpered in protest when Charles broke the seal of their kiss and moved away.

"Shush . . ." he said. Her deep brown eyes echoed his own raw need. His hands went to his chest and he began unbuttoning the wet shirt and peeling it away. He sent it hurling across the room in the general direction of the wicker hamper near the dressing room door.

"Let me," she said urgently, when his fingers lowered to his western belt buckle.

Charles's eyes smoldered with desire and he never lost eye contact with his wife. He shook his head, knowing he could not bear the softness of her hands on him just yet . . . not until he had himself under control. His limbs were actually trembling when he shoved jeans and navy briefs down his legs and kicked them away. He suppressed a groan as he watched Diane's eyes caressing his long male length. His sex thickened and lifted even more as she focused on it. When her tongue came out to moisten her lips, he nearly lost it. He forced himself to look away. She went straight to his head, leaving his body pulsing with the sexual fires she alone had the power to extinguish. He couldn't remember the last time another woman had interested him. It was Diane . . . only Diane . . . always Diane. Since that first night on the ship, it didn't take much encouragement on her part . . . a look, a smile, a caress, and his body was stiff and standing at attention, eager to please her . . . ready to sample her wet, sleek heat.

"Chucky . . ."

He reached for a bath sheet on the heated brass towel bar between the tub and the shower stall. He held it out in front of him . . . waiting. His breath quickened even more as she rose, bubbles cascading down her lush brown frame.

As he wrapped her in the bath sheet, he said with his mouth against the side of her throat, "Join me in the den . . . wear the red thing."

Diane smiled, leaning back against his chest, nodding her agreement.

He wanted to watch her get ready for him, but he knew he didn't dare. He hurried out.

Diane hummed softly to herself, taking her time to prepare. She brushed her thick, heavy curls until they shone. She creamed her skin with perfumed body lotion before slipping into the French-cut silk and lace red teddy Charles had requested. She covered it with a thigh length red silk robe with soft ruffles at the v-neck opening and the sleeves.

She knocked softly on the closed door before coming inside and firmly closing the door behind her. It wasn't difficult to find her man. He was the long, sexy one lounging on a black satin comforter in front of the fire. His dark terrycloth robe was tossed on the seat of the armchair. A brandy snifter was cupped in his palm while his eyes flamed hotter than the sparks leaping behind the screened covered grate. She smiled at him as she loosened the sash at her waist and let the garment glide from her shoulders to the floor.

Charles swallowed a groan. He held out a hand to her. Diane didn't hesitate. She crossed to his waiting arms. Their lovemaking was slow and tender, his mouth soft and sensuous on hers. He gave her all he had to give, and she, in turn, held nothing back. They peaked together in an agonizingly sweet moment of utter bliss.

He lay on his side, his wife cuddled against him. Diane stretched like a thoroughly contented cat, absently stroking his arm, which rested across her waist.

"Getting sleepy?" he asked softly, close to her ear. "Ready to go up?"

"Uh-uh. I like it here in front of the fire." She pressed her mouth along his collarbone. "Mmmm, you feel so good."

"More?" He caressed her from her nape to her hips. He enjoyed making love to her; he never seemed to get enough.

Diane giggled. "I wasn't hinting. It's so good to spend time alone with you. We don't do enough of this. Just you and me, no interruptions."

"I agree," he sighed. "Sweet cheeks, I know I always seem to be at the office or the community center, but . . ."

She pressed her fingertips against his full masculine lips. "I'm not complaining. I wish we could find time to get away. Maybe during the summer? A weekend in Montreal? Just a few days away from the telephone . . . work."

He laughed. "Sounds wonderful. Let's do that."

Diane snuggled closer. "Where was Jeff tonight? Isn't he still on the swim team?"

"Yeah. He didn't show. We stopped by his place, but he wasn't there. Anthia seemed to think he'd gone to the center."

"You sound worried. What are you thinking?"

"I just don't want him getting caught up with the wrong crowd. Jeff's a smart kid. He can go places, with the right kind of support system. Hell, that goes for all the kids."

"Maybe you should have a talk with him. See if you can find out what's goin' on with him."

"Yeah. I think I will."

Diane leisurely smoothed her hands over his muscled chest. She casually caressed a nipple.

Charles caught his breath, saying roughly, "Keep that up, and you'll get more than you bargained for."

"You like?" she asked, flicking her soft, wet tongue over the ebony crest.

"Yeah," he groaned. The telephone ringing caused Charles to swear softly.

"Honey, we'd better get that before it wakes the Sheldons."

"No chance of that. They have their own line in their apartment. But who the hell is calling this late? It's almost midnight." Charles was scowling as he rose to his feet. He picked up on the next ring, saying impatiently, "Randol residence. Yes. Anthia? What's wrong?" he paused. "No! Where are you? Okay, we'll be right there. 'Bye."

Diane could see by his face that something was terribly wrong. As soon as he put down the telephone, she asked, "What happened?"

"Jeff. He's been shot."

"Shot! How? Is he going to be all right?"

"I'm not sure of the details. He's at Henry Ford. I told Anthia we'd both come."

"Yes, of course. Let's hurry and get dressed."

"Okay. But give me a minute. I have to call Dexter."

It was late, and they completed the drive into the city in record time. They found Anthia in the waiting room, and she was not alone. Doug Henderson and Dexter Washington were with her.

Diane hadn't seen Doug since the charity dinner dance.

Anthia greeted them with a weak smile. "Thanks for coming."

"How is he?"

"Still in surgery. Why's it taking so long? They've had him up there for hours."

"These things take time," Dexter said softly. "Would you care for some coffee?"

"No, thank you," she said, mopping her face.

"What happened?" Charles asked.

"I don't know. The police said he was involved in an armed robbery. The store owner claims it was necessary to shoot him in the back," Dexter supplied.

"The back!" Charles and Diane exclaimed.

"It's a lie! My baby's not like that! He's not like that!"

"There's been a mistake," Doug said, sending an accusing glare at the taller, broad-shouldered Dexter.

Diane and Charles exchanged a look before Diane moved forward, putting her arm around the weeping woman. "Why don't we sit down?"

Once they were all seated, Anthia whispered, "It's all a mistake . . . I know it is. Why did they pick on my boy? He's a good boy."

Charles was frowning. His disappointment was acute. "I agree. This doesn't make any sense."

Dexter said, "Jeff had a gun. The store owner claims it was self-defense."

"It's not true!" Anthia insisted.

Doug grated, "Why don't you shut the hell up, Washington?"

Dexter sent the other man a sharp glare. He'd been awake when Charles had called, trying to get through another long, lonely night, avoiding sleep until he was so exhausted that the nightmares wouldn't haunt him. He didn't consider not coming. How could he? He'd seen Anthia Jenkins only twice, this evening when they'd stopped to ask about Jeff, and the night of the dinner dance. There was something in her dark, lovely eyes that had warmed him. Dexter found he couldn't stay away.

"I don't believe it, either," Diane said soothingly, lacing her fingers through her husband's. "There has to be a logical explanation."

"There damn well better be," Charles hissed beneath his breath, but Diane saw the hurt in his brooding eyes.

The time passed slowly as they waited with Anthia for word. It was after two o'clock in the morning when the somber surgeon came to speak with Anthia. The news was not good. Jeff was alive, but barely. They'd removed the bullet lodged in his spine, but until the swelling went down, they had no idea if he would ever be able to walk again. Anthia cried out, suffering both shock and fear for her child. She was sobbing so hard she had to be sedated. They didn't leave until she had calmed, and settled in an armchair to wait out what was left of the night. Diane was prepared to stay, but Anthia insisted she wanted to be left alone.

Charles was quiet on the drive home, it seemed to Diane too quiet. Her heart ached for Anthia and her son. Rather than going up to their bedroom, Charles went into his study, flicking on the light.

"I still can't believe it. He seemed like such a great kid. And smart, too," Diane said from the doorway. The study was very much her husband's domain. It was where he worked, sometimes hours into the night, to keep up with his responsibilities to his company.

"Not seemed! He's a good kid! The police report is wrong! Damn!" As if suddenly realizing he was shouting, he sank into his chair behind the heavy mahogany desk. "Anyone who knows Jeff realizes he couldn't have been involved in some shaky stuff like this. It doesn't make sense!"

The large rug, done in burgundy and gray, covering most of the hardwood floor, provided the only splash of color in the room. The walls were lined with book shelves. A heavy black wingbacked leather chair behind the desk faced a long black leather sofa.

Diane watched sadly as Charles began pacing the confines of the small room. "Honey, it's late. Let's go to bed."

Charles didn't even look at her. He stood staring out the window into the tree-lined yard, seeing nothing but his own helplessness.

"Chuck?"

"Go on up, Di. I'll join you in a few minutes."

By the time Diane had showered and changed into a peach gown and robe, their bedroom was still empty. She found him where she'd left him. He sat behind his desk. The computer screen was switched on, but Charles sat with his head in his hands, his shoulders hunched.

"Sweetheart . . ." She crossed on bare feet to him, kneeling down beside his chair. "Talk to me . . . please."

Charles shook his head, unable to voice his despair, his grief.

"You mustn't blame yourself. None of this is your fault."

Charles lifted his head and looked into her flawlessly beautiful features, but he remained silent. Naked anguish darkened his eyes, deepening the brackets down the side of his face.

Diane ached to help, but she wasn't sure what to do or say. He was taking Jeff's situation much too personally. "Please, talk to me . . . let me share your thoughts. Don't shut me out."

"There's nothing to share. It's not me lying in that hospital room with a bullet wound in my back." His voice was brittle with bitterness and rage.

Diane didn't flinch when he gripped her forearms a bit too forcefully. If only he would share his thoughts . . . his hurt. Like her, he was probably used to keeping his fears to himself. This realization was far more painful than the pressure he unwittingly applied to her soft skin.

What kind of marriage could they have if they didn't trust each other? She wanted to be not only his lover, but his best friend as well. How could she be when she couldn't allow him to do the same for her. Suddenly she cried out, gasping his name.

Charles blinked as if to clear his head. He released her immediately, soothingly caressing her arms. "I'm sorry, baby. I didn't realize . . ." His voice faded as he pushed her robe off her shoulders and frowned at the red marks on her skin. "I didn't mean to hurt you."

"There's no need to apologize," she said, ignoring the small hurt. "We just have to keep praying that Jeff is going to be fine. We have to believe that, never lose sight of it."

Charles nodded. He slowly rose from the chair and helped her up. "You must be exhausted."

Disappointed that he hadn't confided in her, Diane took his hand. They mounted the stairs together. Charles's love-making that night was hot and demanding,and it didn't al-low Diane to hold back any of herself from him. As he held her sleeping form close, he gained what comfort he could from her softness. His pain eventually eased enough to allow him to sleep.

Nineteen

On Monday morning, Diane and Charles left the house at the same time. While Charles assumed she was on her way to the high school, she took it for granted that he was going to his office. They were both wrong.

Anthia was asleep in an armchair in the intensive care waiting room of the hospital when Charles arrived. Dexter was standing at the window, staring down at the street several floors below.

"How is he?" Charles asked softly.

Dexter shook his head sadly. "Not much change. He regained consciousness for a few minutes early this morning."

Charles nodded, his anguish undetectable except for his balled fists. "Do they know yet if he'll be able to walk?"

"Too soon to tell."

"It was nice of you to wait with Anthia."

"She's good people," Dexter said quietly. "She certainly didn't need this kind of pain."

"Is that what you think? That Jeff brought this on himself?" Anthia asked sleepily, pushing away Dexter's overcoat, which she'd been using as a blanket. "You think he robbed that man, don't you?" She didn't give him a chance to respond. "If you have so little faith in my son, then why are you here?"

Dexter scowled, running his hand over his close-cut natural. "I never said that."

"But that's what you're thinking, isn't it?"

"Hell, I don't know what to think. Do you?"

Anthia was tired. Her eyes were the lovliest and saddest Dexter had ever seen. Her voice was stiff with formality. "Perhaps you should take yourself right back to that center of yours and leave us the hell alone."

Charles glanced at his silent friend. He could see the turbulent emotions playing across his strong brown features. He was shocked by what he saw. Dexter was a quiet man, a thoughtful man who shared little of himself with others. He was also devoted to the center and to its aims. He had given up a high-paying job to work for next to nothing to keep the community center operating. He had no family that Charles knew of. But he was a man Charles would've trusted with his life. It was evident, at least to Charles, that Dexter had a personal interest in Anthia Jenkins.

"I'm sure Dex didn't mean what you think," Charles interjected.

"I don't want him here!"

Dexter didn't say a word. He exchanged a look with Charles before he walked out.

"You're wrong, Anthia. Dex cares about Jeff."

Anthia sank down onto the chair like a deflating balloon, her eyes brimming with tears. "Do you think my boy is capable of armed robbery?"

"No."

"Thank you."

"Come on. Let me buy you some breakfast."

"I can't. I want to speak to the doctor. Did you hear that he regained consciousness? It was only for a few minutes, but it's a start."

"Yes, I heard. Come on. We'll ask the nurse to page us in the cafeteria if the doctor comes while we're gone, okay?"

"Okay."

Both were troubled by the uniformed officer stationed at Jeff's door.

It was only after she'd eaten that Charles asked, "What happened, Anthia? Why was Jeff at that store?"

"I don't know . . . I just don't know."

"When did you see him last?"

"Around three-thirty. I was cleaning up when Jeff left for the center. Until then, he was at home with me all day. We did the grocery shopping and the laundry. The only time we weren't together was when I stopped in to see our neighbor, Mrs. Turner."

"Did you two have an argument?"

"No! The only time we argue is when he hangs around with Eddie Walker, a boy from the old neighborhood. But that hasn't happened lately, not since Jeff has been going to the center. He's really been working hard in school. He doesn't give me any trouble at home. He never really did," Anthia sniffed.

"So everything was cool when he left?"

"Yes. He asked for his allowance a day early. I kinda fussed about that, but it was nothin' serious. I gave it to him. Why would he rob that store? He has money. He's received money from Social Security ever since his father was killed. We've been putting every penny of that money into the bank for college. What did he need to steal for?"

"I don't know, but he knows if he needs anything he can come to me."

Anthia nodded. "I'm grateful, but Jeff doesn't want your money. What he appreciates is your friendship."

Charles smiled sadly. "How much money did he have on him?"

"Five dollars."

"What was his mood?"

"He was excited about the swim meet . . . sure the community center would win."

Charles sighed thoughtfully.

"Charles, I know my child. He didn't hold up anyone!"

"How did he get the gun?"

"How do I know? This has to be some kind of terrible mistake. I'm sure of it."

Patting her hand, he said reassuringly, "Don't worry. We'll get to the bottom of this mess."

"You don't think he . . ."

"No, I don't think he robbed that store. I intend to find out the truth."

Anthia smiled for the first time.

"Are you finished?" he asked, gesturing toward her plate.

"Yes." She nodded. "I can't eat anymore."

"Why don't we check in with the nurse? After you've spoken to the doctor, I'll run you home." When she started to protest, he reminded her quietly, "You won't be any help to Jeff or anyone else if you're too exhausted to function."

"I appreciate the offer, but I can't leave until he's out of danger."

"Okay. Anthia, Dexter's a great guy. He cares about Jeff. And he only wants to help. Why not let him?"

"He thinks Jeff is guilty."

"Did he say that?"

Anthia hesitated, then admitted, "Not exactly."

"Give him a chance."

Anthia nodded, suddenly too tired to argue.

"Girl, if you get any bigger, you're going to burst!" Diane teased, struggling for a calm she was far from feeling.

Heather laughed, caressing her protruding abdomen. "If you weren't my best friend, I'd smack you for that! Di, I'm so tired of not being able to see my own feet and not being able to stand up by myself. The absolute worst is, I can't even make love to my own husband," she complained. "And speaking of husbands, mine is driving me nuts. If these babies don't come soon, I'm going to murder their father. He calls me every hour on the hour. Honestly! It's his fault I'm like this anyway!"

Diane giggled. "Oh, really? I was told it takes two."

"Well . . . maybe I had a little something to do with it." Heather blushed.

Both women giggled like the freshmen they'd been back in Hunter Hall on Central State's campus, where they'd been roommates.

"Excuse me." Miss Mattie, an elderly friend of the family the Montgomerys had welcomed into their home, knocked softly on the door before entering. "Honey lamb, what can I get for ya? Pillow for your back?"

"Nothing, Miss Mattie, but thanks."

Diane and Heather shared a smile. The two were seated in the Montgomerys' family room.

"Honestly," Heather exclaimed, once they were alone. "I'm so sick of being fussed over. Di, I feel like running away from home. Only trouble is, I can't make it to the front door without help."

Diane had been trying to maintain the light-hearted mood when she was anything but joyful. She was shaken up by what she'd just learned about her mother. The situation was getting worse. She couldn't solve this alone. There was only one person who she could tell about this . . . one person she dared trust with this horrible secret. The trouble was how to go about admitting to her best friend that she'd been lying to her since the day they'd met. Fidgeting, Diane crossed, then re-crossed her legs, unable to find a comfortable position.

"Do you mind if I close the door? I need to speak to you privately."

As Heather shook her head, her shoulder-length ebony braids swung freely. Her normally smooth brow was suddenly wrinkled with concern. "Uh-oh, what happened? Surely you're not still worried about Charles's sister? Diane, Eliz is just a bit protective when it comes to her big brother. Give her time. She truly loves him and only wants him to be happy. Eventually, she'll realize that you two are right for each other. Anyone with an ounce of sense can see how deeply you two love each other."

"It's not Eliz," Diane said, as she returned to her seat across from where Heather was stretched out with her feet propped up on an ottoman. "It's personal . . . something I never told anyone. It's about my past. And quite frankly, I'm having a rough time talking about this."

"We've been friends for over ten years. We lived in the same dormitory room for four years. What could be so personal?" Heather teased, "Honey, I remember when we were both flunking physical science and you batted your pretty brown eyes at the professor while I cried all over the poor man. Somehow, he felt sorry for us and gave us a D rather than the F we deserved."

Diane laughed in spite of her anxieties, but she quickly sobered, swallowing back the tears. "Do you swear you won't tell Charles?"

Heather nodded.

"Thank you. I've hid so much of my life from Charles . . . from everyone. If he ever finds out I've lied to him, he'll never forgive me. I might as well kiss my marriage goodbye."

Heather's professional training as a counselor warned her that Diane was near the breaking point. Unable to keep the worry out of her voice, she asked, "What's wrong?"

"I don't think I can do this." Diane hesitated, close to tears. Finally, she blurted out, "My whole life is a lie."

Heather blinked in surprise, but she didn't interrupt.

"Nothing I've told you about myself is true. I've been so ashamed of my past that I made up one for myself. I grew up in Chicago, but I didn't have the normal middle-class childhood I told you about. My mother hasn't been married four or five times. She doesn't spend her time looking for a new husband and traveling."

"There is nothing you can tell me that will change how I feel about you. We're friends . . . forever."

"Thank you." Diane said nervously. "I probably wouldn't be telling you this now if my past wasn't threatening my relationship with Charles. I need your help, Heather. I have to do something before he finds out. I don't want Charles to know any of this!"

"Charles loves you, Diane. That's not going to change."

"Don't you see, I'm just not willing to take that risk," she insisted. "I feel like my back is rammed against a brick wall." She impatiently brushed the tears from her eyes. "Please don't be angry with me for not telling you before . . . I couldn't." Diane plunged right in before she lost her nerve. She told Heather about growing up in tiny apartments, totally dependent on a mother who wasn't there for her emotionally because of her own struggle to survive prostitution and addiction. Diane told her about her brother, who'd eventually lost his battle with cystic fibrosis. When she finished, her heart was pounding with dread.

"Diane, I'm sorry."

Heather was horrified by the unhappiness Diane had faced at such an early age. She hadn't had a childhood . . . hadn't known the love and support that both Heather and Charles had always taken for granted.

"I'm not looking for sympathy. In a strange way, it happened so long ago that it's almost as if it happened to someone else, not me."

"I wish you had shared this with me, rather than keeping all of it bottled up inside," Heather said, although she knew the reason. Diane didn't trust anyone with her secrets. "How old were you when you left home?"

"Sixteen."

"But why didn't you feel as if you could go live with your aunt?" Heather was disturbed not by what she heard, but by the fact that it had happened to her best friend and she'd felt the need to hide this part of herself from those who loved her.

"Aunt Jean's would be the first place Lillie would have

looked for me. The night I left home, I swore I'd never go back." Diane shivered from the horrible memory. She'd been so afraid, but she knew she had to leave. "It has taken me years, but I've made a good life for myself, Heather. I'll be damned if I'll allow Lillie to interfere with what I have now with Charles. I won't let her blackmail me, either."

"Blackmail!"

"Exactly. She's quite capable of worse, especially when she's high. I'm sure she's been drinking heavily again. Although I have no proof that she's back on drugs, I have to find out. Damn it! It's enough that she's ruined her life and Danny's. Must she destroy mine?" Diane wanted to lash out, but she was very controlled when she said tautly, "I found out this morning when I went by her place that she hasn't been home for days. I don't know where she is."

"Hold it! You're taking me too fast," Heather begged. "Your mother isn't in Chicago?"

"No. Lillie followed me here to Detroit about four years ago, after being in a rehab center. We made an agreement. I would help her with her expenses as long as she remained sober and stayed out of my personal life. She kept up her end of that bargain—that is, until recently." Diane sank down onto the sofa. "I've got to find her before she finds me. She's capable of anything. This morning I went to try and talk some sense into her." Her voice was soft with despair when she said, "She knows where I live and where I work. She came to the house on Saturday, wanting money. I was so scared. Charles was right upstairs. He could have come down at any moment." Tears filled her eyes.

"Oh, no." Heather's own eyes filled with tears. "This must be awful for you."

"Please . . . help me."

"How?"

Diane sighed, brushing impatiently at her tears. "I need to know who to contact about getting her into a treatment program. I'm willing to pay whatever it costs. I have some money saved. If necessary, I can always put up the condo for sale."

"I know of a very good treatment center. That's the easy part. The problem will be, can you get her to go in voluntarily. It's a live-in facility at first, then later on, it works on an outpatient basis. The problem is do they have room now and do you think you can get her to agree to go for help?"

"She won't be given a choice. She'll either go, or I'll cut her off without a cent," Diane said firmly. "Once she's in treatment, she'll no longer be a threat to me. Thanks, Heather."

"No need to thank me. We're friends."

Diane smiled, overwhelmed with emotion. Heather still cared about her. She hadn't condemned her, as she'd feared. It was too much to take in all at once.

"Alcoholism isn't something to be ashamed of. It's a disease and it can be treated."

"I know all that. But it doesn't change my situation. My mother is still a threat to my happiness unless I can get help for her."

"You're wrong. She'll always be a threat to you unless you reverse the situation."

Diane clearly didn't like the sound of that declaration.

"You have to tell Charles. That's the only way you can have any peace," Heather insisted.

"Peace! You're talking about destroying my marriage. Can you imagine how elated his sister would be if she learned she'd been absolutely right about me? She practically told me to my face that I'm not good enough for her brother. No! Charles won't learn about this from me!" Diane shouted, close to tears.

"Girlfriend, the truth can't hurt you. It's the lies that may destroy your marriage. Think about your husband. His love isn't of the fair-weather variety. Charles will be devastated if he gains this information from anyone but you."

Absently twisting her engagement and wedding rings, Diane finally whispered, "I can't . . ."

"If you can tell me, you can tell Charles. I haven't stopped caring about you. Why should he? What happened in the past wasn't your fault."

Tears filled her eyes, but Diane refused to let them fall. Now was not the time to give in to weakness. She needed a clear head. Her voice was steady when she said, "I can't do it. I love him too much. He'll lose his faith and trust in me. Without those two ingredients there can be no love." Diane went over to Heather's chair and knelt down beside her. She took her hands. "Please . . . I'm begging you. Please, don't tell him. I need you to be my friend."

Heather hugged her. "We'll always be friends, no matter what. That's why it would be wrong of me not to tell you what I think." Heather smoothed her hair. "Di, you've got to be the one to tell him. And soon."

"Why don't we go over these figures at another time?" Elizabeth said, after her third attempt to obtain her brother's attention. "Chuck, what is it? You've been in a funk all day. You bit off Ginny's head for no reason. Keep this up and you'll be looking for a new secretary."

Pushing back his chair from the conference table where they'd been working in the corner of his office, Charles began pacing back and forth in front of the floor-to-ceiling windows behind his desk.

"This is about Diane, isn't it? The honeymoon is over so soon?" Elizabeth could have bitten her own tongue, suddenly realizing she'd spoken her thoughts aloud. "I'm sorry. I didn't meant that."

Charles sent her a sharp, penetrating look. "Oh, you meant it. You just shouldn't have said it. And no, my mood has nothing to do with my wife. Diane and I are fine . . . better than fine. It's Jeff Jenkins, the kid I sponsor at the community center. He's lying in Henry Ford Hospital with a bullet in his back."

"Shot? How?"

"According to the police, by a convenience-store owner during an armed robbery."

"You mean he was trying to rob the store?"

"That's what the police report says." Charles had stopped at the police station before going to his office. The officers seem to view it as an open-and-shut case, even though the clerk indicated there'd been two robbers."

"But you don't believe it?"

"No. Jeff isn't a criminal."

She walked over to her brother and placed a comforting hand on his arm. "How serious is it?"

"Very. Jeff is fighting for his life. He took a bullet in the back as he was leaving the store. The cash register was empty, yet no money was found on Jeff. It'll be his word against the store owner's."

"He had a gun, didn't he?"

"He was holding one, but it hadn't been fired."

"Shot in the back, you say?"

"That's right," Charles said tightly. "The life of a black male isn't worth a dime in this society."

"Have you spoken to Jeff? What does he have to say?"

"Nothing. He regained consciousness only this morning, and then for just a few minutes. Sis, if he lives . . . he may never walk again. He's facing felony charges."

"We have to help him."

"I intend to. The problem is how."

"The most obvious is to find him a lawyer . . . the best."

Charles looked at her and then suddenly he grinned. "Thanks, Sis." He gave her a kiss on the cheek.

"Hey! Where you goin'?"

"Taking your advice. Ask Ginny to cancel my appointments for the rest of the afternoon. I'm not sure when I'll be back."

Charles's next stop was downtown Detroit. Charles didn't have to wait while Quinn's secretary announced him. Quinn was at his desk, shirt sleeves rolled up, a deli sandwich beside him.

"That's a good way to get an ulcer," Charles said, knocking on the open portal.

"Too late—I already have one." Quinn got to his feet, extending his hand. "What's up?"

"Trouble." They shook hands, then Charles dropped into the leather armchair in front of the cluttered desk. He filled the other man in on what had happened. It paid to have friends. Quinn Montgomery was one of the most highly respected black criminal attorneys in the country. In spite of his success, Quinn had come up the hard way. He'd lost a brother to the streets, and he put not only his money but his time into black community-based programs.

Quinn leaned back in his chair, recalling the time when Charles and he were not so friendly. The cause was Heather. Quinn couldn't stand Charles, viewing the man's friendship with Heather as a threat to his very personal interest in the beautiful young counselor. Thank heaven that time was behind them. Heather was on leave until after their babies were born. And his daughter, Cynthia, was close to finishing high school with honors.

"Will you take the case?"

"Of course. Whatever the kid did, he didn't deserve to be shot down like a dog."

Charles slowly released the breath he'd been holding. "Where do we start?" There wasn't a discussion of fee. There'd be none.

"With the police. I have a few friends in the department. I'll see what I can find out. We need to know what was on the surveillance camera.

"I didn't think of that."

"That's what you have me for. The problem is, who was with him?"

"Good question. How can I help?"

"As soon as you can, see what you can find out from Jeff," Quinn said, reaching for his suit jacket.

Charles nodded, getting to his feet. He'd come to Quinn seeking legal advice. When, or rather if, Jeff was released from the hospital, he was going to need all the help he could get. Charles planned on giving Anthia and Jeff both financial and emotional support.

Twenty

At dinner that evening, Diane said, "I visited with Heather today. With the babies overdue, she's putting the blame on Quinn." Diane forced a giggle, trying to lighten the mood. Charles's strong, distinct features were not arranged in their usual relaxed countenance. His somber, thoughtful manner barely eased at the mention of their mutual friend's name.

"How was your day?" she asked hopefully, thinking his couldn't have been as awful as hers.

"Busy," he grumbled, eyeing the smoked salmon on his plate as if it were some foreign substance that might attack at any moment. "I saw Quinn today. He agreed to take on Jeff's case."

"Do you think it's that serious?"

"Absolutely. Jeff may be facing a prison term. He's going to need legal counsel . . . the best . . . if he makes it."

"Excuse me, sir. Telephone call for you. Mr. Montgomery. Will you take it in here?"

"Yes." Charles took the cordless phone, nodding his thanks to the older man. The conversation was quick and to the point. Charles was scowling when he put down the telephone.

Giving up all pretense of eating, she replaced her fork. "More bad news?"

"The cops don't have the tape from the security camera mounted in the store. It seems, according to the owner, that the camera was broken and he hadn't gotten around to getting it repaired." Charles swore. "It'll be his word against Jeff's. Who in hell is going to believe a black kid with a gun?"

"Oh, no! Honey, I'm sorry. Did you have a chance to speak with Anthia today? I tried her at home but couldn't get her. I wondered how she has been holding up."

"She's doing as well as can be expected, considering that her son is hooked up to all those machines. He'll be lucky if he lives. Excuse me," he said, tossing his napkin beside his barely touched meal. "Don't wait up, I'll be late."

"Charles . . ." Hurrying, she caught up with him in the foyer.

"Yeah?" He turned, his heart heavy with feelings of guilt and grief . . . feelings he wasn't ready to share with anyone, not even his wife. He was barely able to admit them to himself.

Suddenly unsure of herself and of him, she hesitated. She craved his warmth . . . his strength . . . his love. "Don't rush off. Let's talk about it."

"I can't."

Charles, expecting some form of reprisal for his abruptness, let out a breath when she slipped her arms beneath his and circled his waist. Diane pressed her soft, sweet mouth against the side of his throat in that tender spot guaranteed to gain his attention. Charles shivered, holding her against him in an effort to soothe the rawness deep inside him.

"I'm sorry . . . so sorry about Jeff."

He lowered his head until he could cover her mouth with his. His kiss was dark and husky, deep and throaty. Her mouth opened to accept all that he was unable to voice but felt so deeply. He squeezed Diane one last time before breaking the seal of their kiss.

His voice was rough with emotion when he whispered, "I love you." Then he left.

Diane sighed wearily, sitting down on the staircase. So many lies stood between them, too many to count. They just kept on mushrooming, one right after the next, as Diane struggled to hold her world together.

Diane still had not gotten over Heather's calm reaction to her revelations. She hadn't known what to expect. Certainly not Heather's generous acceptance. Never in a million years could she have guessed.

What if Heather was right? What if she was risking everything by keeping the past from him? Heather had seemed so certain that Charles would understand. Diane was equally certain the risk was one she wasn't strong enough to face. Their whole future was at stake. How could she take that gamble? What man in his right mind would want to be married to a woman who was the daughter of a prostitute . . . a junkie?

It was not as if she doubted his love for her. Yet she would be foolish not to accept the truth. Charles was in love with the new Diane. She'd left Chicago; she'd never looked back. She was not the same girl-child who had endured years of neglect. She had left that part of her life far behind. She would help her mother, but she could not step back in time.

Dexter was on the telephone when Charles paused at the door of the community center's business office. He waved Charles in, pointing toward the battered armchair in front of his desk. He placed his hand over the mouthpiece. "Anthia," he whispered, before continuing his conversation. "That's great. Yes . . . yes. Please. I'll be happy to give whatever help I can. Yes . . . yes. I'll tell him. Goodnight."

"How's Jeff?" Charles asked, as Dexter ended the call.

"Better. He's awake, stabilized. It looks like he's gonna make it."

Charles sighed heavily. "Thank God."

"Hey, man . . . where are you goin'?"

"To the hospital. There are some things I need to know."

"Hold up there, Randol. It's way past visiting hours. Besides, they aren't going to let you see Jeff. He's still in intensive care . . . family members only."

"I'll tell them I'm Jeff's uncle."

"Don't you know the kid is in no shape to answer questions?"

"Dex, I don't intend to let that kid spend so much as a half hour paying for something he didn't do."

"How can you be so sure?"

"So you *do* think he's guilty?"

"Hell, I don't know. I took that go-round with Anthia this morning, remember? At this point, there's not a lot we can do. Other than give them our support."

An image of the soft-spoken, shapely Anthia suddenly flickered through Dexter's mind. That smartass Doug Henderson she called a friend was doing his best to get into her panties. Damn it, who she slept with was none of his business! He had his own unresolved issues with women. He didn't need to be thinking of Jeff's mother as more than just what she was—if he was lucky, a friend. But she had the prettiest eyes . . .

"Now, look here . . ."

"No, *you* look. Man, Jeff isn't the only kid we have here. There are others depending on us to be there for them, show them what it is to be an African-American man. Are we supposed to forget about them?"

Charles swore softly, shoving his hands deep into his pockets. "I know that. I'm not about to give up on Jeff! The store clerk says Jeff wasn't alone. I intend to find out who was with him." His forehead wrinkled in concentration, "Tell me about this Eddie the guys were talkin' about before the meet."

"He and Jeff grew up together. Eddie has gotten himself

involved with a rough crowd. Nowadays he runs with a bunch of crackheads, man. Word is Eddie is bad news."

Charles asked, "You think he's connected to this robbery?"

"He's capable of it. He and Jeff were really tight once. Ain't no way of tellin', man."

"Jeff isn't going down for this. He might have been there, but he didn't do it."

Dexter shrugged his powerful muscled shoulders. I hope not, man."

"Where can I find this Eddie?"

Dexter sat up. "That's not a good idea."

"If he has something to do with what happend to Jeff, why not? There may be no other choice."

"You'll find trouble, whether you're looking for it or not."

"An address, Dex."

"Last I heard, Eddie hangs out at the Starmore Lounge on Davidson. But you can't go there alone."

Charles shrugged.

"Talk to Jeff first, man. You may have this whole thing wrong." When Charles didn't respond, Dexter said, "Charles?"

"Yeah, you're probably right."

"I know I'm right. When and if you need a back-up, call me, man."

"Thanks. I'd better get to it. Later."

It was late, too late for house guests. Charles, nevertheless, knocked on Anthia's door.

"Who's there?"

"It's me, Charles. I know it's late. But I'd like to talk to you."

"Just a minute," she said, unlocking a series of deadbolts. "Hi, come on in."

"I'm sorry . . ."

"Don't worry about it. I was up anyway. I just hung up the phone from talking to Diane. She's so sweet."

"She's concerned about you. I know you've got to be beat. I promise I won't stay long."

"It's all right, Charles. I know I need to sleep, but I can't even lie down. Sit with me for a little while." She gestured toward the sofa. Her eyes filled when she thought of how Jeff wouldn't be needing the sofabed for some time . . . if ever. Swallowing back tears, she asked, "Can I get you something? Decaf?"

"No, thanks."

Once they were seated, he asked, "How was Jeff when you left the hospital? I heard Dex say he was fully awake for a while tonight."

"Yeah. He's responding to treatment." Anthia beamed "I can't tell you how grateful I am to you. If you hadn't gotten Dr. Grant to take over his case, I'm sure he wouldn't have pulled through."

"We're friends, Anthia. Friends help each other."

"You and Diane have been so kind . . ." Anthia's eyes brimmed with tears that she quickly wiped away. "I'm sorry. I'm a mess." She sighed. "Oh, Charles, I don't know what's happening from one minute to the next. Nothin' will make me believe that my boy held up that store!"

"Anthia, I'm with you on this. Jeff couldn't have done this. Anyone who knows Jeff realizes he has problems, but he's not vicious, and he isn't hard enough to rob and then try to kill anyone," Charles said.

"That's not what your friend Dexter thinks!"

"Hey, wait. We've gone over this before. Dex doesn't believe Jeff is guilty any more than I do. You have to remember, Dex grew up on the streets, and he has a hard edge. Not once has he said he believed Jeff is guilty . . . not once," Charles insisted.

"I suppose because of the gun they found . . ."

"It didn't help, that's for sure. I've got Quinn Montgomery to represent Jeff. He's the best. I hope that's okay with you?"

Anthia gasped. "His reputation is formidable. I can't afford him."

"He's a friend, so there won't be a fee."

"Oh, Charles. I can't ask that of you."

"You didn't ask. Besides, Quinn is good people. You'll like him."

"Thank you."

"Glad to be able to help." Glancing at his watch, Charles rose to his feet. "I just stopped in to hear how Jeff's doin' and to check on you." At the door, he advised, "Try to get some rest."

"I will. Give Diane my love."

Charles smiled, " 'Night." He took the stairs two at a time. He wanted to ask about Eddie but decided she'd been through enough. Anthia was clearly in no condition to be cross-examined.

He reached his car just as a familiar car eased to a stop behind him on the dark street. He hid his surprise when Dexter Washington slid from behind the wheel. He had a large bag of takeout food under his arm.

"Hi. Kinda late for a social call, isn't it?"

"Yeah." Charles hid a grin.

Dexter grunted. "Well?"

"Well, what?"

"What brought you here at this hour?"

Charles recognized jealousy . . . he'd suffered enough from it. Talk about pain. Charles ignored the challenge in the other's dark eyes. "My interest is solely Jeff. Besides, Anthia is a good friend of both my wife, Diane, and myself." Charles quietly reminded him.

"Sorry," Dexter said softly, knowing he'd given his own interest away. "I thought Anthia might be hungry. I hadn't planned on staying but a moment."

Charles grinned. " 'Night," he called, as he got into his

car. Laughing as he drove away, Charles was amazed by the discovery. Dexter was such a reserved man, preferring to keep to himself. Charles knew he'd been hurt very badly in the past, knew he had done hard time for something he hadn't done. Charles was pleased Dexter was attracted to a woman as caring and loving as Anthia. Now, if the feeling was mutual, maybe those two could get something going.

Charles chuckled, deciding that Diane would be very interested in the possibility of romance. Women seemed to find that sort of thing fascinating. Heather and Elizabeth had always had plenty to say about his love life. Neither seemed to care how annoyed he'd been by their meddling.

The thought of his lovely wife had Charles pressing down on the accelerator. He'd been a real bear at dinner. He had some sweet-talking to do. Suddenly he was eager to see his beautiful wife.

Diane nearly jumped out of her skin when Charles placed a kiss in the space where her neck and shoulder joined. He chuckled at the look of alarm she sent him, having dropped the telephone she'd been holding to her ear.

"Sorry, baby. I thought you heard me on the stairs."

"No . . ."

She had been so upset by her inability to reach her mother that she hadn't known he was even in the house. Diane quickly retrieved the earpiece from the bedroom carpet. Berating herself for calling from home, she knew she should have driven over to her mother's rather than repeatedly calling every half hour. She wasted hours and she still didn't know if Lillie was all right. More important, she didn't know if Lillie was passed out drunk, or worse, shooting heroin again. The only thing she'd accomplished tonight had been to arrange for an appointment at the private clinic that Heather had recommended.

The rehab clinic was willing to help Lillie, but only if

Lillie checked herself in . . . that was a huge "if" that left Diane terrified at the possibility of failure. She had no choice. She had somehow to talk Lillie into it.

Charles's appreciative eyes wandered over the cream ruffled layers of the silk chiffon nightshirt she wore. It was cut high on the sides and stopped at the middle of her shapely thighs. The sheer fabric left very little of her soft brown skin hidden. His hot gaze lingered at the apex of her thighs, where the lush nest of black curls was visible against the cloth. His own sex rose, thickening, driven by an old, so familiar urgency to be a part of her.

"I expected to find you curled on your side fast asleep, sweet thang. Who were you . . ."

He didn't complete the question because Diane encircled his waist and pressed her sweet open mouth against his while rubbing her breasts into his chest. He accepted the invitation without hesitation. His full masculine mouth responded to hers. Not for an instant did he consider resisting her sweet magic. Charles teased each corner of her mouth with a quick flick of his tongue. She moaned softly. The exciting, pleasurable sound inflamed his senses even more. The tantalizing feel of her cushiony soft breasts against his chest caused him to tighten an arm around her, bringing her even closer.

"Did you wait up for me?" he asked a split second before he deepened the kiss, plunging into the honey recesses of her mouth. Over and over he drank from her mouth.

"Oh, yes . . . yes."

Charles lifted her and placed her in the center of their bed, his mouth ravishing hers. The comforter had been turned back, but he didn't notice as he settled against his wife's soft length. She parted her thighs as he pressed his throbbing erection against her mound. Her trembling responses were so wonderfully welcoming that he stroked her silk-covered sex with his own. Diane shivered, her hands pushing and pulling at his clothing, impatient to feel his warm dark supple skin against hers. Diane gasped aloud as his sizzling hot hungry mouth dropped to the base of her throat and warmed the fragrant, delicately boned hollow.

"I want you . . . every soft, sweet-smelling inch of you," he whispered.

Diane's eyes never left him as his shirt dropped to the carpet. His long, strong fingers hands made short work of the leather belt, jeans, socks, and black silk briefs. Diane's breath accelerated at the fullness of his sex as he returned to bed.

He put one knee on the bed, extending his hand to her. His fingers locked with hers and she rose to her knees. Charles's breath quickened as he lifted the nightshirt over her head. She was lovely . . . so damn beautiful. He still couldn't believe she was his. His gaze was captivated by the fullness of her breasts.

Diane rested her arms on his shoulders, her hands cradling his head, her fingers in the crisp ebony thickness at his nape. His lips were warm and exciting and wonderfully firm beneath hers. She flicked his fleshy bottom lip with her tongue, dipping inside to lick the enticing vulnerable interior before tugging his bottom lip into her mouth and suckling.

Charles shuddered with excitement. His caressing hands cradled her breasts, savoring their incredible softness. He slowly flicked his thumbs over the large brown tips, watching with pleasure as they hardened even more and she moaned her enjoyment. He did not stop until they were fully erect, begging to be tasted.

"Want me?" he asked, his body hard and aching.

"Yes . . ." she sighed, sweet flames of desire flicking her loins. She trembled as he dropped his head and replaced his hand with his mouth. He sampled the entire sweet globe before he tongued the sensitive peak. As Charles licked her, his breath quickening by the sexy sounds of her increasing passion. Diane cried out when he finally sucked her nipple with exquisite care. She lay over his arm, her back arched, offering as much of herself as she could to him. His hands moved over her, caressing down to her silky thighs.

She said his name aloud when he cupped her softness. Her body pulsed with desire. She knew he found her wet . . . ready for him. She could feel the strength of his arousal against her side. Her hands were trembling as she caressed him.

"Chucky . . . please . . . now . . . I want you, now."

"Not yet . . ."

"Now . . ."

"Not until I taste your sweet honey."

Without his support, she could have fallen. Charles held her in place as he spread her wide for the hot, sizzling strokes of his tongue. Diane quivered from the unrelenting pleasure as he laved her. There was no hesitation as he pleasured Diane until she sobbed his name while wave after wave of dazzling sweet release rushed over her.

Charles didn't give her time to catch her breath as he settled her over his hard length. She seemed to have lost her ability to breathe as he surged forward, entering her in one long, deep thrust. Charles's senses reeled, overwhelmed by her welcoming, tight heat. Never would he get his fill of this woman. She made each day brighter, each moment together sheer wonder. She made him feel as if he were a black warrior . . . strong, invincible, the best lover on the planet. She gave him more and more of herself each time they made love. He worried her sensitive nub as he surged over and over again deep inside her, desire whirling out of control until they shared a breathtaking, heart-stopping climax. Slowly the room came back into focus and their breathing slowed.

Diane hugged Charles, not wanting to ever let him go. Gently she pressed sweet, tender kisses against his warm lips.

"I'm sorry I was so impatient at dinner. It wasn't you, it was me," he said quietly.

She lay nestled against him, her back to his chest. "It's okay," she sighed. "Love you."

"Love you . . ." he murmured, then dropped into a deep slumber.

It took Diane considerably longer to relax her mind enough to sleep. While her body felt languorous and satiated, her thoughts were crowded with worry as she relived those tense moments when Charles had walked into their bedroom. She'd been paralyzed with fear . . . sickened by the possibility of discovery. And she had been very lucky. She'd managed to divert his attention, thus saving herself the agony of making up more lies.

Heather was wrong. She didn't understand. Diane had no choice but to continue on the path she had chosen and pray that Charles never found out the truth. Tomorrow, she would find Lillie. Tomorrow, she would take her to that clinic. Diane knew she couldn't feel safe until Lillie was in treatment.

Twenty-one

Although Jeff was moved out of intensive care by the end of the week, he refused all visitors accept his mother. He remained mute when Quinn tried to question him. Anthia tried to persuade him to cooperate but eventually gave up. He would not even talk to her about the robbery.

Frustrated, after over a week of refusals, Charles decided to take matters into his own hands. He walked right into Jeff's room as bold as brass.

"Hi, kid."

Jeff looked up in surprise. But instead of answering, he turned his head toward the window.

"How are you feeling?"

Jeff's eyes remained glued to something outside the window as he fought for control. He blinked back tears and swallowed the sob lodged in his throat. After the mess he'd made of things, Jeff was unable to so much as look at his mentor . . . his friend.

"Compared to what you looked like when they wheeled you in here, you're doing great, son. We've all been concerned about you."

"It don't matter," Jeff mumbled. Nothing mattered. He knew he was going to end up in a wheelchair.

Taking the seat beside the bed, Charles said, "You're man enough to carry a gun but not man enough to look me in the eye?"

"Hey! You don't know nothin' about it, man!" Jeff retorted, then winced at the sharp pain from his having moved too quickly.

"What I do know I don't like." Charles scowled, crushing the tender emotions he felt for this young man. If he had a hope of reaching him, it wouldn't be through sympathy. "By the way, the store owner says you were trying to rob him. He says he shot you in self-defense."

Jeff held his lips taut. What was the point? It was because of his own stupidity that he was going to spend the next couple of years behind bars instead of in college. All that hard work for nothing. He didn't have a future anymore. Hell, he didn't know if his legs were ever going to work properly again.

"Jeff, we're talking about your life here. Staring out the window and pretending this mess will go away is a waste of time. I've got news for you, kid. You've been charged with armed robbery. Son, they're talking about prosecuting you as an adult." Jeff didn't so much as blink as Charles went on. "The choice is yours. Quinn Montgomery is a damn good lawyer, but without your help his hands are tied."

"It doesn't matter!"

"It matters. *You* matter! If you don't care about your own skin, think about your mother. Anthia has worked long and hard to provide for you. You plan to let all that effort and love disappear down the drain like dirty bath water? Huh? It's time you started acting like you cared about her . . . about yourself?"

"Leave me alone!" Jeff wailed disgusted with himself when tears filled his eyes.

"Not a chance. You think because you have a bullet in your spine you'll never walk again? I don't care *what* the doctors say. If you want to walk, you will. It may not happen overnight. It may take some awfully hard work, but it *will* happen, if you want it badly enough." Charles clasped the boy's hand and squeezed. "You can beat this."

"It would have been better if I had died!"

"No way. You're not getting off that easily. It's going to be okay . . . you'll see. Have some faith."

"Nothin' is going to be right! Hell, I'm in a hospital bed while the other kids are walking around without a care in the world."

"It's your choice. You're the one keeping your mouth shut. Your mother and I have tried to talk some sense into that hard head of yours. You want to take the rap for someone else, don't you? Go on, be a fool—do the time. Your buddy isn't doing a blasted thing to help you out of this jam. It's all on you, my man." Charles's heart pounded with nervous apprehension as he waited for the boy's decision.

It seemed to take forever for Jeff to answer, but in truth it was only a few minutes before he said, "Eddie Walker stopped me on my way to the center. I was going to the bus stop when he pulled over and asked for money. I let him have what I was carrying . . ." He went on to explain how he'd been tricked. "Next thing I knew, he said 'catch' and tossed the gun. I caught it without thinking. He started emptying the cash drawer. When he ran, so did I. I didn't know what else to do. It happened so fast. I felt the pain, then I don't remember anything until I woke up in the hospital."

"Why didn't you tell this to the police?"

"What good would it do? Man, did you forget I'm black? I was in the wrong place at the wrong time."

"You plan on taking the rap for this, Eddie? That's what will happen if you keep your mouth shut. Seems to me that if this guy was a real friend, he wouldn't have set you up."

Jeff laughed bitterly. "He's probably totally spaced out, especially since he got all the money."

"Quinn's a friend, Jeff. He knows how to help you. Will you talk to him? Tell him what you told me? Jeff?"

"Okay," he mumbled, his dark eyes filled with pain and regret.

"Don't worry about anything. Concentrate on getting well."

Jeff hung his head. "Look, I know now I should have kept walking. I messed up. I'm sorry I let you down."

"We all make mistakes, Jeff. Hopefully we learn from them."

"Sorry, sir. But I have to take him down to X-ray in a few minutes," a nurse said, as she came into the room. "I need to get him ready."

Charles got to his feet.

Before he could leave, Jeff said, "About the money you're paying for the doctor and the lawyer—I'll pay you back."

"We're friends; friends help each other out. Now I'd better get out of here. See you soon."

Charles was elated as he left the hospital. Jeff had verified what he suspected. Jeff had made a mistake, but he had not committed a crime. He had been in the wrong place at the wrong time. He never should have gone with Eddie. Charles intended to see that Jeff did not ruin his life because of it.

Charles made a call on the car phone to Quinn before he started the engine. He filled him in on what Jeff had told him about Eddie. Quinn was as pleased as Charles when they hung up the telephone.

Kids like Jeff were the very reason Charles had become involved in the mentoring program. The statistics were staggering when it came to the number of African-American males lost in a world of drugs, crime, and violence. This wasn't just a national problem, but a global problem. Charles viewed it as a personal challenge that frankly he wished more brothers would take on.

Now that he was married, it was becoming more and more difficult to devote the time the project demanded. It was time-consuming and often heart-wrenching work. Despite the horrible odds, it was something he couldn't turn his back on.

Unfortunately, his bride was the one losing out because of his involvement. There seemed to be so little time left for them. Thank goodness, Diane understood how much the project meant to him and supported him. He was damn lucky. She deserved better than he'd been providing lately. They hadn't gone out for a candlelit dinner and dancing since they'd returned from their honeymoon.

A picture of her with soft eyes burning with desire, her skin flushed with heat as they pleased each other, flashed through his mind. She was exquisite when her breath caught and she said his name as she reached fulfillment. Her climax usually triggered his own.

Diane . . . the corners of his mouth tilted as he put the car into gear. There was no better time than the present to show her how much she meant to him. His smile widened into a grin as he decided to surprise her by taking her out for a romantic lunch. Perhaps the Omni Hotel?

He chuckled at the thought of convincing her to play hooky with him for the rest of the day. They could spend the afternoon in one of the hotel's luxurious rooms. Charles's body tightened, swelling from the mere thought of making love to his wife. Concentrating on the late-morning traffic, he made a telephone call to his secretary canceling his afternoon appointments. Then he called the hotel and arranged for a table for two, reserved a room for later, and ordered champagne and a spray of pink orchids . . . a reminder of their wedding day.

Just as the bell rang, Diane added, "I want you to review chapters nine, ten, and fifteen. Be ready for a quiz tomorrow." She suppressed a smile at her students' collective groan.

As the class began to file past, she collected their homework assignments.

"Ms. Rivers . . . aw, I mean, Mrs. Randol. We had a

game last night. I didn't get a chance to do the assignment. Can I turn in my spreadsheet tomorrow?"

Diane lifted her gaze to the six-five tenth-grader. "That's not a valid excuse, Johnny. Coach Brown expects you to keep your grades up, and so do I. This isn't the first time this semester you've missed an assignment."

"But Mrs. Randol . . ."

Diane's glance moved to the wall clock. "Don't you have study hall last period today?"

"Yeah."

"Then I expect to see you in the computer lab by . . ." Diane stopped in mid-sentence.

Lillie was hovering at the door that led into the central hallway. Not only did she look nervous, but she was clearly agitated. She was also disheveled, her hair standing on end. She wore a badly wrinkled green blouse and slacks that looked like she'd slept in them. Diane was so shaken she nearly dropped the pile of papers she held.

"What?" the teen prompted, shifting from one large sneakered foot to the other.

"I-I-I'll let it slide for now. But do your reading tonight," she said absently. It seemed to take forever for her classroom to clear. Thank goodness she didn't have another class until after lunch.

Dropping the papers on her desk, Diane hurried over to the door and urged her mother inside, closing the door quickly behind the last student. "What are you doing here?"

"I needed to see you, baby. Couldn't wait . . ."

"You look terrible. When was the last time you had something to eat? Where have you been? I've been trying to reach you for days. Are you okay?" Diane ended out of breath. She recognized the stupidity of the question. Lillie reeked of alcohol and neglect. She was barely able to stay upright.

"You been looking for me, baby? That's a first." Lillie laughed as if she'd told a joke.

"I told you never to come here. How could you forget? How did you find my classroom?"

"Someone in the hall told me where you were." Her speech was slurred.

"You didn't tell them you're my mother, did you?" Diane said in near panic, her eyes continuously moving toward the door. All she needed was for one of her coworkers to appear at her door.

"Relax, no one guessed."

Diane was anything but tranquil. All kinds of horrible things had gone through her mind during the week she'd been trying to reach Lillie. At least now she knew she had not been injured.

"I need some money. A couple of dollars . . . whatever you have on you. Please, baby. You know I love you."

Diane hated it when she started the "caring mother" bit. It was wasted on her. She automatically started moving toward where she kept her purse in the coat closet, then suddenly she thought better of it. She couldn't just give Lillie money to get rid of her. Lillie was going down fast, and Diane knew that she was the only one who might be able to help her. But, damn it, Diane had to get her out of the school, and quick. What to do?

She turned to Lillie. "I was on my way to lunch. Meet me at my car in, say, five minutes. We'll get some food, then go to the park where we can talk."

Lillie looked at her suspiciously when she didn't just hand over the money. "I need cash . . . not food."

"I don't have much with me. We'll stop at the teller machine. There is one right around the corner. Shouldn't take long. I need to go to the school office for a minute. You go on out to the car," Diane urged.

"Just give me what you got." Lillie shifted from one unsteady foot to the other.

Diane was close to ringing her hands with anxiety. Her eyes kept returning to the door. This was not the place to tell her about going in for treatment, let alone convince her to admit herself.

"Five minutes." Diane took Lillie's arm and firmly steered her into the hallway. Thank goodness it was nearly empty. She said quickly, "My car is parked in the staff lot. Turn left at the end of the hall. The rear door is at the end of that corridor. I'll meet you there."

"Five minutes!" was Lillie's parting shot before she left.

Diane quickly switched off machines in the glass-walled computer lab connected to her classroom. Shoving the homework papers into her briefcase, she slipped on the suit jacket to her cream coatdress and retrieved her black leather shoulder bag from the closet, all in record time.

As Diane hurried to the school office, her mind raced to the challenge ahead. So many things could go wrong. She felt compelled to quicken her steps even more.

Diane was almost certain that Lillie was very close to using again. Maybe, if she was lucky, it was only alcohol, and not heroin. Lillie must have been desperate to have come to school.

"Mrs. Slivers, may I speak to you for a minute?" The principal had just hung up the telephone when Diane, having hung her keys in the cabinet behind the office counter, peeked into her office.

"Certainly. I hope nothing is wrong. You seem a little flushed."

"I'm not feeling well. I think I'm coming down with the flu. Can you get someone to cover my classes this afternoon?"

"Of course, dear. But only for this afternoon? What about tomorrow? Surely you need a few days to rest. These viruses are nothing to take lightly."

"I'll call you in the morning if I am not feeling any better. Thank you." As she hurried out of the building, she knew the lie wasn't far from the truth. She was developing a tension headache and her stomach was in knots at the idea of convincing Lillie to go into treatment. She hadn't allowed herself to question her own motivation or the past days of real fear when she'd been unable to reach Lillie.

She told herself she was only doing what was right. Her disdain and resentment toward her mother hadn't diminished . . . nothing could change the past. Her resentment was rooted in years of pain and unhappiness. Yet Diane raced toward her car, determined to get help for Lillie.

"Hey, man, what are you doin' around these parts?" Kenneth Brown asked.

"Checking up on you, what else?" Charles teased the man who had taken over his coaching job at Lawrence. "I heard you were doing a class A job, my man. Track team was really doing it against Brookman the other day."

"You made the meet?"

"Nope, but I heard about it."

"Hey, why don't you come around to practice? The kids would love to see you."

"Sorry, not today. I thought I would surprise Diane. Take her out to lunch. Have you seen her?" Charles was unaware of the smile that came to his mouth automatically at the sound of his wife's name.

"I saw her a few minutes ago in the office. So how's married life, my man?"

"Great. Just a little difficult to manage our schedules. How are things going around here? A few more weeks and it will all be over but the shouting."

"Yeah! And I can't wait. *Summertime . . .*" he sang, then laughed. "Nothin' changed around here. These rich brats think they can get away with murder. Slivers isn't about to expel anyone. It all comes down to the mighty dollar."

Charles almost laughed aloud, but he caught himself just

in time. Brown was right. Nothing had changed, including the other man's negativism. Every school had its problems, even the affluent private ones like Lawrence.

"If you get bored this summer doin' nothin', come on over to the community center. We can always use the help." Before Brown could formulate a reason why he could not possibly spare the time, Charles waved, moving on. "It was good seeing you."

Brown didn't have a clue to the daily struggle that too many minority students faced just to stay on the right path. A week at the community center might open the man's eyes to the real world. Brown would, no doubt, cut his own throat before he did any volunteer work in the Detroit 'hood.

Charles was stopped several times by members of the staff and former students. It took longer than he expected to reach the main office.

"Hey, good-looking," he teased the school's secretary, Barbara Gardener, who was standing at the counter.

"I might say the same, Mr. Executive. Congratulations on the marriage."

"Thanks. Have you seen my bride?"

"You just missed her. She left for the day. Not feeling well. A bit of the flu is my bet. Everyone in my house had it last week."

Charles frowned. "Thanks, Barb."

"If you hurry, you might catch up with her in the staff parking lot."

"Okay. Take care."

Charles didn't pause to talk. He waved at familiar faces he saw as he moved through the crowded hall. Once he reached the back door, he spotted Diane. Her car was parked near the fence on the far side of the lot. Before he could call her name, he saw her struggling with a woman. What the hell? He started sprinting across the lot.

Twenty-two

"Lillie, please," Diane begged. "Get in the car! I promise I'll take you anywhere you want to go."

"You think I'm stupid, don't you? All of a sudden you're trying to be so nice to me. You trying to get me in the car so all your high-class friends don't see me? Well, I don't care who sees us. I ain't goin' anywhere with you. Give me some money! You little bitch!" She made a grab for Diane's purse.

"I told you I didn't have any. Let go!" Diane was starting to panic, scared one of her co-workers would see them struggling out in the open. "Just get into the car. We'll drive to the bank. Honest!"

"You think I'm that big a fool? You just want me to get in that car so you can take me to some hospital or one of those treatment centers. Hell, no! I don't trust you! Give me that!" She made a grab for Diane's leather briefcase. "You're rich, now that you've tricked some fool into marryin' you. He's keepin' your ass in that big, fine house. Think you better than me. You ain't nothin'! You're no different than me. Selling your body for the money he gives you. When you gonna stop pretendin'? We are the same. You came from my body! Mine! You little whore . . . whore!"

"What is goin' on here?"

Diane swung around in absolute horror, dropping her briefcase and purse. Lillie grabbed the purse and ran. Diane didn't know what to do. All she could focus on was her mother, and not the bewilderment in her husband's dark eyes.

"Stop her . . . please."

Charles gave Diane a hard look before he took off after Lillie. His long legs quickly eliminated the distance. He'd didn't need to listen to the woman's tirade to know that she was Diane's mother . . . the physical resemblance between the two of them was unmistakable. In spite of the ravages of time and hard living, Diane's mother was still a striking woman.

"Let me go, damn it!" Lillie fought him.

Charles held her as gently as he could. He, unlike Diane, ignored the curious onlookers.

"Who the hell are you?"

"Hush, Lillie. He's my husband. He won't hurt you," Diane said. "Please help me get her into the car." Diane discovered that she was way beyond mere embarrassment. Tears burned her lids, and her stomach was tangled into knots of pure fear. She was terrified of her husband's reaction. Now was not the time to focus on that, either. She had to be strong in order to deal with Lillie in the most effective manner.

Once they had her in the car and relatively quiet, Diane would have climbed behind the wheel if Charles hadn't stopped her. "Move over, I'll drive." His voice was taunt. "Where to?"

"Anywhere, as long as it's away from here!" Diane said between clenched teeth. She held her shaking hands in her lap.

They went a mile or so when Charles eased the car to the side of the road. "Well?"

"Sanderville Clinic on East Jefferson."

"No! I'm not going!"

"Lillie, you need help. You can't just keep going on like this. The people at Sanderville are very nice. They'll see that you have the best care."

"Hell, no! I'm not going to no dumb-ass rehab clinic. Let me out of here!" she yelled from the back seat.

Diane, flushed with acute embarrassment, gave a silent thanks for the two-door Buick. Charles's strong hands gripped the steering wheel with far more pressure than necessary. He managed to contain the furious questions and the outrage boiling inside him.

Diane sighed, knowing that even though Sanderville was a highly recommended private facility and they were willing to take Lillie, their hands would be tied without Lillie's consent.

"Her apartment is on Woodward in Highland Park," Diane finally volunteered, shivering from the cold glare he issued before easing back out into traffic.

The drive across town was the most uncomfortable Diane could remember. The only sound came from Lillie mumbling to herself about her rights while Diane fretted.

Lillie occupied the rear apartment in the older building. As they entered the dank, dark dwelling, the landlady stopped them before they reached Lillie's door.

"Ain't no sense in trying to get in. I had the lock changed this morning."

"You can't do that!" Lillie screamed, releasing a litany of swearwords.

"You haven't paid your rent in three months. I can do anything I damn well please. I figure that stuff you got in there is mine now." The plump older woman huffed indignantly, glancing at Diane. "Ain't you the gal came looking for her last week?"

"Yes. How much does she owe you?" Diane asked, searching for her wallet in her purse.

"Six hundred and seventy-five dollars."

Diane stared at the woman for a moment before her gaze swung to her mother. "How? How could you possibly owe so much?"

"I paid her last month," Lillie wailed like a wounded child. "She's lying! Bitch!"

"Who you calling a bitch! You're nothin' but an old drunk. Smelling like the inside of a bottle all the time. Don't know what you doin' half the time. Probably an old drug addict, too!"

Lillie swore profusely and the landlady joined in. Diane wanted to cover her ears and drop through the floor, more ashamed than she ever dreamed possible.

Charles stood behind Diane, a frown marking his dark features. He spoke with so much authority, both women immediately obeyed. "Both of you, stop this now!"

Diane was so rattled that it took her a few moments to realized she didn't have her checkbook with her. "I left my checkbook at home. I don't have that much money on me." She had no way of paying her mother's rent. What in the world was she supposed to do now?

Charles reached into the inside pocket of his suit coat and extracted a checkbook. He wrote out a check without comment, his mouth tight with suppressed emotions while Diane wished the earth would kindly open up and swallow her whole. She didn't want him to know about her mother, let alone about her supporting Lillie.

The landlady handed Charles the key without further comment and made a point of slamming the door in Lillie's face. Charles used the key to open Lillie's door but stepped aside for Diane and her mother to enter first.

Diane didn't think she could be more embarrassed, but one glance around proved her wrong. The one-bedroom apartment was in a shambles. It was only the second time Diane had been inside the apartment.

"If I had known you and your husband were coming, I would have straightened up." Lillie began picking up the scattered clothes, beer cans, and liquor bottles from the floor. Diane stared at her in disbelief. Her mouth nearly dropped open when Lillie actually giggled. "My baby's here with her man and my place is a mess."

Diane wanted to scream. Apparently, all this was to impress her new-son-in-law. "Sit down, Lillie. We're not here to be entertained," Diane snapped impatiently, wishing to die on the spot. Nothing could be worse than this, especially the not knowing what he was thinking. The cold fury she had seen in his eyes earlier was enough to convince her that the bottom had dropped out of her world. No, she must not think about that now. "About the clinic . . ."

"I ain't goin'," she said, slumping tiredly into an armchair already filled with clutter.

"You can't keep on drinking. Do you even have food in this place?" Diane asked impatiently.

"Ain't been hungry."

Diane sighed tiredly.

"Give me a few dollars, baby. I promise I won't ask for more. I won't bother you again, I promise. You know I love you. I didn't mean for him to find out . . . honest, baby. I won't go back to the house. I'll keep all my promises. Please, baby, don't be mad at me. Tell me you ain't mad? Tell me . . ." Lillie broke down and sobbed.

Diane had nothing to say.

"Tell her, damn it," Charles said between clenched teeth, his hands shoved into his pockets from where he leaned one shoulder against the wall.

Diane was too upset to feel anything beyond the despair weighing her heart down. Charles didn't have to say the words. She knew Lillie wasn't the only one in need of forgiveness.

"Diane!"

"I'm not angry. But I refuse to give you any more money. I won't support you if you don't agree to sign yourself into a rehabilitation center."

Diane didn't even wait for her husband. She went out the door and down the hall, intending to wait for him in the car. It no longer mattered if he was left in the room with Lillie. What more did she have to lose? She had already lost it all. Lillie had finally managed to ruin Diane's life as she had ruined Danny's and her own.

She waited nervously until he appeared and unlocked the passenger door of the car. "Charles . . ."

His gaze was frosty as he said, "We'll discuss this when we get home."

Emotionally exhausted, Diane climbed into the car, suddenly too drained to do more than lay her head against the headrest.

It wasn't until they'd reached the expressway that Charles broke the silence. "How did you find out about this clinic?"

"Heather recommended it. They have an excellent in-house facility."

"I see," he said tightly.

Diane didn't even notice the passing scenery. She didn't have a clue as to how to explain all this to her husband. There was no doubt in her mind that he would demand a full explanation once they were home. Charles made a brief stop at school to pick up his car.

"I'll follow you home," was all he said, as he got out of the car.

Diane's nerves were so rattled by the time they parked in their driveway that she would have preferred to spend the night in the car. Anything but face her husband.

Charles didn't open his mouth until they were in the family room, the double door closed. He walked to the liquor cabinet and poured himself a whisky neat.

Diane's eyes went wide with surprise. Charles very rarely drank anything more potent than beer.

"Why didn't you tell me about her? Why did I have to find out about her in the damn school parking lot?"

Diane had never seen him so agitated. His handsome features looked as if they had been carved into a bitter, angry mask. Trembling, Diane shook her head. "No, you aren't ready to listen with an open mind."

"I plan to listen to every damn word you have to say.

Neither one of us is leaving this room until you've said it all."

Diane rung her hands in frustration. "I don't even know where to start."

"Start with the truth! Start with the damn truth!" Charles snapped, feeling as if his heart had been ripped from his chest.

Diane was familiar with fear. It had been a part of her life for as long as she could remember. This was different . . . it was paralyzing. Even though she knew he wouldn't hurt her physically, Charles could devastate her emotionally . . . if he walked way from their love, their marriage. There would be nothing left to cling to . . . all the dreams would be shattered.

"How could you? All this time she's been right here in Detroit. How could you deny your own mother's existence?"

"Very easily." Although she knew she'd shocked him, she didn't look at him. She couldn't face him knowing that she must tell him everything. No, she could not look at him, for she could not bear to see the disgust . . . the disillusionment . . . and ultimately the abhorrence on his handsome face.

"I've spent most of my life pretending that woman, the one you met today, wasn't my mother." She lifted her chin before saying, "My earliest memory of her was of shame. She wasn't like the other kids' mothers. She was crude . . . flamboyant . . . a prostitute."

"What!"

"You heard me! You wanted to hear the truth, so shut up and listen!" Diane shouted at him, but she couldn't look him in the eye. She hugged herself as she sank into an armchair, her head down. Her voice was barely above a whisper when she said, "I thought she was beautiful, so perfect, although a four-year-old doesn't really understand that word. She had so many friends . . . all men. It wasn't until I started school that I learned she was different . . .

bad. That made me feel different . . . feel bad, like her. I didn't want to feel that way! It was horrible."

Diane didn't even glance his way as she recounted the past. "So I learned to keep secrets. Yes, some people do call it lying, but to me it was pretending. By junior high school I'd gotten quite good at it."

"Diane . . ."

"No, you wanted to hear this. So let me tell it . . . all of it."

Charles nodded, his body tight with tension and disappointment.

"There were happy times after my little brother was born. I loved Danny so much. Things weren't so bad, unless Lillie had been drinking or using drugs. You see, my mother was also a heroin addict. For the most part she kept the men out of the apartment . . . only when she was really strapped for money did she bring men home with her.

"When she was arrested and placed in rehab, Danny and I were sent to live with my mother's older sister. It was heaven for us. Finally, we felt safe. For the first time I learned how the rest of the world really lived, and I loved it. We went to church and made friends who could come over to play. It was crowded. Aunt Jean had five kids of her own to take care of." Diane almost smiled at the memory.

Her voice was without expression when she went on to say, "Once Lillie was released, we went back home. It took awhile, but before too long, she was once again dealing with the wrong people and making money the only way she knew how . . . by selling her body. Thank goodness, I was old enough by then to pretty much look after Danny and myself. I used to shop for our food on my way home from school and prepare our meals. As time went on, I took on more and more responsibility. I lost myself in my schoolwork and my books. I loved to read and daydream. Fortunately for me, I was an excellent student."

"Diane, why couldn't you share this with me?"

Diane didn't allow herself to respond, to feel, or she would have shattered like spun glass. She went on as if he hadn't spoken. "It was after Danny's death that Lillie stopped trying to be a mother. By the time I was in high school, it was dangerous for me to stay on with Lillie. She was bringing her men home at all hours of the day and night. I knew then I would have to leave."

"Diane . . ."

She knew she couldn't let her guard down. She couldn't respond to the pity she thought she heard in his voice. "I was sixteen. I've been on my own ever since. And I was very, very lucky. I was able to maintain good grades and a full-time waitressing job at night. After high school, I got lucky when I was accepted at Central State with a full academic scholarship. I also worked to cover my other expenses. I never had time to worry about the past. As you know, Central was where I met Heather. When I left Chicago for Wilberforce, I never looked back. I started a new life for myself. It was after college when I moved to Detroit and started teaching at Lawrence. The rest you know."

"No, I don't know, Diane. How could I? How did your brother die?"

Suddenly, tears distorted her vision. She wiped them hastily away. "Danny had cystic fibrosis. He died because we couldn't afford the medication he needed. Funny, how we had enough money for the drugs Lillie needed to maintain her high," she ended sarcastically.

"I'm sorry."

"Me, too. Danny didn't deserve to die. He was so young."

The brass clock on the mantel was the only sound in the room. Charles stared into the empty grate, trying to understand while attempting to ignore the keen sense of betrayal he felt. How could there be love without trust? Without love, what in the hell did they have? Diane sat nervously biting the tender flesh on the inside of her lip. There was nowhere to go . . . nowhere to hide from the shame she had tried so desperately to leave behind.

"Was it your idea for your mother to follow you to Detroit?"

Diane laughed with a marked lack of humor. "Hardly. I'd been in Detroit several years and I was feeling sentimental around the holidays. I sent my Aunt Jean a Christmas card with my return address. Lillie showed up on my doorstep before the snow had melted that year. The only good thing I can remember about her coming was that she was clean . . . no drugs or alcohol. She hadn't a clue about how to take care of herself without resorting to the old habit. So I got her an apartment and a job working in a nursing home. She kept that job about six months. It was the last time she worked."

"So you've been supporting her and lying to everyone you know about your absent mother," he said dryly.

Diane nodded. "As far as I'm concerned, I still don't have a mother. All I have is an obligation."

"Well, what are you planning to do about her? She's going down fast."

"I don't know. I just don't know. I can't make her get help if she doesn't want it."

"I see," he said quietly.

"No! You don't see." Her temper flared. She was tired of him judging her . . . tired of his lack of understanding. "You don't even know what it is to do without. You don't have a clue!" She was on her feet now, trembling from head to toe.

Charles was just as agitated as he paced in front of the fireplace. Abruptly, he stopped and came to stand directly in front of her. "Diane, this is not about me. It's about you. You're the one who didn't trust me enough to tell me the truth. I don't know what you call what you claim to feel for me, but it ain't love, that's for damn sure."

She still couldn't meet the challenge in his dark eyes.

She stared down at her tightly clasped hands when she said, "I love you with all my heart. You're not being fair!"

"Don't you *dare* talk to me about fairness or love. You possess neither. Hell, Diane, you can't even look me in the eye."

Diane heard the fury and hurt in his voice. He was right: she couldn't face him. Yet somehow, she had to make him listen. "Chucky . . ."

"Don't call me that!" Charles was so torn up inside that he couldn't bear to have her call him by the name she used when they made love. Love. Obviously it didn't have a damn thing to do with what had happened on board that cruise ship, or since, for that matter. How could she have married him when she didn't trust him enough to tell him the truth? She had promised that there would be no secrets between them.

"I'm sorry. I never meant for you to be hurt by this or embarrassed as you were in the school parking lot." Diane pleaded with him, "Please, honey. I nev—"

"You never meant to tell me!" he snapped, his hands balled into fists and his mouth pinched with anguish.

"I'm so sorry."

"Not half as sorry as I am, Diane." He slammed his glass down on the table so hard it broke. He didn't even feel the cut on his hand.

"Charles, please. Can't you try to see my side of this?"

"I've heard enough. I need time, and you don't have any other choice than to give it to me."

Diane's lips were raw from the way she'd been biting on them to hold back the tears. She refused to cry in front of him. There would be time for tears later.

Charles pulled on the black suit coat he'd thrown on the sofa earlier. "Just tell me one thing. Why did you trust Heather with all this, but not me? Why?"

"How did you know?"

"You told me in the car that Heather recommended the clinic."

"Oh."

"How long has she known? From the first?"

Charles stood near the door, waiting for Diane's answer.

"No! I only told her recently, when I became really concerned that Lillie might be using drugs again. Lillie started asking for more and more money, and she was drinking. I'd already given her money for her rent and living expenses. Charles, I had to get her into treatment. So I went to Heather for help." She could see by his expression that her revelation had caused him even more pain. "I'm sorry. I couldn't come to you with this."

"That's what hurts the most," he said, walking out.

Diane's knees were quivering so badly that she dropped down to the sofa before she fell. She curled her legs beneath her, listening to his feet as he climbed the stairs.

She was tired, so tired . . . beyond that, she was numb. Heather had been right. She should have told him all this herself. Perhaps, if she had followed him upstairs and kept right on explaining until he could see her side . . .

Diane wasn't sure how long she sat there disheartened. It was his footsteps in the foyer that alerted her to his presence. Her eyes went to the open double doors. Charles had a duffel bag in his hand.

"Charles." She reached the front door a few steps behind him. "Where are you going?"

His face was devoid of emotion, hard with purpose. "It doesn't matter. I have to get out of here."

"But . . ."

"I need to think. Sort this out for myself."

"Please, honey," Diane whispered, as her world tilted on its axis. "We can't solve anything apart."

"There is no 'we'. There is you, and there is me. There has never been a 'we'."

Twenty-three

Diane sat staring at the food on her plate. She couldn't seem to gain enough enthusiasm to lift the fork.

"May I get you something else?" Sheldon asked. When she didn't respond, he prompted, "Mrs. Randol?"

Diane was seated in the small breakfast area just off the large, cheery kitchen. She preferred its cozy comfort to the large formal dining room.

Sheldon patiently repeated his question, a bit louder.

"I beg your pardon," Diane said, flushed with embarrassment.

Once more he inquired about her appetite, eyeing the uneaten food in front of her.

"No. I'm not very hungry."

"Coffee in the family room?"

"Yes . . . please." Diane knew better than to offer to help. Sheldon would consider it an invasion of his domain.

Seating herself on the sofa in the family room, she absently focused on the logs stacked in the fireplace. It was too warm for a fire. She was surrounded by all the comforts of a real home. The irony was, this wasn't her home. It was not where she belonged. That was Charles's family portrait that graced the wall above the mantel. His desk and computer were in the small study down the hall. His pool table and pinball machines were in the recreation room. His books were on the shelves in the cozy library off the living room. He'd left it all behind in his effort to get away from her. Why hadn't he sent her away, instead? She was what didn't belong in his world.

Diane had come home this evening to find many of his personal belongings gone from their bedroom. She had been too sick at heart to even broach the subject with Mr. Sheldon. What was the point? No doubt she would end up crying herself to sleep tonight, an unfortunate habit of late.

She sighed wearily. The entire day had been a trial, her first one back at work after more than a week at home, grieving over the dissolution of her marriage.

She'd been a nervous wreck this morning, not knowing what to expect from her co-workers after the scene her mother had put on in the staff parking lot. Everyone had assumed she was out because of the flu bug sweeping through the school. Diane didn't dispute the claim. The most difficult times hadn't been because of inquiries about Lillie, but about Charles. Holding back tears time and time again, she'd given a vague response, then hurried away.

Diane barely noticed as Sheldon left a tray on the table next her. She moved to study the photograph of the two of them on their wedding day. They had been so happy then . . . so much in love.

Diane shivered, rubbing her hands up and down her arms. She wasn't really cold. She couldn't get used to being in this house without him. She found herself listening for his key in the lock. She wandered from room to room, feeling out of place. The only comfort she gained was in sleeping in their bed with his things around her. Most of the furnishings in the house had been in his family for years, except for those in the living room, where her things were mixed with his. Everywhere she looked she was reminded of him and what they'd once shared. It was all lost.

"Well, Elizabeth must be thrilled," Diane mumbled to herself, the words leaving a bitter taste in her mouth. Their separation was exactly what his sister had been hoping for from the first. She had made it clear that Diane wasn't good enough for her brother. It seemed time had proved her correct. "Oh, my love," Diane whispered, as she gazed at his face through the veil of tears clouding her vision. "I miss you . . . so much."

As the second week slipped into a third, Diane's hopes of reconciliation diminished. She went through the motions of living, but her heart wasn't in it. Mornings were the worst. She suffered bouts of nausea that often forced her to leave the haven that only sleep provided. At least when she slept, she didn't have to remember . . . didn't have to blame herself. And blame herself she did, from the time she got up to the time she went to bed.

As the weather warmed and the end of the school year approached, Diane found she was not looking forward to the summer vacation ahead. She tended to concentrate her thoughts on reliving their cruise . . . their honeymoon . . . their first few weeks of married life. She didn't allow herself to dwell on the accusations Charles had hurled at her. It was too painful.

Yes, she had lied to him. What choice had she had? He was a highly respected member of the community. How could she have told him the truth? The pretense had started so long ago . . . long before she'd even left home for good. In all honesty, Diane had never expected Charles to understand. Perhaps that was why she couldn't tell him.

The most surprising thing of all was that Charles's condemnations had been due to her lack of faith in him, not because of the circumstances of her birth. What he couldn't stomach was her lack of trust in him—that was what he couldn't forgive.

Well, she'd started a new life when she'd left home . . . a life where she could hold her head up with pride, where she could be considered an equal to her friends and coworkers. She could do it again! The trouble was, she didn't want a new beginning . . . what she wanted was her husband.

Damn! It wasn't her fault that the mother she'd left behind had followed her to Detroit. Not only had Lillie interfered with Diane's life; she had destroyed what it had taken Diane years to build. The love was gone.

Yet with each new dawn, Diane fortified herself with the hope that this was the day Charles would forgive her . . . come home to her . . . and every night when she went to bed alone, her heart would be filled with the bitterness of disappointment.

At the beginning of June, Diane was shocked to discover that all the household expenses, including the staff's wages, had been sent to Randol Pharmaceuticals. Charles not only maintained their household, but Diane's mother's expenses as well. Diane was overwhelmed with emotion. Charles was the only person who had ever taken care of her.

The mortgage on her condo had been paid outright. Diane now owned the property free and clear. Her husband had also deposited a hefty sum in her checking account, all without her knowledge or consent. The question uppermost in her mind was why, especially considering their separation.

There was no one to ask . . . no one to see her tears . . . no one to hold her close to his heart. Charles had, in effect, disappeared from her world, abandoned their dream of a shared future.

Diane considered moving out of their home . . . his family home. She couldn't make herself go, not yet. The move, when it came, would clearly signal the end. Emotionally, she wasn't ready to give up on their marriage. Despite everything, she loved him and couldn't let go.

One of the hardest tasks for Diane was to visit her mother. As time passed, she found herself wondering how Lillie was managing. The thought of her alone and out of control was frightening.

* * *

Lillie was as surprised to find Diane at her door one Saturday afternoon as Diane was to be there.

"May I come in?" Diane said formally.

"How you feelin', baby. You don't look too good." Lillie stepped back, allowing Diane to enter.

Diane blinked in dismay at the concern etched across Lillie's toffee-toned features. Lillie's eyes were clear. Her speech wasn't slurred, though her movements were somewhat unsteady. She wore a plain denim shirtdress and smelled of Ivory soap. For the first time in weeks, Diane found her mother sober and in control of herself.

"I'm fine," Diane said, her eyes traveling over the clean, orderly apartment. "I stopped to see how you're doing and find out if you had everything you need."

Diane made no effort to remove her wet raincoat and hat. She wasn't sure why she had come. She had expected to hate her after what had happened in the parking lot. She wanted to hate Lillie, but no matter how she tried, she couldn't. Maybe she felt sorry for Lillie? All Diane knew for sure was that she felt a certain measure of responsibility for her.

Lillie reached for her daughter's things. "Sit down. I'll make some coffee while you dry out. That rain been goin' all day. Don't seem as if it'll ever stop."

Diane was too tired to argue. She handed her things over without comment. But she didn't sit in the living room. Instead, she followed Lillie into the small kitchen. She sat at the tiny table wedged beneath the window. Every place she looked gleamed with care.

Lillie put water on to boil, explaining anxiously, "I only have instant."

"Doesn't matter."

Once her mother was seated across from her, Diane asked, "You're not drinking. What happened?"

"I don't know what ya mean."

"Lillie, I don't have the energy to play games. I haven't

heard from you in weeks. Then, when I come here, I find you looking like Mrs. Clean."

"What you mean is, you can't remember last time you saw me sober. I've gone back to the church and to AA."

"The church!"

"Yes. After what I did that day at your school, I knew I needed help. I was out of control that day. Thank goodness you didn't give me any money . . . I know I would have used it to buy drugs." Lillie clasped her hands nervously. "I'm tryin', baby, really tryin' to make it this time."

Diane stared at her for a moment. She didn't dare hope that Lillie had really changed. She'd heard it so many times before. Reluctantly, she said, "Congratulations."

Lillie shrugged, knowing her daughter had good reason for her doubts. She'd fallen off the wagon more times than she could count. Yet this time was different. This time she had not just hurt herself, but her baby, too. That she found intolerable.

"I'm gonna do it this time, baby."

"We'll see," was all Diane was prepared to say. They both knew the major test would come with time.

"I'm sorry . . . so sorry about the fool I made of myself in front of your husband. I don't expect you to forgive me . . ." she said, fighting tears. She took a deep breath before she forced herself to go on. "But I hit bottom, and I hit it hard. Please, believe the last thing I wanted to do was hurt you. Diane, I do love you, even if I've been a terrible disappointment to you."

Diane was too tired to even act on the anger inside her. She shook her head. "Doesn't matter now . . . none of that matters," she said, staring into the murky depths of her coffee mug. "I've lost the only man I ever loved. As far as I'm concerned, nothing else matters."

"You mean, your husband?"

"Yes, my husband!" Diane snapped, glaring at her mother. "He's left me."

"Oh, baby . . . no." Lillie's eyes were wide with pain and tears. "He seemed like such a fine man."

"He is a fine man. He paid your rent through the end of the month, didn't he?" Diane suddenly found herself defending Charles. No matter what he had said and done, she knew she could not stop loving him.

"But he hurt you!"

"No. I hurt myself, by lying to him. I should have told him the truth." All the old hurt suddenly welled up inside her. Diane lashed out, "Look, don't go acting all concerned. It's much too late for that. I learned the hard way that I can't depend on you. Unfortunately, Danny had to learn it, too. Only he wasn't as lucky as I've been."

"You still blamin' me."

It was as if the years had slipped away and she was still that same frightened little girl, left alone to cope with her beloved brother's illness and death. "No, blame is too gentle a word. I hate you for it. Never, ever can I forgive you for allowing my brother to die like he did . . . alone, with only me to hold him. You knew he was sick that night and you left us alone anyway. I was only a kid. But I was the one who took him to the hospital. Not you! Never you, Lillie!" Diane swallowed down bitter tears.

Lillie sat with her head bent, her shoulders hunched. She made no effort to defend herself as Diane heaped yet another accusation on her stooped shoulders.

"Why did you even bother to have us if you didn't want us?" When Lillie didn't respond, Diane shouted, "I have a right to know!"

"It don't matter now," Lillie whispered, her eyes brimming with tears. She was trembling so, she had to put her cup down on the table.

"It matters to me! It would have mattered to Danny."

"I'm sorry, baby . . . I'm so sorry. I love you, and I loved Danny. I didn't know how to be a good mother. I almost gave you up for adoption the night you were born. You were so tiny, so beautiful . . . I couldn't let you go."

"Why?" Diane was trembling from an enormous sense of disillusionment. "Why did you sell yourself? Didn't you want a decent life, if not for us, then for yourself? Didn't you think you deserved that much?"

Lillie looked at Diane, really looked at her beautiful, beautiful daughter, who looked as she herself had once looked a long, long time ago, before the alcohol and drugs, before the heartache.

"You've never asked me that before. You never wanted to know about me . . . my life."

"I've always wanted to know. I've always wondered," Diane mumbled, thinking of the pain and empty years separating them. "Why?"

"I didn't start out in the streets. I had a mother, a father. Parents who raised me and loved me. My father was a religious man, a minister, a devout Bible-carrying Baptist."

Diane was shocked, but she didn't interrupt.

"I was a good girl until I made the mistake of fallin' in love with the wrong man . . . your father."

"I honestly didn't know I had one." Diane wanted to laugh sarcastically. "Or rather, I didn't know you knew the man's name."

Lillie whispered, "I deserve that. But I loved him." She swallowed back tears. "I was so young. I remember the first time I saw him in church. He was so tall, so handsome. He was a deacon, a very important businessman in the community. A family man. But that didn't matter . . . nothin' mattered but the way he made me feel."

Diane listened, really listened, trying to visualize the images Lillie painted.

"I was sixteen and real shy. He began tellin' me how beautiful I was, buyin' me things . . . pretty things. I knew my folks would be furious if they found out. But it didn't seem to matter.

"I used ta meet him in the park behind our house. Tuesdays and Thursdays after school." She stopped suddenly, then swore. "I was so stupid, just a baby. I loved that man. And he started wantin' more than walks in the park. I would have done anythin' for him. He found us a place where we could meet . . . a tiny little studio apartment. I began sneaking out at night. One night Daddy came home from evenin' prayer meetin' early and caught me all made up. He hit me when I wouldn't tell him where I'd been or who I had met. When I wouldn't stop sneakin' out to see your father, Daddy threw me out of the house." She paused, then said, "Mama and Jean tried to help, but Daddy's word was law in that house."

Diane was stunned. She never thought of her mother as a girl . . . as someone's daughter. "How scary for you."

"I called your father. And he moved me into our little love nest. I quit school and devoted myself to him. Any time he could give me was good enough. It wasn't long before I got pregnant with you." Lillie laughed bitterly. "I was such a fool. I was so excited, sure he would leave his wife and marry me. I was so blind, so stupid. I was desperate when he refused. I wanted to marry before you was born. I threatened to tell his wife. That threat ended everything. He paid the rent for several months and left me with enough money to last until after you were born."

"What was his name?"

Lillie didn't hesitate. "John . . . John Harvey."

"Thank you." Knowing his name made him seem real to Diane for the first time. Her parents had actually had a love affair. All this time she'd assumed her birth had been nothing more than a result of accident.

Lillie went on. "By the time you were six months old, I was broke. I went to my parents. They wouldn't even talk to me. As far as they were concerned, they only had one daughter, Jean."

"That was wrong," Diane whispered, surprising them both.

"I really did try to take care of us. I took whatever work I could, but I had you. Baby, I loved you. I didn't want to give you up. I fell for the first guy who was nice to me after your father. He convinced me of what I had to do to survive. After a while it didn't seem so bad. I was usin' alcohol; it helped to make it easier. The more I drank, the easier it became. The rest you know."

"I wish you had told me long ago. Not that it changes anything, but it helps." Diane surprised her mother when she asked, "Why did you start drinking again?"

Lillie shrugged. "I got scared . . . thought I was losing you again. When you moved and wouldn't give me your number . . ."

Diane nodded sadly. Slowly, she got to her feet. "I brought you some money. I've also arranged for you to move into my condo. It's vacant and rent free, so you might as well take advantage of it." She didn't add that it was only a matter of time before she would be moving in, too. She didn't know how long she had before Charles would throw her out of his house, out of his life. Diane reached into her skirt pocket and dropped four hundred dollars on the table.

"I don't want your money."

Diane's head jerked up. "What?"

"I've got a job."

"Doing what?" Diane asked skeptically.

"As a clerk in a small bookstore downtown."

"You went out and got a job on your own?"

Lillie flushed. "I had help. The store owner called, said he was a friend of your husband's." Lillie said proudly, "I started workin' last week. I get paid on Friday. But more important, I like the work."

Diane didn't know what to say. She could see by Lillie's

face that she was waiting for praise. Finally, she said, "Congratulations."

"You mean it?"

"Yes. I wish you well."

"Thank you, baby girl. That means a lot to me to have your support."

"I have to go."

Lillie followed her to the door. "You forgot this." She held out the money.

Diane shook her head. "Use it toward moving expenses."

"No. For now, I want to work on one thing . . . stayin' sober." She pushed the money into Diane's hand, curling her fingers around it. "Will you come and see me again? Just to visit?"

Diane hesitated, looking into her mother's eyes for a moment. The substance abuse and passage of time had aged her beyond her years. But her dark eyes were filled with emotion . . . the warmth of which Diane wasn't sure she had ever seen before. After thirty-two years, it seemed she wanted to be her mother.

"Please?"

Reluctantly, Diane found herself agreeing before she hurried out.

Twenty-four

"Hey," Dexter said, as he took the barstool next to Charles.

Charles didn't spare the other man more than a glance, his attention returning to the nearly empty beer bottle in front of him. "What are you doin' here?" Charles asked, comfortable in the dank, dreary place. Although he had a purpose, hoping Eddie would show himself, the place certainly fit his mood.

"Looking for you." Dexter motioned to the bartender. "Give me the same as my friend here." Once they were alone, he said, "I—spoke to the kid's grandmother."

"Eddie?"

"Yeah."

"And?"

"Got an address. Thought you might want to go with me. Check it out."

"Let's ride," Charles said, tossing a bill down on the bar.

They decided Dexter's older model car would attract less attention than Charles's Jaguar.

"What did his grandmother say?" Charles asked, once they were under way.

"Usual. Eddie was really a good kid. He just never had been given a chance to prove himself."

Charles shrugged. "She's probably right. From what Jeff told me, the kid was a whiz in school. He got mixed in with the wrong crowd. Got caught up in that gang thing."

"It happens far too often," Dexter grumbled, as he slowed for a traffic light.

"We can't save them all, man."

"I suppose."

Luck was with them. They arrived at the two-story house on the northeast side of the city to find the place sealed off by police.

"What's goin' on here, Al?" Charles asked one of the officers who often volunteered at the community center.

"Drug raid."

Dexter and Charles exchanged a concerned look. They needed Eddie alive so that he could testify at Jeff's trial.

"What are you two doing here?"

"Looking for a kid, what else?" Charles said tightly, his eyes on the house.

"Anybody down?" Dexter asked.

"Two."

Charles swore impatiently.

"Hey, what's with you, Randol?"

"We can't help them, Al, if they're dead," Dexter said with a scowl.

They watched as several teenage boys were led out in handcuffs.

Dexter grinned and slapped Charles on the back. "That's Eddie in the blue shirt, man. Looks like the kid could use a lawyer," Dexter speculated.

"Sure does," Charles said, as they walked to the car. "Now all we have to do is let the cops know they need to hold onto this one. Let's get to a phone, man. We need to get Quinn moving on this one."

"Sure thing. The store owner's testimony should nail him."

They pulled into a gas station. Charles made the call while Dexter waited in the car.

"All set?" Dexter asked, when Charles had returned to the car.

"Looks that way. Quinn is on his way down to the precinct. This is the break we needed, man. Anthia will be thrilled."

Dexter nodded. "You going over there tonight?"

"I thought I'd wait until everything is in place."

"That'll work."

"Would you like to be the one to tell her?" Charles was careful to keep his gaze on the road ahead.

"I think you should do that, but I'd like to be present."

"Deal."

It was late when Dexter eased to a stop behind Charles's car.

" 'Night," Charles called. Instead of getting inside his car, he headed back toward the bar.

Dexter was right behind him. "What are you doin', Randol?"

Charles's brow arched. "What does it look like? I need a beer."

"What you need is to take your butt home."

Charles didn't comment.

"What's the problem, man?"

"No problem, brother man."

"For a guy with the world wrapped around his little finger, why you riskin' your neck? This ain't the new center area" Dexter said impatiently.

"It's my neck."

"Look, man, I don't want to have to scrape you off the sidewalk. These punks in this neighborhood don't play. Go home to that pretty little wife of yours."

Charles stopped walking and looked at Dexter then. His eyes were glacier-hard. "Mind your own damn business." He went inside, reclaimed his barstool, and ordered a brew.

Dexter sat down next to him. "I heard you have a new address. Trouble with your lady, man? My advice is to plead temporary insanity and beg her to take you back."

"I don't remember asking your opinion," Charles snapped. A muscle jumped in his jaw. He felt like pounding his fist on the bar. Instead, he tried to sip rather than down the beer.

"Well, you are gettin' it. Maybe, if I'd had a loyal woman like yours a few years back, I wouldn't have ended up in the joint. You're damn lucky, man. You got a special lady. Time to start concentrating on putting your life together."

Charles heard the concern in the other man's voice. He said tiredly as he rose, "Stay out of it, Dex. Night."

As Charles drove slowly back to the hotel, he knew he was no closer to getting past the hurt and disappointment than he had been the day he'd found Diane struggling in the school parking lot with her mother.

He'd have given anything to alter his steps on that fateful day when he'd discovered his wife's nasty little secret. He would have done anything to avoid the glaring truth that had smacked him in the face. It hurt like hell, discovering that Diane hadn't meant a word of the vows exchanged during their wedding. He had married a woman incapable of trust. She had lied to him from the day they had met. Why was he so surprised? She hadn't even trusted him enough to tell him the truth about her sexual history. He could have made it so much easier for her if he had only known she was a virgin. Yet, that had been part of the facade she had skillfully created for herself. The globe-hopping gay divorcée had been a brilliant explanation for her mother's absence and their apparent lack of closeness.

Her whole damn life was a lie. Apparently, she was not capable of recognizing the truth if it bit her on the behind.

His way of coping had been to increase his time at the community center and his hours at the company. He had very little time left to do anything other than sleep and eat. That was the way he preferred it. No time for regrets over the dissolution of his marriage. Yet the hours between bedtime and sunrise were the most difficult to endure. He spent many a night doing laps in the hotel pool until he was too tired to think when his head finally hit the pillow.

Even his sister had stopped asking what was wrong. He couldn't so much as hear Diane's name without hurting. Consequently, he flatly refused to discuss his personal life with anyone . . . not his family . . . not his friends . . . not anyone. He found it easier to keep the pain deep inside.

Unfortunately, his subconscious managed to lay claim to his thoughts. He would often find himself submerged in the pleasure of once again making love to Diane. His dreams were so vivid, so real, that he would wake shaking with need, her sweet taste lingering in his mouth, her tantalizing scent flooding his senses, his body painfully aroused, aching for her. Neither distance nor time was doing a thing toward eliminating his hunger for Diane.

He recalled the night he had given in to his loneliness. He had convinced himself that all he needed to straighten out his head was a willing woman. With the singular thought to get laid burning in his brain, he had entered the hotel's dimly lit bar.

"Hell," he had muttered to himself, wiping at the beads of perspiration dotting his forehead as he took a seat at the circular bar. He didn't have to wait long.

"May I join you?" A very attractive woman had asked.

"Certainly," he'd said, motioning to the bartender. "The lady needs a drink."

"Thanks," she'd said in a deep, sexy voice laced with a southern drawl.

He'd nodded, glad he had thought of it. Evidently he hadn't completely forgotten the knack of picking up a woman. "Where you from?"

"South Carolina. Is it so obvious?"

Charles had smiled. "Charmingly so. What's your name?"

"Sarah . . ."

"Nice to meet you. I'm Charles." Physically, she had been nothing like Diane. While Diane was tall and curvy, this lady was petite and slender, almost childlike. She had long, thick dark-brown hair and soft, pale creamy light-brown skin. Her eyes were large and dark brown, her mouth small.

"Are you waiting for someone?" she'd asked, pretending she didn't see the gold band on his left hand.

"No. How about you?"

"My girlfriend and I plan to have dinner in the restaurant. I'm early." She had crossed her shapely legs, bringing his eye downward. The smile she flashed his way was an open invitation. She wasn't the least bit shy. She soon had him laughing as she told him about her adjustment to big-city life. She was from a small town and claimed to just adore tall, dark, and handsome northern men.

When her soft fingers had caressed Charles's hand holding the beer glass, he had not pulled away. He'd stared down at her hand, finding the small, slender fingers with extremely long vividly painted nails unappealing. Her hands didn't look right against his skin. The tone hadn't been deep enough, the feel not soft enough. Her drawl, instead of being soothing to his ear, had gradually seemed to grate on his nerves. Her laughter had been shrill—too girlish, too silly. Even the shape of her mouth had begun to offend him. Her lips were full, the upper lip fuller than the bottom, lovely but not wide enough, not soft enough looking for his taste. Charles preferred softer rose-tinted lips with the bottom lip more succulent, fuller. Her perfume had been heavy, seductive, but it hadn't caused his pulse to quicken . . . the scent had been too potent, not the alluring scent of lilacs. He'd discovered he had no interest in what was beneath her short, tight black dress. Charles had scowled, realizing there had been absolutely nothing wrong with that beautiful woman. The problem had rested with him.

There was only one woman who suited him in every way,

only one woman who sent his senses soaring by a mere glance from her dark, sultry eyes. That woman had gained his name and his trust and his love, only to have crushed them beneath her three-inch heels. He knew then that he could not control his hunger for Diane any more than he could stop the flow of air filling and emptying his lungs.

Charles, much to his annoyance and his companion's surprise, had left the bar as he'd entered it . . . alone.

The only bright spot had been when Heather and Quinn had become the proud parents of two healthy, identical twin boys. Charles had stopped in to see Heather and the babies. He hadn't lingered as he once might have. He had not wanted to risk running into Diane. Even more, he had not wanted to discuss Diane with their closest friend. Thank heaven, Heather hadn't forced the issue.

Charles did not allow himself to wonder about Diane . . . to dwell on the possibility that she might be carrying their child. He had no idea whether she'd been able to convince her mother to admit herself into a treatment center.

As far as he was concerned, it was only a matter of time before Diane filed for divorce. When she did, she would find it remarkably easy, since he had no intention of contesting the divorce. She could have any damn thing she wanted, so long as she stayed the hell out of his life.

Twenty-five

"You're making a mistake, babe. Charles won't appreciate your meddling in his life."

Elizabeth's soft, dark eyes begged her husband to understand. "I have to try. Chuck is miserable. Since I can't talk any sense into him, maybe I can reach her."

"You've got to be kidding. Sweetheart, you'll be lucky if she doesn't slam the door in your face."

Her eyes filled with tears, but she lifted her chin. "Honey, I can't stand to see him like this. He's in so much pain."

Bernard took his wife into his arms. "I suppose it's worth a try. Do you want me to come with you?"

Elizabeth shook her head. "No, but I'm glad of the offer. Wish me luck?"

"You have that, and my love," he said, placing a tender kiss on her soft lips.

Diane's limbs were barely able to support her. She breathed a sigh of relief as she eased behind the wheel of her car. She still held the list of vitamins and eating instructions that the doctor had given her. It took all her energy to tuck it inside her purse. She had none left over to start the car.

She was in a daze. She couldn't believe it! She was pregnant! She and Charles were going to have a baby of their own. She wanted to laugh; no, she wanted to cry. She had done both in the doctor's office.

She had been too upset by their estrangement to pay attention to the changes in her body. It was the continued bouts of nausea that had forced her to take notice. She had to be certain, so she had made an appointment to see her doctor.

Well, it looked as if she and Charles had gotten one thing right. They had once been so confident in their love that they had decided to start their family without delay. They had created a precious new life. For the first time since the separation, Diane realized that she was happy. She refused to let thoughts of Charles diminish her joy. It was pointless to wonder what he would say or how he might feel about the news. She could not very well rush home and tell him. They no longer shared a home . . . they no longer shared anything.

As she moved to turn the key in the ignition, she paused. The sweetest memory flickered through her mind. Their last night in Saint Thomas had been magical. They had made exquisitely tender love. It had been thrilling, as all their loving had been on their honeymoon. It had also been so romantic. They'd been surrounded by the beauty of the island. Charles had taken his time in his efforts to pleasure her . . . they had found release together as one. The experience was unforgettable. Even later, when she lay against him while his arms kept her close, Charles had whispered how much he'd hoped he'd made her pregnant just before he'd gone to sleep. Could that have been the night they had made their baby?

Tears ran down Diane's face, even though she tried to hold them back. There was no stopping the flood of emotions. Her sobs didn't slow, and she was powerless to stop them.

"Oh, Chucky . . ." she sobbed, heartbroken. Eventually the storm of agony eased and she composed herself enough to put the car into gear. It was rush hour and the expressways were maddening. When she finally stopped in the circular drive, she was exhausted. Unfortunately, the long, emotionally draining day was far from over. Elizabeth's van was parked in the driveway.

"What now?" Diane said wearily, uncertain how much more she could take. Why was Elizabeth here? Had she come to gloat over her victory? Taking a few minutes to repair her make-up as best she could, Diane closed her compact with a snap, unable to do much about her swollen eyelids.

Sheldon opened the door before she could place her key in the lock. "Good evening, Mrs. Randol. I trust you had a pleasant day?"

"Good evening." Diane forced a smile, handing him her briefcase and purse. "We have guests?"

"Mrs. Bennett is in the kitchen with Mrs. Sheldon."

Diane nodded, smoothing the skirt of her coral silk suit as she slowly followed the central hall to the rear of the house.

Elizabeth, very much at home, was leaning against the gleaming counter, chatting to the elderly cook and housekeeper. Why shouldn't she feel welcome? This was her family's home. Diane was the one who felt like the outsider. Was she wrong to remain, hoping against hope that her husband would change his mind and return?

"Hello, Mrs. Sheldon, Elizabeth."

"Good evening, Mrs. Randol." Mrs. Sheldon reached for the kettle. "Would you care for a cup of tea?"

"Nothing for me, thank you." Her gaze swung to her husband's sister. As usual, Elizabeth was fashionable in a gray silk pant suit and white silk blouse. A rope of creamy pearls circled her graceful neck and diamonds adorned her earlobes. "Eliz, I wasn't expecting you."

"It's good to see you."

"I bet." Diane didn't try to conceal the sarcasm. Abruptly

deciding she just was not up to a confrontation, Diane said, "Excuse me," and turned on her heels. Let Charles's sister find her kicks somewhere else. Diane was tired of being her punching bag.

Hurrying after her, Eliz called, "Diane, wait. I'd hoped we could talk."

"Whatever for?" Diane asked, genuinely perplexed. They were in the foyer between the family room and the living room.

"Please. Can we sit down?"

Diane nodded, then reluctantly led the way into the elegantly furnished living room, the only room in the house that reflected her taste. "Have a seat."

Elizabeth looked around in surprise. "You've redecorated."

"We . . ." she started, then closed her mouth. There was no longer two of them. She was alone now. Diane dropped gracefully into the nearest armchair. "Have a seat."

"It's lovely," Elizabeth said, sitting on the sofa across from Diane. "Isn't it wonderful about Heather and Quinn? Have you seen the babies?"

Diane smiled for the first time. "Yes, they're beautiful." Then she said, "Look, we both know you aren't here to explore the old homestead or talk about mutual friends. Why did you come, Eliz?"

"Please . . ."

"I don't see the point in pretending." Diane crossed her arms beneath her breasts and her legs at the knees, and one foot swung agitatedly. "You don't like me, and furthermore, you decided before you even met me that I was wrong for your brother. You have never made a secret of it. So I really cannot imagine what you and I might have to discuss. Or is that why you're here, to tell me how pleased you are that Charles and I have separated? Or are you here because you want me out of your childhood home?"

Elizabeth didn't flinch at the unadorned truth. "No matter

what you think about me, please believe that above all else, I love my brother. His happiness means the world to me."

Diane didn't feel up to a debate. Nor did she feel the need to defend herself. She was tired. Once she had longed for this woman's acceptance and possible friendship, but not any longer. All she wanted now was to be left alone. She had so much to think about. She needed to decide what to do, now that she knew she carried their child.

"Would you please come to the point of this visit?"

Elizabeth shifted and her eyes flashed indignantly, but her reason for being had nothing to do with her own comfort. "I'm here because of Chuck."

Diane waited for the accusations and condemnations to rain down on her head. Surely that was her purpose in coming. Charles had evidently told her why they had broken up. Diane lifted her chin, refusing to appear as if she had some reason to be ashamed of the way she treated her husband. She had showered him with love. It was true that she had lied, but her reasons for doing so had nothing to do with her feelings for him. Why couldn't he see that?

"Chuck's very upset, Diane. I've never seen him so unhappy."' Elizabeth waited for a reaction. When none was forthcoming, she said impatiently, "Please, Diane, won't you call him? Maybe if the two of you could talk, you might be able to work it out."

Unable to remain seated a second longer, Diane went over to the picture window. She stared out at the perfectly groomed lawn. The sun would be setting soon. The empty hours of the night stretched ahead.

"It's worth a try. Don't you want to settle your differences?"

Diane turned and said, "Since you know the circumstances of our separation, then you know what you asked is impossible."

"Is that what you think? That Chuck has discussed your problems with me?" She shook her head vehemently. "I'm the last person my brother would confide in, especially after my gloom-and-doom prediction concerning your marriage. Knowing him, I doubt he would talked to anyone in the family or even his friends about what's gone wrong between you two. He's probably keeping it all locked inside."

"You don't know?"

"No. All I know is that my brother is in a bad way. Please, please, won't you consider taking him back? Even if you aren't willing to share your bed with him, can't you at least share the house with him? How are you two ever going to solve anything with him living in a hotel and you here?"

Diane tried but failed to slow the tears. They were in her throat when she said bitterly, "You have it all wrong. I didn't put him out of his home. He's the one who left me."

"You're kidding!"

"I wish I were."

"It makes no sense! My brother is crazy in love with you, Diane. That hasn't stopped because of a disagreement."

"Love isn't always enough." Diane mopped her tears with the back of her hands. "He can't forgive the lies . . . the secrets I kept about my past. To be perfectly honest, I don't even blame him."

Hearing the anguish in the other's voice, Elizabeth whispered, "I'm sorry. I thought . . ." Her voice trailed away. Thoughtful for a while, she eventually said, "If you two could just get together and talk about it . . . try to work it out."

Diane hugged herself, trying to contain the pain, the despair, filling her heart and tearing her apart. "If only it were that simple. Charles made his decision. I just have to learn to live with it . . . somehow." Feeling like she was about to collapse, Diane welcomed the support of the same armchair she'd found confining only moments ago.

Losing patience, Elizabeth said, "I don't understand you. Why aren't you putting up a fight? Why are you just giving up? Don't tell me you don't love my brother. Your feelings are as plain as the nose on your face."

Diane couldn't believe her ears. "Who do you think you are, coming in here, telling me what to do? I've had about as much as I can take of you, lady. You've never gave me a chance. You didn't even try to get to know me. Shall we cut the crap? I've as much use for you as you have for me."

"Go, girl!" Elizabeth laughed. "I deserve that, and worse. Diane, I'm sorry I've been so dense. Stubbornness is apparently a family trait. I'm just realizing how foolish I've been by not trusting my brother's judgment. Chuck made himself quite clear when he married you. He loves you." She hesitated before saying, "I was wrong not to welcome you into the family. I'm apologizing for it. Can you forgive me, Diane?"

"I don't believe this!" Diane said, shaking her head.

"I don't believe it, either, but I'm woman enough to admit when I've made a mistake."

"Eliz, you don't even know what really happened between us."

"We all make mistakes. If Chuck wasn't being so pigheaded at the moment, neither of you would be so miserable. You two love each other. You should be together."

"You're wrong, Eliz, none of this is his fault." Not so very long ago, Diane had desperately wanted his family to accept her. It should be laughable, only she wasn't the least bit amused. Here Elizabeth was, finally welcoming her into the same family her husband was throwing her out of. How long did she have before he started divorce proceedings?

"I love my big brother with all my heart, but he's not sporting a halo."

Diane studied her, really studied her dark eyes. What she saw there made her ask, "You mean it, don't you?"

"Yes, I do. I thought you were trying to take advantage

of my brother. I was wrong, I can see that now." Elizabeth said softly, "I hope you and I can start over."

"Do you always change your mind so unexpectedly?"

She giggled. "Occasionally. We're sisters now, and sisters stick together."

Suddenly, Diane wanted to share her news, share it with someone who would be as thrilled as she was. Elizabeth was his sister. The situation being what it was, Diane could not take the risk of him finding out about her pregnancy. He had to be told eventually, but not yet. She still hadn't had time to adjust to the news herself.

"I appreciate your wanting to help. Charles was correct about me all along. Because I didn't trust him, I ended up hurting him . . . badly."

"So you're just going to give up?"

"This is not a contest, Eliz. This is my life we're discussing." Diane started crying. The tears came quickly.

Her sister-in-law didn't hesitate to offer a comforting shoulder. "There . . . don't cry. It's going to be wonderful again. You'll see."

Diane cried her anguish out, letting all the fear pour out. She was babbling by the time she said, "I never meant to hurt h-him. I just didn't want anyone to know about my m-m-mother."

"Diane, you don't have to tell me," Elizabeth said, handing her a tissue.

"I know. You might as well know the worst," Diane said, then recounted that horrible day at school. When she ended, Elizabeth's shock was written all over her face.

"Oh, Diane. I'm so sorry. It must have been horrible for you, feeling as if you had to keep all this hidden."

"I grew up pretending that Lillie was like my classmates' mothers . . . always pretending. You were right. We made a terrible mistake by rushing into marriage. Probably all the moonlight and sea air," Diane ended unhappily.

"You're not responsible for who your parents were . . .

none of us is," Elizabeth said, clasping her hands with Diane. "I can't believe my brother has turned into a snob. He has always been so opened-minded."

"He's not a snob!" Diane was quick to defend him. "He was furious, but not because of my mother. He can't forgive me for not having faith in him . . . not telling him the truth."

"What now?"

"I don't know. I just don't know."

"Maybe I can talk some sense into him?"

"I can't let you do that," Diane said quickly, amazed that Eliz was taking the secret that had tormented Diane's life in stride. No one she cared about had reacted as she'd expected . . . not Heather, not Elizabeth, and especially not Charles. How could she have been so wrong? How could she have misjudged them so?

"I'm not asking permission."

"No! It will only make things worse."

Not wanting to upset Diane more, Elizabeth finally nodded her agreement. "I know I have no right to ask, but I'd really like it if we could be friends."

Diane smiled. "Yes, let's try."

The two hugged.

"We'll work on the sister part, okay?"

"Agreed." Diane nodded.

"I'm hungry. Let's raid the refrigerator," Elizabeth giggled, pulling Diane along with her.

During dinner, Diane was unable to contain her joyful news. Her eyes sparkled with excitement when she told Elizabeth about her pregnancy.

Elizabeth squealed with pleasure, giving Diane a hug. "Congratulations! Chuck will be ecstatic!"

Having lost her smile, Diane said apprehensively, "Maybe . . . but I don't plan on telling him. That is, not until he has made a decision about our marriage. If he wants a divorce, I'm not going to try and fight it."

Horrified by the possibility, Elizabeth was about to argue the point when Diane interrupted. "I don't want him back because of the baby. If you were in my situation, would you want that?"

"No, I wouldn't want that, either."

"Promise me you won't tell him about the baby," she insisted.

"Of course I won't tell. That's something that should come from you." Determined to help, Elizabeth said, "Thanks for sharing the news with me. I just wish that somehow the two of you could make things right between you. You both love each other too much to be apart like this. Think about it. How long will you be able to keep your pregnancy a secret?"

"I'm not going to hide it from him. Oh, Eliz, I was so excited today when I left the doctor's office. I wanted so badly to share the news with Charles. I can't. I don't even know where he's staying. He could have moved in with one of his old girlfriends, for all I know."

"He's downtown, at the Omni."

Diane blinked in surprise. "You shouldn't be telling me this. If he wanted to be with me, he'd be here at home, where he belongs, not living it up in some hotel. Damn him!"

"Nothing can convince me that he doesn't wants you. There is only one sure way of find out, my dear."

"Forget it! I already know how he feels."

"Prove it." When Diane would have interrupted, her sister-in-law said, "Go to him . . . talk to him. Tell him how you feel. This time, make him understand why you did what you did."

Diane dropped her gaze to her lap, where she been twisting the linen napkin. She carefully smoothed it out as if the task was extremely important. Finally, she said, "I don't think I can."

"Forgive me for being stupid, but aren't you the same

woman who boarded a ship for the Caribbean determined to go after the one man you loved? You're going to tell me a few months later that you're ready to give up on that love while you're nurturing his child in your body? Please! Girl, you're still wearing his ring on your finger. You took a big risk once . . . you can do it again."

"What if he can't forgive me?"

"Then try again and again. Personally, I don't think he's going to be able to get around his feelings for you," His sister ended with a confident grin.

"I hope you're right."

"Are you going to try?"

"Yeah."

Twenty-six

Charles was so tired by the time he passed through the hotel lobby, all he could think about was a hot shower and bed. The day wasn't unlike the one before it. He'd managed to get through many such days since moving out of his home.

His brow was creased in a frown as he waited for the elevator. Elizabeth had tried again today to talk to him about his personal life. She'd been hurt by his abrupt refusal. Why didn't she mind her own damn business? She had a life of her own. Why didn't she concentrate on driving her husband crazy?

Talk about a rotten day, he'd even gotten into a disagreement tonight with Dexter after the executive board meeting at the community center. Privately, Dexter had suggested that if Charles went home and made love to his wife, it might improve his disposition considerably. Charles saw red. Only their longstanding friendship had kept Charles from decking the guy. Man! Why didn't everyone leave him the hell alone?

His eyes didn't even linger on the opulence of his surroundings as he let himself into the suite. He was acutely aware that an impersonal professional had remade the bed and tidied the bathroom. Everything would be in its place. There would not have been love or affection involved in the action. Not a single throw pillow was out of place in the living room. Only his clothes hung in the roomy closet, only his toiletries graced the dresser top, and his was the only head that would eventually disturb the pillows on the king-sized bed. In the weeks he'd occupied these rooms, he'd come to detest everything about them.

As he stripped off his clothes, he purposefully left them in a chair, hoping to add a lived-in feel to the bedroom. He exercised strict control over his thoughts, not permitting them to wander. He'd gotten quite good at it, especially during the daylight hours. It wasn't until the wee hours of the night that his control would vanish and his hunger would surface. His dreams were full of Diane. When he woke each morning, his arms were as empty as when he'd fallen asleep.

Charles had just soaped himself when he heard the knock on the outside door. He swore softly, pausing to let the heated spray run over his tired body before shrugging into a burgundy terrycloth robe. His feet were soundless on the thick carpet as he crossed to the door.

Diane tried not to be thrown by the unrelenting fury burning in his dark eyes. Her heart raced as she drank in the sight of him and her nostrils flared as she inhaled the clean male scent of him. Oh, how she missed him.

"Hello, Charles. May I come in?"

"What are you doing here?"

"So much for small talk," she said, her voice edged with sarcasm. "I should have called, but I was uncertain of how I'd be received, so I decided not to risk it. May I come inside?"

He stepped back, keenly aware of her beauty. The pink knit dress complimented the soft curvy lines of her body and the smoothness of her complexion. What had she done to herself? His experienced eye took note of the subtle changes. Her skin seemed to glow with an inner richness. Her thick hair had recently been cut and shaped. Her soft mouth was covered in a luscious rose shade, while her dark, long-lashed eyes seemed larger. There were shadows beneath her eyes which spoke of a recent lack of sleep. She was thinner and even more beautiful than the photograph he carried inside his head.

Diane's gaze was equally hungry as it ran over him. His shoulders seemed wider and his waist leaner. He looked as if he'd lost weight. His legs were just as long and well-muscled as she remembered. She forced back tears as she recognized how desperately she needed him in her life. Instead of launching herself into his arms, she nervously inspected the spacious living room. Eventually, she had no choice but to face him. Lifting her chin, she said, "I'd hoped we could talk."

"Have a seat. It won't take me a moment to throw on some clothes." Charles didn't bother closing the bedroom door. He pulled on a pair of faded jeans and a white cotton T-shirt. Diane didn't hear him when he reentered the room. His feet were still bare. He found her standing in front of the window, gazing down at the street far below.

Why had she listened to Elizabeth? She was wrong to come here. He was still clearly furious with her. He wasn't ready to hear anything she had to say. Nothing had changed in the weeks they'd been apart. Just looking around she could see he had all the comforts of home. The man hardly looked unhappy to her.

Diane spun around when she heard the fizz of a beverage cap being twisted off. Charles stood at the breakfast bar where a small refrigerator had been built into the base.

"Sorry, I only have brew. Care for one?" He lifted the narrow-necked bottle to his lips, taking a deep swallow. His eyes never left her face.

Diane couldn't fail to miss the way his jeans hugged the masculine lines of his hips and his undershirt stretched over his broad chest. "Nothing for me." She took a deep breath before she said, "I suppose you're wondering why I'm here. I owe you an explanation . . ."

"You owe me a whole lot more than that!"

"I never meant to hurt you."

"How do you think I felt when I learned that not only did my wife lie to me, but that she had more trust in our best friend than she had in me? How do you think that made me feel?"

Pure rage and raw emotion poured out of him like an open bloody wound. "Look, your coming here wasn't such a hot idea. I can't discuss this calmly. I'm still too damn pissed." Charles was careful to put the bottle down before he flung it against the door. His hands were shaking. In spite of his fury, in spite of everything, his senses were sizzling with hot, pulsating desire. He was erect and aching with need.

"Chuck, please, believe . . . I am truly sorry. I never meant to hurt you. Never!" Diane said, her throat choked with tears. "I was trying to protect myself . . . not hurt you. I love you."

"Don't! Don't talk to me about love," he said, slamming his fist down on the top of the bar. With quick strides he was in front of her and jerking her into his empty arms. His mouth settled over hers, hard and insistent. He tasted the salt of her tears; he sampled the sweetness.

Diane didn't even consider pulling away. This was where she belonged. Sparks flew as his tongue sponged over her lips, parting them and sliding deep inside to stroke her tongue. His tongue was like velvet, exquisitely rough while being wondrously soft and deliciously wet. She quivered from head to toe, pressing her aching breasts into the muscular wall of his chest as his sensuous assault on her mouth continued.

Suddenly he tore his mouth away, furious with himself for losing control. His voice was rough with impatience when he said, "Go home, Diane. Tonight isn't the right time."

"When is the right time? I haven't seen you in over a month. Tell me when." Pride be damned, she didn't have any when it came to this man. He was her heart, and she was dog tired of their separation. "Come home, Chuck. Please."

Charles's hands were deep in his pockets. He rocked back and forth. His sex was thick and uncomfortable pressed against the fly of his jean, throbbing with unfulfilled longing.

"I said not tonight!"

"We need to talk."

He spoke through tightly clenched teeth. "At the moment, all I can think about is how soft your mouth is and how hard I am."

If he thought to shock her, he'd failed. Diane missed him desperately. She hated that he was doing his utmost not to give in to his desire. He'd rather pretend he didn't have any feelings for her.

"I've missed being with you, too," she whispered.

Charles fought the power of his desires. "Sex has never been a problem for us. We've always been good between the sheets, Diane. Our difficulties start when both feet hit the floor. You lied to me, damn it!"

"Stop it! Stop pushing me away. You're determined to punish me for hurting you. We can't make things right between us this way!"

"What will make it right? More lies?"

"Just listen to what I have to say. Please . . ." Her eyes were brimming with tears of grief and fear.

Charles released a rush of air from his lungs before he relaxed his body and moved to an armchair. He sat down, propping one leg over the other as if he'd resigned himself to hearing her out.

Diane's stomach twisted into a ball of tension as she tried to sort out her thoughts. When she finally spoke, her voice was only a notch above a whisper, "I've been hiding the truth about my life since I was in elementary school. It's been so long that it has become second nature to me. You have no idea what it was like growing up, being so different from all the other children in school. I wanted so badly to be accepted. I learned early not to tell anyone how we lived. That was my way of coping."

"You should have told me the truth."

"Yes, I realize that now. I was afraid . . . afraid you wouldn't feel the same way about me. I'm sorry, Chucky . . . so sorry," she whispered, looking into his dark gaze. She had no way of knowing what he was thinking.

It was Charles who said, "Tell me what it was like for you."

Diane laughed, a raw, pitiful sound. "Lillie never allowed us to call her mother. She was correct. She was never a mother to either one of us." As the years seem to slipped away, the fear returned. Tears rolled unchecked down her cheek. "Did I tell you how I was with my brother when he died? I couldn't find her, Chucky. It was awful. I knew how desperately ill he was, and I was so scared . . ." Diane wasn't even aware of the tears. "I was the one who took him to the hospital. I was a kid myself. Alone . . . so alone. Yes, I still resent her for it . . . I can't help it. I'll never forget how it felt to be holding him when he took his last breath."

Charles scowled, as he listened with not just his ears, but his heart as well. He couldn't imagine the kind of despair and fear she'd faced as a youngster. He, too, had lost his mother at an early age, but she had always been a proper mother to him and Elizabeth. They'd never had reason to doubt her love. After she was gone, Aunt Helen was there for them. It was his father and his Uncle Alex who'd taught him what it was to be a man. It was his Aunt Helen who'd taught him how to love and how to trust. Diane had never had an Aunt Helen.

His heart wrenched as he saw the anguish in her dark, beautiful eyes. He wondered if she was even aware of the stream of tears that rolled down her soft cheeks. She'd faced so much alone, including his rage. That realization tore at his heart. Purposefully, he rose and went quietly over to her. He settled her against his chest She was right . . . he'd never even come close to walking in her shoes. How could he judge?

Suddenly he understood why it had taken so long for her to allow him to get close to her. Charles recalled the empty years of loving and wanting this woman. It was a miracle that she had been able to trust anyone with her tender emotions. She had eventually trusted him with her love . . . trusted him enough to risk marriage.

"Shush, baby," he whispered, stroking her back. "It's over. You don't have to tell me any more."

Diane shook her head. "I need to finish . . ."

Charles used the hem of his cotton shirt to dry her face, not certain he could bear to hear more of her suffering.

"After Danny died, things deteriorated even more between Lillie and me. I was growing up, and it became increasingly difficult for me to feel safe in my own home. My mother was so out of it, caught up in drugs and the men that were necessary to support her habit, that I'm not sure she even knew what I was going through."

Diane shuddered. "One night I woke with one of her men in my bed. His hand was over my mouth as he tried to pry open my legs. I was so scared. I couldn't breathe . . . I couldn't think. I fought him. I'm not sure how I got far enough away from him in order to get the baseball bat I kept hidden under my bed. I hit him and kept right on hitting him until he let me go. I remember screaming and screaming until he left the apartment. After locking the door, I ran into my mother's room, crying hysterically. She was passed out cold on her bed. I'm not sure if it was from the alcohol or the drugs. All I know is that she didn't move. She would have died that night if I hadn't called for help."

Horrified, Charles held her protectively close, soothingly caressing her shoulders and back. "How old were you?"

"Sixteen. I couldn't take it anymore. I left while she was in the hospital. I had to go. I wanted a decent life for myself."

"How did you survive on your own? How come you weren't placed in foster care?"

"I lied about my age. I took a room at the YWCA and I stayed in school and out of trouble. I used to study during the day and waitress at night. I was very lucky. I was able to get modeling jobs. I looked older. My boss at the diner didn't know or care how old I was. All he cared about was that I was reliable. He had illegals working for him because he paid in cash. I made enough to keep my room and keep myself in clothes. I had my biggest meal at the diner. I studied or slept whenever it was slow. I saved my tips. I was very careful not to let anyone from school know I was living alone. All my records had my old address until the end of my senior year."

"You were lucky to finish high school, but to go on to college! It's unbelievable. You beat the odds, baby." He shuddered when he said, "So many bad things could have happened to a teenage girl on her own."

"My life turned around when I won that scholarship to Central State. I was always a good student. I worked my tail off to keep my grades up. I just wish Danny could have made it, too. He deserved a decent life."

"Yeah, he did." Charles slowly digested all she'd told him. He'd heard it before, but this time he'd understood . . . this time he was able to keep his own sense of betrayal out of it.

"I'm sorry, baby, that you had to go through this. For too many years you've had no one to depend on but yourself."

"I used to feel sorry for myself because I didn't have the life you and Heather had growing up. Now I realize that there's nothing for me to feel sorry about. The experience made me the person I am today. It has made me strong. I learned how to take care of myself."

His voice was gruff with emotion when he said, "I'm proud of you, baby."

Diane lifted her head until she could look into his eyes. That declaration meant the world to her. It was the first time anyone had ever said those words to her. It filled her heart with sheer joy. "Thank you."

"Now, I can fully understand why you never let any man get close to you. You never had a reason to trust men."

Looking deep into his dark eyes, she said, "Trust has always been difficult for me. But I'm learning . . . I swear, honey, I am learning."

"Yes, you've proved that tonight."

"Chuck, the lies I told you weren't designed to hurt you. You must believe that. I've been so scared of anyone finding out about my mother. I tried to bury everything that reminded me of the past. The one reminder that I couldn't change was my looks. I look like her . . ." She bit her lip. Her eyes were wide with dismay. "I hate looking like her. I'm not like her . . . I'm not."

"No, you're not, baby. Her shame is not yours." He sensed how important his reassurance was to her.

"I was a coward. That's why I never told you about Lillie. I couldn't bear it if you looked at me differently, if you lost respect for me or if you no longer wanted me." Tears brimmed over and spilled down her cheeks.

"Don't . . ." he said, rocking her until she calmed.

Diane snuggled even closer, her soft breasts pillowed against his chest, her face buried against his throat. It took all her courage to ask, "Please, can . . . can . . . can you ever forgive me?"

Charles sighed heavily, struggling to focus on anything but her softness. Oh, how he had missed her. He knew they were at a critical point in their relationship. Despite the depth of his feelings for her, he couldn't just dismiss what she'd done.

He was silent for so long that Diane, unable to bear the escalating tension, whispered, "Honey?"

"It isn't a question of forgiveness," he said evenly, dropping his hands to his sides and easing away from her.

He couldn't think with her in his arms . . . all he could do was feel. Charles needed a clear head. Although they weren't touching now, they maintained eye contact.

"More than anything I want our marriage to work. Hey, I know I've contributed to our problems. I've made some bad mistakes, too. My jealousy of your past friendship with that guy on the phone was really stupid. It caused a rift between us before we could even establish our married life together." He paused, absently rubbing the evening stubble on his chin. "Di, I'm sorry about that. It has taken me a while to get past my jealousy and start using my head. Logically, I knew that if you wanted to be with that guy you'd have stayed in Detroit and never boarded that cruise ship in Miami. Nor would you have put up with me flinging one nasty accusation after another at you when we met aboard the ship."

"Chuck . . ."

"No, please, let me finish. Only now am I able to recognize the significance of you loving me enough to move beyond the horrors of the past. If your feelings for me weren't deep, we could have never reached the level of intimacy we have."

As Charles sorted through his ambiguous emotions, Diane fought to hold onto her dreams. Because of their feelings for each other, they both had the ability to twist each other into emotional knots.

When he said, "Di, I need to say this and I especially need for you to really hear me," her heart started pounding with dread. Instead of continuing, he stood and began pacing. Diane was close to tears once more when he stopped and said, "I love you, but what kind of marriage can we have if we don't have complete faith in each other?"

"I have faith in you."

"Enough to turn to me in the bad times? That's what I need, Diane. Hell, you think I don't know I'm the one who rushed you to the altar? It was wrong. We needed more time to get to know each other. We needed to find out what we both wanted from marriage."

His voice held so much regret that she gasped his name aloud while fear rose in her throat.

"We've been apart for a while. Perhaps we should take more time so that we can really think this thing through."

Twenty-seven

"No!" She bit down hard on her lip, determined to stop crying. She needed all her wits about her now. She was fighting for her marriage . . . for her man. Diane stood in front of him, her head held erect when she said, "My living at the house and you being here is not solving anything! Honey, please. We're talking now, listening to each other. Chucky, I trust you. I have absolute faith in you. I wouldn't have come here tonight if I didn't. I promise . . . no more secrets."

Charles ached to hold her. She had finally said what he'd been longing to hear, yet so much had still been left unsaid. He took her hand and led her back to the sofa. They sat side by side, but he no longer touched her. "Tell me what you need from me."

Diane worried her fleshy bottom lip with her teeth as she concentrated. She loved him so much and wanted to stay married to him more than anything else in the world. Yet she didn't know what could halt the downward spiral they seemed to have fallen into.

Charles, feeling vulnerable and emotionally exposed, wasn't encouraged by Diane's silence. When he began to rise, she circled his waist. "Don't, please . . . this is all so new for me. I hadn't even seen the kind of relationship you're describing until I was an adult, and only then from the outside, looking in. I never had anyone to share my most intimate thoughts with before you . . . never lived with a man and certainly never trusted one . . . not until I fell in love with you. I don't want to lose you."

Charles couldn't help himself. His arm went around her and he allowed himself the pleasure of caressing her soft nape. Finally he said gruffly, "I'm willing to give you all the time you need, Di."

She shook her head. "By time, you mean continuing to live apart? No, Charles. I hate not being able to be with you . . . sleep with you."

"So do I," he confessed.

"But you're the one who left. You left me!"

"I know that!"

"You're still angry with me. I can hear it in your voice," she accused softly.

"I want us to be a unit, a family where everyone else is on the outside. I want us to be best friends, lovers, and soulmates," he insisted.

"I want that, too," she said, staring at her hands, afraid to meet his gaze. "I'm sorry I didn't handle things differently. Our time apart has forced me to face things about myself I don't like very much. I don't know if I can be the way you want me to be. All I know is that I love you with all my heart and I respect you. Honey, I need you in my life . . . you're the one who makes my life worth living."

Charles waited, his heart pounding loudly.

Diane looked deep into the depths of his eyes when she whispered, "When I was a little girl, I daydreamed about someday meeting a special man like you. A decent, honest man who genuinely cared about people. A man who would love me . . . really accept me as I am. I longed for 'happily-ever-after.' I suppose that because I spent so many years too afraid to even reach out it has affected our marriage. I've had time to think. I'm not afraid anymore, my love."

"From now on we'll face our problem together?"

"Yes . . ." she murmured, brushing her soft mouth along

the deep grooves in each cheek, then she touched his wide mouth, tracing its bold contour with the tip of her tongue. "I've missed you."

His reaction was immediate. His breath quickened, his nostrils flared, and his heavy shaft throbbed, readying to join his body to hers. Charles closed his eyes briefly, savoring the sweetness of the caress, yet not allowing her to deepen the kiss. There was no room for misunderstanding, especially with their entire future hanging in the balance.

"Not so fast." His voice was rough, thick with desire. "You haven't answered. What is it you need from me?"

Suddenly feeling more confident and more courageous than ever before, she boldly answered, "I want us to spend more time together . . . away from work, the community center, and other people. Just the two of us."

Charles nodded, his smile easy, engaging. "Yes, if we put our heads together, I think we can arrange that. You're right, we didn't spend nearly enough time together. This summer, would you consider teaching a computer class at the Community Center?"

Diane smiled, nodding.

"Now, Mrs. Randol," he said, dropping his gaze to her beautiful mouth, his heart pounding wildly in his chest. "I interrupted you earlier."

Diane laughed, wrapping her arms around his neck. She flicked her tongue over his bottom lip. He sighed heavily at the action, causing a shimmer of heat to flood her senses. As he parted his lips, opening for her, she moaned, sliding her tongue into the moist haven of his mouth. She licked the sleek inner lining, exploring the hard, cool surface of his teeth before dipping her tongue deep inside to rub against his tongue again and again. Diane licked him until he growled his enjoyment, their tongues dueling until, unable to bear it any longer, he urged hers into his mouth to suckle. She was much sweeter than any candy. The flaming heat he generated caused her nipples to pucker into hard peaks. She rubbed her breasts into his chest, annoyed by the cloth that separated them.

Charles took one kiss after another, the thrusting of his tongue inside her mouth a prelude to the eventual thrust of his sex into her tight, wet sheath.

"I love you," he said, his mouth settling at the base of her throat. He licked her skin as his hands cupped and squeezed her soft, full breasts. Diane's breath quickened even more; her eyes were closed in order to savor the pleasure of his touch.

"Oh, baby, I've missed you . . . so much," she said, as she moved her hands beneath the hem of his T-shirt to caress the smooth, warm expanse of his back and shoulders. She cried his name when he squeezed the hard tips of her breasts. Even through the barrier of her dress she could feel the heat . . . a heat that only he could generate within her.

Charles groaned his frustration. Unable to wait a second longer to feel her soft skin against his, he yanked down the zipper at her nape. Within mere seconds, he'd eased the material down her arms until the bodice had dropped to her waist.

Diane's heart fluttered in her chest as she watched his dark eyes smolder with hot flames. She wore the lacy red teddy he so admired. The silk didn't conceal but rather draped the lush swells of her breasts. He dropped his head and flicked the upper curve of her breasts, warming the valley between them before moving to draw an elongated tip into his mouth. She cried out in pleasure. He created such a marvelous suction that she could feel the sensation all the way down to her toes. Diane gasped, feeling as if her insides were melting as the erotic caress continued. She wanted to scream in frustration when he stopped.

"Please . . ." she begged, arching her back, offering him even more of her softness.

Charles overlooked the insistent pressure against the teeth of his fly as his body pulsed, matching the rhythmic beat of his heart. Determined to give her absolute pleasure, he peeled the fabric away from her body until she was exposed to his eyes, his mouth, his hands, his hard masculinity.

"Please, what?" he said huskily. "Tell me what you've missed the most."

"I've missed making love with you." She stopped, embarrassed to say more.

"In what way, sweet cheeks?" he teased, squeezing her fleshy bottom.

Diane exclaimed, blushing even more, "Charles!"

"Tell me," he said, hotly fighting his own arousal.

Diane flung back her head, her torso arched, and her aching breasts lifted toward his mouth. When he didn't touch her, she closed her eyes and slowly cupped her own breasts, offering them to him.

Blood rushed into his head so quickly he felt dizzy with longing. He dropped to his knees in front of the sofa. She lifted her arms to his shoulders and opened her soft thighs for him. Charles knelt between them. His mouth was unrelenting in his hunger for her.

"You're so beautiful," he whispered between kisses as Diane caressed his nape, his shoulders, and whatever she could reach while rubbing the hard tips of her breasts against his cotton-covered chest, her feminine heat pressed against the cloth covering his arousal. They were both out of breath when he finally lifted his head. "Tell me . . . please," he said against the side of her throat.

"My breasts."

"What about your breasts? They are beautiful," he whispered throatily.

"Caress them . . . please . . . with your tongue."

Charles shuddered with desire. He kissed her breasts. Only then did he finally return to the diamond-hard center and circle it, his tongue wonderfully rough and wet on her silky skin. He groaned his enjoyment. Her nipple looked and almost tasted better than dark sweet chocolate, he decided, as he rolled his tongue around it, then finally suckled deeply. Diane, trembling from head to toe, gasped aloud when he scraped his teeth over the sensitive peak.

"Is this what you want, baby?"

"Yes . . . oh, yes."

As Charles returned his sensual attention to her other breast, Diane moved against his muscular thighs. That sweet pressure almost drove him over the edge. He maneuvered her until she lay back on the long sofa while continuing to lave her breast. His large hand trembled as he cupped her, discovering her liquid heat. He applied such a sweet rhythmic pressure that she called his name frantically.

Diane felt as if she would die if he didn't touch her fully. She moved against his hand, trying to persuade him. When he finally parted her softness, she was as damp as the dew-kissed petals of a fragrant rose. Diane cried, "Yes . . . oh Chucky . . . oh, yes . . ." as his blunt fingers applied the exact pressure she craved. He stroked the ultrasensitive feminine pearl at the top of her thighs over and over again, then suddenly replaced his hand with his mouth. He loved her until Diane screamed his name as she convulsed in a quick, intense release.

He didn't give her time to recover her senses. He began a sensuous assault once more, and each soft stroke of his tongue was hotter and more intimate than the one before it. He didn't stop until she climaxed yet again. She recovered slowly as he lay sprawled on the carpet. Diane dropped down beside him, longing to give him as much pleasure as he'd given her.

She pulled and tugged at his T-shirt. With his help it was soon gone, leaving the brown expanse of his chest open for her caresses. She teased his nipples with her soft palms, then, with her wet, soft tongue, licked each in turn. She didn't stop until his nipples stood up like tiny raisins stretching toward the morning sun and he was moaning deep in his throat. Her hands went to his waist and she pushed the heavy metal button through the buttonhole, then carefully unzipped him, parting the material stretched taut by his erection before pushing it down his long legs.

Her lips were soft and warm on his chest as she slowly made her way down his chest to his waist. She stroked the thick nest of ebony hair before she dropped her head and caressed him fully. She pleasured him as thoroughly as he'd pleasured her earlier. She brought him right to the edge of release, a mere heartbeat away.

Charles, unable to think, let alone speak, while his body pulsed with unyielding urgency, pulled her up so he could enjoy her soft mouth. With each generous stroke of his tongue, he let her know in no uncertain terms how much he wanted her . . . needed her.

"It has been too long, I've been without you for too damn long. Touch me . . . Please, Diane. I want to feel your soft hands on my body."

His heart was beating with all the thunder and power of an ancient African drum as she caressed his chest, his arms, his stomach, then the sensitive flesh of his inner thighs. He said her name aloud when she palmed his heavy shaft and stroked him from base to the tip.

"No more . . . no more," he whispered, close to losing what little control remained. He had to get inside her . . . had to feel her tight, moist heat. Charles's strong hands spanned her waist and easily lifted her over him. He grinned at her expression as she blinked in dismay.

"Honey . . ."

"Make love to me, baby . . . take me deep inside," he crooned, then shouted her name as she lovingly accepted him, sheathing him . . . gloving him as if they had been created for none other.

Diane shuddered from the force of her emotions. He locked his hands around her waist, cradling her breasts against his chest until his face was nestled where her shoulder and throat joined. She said his name over and over again as she sought his mouth for tender loving kisses.

He delighted in the sheer pleasure he'd denied himself for so long. Charles closed his eyes, aching for her to take all of him . . . all his love . . . all his hopes and dreams . . . all that made him Charles. Cupping her hips, he relished her slow movements along his length. Much too quickly he could feel himself losing the struggle as his emotions eroded his control. Charles sensed she was not anywhere near release. He rolled with her until she was beneath him. His thrusts were long and deep as he cupped her breasts, worrying the sensitive nipples with his fingertips. Soon Diane's breath matched his, quick and uneven, as the tension built inside of her. He intensified each stroke until they both were quaking wildly in the blazing heat of a white-hot climax.

Diane recovered more slowly than her husband. She was so quiet that he asked, "You okay?"

"Mmmm," she smiled, snuggling closer to him.

Charles grinned. "Too tired to share a shower?"

It wasn't until later, when they were snuggled in the large bed, that Diane told Charles how much she loved him.

He smiled. "That's great, because I am crazy in love with you, girl."

"Oh, honey." She kissed him softly. "How could you stay away so long?"

"I was busy nursing my anger. You were probably better off without me. I wasn't pleasant to be around."

"Eliz told me."

"My sister? You've spoken to my sister?" He looked incredulous. "How did that come about? I thought you two couldn't stand each other."

"Not any longer. We've become friends."

"Friends?" Charles rolled onto his stomach so he could look into her eyes. "Hey, I missed something?"

"Eliz came by the house earlier this evening. We had a

long talk. She was worried about you, honey." Then Diane chuckled. "You can imagine how pleased I was to see her."

"Yeah. So?" he encouraged.

"She assumed the separation was my idea and hoped that if she could get us talking we could work out our problems."

He frowned before he asked softly, "Is that why you came here tonight?"

Diane pressed her mouth against his, saying emphatically, "I came to you because I love you and couldn't bear this separation. Your sister *did* give me the push I needed. She let me know that you still cared about me and that you were as miserable as I was."

Charles shook his head in disbelief. "Who would believe? Thank her for me, will you?"

Diane slowly traced the full, sensuous curve of his lower lip with a fingertip. "You have such a beautiful mouth."

Charles swallowed, his voice thickening with desire. "Oh . . . do you have any idea how much I've missed you?"

Diane shook her head, "Show me."

He lifted a brow. "Show you, huh? Some babymaking practice is in order."

Diane shivered as his kisses trailed down the tender side of her throat. "I have something to tell you."

"Tell me after . . . I have an urgent matter to take care of." He sponged the base of her throat with the hot velvet heat of his tongue.

Diane's eyes closed as she trembled in his arms. He cupped a breast, teasing the tip with his thumb. She said his name again, unable to stop the rush of tender emotions or the wave of desire flooding her senses. The joy she felt won out and soft tears trickled down her face. Charles tasted the salty moisture on her lips.

"Sweetheart, what is it? Why are you crying?"

"Oh, Chuck . . ." She pressed her lips to his over and

over again with tears steadily trailing down her cheeks. "I'm so happy."

"That's why you're crying?"

Diane nodded, then shook her head, further confusing him. "We don't need to practice."

Charles stared at her completely baffled, then suddenly his eyes bore into hers. He said in a sudden rush of words, "You're pregnant?"

Diane nodded, her gaze locked on him, her heart slamming frantically in her chest.

Charles sat up quickly, staring down at his wife. "We're having a baby?"

"Yes. I found out this afternoon."

He let out a whoop, then he gave her a warm hug and gentle kiss. "We're really pregnant?"

"Yeah."

Charles laughed exuberantly. "How? When?"

"You need me to tell you how?"

Chuckling, he nestled her cheek. "Smart mouth! When?"

"I'm not sure. I think it was on our last night in Saint Thomas. Or perhaps it was early that morning, before we left. Or maybe . . ."

He laughed, recalling the frequency and the heat of their lovemaking. "I get the picture. Baby, how are you feeling? What did the doctor say?"

"I feel fine," she beamed. "Except for the morning sickness. Our baby is due after the first of the year."

Charles held Diane close. "You've made me so happy. Do you have any idea how much I love you?"

They talked of a future bright with promise and love. Diane announced she was hoping for a boy, while Charles put in a bid for a daughter. They looked at each other in shock before dissolving into laughter.

They made slow, leisurely love. Afterward, Diane declared she was starving and insisted that he feed her. He laughed, picking up the phone and ordering a huge pizza, beer for him, and milk for her. They had a picnic on the bed.

"How's Jeff?" Diane asked, ashamed that she hadn't called Anthia recently.

"Much, much better." He told her about Eddie's arrest.

"That's wonderful. Do you think they'll drop the charges against Jeff?"

"There's no way of knowing at this point, but I think so."

"Congratulations." She gave him a soft kiss.

Drowsy with sleep, Diane curled against his side. She was instantly alert when Charles asked about her mother.

"She's clean, sober, and gainfully employed, thanks to you."

"So she told you," he said, holding her close.

"Why did you do it?"

"She's your mother—that was reason enough to help her. I should have gone to see her, lend my support," Charles admitted. "I was lost in self-pity and anger."

"You've done so much already." Diane told him what she only recently learned about Lillie's past and her father. He listened thoughtfully.

"I hear from her boss that she's doing very well," he said softly. "She's been showing up for work on time and working very hard while she's there. You should be proud of her. She's certainly proud of you. I'm glad you went to see her. She's family, Diane."

"I don't like talking about her . . . I don't even like to think about her," she confessed.

"She's a part of you and you're a part of her. Di, she may not be the mother you'd have wished for yourself, but she certainly loves you very much. I think you love her, too." Charles soothingly stroked down the curve of her spine, in hopes of easing the sudden tension in her soft frame. "Give her a chance."

"She killed my brother. She let him die . . ." Diane

whimpered, tears pooling in her eyes. "She wasn't there, Chucky. How can I forgive that?"

Charles held her until she quieted, then whispered, "I'm sorry about Danny . . . so sorry you lost him. You've been blaming your mother all these years, punishing her. Maybe she's been blaming herself, too? I don't know. I think once you understand her reasons . . . perhaps then you can let go of the resentment . . . the pain you've been holding onto. Huh?"

"Maybe," Diane mumbled.

"We'll work it out, my love . . . work it out together."

"Together . . ." she smiled.

"Yes, together. Now about the cruise, sweet cheeks," he crooned in her ear. "Admit it. You followed me, didn't you?"

"Maybe," she laughed at his frown. "I might tell you in, say, forty or fifty years."